Eden Found

Eden Found

A Novel
By
Steve Hart

Hart-Burn Press, Inc.
PO Box 99
Newton Jct, NH 03859

First Hart-Burn Press Edition, July 2003

FIRST EDITION

10 9 8 7 6 5 4 3 2 1

Published in 2003 in the United States by
Hart-Burn Press, Inc., PO Box 99,
Newton Jct., New Hampshire 03859

Library of Congress Information: LCCN 2003103793

Additional LCC information available at
www.stevehartbooks.com

Hart-Burn ISBN 0-9740318-0-1

For

Roxanne

Couldn't have done it without
your love and support,
Darlin'

"We have just enough religion to make us hate,
but not enough to make us love one another."
— Jonathan Swift

Sincere people are unafraid of the critical examination
of their true convictions and noble ideals."
— The Urantia Book

Prologue

They wait in the dark, a cool, dry, airless alcove deep within an ancient cave structure. Fashioned in the light of day from a mixture of clay and water by hands that have long since returned to dust, they remain consigned to the blackness.

The twenty-four earthenware jars, artifacts of a long gone generation, sat untouched by humans for thousands of years. To the occasional scorpions, moles and other underground life forms that spend passing moments in their presence, they mean nothing, for the nourishment they contain provides no sustenance for the body.

The tightly sealed vessels serve one purpose, to house and protect twenty-four scrolls of leather, manuscripts created to preserve knowledge etched upon them in a long dead language. The information they store, of origins, meanings, and destinies, has survived in the outside world as only faint reflections in shadows cast by ancient scriptures. Myths and legends of why and how they were created, when and under what circumstances they were placed in the hidden location, have morphed into fantasies blended with tales. Originally preserved as oral folklore, the stories became lost as rewritten history prevailed and family lines died out. None still living on earth know they exist. Just one family tradition mentions them in even the vaguest terms. Hundreds died to protect and preserve them in the times before history. Now the scrolls bide time, as the day of their emergence nears.

ONE

The Warning

Fall, 1985

Established three thousand years ago by King David, Jerusalem is a place of contrasts and varieties. Situated high in the Judean Hills, about midway between the Mediterranean Sea and the Dead Sea, the Capital of Israel is one of the world's most extraordinary cities. But its disparities and variations create a volatile mixture. Should the Great Chef in the Sky desire a recipe for chaos, (S)He need look no farther for inspiration.

The ingredients are diverse people, adversarial politics, and clannish religions, spiced with fiery rhetoric, flowery languages, and flamboyant behavior. Marinated in a sauce of deep hatred, innate suspicion and determined revenge, they simmer under the relentless sun into a cultural stew that captivates, fascinates and intimidates. The result is disaster squared.

Jerusalem is a place where architecture; old and new, holy and secular, natural and manmade, permeates the atmosphere with a near-breathable sense of history.

Sacred to three of the world's main religions, it is a city with visitors moved and inspired by the shining glow of its religious shrines, picturesque scenery, and golden limestone. The sights, sounds, and smells of this unique creation add subtle flavor to an experience that brands the psyche of even the most jaded world traveler.

Physical jeopardy is also a component. Concealed within the panoramic beauty, multicultural citizenry and historical setting, lies the specter of death, an omnipresent invisible fog. The Grim Reaper accompanies those unfortunate enough to become trapped in the animosity that has been an interwoven part of the city's fabric since before Jesus walked its streets.

The city David founded in tribute to God has shamefully become a witch's brew of hatred, revenge, and turf battles ready to engulf the unwary faster than a downtown bazaar feeds on a naïve shopper.

Lenny Cronin, a recent arrival to the world's most disputed capital, walked the dark empty streets of Jerusalem's "Old City" section at four A.M. on a Wednesday.

Ignoring the ancient sandstone buildings, with their shuttered offices and shops surrounding him like man made cliffs, he wasn't thinking about architecture or history. Notwithstanding the government agencies housed here, politics was not on his mind. He looked in the faces of the synagogues, mosques and churches that he passed, but reflected not on religion. What Lenny did think was that should one of God's angels decide to rain Biblical fire and brimstone here and now, only two people would burn and die, him and the guy on his tail.

Lenny had noticed the man four blocks back. Two random turns had not shaken him; the shadow's stealth tactics were crude but determined. No doubt about it, someone was following him.

A disgraced former investigative reporter seeking to redeem his reputation and ransom his career, thirty-six year old Lenny Cronin was on assignment for his Boston newspaper. He glanced furtively back over his shoulder. The stalker lurking in the shadows now had him wondering what the hell had possessed him to take this gig in the first place. Did his old job mean so much to him that he was willing to risk his life to get it back? Of course not. Yet here he was following secret instructions on a dark deserted street like a damned spy.

The note had been clear about what to wear and where to go but said nothing about an escort. Why was this guy up his ass? He was wearing clothing similar to Lenny's, right down to the jacket and necktie. He was tall and lanky like Lenny, and dogged his every footstep.

He tossed a mental tennis ball back and forth. Should he turn around and confront his shadow? Or was breaking into a dead run, hailing a cab, and getting the hell out of there the best bet? Faith and redemption won out over both choices. He just kept walking, following instructions; fervently believing his editor would pay up big-time when this was over.

* * *

Two hours earlier a soft knock had landed on Lenny's hotel room door.

"Who is it?" he called out.

When there was no answer, he cautiously rose from the franchise hotel's back-destroying bed and approached the peephole. He saw only the door across the hall. *What the hell's going on*, he thought.

"Who's out there?" Tougher this time, but still no answer. He looked again and saw nothing. He eased the door open a crack and looked left. No one there. He peeked around the door and checked right. More empty hallway. He was about to close the door when he noticed an envelope on the floor. He picked it up. It was blank.

Back safely inside the room with the door bolted, Lenny ripped open the envelope. The note inside told him to be at the intersection of David and Jeremiah streets at exactly four A.M. He was to wear a jacket and necktie, leave the jacket unbuttoned, and wear the tie draped over his right shoulder. He would be met and taken for a ride. 'Tell no one and be alone', it finished.

Lenny looked at his watch. He would barely have enough time to dress and reach the intersection at the appointed time. Apparently, they didn't want to give him a chance to set anything up.

The note was unsigned. Lenny had no way to verify that it was from his editor's underground Palestinian contacts. What if it was a trick? He remembered the night of his arrival when his hotel room had been ransacked, and wondered if this note was related to that event.

He'd been hesitant to take on this assignment. Had tried to turn it down, actually. He didn't like to travel for one thing. And dealing with terrorists wasn't exactly a huge enticement. But his editor had kept at him (coerced him, Lenny thought), and eventually he did accept it.

But nobody had mentioned hotel room pillaging. Could that be a deal breaker? He considered this for a moment. Screw it. Lenny Cronin decided he wanted this story about recent tourist kidnappings and the opportunity it presented to restore his journalistic standing. He knew if his professional life were a poker game, he'd be just about cashed out. But now he'd been dealt a decent hand with a good-sized pot and he would take his chances. He dressed as the note instructed, locked his hotel room (for all the good that did), and took off at a brisk pace to make the appointment.

* * *

The green glow of his cheap Timex told Lenny it was exactly four A.M. as he turned the designated corner, tie over shoulder as per instructions. His double was still a block behind him and Lenny was afraid this guy, whoever he was, might screw things up. Would his contacts see the man and cancel their plans? Worse, what if they mistook his stalker for him and they picked up the wrong guy? *Well,* he thought, *at least only one of us looks like a putz with his tie slung over his shoulder.* Then he had an even more frightening thought. Would they think he had betrayed them and shoot him dead in the street? He'd been warned of just such a possibility during his initial contact with the terrorists.

Lenny had worked as an investigative reporter for eight years. But even factoring in the small amount of covert training he'd received in Vietnam, his biography lacked guidance for a situation like this.

He continued walking in the direction instructed by the note, searching for other people on the one-way street. No one, except for his mimic of course, but what the hell did he expect at this hour of the morning?

He tried to secretly snatch glimpses of the man. The guy was doing a good job of keeping in the shadows and doorways. It occurred to Lenny that anyone watching HIM wouldn't see this other man. With each step he felt more and more like he'd overdosed on caffeine.

The stillness of the night was broken by the sound of screeching tires, followed by a metallic crunch. It came from behind Lenny, where he'd just been. He whirled toward the noise and saw two cars, nose to bumper at an angle that blocked the entire street not two blocks behind him.

Shit. Now what?

Just then, from around the same corner Lenny had just turned, he saw a large newspaper truck approaching rapidly. It had a black and red motorcycle hugging the near side like a well-trained dog. The truck took the corner just wide enough for the cycle to stay beside it yet remain unseen from nearly anywhere on the street. The two vehicles stopped beside Lenny in a well-choreographed maneuver. Someone from inside the back of the truck threw a newspaper bundle onto the sidewalk beside him. Lenny stared, frozen, surprised.

"Get on," the driver of the motorcycle yelled over the sound of the engines.

"What?" Lenny said, feeling like a first grader caught daydreaming.

"Get on now, Mister Cronin, or I leave you standing here."

He shook off the sensory overload and mounted the cycle, which then took off in tandem with the truck.

Lenny looked back to where he'd been standing only seconds before and was amazed to see his twin standing in the exact location he had just vacated.

The man even wore his tie over his shoulder now. The whole maneuver had taken under fifteen seconds, including the apparently staged car crash that blocked the street. Lenny realized that anyone observing the action would merely have seen a newspaper truck making a delivery. An observer wouldn't know Lenny was even gone. His substitute continued to walk down the street as if nothing had happened. The dance had been timed perfectly and executed with military precision. Lenny was impressed as hell, and realized like he'd been hit with a hammer that he was in way over his head.

The truck/cycle combo sped two blocks north through the hot dry night air, then one block east, and another two north. The motorcycle stopped beside an old Mercedes sedan as the truck continued on into the night.

"Get in the back seat and lie down with your eyes closed," the motorcycle operator said. The tinted shield on the helmet prevented Lenny from seeing his face and made his thickly accented voice sound hollow.

Lenny got off the cycle and opened the car's rear passenger door. There was no one inside. He followed the instructions to lie down. After closing his eyes, he heard two people jump into the front seat. A raspy Middle Eastern voice told him to stay down and keep his eyes closed.

"We will be taking a long ride, Mister Cronin," he heard over the starter motor. "So that you are not tempted to open your eyes, I am going to cover them." Lenny felt a pair of hands tie a cloth over his eyes and then remove his watch. Inertia rolled him into the seatback as the car screeched away. The sweaty smelling blindfold and his own perspiration mixed with the leather seat to form a gaseous cocktail. Movies about kidnap victims came to mind; his jackhammering heart and the racing car engine provided the sound track.

"Where–" he began, but was quickly silenced by a calloused hand that covered his mouth.

"There will be no talk, Mister Cronin," the man said. Lenny felt hands adjusting the sightkiller around his eyes. "If that is clear say yes and no more."

"Yes," Lenny said softly, and neither man spoke another word.

Back in the cookie-cutter hotel room, the man who had taken his place on the street corner was packing Lenny's suitcase. Moments later, the same man was checking out of the hotel in the reporter's name.

"I'm sorry you have to leave so suddenly, Mr. Cronin," the night clerk said.

"So am I," the imposter replied. "Unfortunately something has come up and I must return home for a few days."

In the back seat of the Mercedes, the real Lenny Cronin, who'd often wondered whether his ability to nap anywhere anytime was a gift or an affliction, had become so disoriented by the darkness and maneuvering of the vehicle that he'd fallen asleep.

He woke after what seemed a short time and was startled by his missing vision. Then the memories flooded in on the tide of odors, and concern displaced amazement. He wondered again whether he'd been foolish to play this hand. This wouldn't be the first time his penchant for thoughtlessly jumping into dangerous situations, before weighing potential consequences on the scale of common sense, had gotten him into trouble. Caution was not his strong suit. It was why he'd been demoted in the first place. Not to mention why he lost so much money at poker.

Shortly after he waked, he felt the car slow to a near crawl. The driver's window opened and Lenny could hear the sound of rushing water. It seemed to be coming from below. Were they on a bridge? The car stopped.

"Do not move, Mister Cronin," Raspy Voice whispered.

Lenny could hear the crisp click of boots on pavement and muffled voices over the background noise of the water. He tried to smell the air but got only blindfold-sweat and leather. He heard mumbled Arabic and then? Was that the jingle of hard money?

He decided they must be crossing the Jordan River and considered the implications. It meant they were leaving Israel. If possible, he felt even more insecure. It also implied the group he was being taken to meet was based in Jordan, although Syria was a possibility as well; that country was only fifty or so miles from where Lenny guessed they were.

He heard the window slide shut, listened as the outside world died.

The car began moving, picked up speed, and within minutes was travelling at what Lenny thought was fifty or sixty miles an hour.

About an hour after the bridge crossing, Lenny felt the vehicle slow then turn onto a rough, unpaved road. The tires kicked up a steady barrage of gravel, beating the undercarriage beneath him. The sound of the rocks raining upward reminded him of the driveway to his grandfather's farm. He hadn't thought about that place in years. *Funny,* he thought, *the things that pop into your head when you're blindfolded. Confused. And scared shitless.* Suddenly the boredom he'd been fleeing when he accepted this assignment didn't seem all that bad. A few minutes after gravel entry, the car stopped.

"We have arrived at our destination, Mister Cronin," Sandpaper Voice said. "Do not remove your blindfold until you are told to do so."

Lenny felt two sets of hands help him exit the Mercedes. Then he heard the car pull away. He was guided about ten paces. One careful step up and they seemed to be entering a building. Wooden floors squeaked beneath his feet and strong, foreign odors invaded his nostrils. Someone from behind him ripped away the blindfold.

Lenny squinted. He was surprised that it was daylight, dawn really. Apparently, he'd slept longer than he thought, which meant they'd driven farther than he thought too. The brightness made his eyes water. After a few seconds his eyes adjusted and he was able to look around and assess his situation.

He found himself standing between two khaki-clad, machinegun-toting Arab escorts in the kitchen of what appeared to be a simple farmhouse. There was a wood-burning stove in the center, with the smokestack rising straight up through the ceiling. Lenny thought this unusual, given the scarcity of wood in the region.

The room was small, perhaps twelve by twelve feet. The only furniture was an unfinished dark wooden table with four matching chairs, each scarred by decades of use. The sink's water source was a hand pump. He saw no evidence of electricity, but there were oil lamps on the shelves and table. The cabinets above the sink had no doors, displayed some canned foods, and had a few cups and plates stacked like sloppy poker chips.

The air was fat with body odor, burned wood and some putrefaction he couldn't identify. The house smelled as though it hadn't been scrubbed in years. The phrase, *cleaning lady*, entered his mind. His internal editor changed it to *disaster recovery team.*

Lenny's weaponed escorts led him through a narrow doorway, down a dark hall, and into a small sitting room. It was about the size of, and furnished just as sparsely as, the kitchen. There was a card table in the center, surrounded by four rough-hewn chairs, and nothing else. And it smelled like the mother of all the other odors lived in this room. He wondered if something had died in the walls. There were a couple of shelves bearing the same type oil lamps he'd seen in the kitchen.

Sitting in the least rickety looking of the four chairs was a third man. Lenny noticed everything; his long legs, dark olive skin, well-trimmed beard, and black eyes set deep in spiderwebbed depressions. The man looked to be about forty, but Lenny knew these men lived lives that took a toll. He could have been twenty. He wore green military issue pants and shirt, with black combat boots. Lenny wondered if Fidel Castro was the guy's fashion hero.

The man seemed to be comfortably awaiting the arrival of his guest, sitting ramrod straight with hands on knees. He looked up as they entered the room, and met Lenny's eyes with a hard, unflinching stare. *Young or old*, Lenny thought, *he's a player. Time for your game face.*

"Welcome to this humble house, Mister Cronin," the fierce looking man said. "May the blessings of Allah be upon you and yours forever. May you die a wealthy man."

He had heard about the effusiveness of Arabic and of its speakers, but this was his first encounter with it. Was the guy for real, or did Lenny's bullshit detector need a tune-up?

After standing to shake his hand and pointing to a chair for Lenny, the man returned to his seat and continued. "I hope that your journey was not too uncomfortable or frightening. I am quite sure you understand that we must take precautions to ensure that you will be no threat to us after your visit. After all, Allah guides us and watches over us, but He expects that we remain diligent. The ungodly surround us."

Despite the man's menacing appearance and the Russian AK-47 leaning against the side of the chair, his tone and mannerisms succeeded in helping Lenny relax. The fact that this man didn't smell as bad as his unkempt teammates helped too. Actually, his clothes were cleaner and in better shape than Lenny's. Maybe this gig wasn't such a bad idea after all. It seemed these guys were just being very careful. He sat, feeling better than he had since he'd locked his hotel room door. "I was a little nervous there for a while. But I understand and no apologies are necessary."

"We must protect ourselves at all costs. Infidels seek our death at every turn," the man said. "With that in mind, let me impress upon you that you must not leave this house for any reason whatsoever unless we escort you. As long as you abide by that simple rule, you will have no problems. Should you be so foolish as to try such a thing, the consequences will be most serious. Is that clear?"

"That's perfectly clear," Lenny said. He meant it too.

"That is very good, Mister Cronin," the still seated man told him. "You will now be led to the room you will be using while our guest. You will find pencils and papers to use for your articles. I trust our humble offerings will be suitable for your needs."

"I'm sure everything will be fine." Questions came naturally to Lenny, so he couldn't resist posing one. "You speak English very well. Where did you learn?"

The man's lips curled slightly upward. He nodded almost imperceptibly. The eyes looked far away. "The best way to know your enemy is to understand his language. I insist that all my men learn English. Where is not important." He snapped out of his mini-trance and refocused on Lenny.

"You will wait in your room for the rest of the day. I must leave and will return this evening. When I do, you may start your interviews. Do you have any more questions, Mister Cronin?"

Lenny wondered how English was the language of the enemy, but asked instead, "What should I call you?"

"You may call me Assad."

Assad got out of the chair and, with one of Lenny's escorts, started to leave the room. "Now, if you will excuse me, I must go."

After the two men left the house, the remaining escort said, "Your room is through that door. I will be out here if you need anything. Food or water, perhaps?"

Lenny had been so engrossed by the sandstorm swirling around in his stomach he'd forgotten how hungry he was. But with the mere mention of food his gut suddenly felt quite empty. "As a matter of fact, I'm starving."

The man gave Lenny a look that nearly sent his appetite scurrying away like a frightened squirrel. "You Americans do not know the meaning of the words you use so lightly. If you want to know what starving is I will show you. Would you like that?" He stared at the reporter in complete silence. Seeing Lenny's contrite look, the terrorist continued, "I did not think so. Wait in your room and I will get something for you".

Lenny entered the room. The door was slammed and locked behind him. *You're out of your league with these guys, Cronin. Better watch yourself.*

Lenny looked around and saw that this room was even smaller than the other two, maybe ten feet by ten feet. In America it would be a closet. There was a tiny cot against the far wall. Far? It was so far he could almost touch it. The only other furniture was an old broken-backed wooden chair sitting by an empty fig crate. There were worn down pencils and lined paper on a board that covered the crate. He sat on the chair, which complained with a moan, picked up a pencil, and began writing what he hoped would be one kick-ass article.

TWO

A Retrospection

Summer, 1985

At six A.M. the alarm clock screamed. The piercing, mind-shattering tone awakened Lenny Cronin, who rolled over, grabbed the sleep killer, and jabbed the off button. He was sorely tempted to throw the piece of crap out the window, but granted it a reprieve. Even hung over, he knew he'd just have to buy another one. As a reward for his self-control, he snatched a cigarette from the pack on the floor by the bed. Robotically, his body went through the motions, a mindless, smoke-breathing automaton.

His head felt like an unpeeled onion with alternating layers of awareness and blunted thought. It was as though he were a newborn baby, but seeing through the eyes of a man. No coherent thought, only a fuzzy awareness.

Then the real world smacked him upside the head big-time. His mouth tasted like a bird had nested in it. Even his tongue felt like the bottom of a birdcage. He was sure his eyes were exploding. The anvil that was pounding in his brain, timed to the throbbing pulse that coursed through his veins, had him wondering where the blacksmith was.

With a half-sigh, half-moan that equaled a total lament, Lenny sat up on the edge of his never varnished pine bed. He rubbed at his itching, burning, and nearly detonated eyes, deriving no relief. A waste of calories. The anvil pounded on. He took a drag from the cig and stood with forced determination.

It was time to prepare for another day of exposing crooked politicians, investigating bribery allegations, digging up scandals, unearthing false testimonies, and otherwise chronicling proud moments in Boston's storied tradition of civic pride and accomplishment.

Then a layer of the onion peeled away, and a layer of thought was revealed. Lenny remembered he didn't have that job anymore. *Son-of-a-bitch.* How many mornings was this going to happen? Losing the job once was bad enough. But to re-lose it again and again, day after day? That was positively Jobian.

He had been consigned to reporting on science and technology. He imagined how unlikely it would be to win a Pulitzer on this duty. Would it be for revealing to an eternally grateful public that some hot new computer didn't actually perform at a speed of ten billion giga-whatchacallits a second? Yeah, sure. Or maybe exposing some pimply-faced, sexually frustrated, virus spewing geek as civilization's latest scourge would provide the enervating, edge of your seat experience he'd grown accustomed to and missed so dearly. Uh huh, and maybe President Reagan would return to acting after politics in the breathlessly awaited sequel, 'Bad Time for Bonzo Too.' Fat chance.

Lenny sat up and placed his elbows on his knees, allowing the weight of his head to give in to gravity's relentless tug. He felt like a dump truck had run over him. A fetid cloud wafted from his armpits, informing his nostrils that he smelled like it too. The man who never met a poker game he didn't like, chastised himself for having stayed so late at last evening's rendition of the weekly cardfest, especially since he'd been losing all night. He vowed abstinence from drinking and gambling. Well, simultaneously anyway. He thought about this for a moment, then realized he'd sworn the same oath too many times to count. *Ah,* he thought, *who the hell am I kidding? Booze and cards go together like sex and cigarettes. . . . , where the hell are my butts?* He lit another one.

He tossed the pack on the light pine nightstand with its discount store lamp. The mismatched furnishings evidenced his lack of interest in decorating. It wasn't that he was colorblind or stupid; he just didn't care enough to spend good money on stuff that didn't matter. His friends called him cheap. Hell, maybe he was.

He sat upright and took one big drag before standing and shuffling slowly toward the coffee brewer. The tobacco made his mouth taste even more fowl, but the nicotine was having the desired effect on the anvil-pounding blacksmith. With no more thought than he needed to take his morning dump, Lenny made a pot of drip grind coffee for his daily caffeine fix.

Two long minutes and half a mug later he took the last drag on the butt, and dropped it in the toilet. He reached into the shower and adjusted the water temperature. *In you go, boy,* he told himself. *It only hurts for a little while.*

"Yowza," he yelped, as he stepped into the icy water. His nipples hardened and his balls shriveled. But by God he was awake. Alive and awake. He turned up the water temperature. As his testicles thawed, how he'd managed to turn four of a kind into a busted hand flashed through his mind like a recurring nightmare.

Lenny Cronin had been the star investigative reporter for Boston's largest newspaper, the *Chronicle.* Getting that job had been the achievement of a lifelong goal. Ever since Woodward and Bernstein had helped bring down President Nixon, he'd dreamt of ejecting corrupt and malfeasant actors from the public stage like a talent show judge wielding a shepherd's crook. He considered public trust a priceless treasure and anyone betraying something so sacred was lower than a mole and deserved whatever punishment society prescribed. But recently he had been relegated to the demeaning position of science reporter.

How he hated his new job. How he missed his old one. And he still loved the *Chronicle* too, in spite of everything. He had hopes of becoming editor someday, or at least he had until the fiasco. Now he was a 'used to be'. He'd been demoted because he committed the cardinal sin of his craft. Lenny Cronin, Boston's best known and most respected investigative reporter, had neglected to verify his source of information.

Lenny knew it was risky when he wrote the article that would become his albatross, but time was critical and the payoff irresistible. He'd been told the *Chronicle's* main competition was about to print the same news. For a chance at beating the *City Crier,* he'd do cartwheels in a tutu. And besides, what were the real chances? His informant was someone who'd been very reliable in the past. The story was a juicy one involving kickbacks for the building inspector, which also implicated the mayor who had appointed the man. Thinking he hadn't the time for his usual legwork, Lenny grabbed the bull by the horns and ran with it, mixaphorically speaking.

The information, though, had been fabricated. Someone intent on ruining the mayor's reputation had coerced Lenny's source into telling the lie. The *Chronicle* was currently involved in a huge lawsuit over his slip of the pen. And now, the *City Crier* had daily forty point headlines screaming to make sure the reading public was duly informed. And informed. And informed. Lenny had never considered himself ironic, but now he was its poster boy. Hell, there was so much irony in his blood now, every time he got near a magnet he felt its pull.

The punishment for Lenny's lack of judgement was an indeterminate sentence to the gulag of techdom. Only his talent and his record of great scoops had kept him from being fired outright. An out-of-court settlement was rumored to be in the works. Lenny had no idea how much that would cost the *Chronicle*, but his editor had threatened piecemeal salary deductions for the next six hundred years. He hoped that was a joke, but you could never be sure with a man like Perry Hazzard. Crusty old bird, but with a good heart; the guy was a walking, talking cliche'.

As Lenny toweled off, he wondered how much longer he would have to write "science stories". What an oxymoron that was. They bored him to near death. Once while trying to think of something (anything), interesting to flavor the latest bit of tech-news, he swore he saw his grandmother waving from the light at the end of a long tunnel. Adding weight to his burden of guilt, the quality of the *Chronicle's* investigative reporting had tumbled downhill faster than Jack 'n Jill since his chastening, at least in Lenny Cronin's humble opinion.

Lenny emerged from the shower and took a good long look in the mirror. His light brown hair, still wet, reminded him of a bush that had been fed too much fertilizer. It stuck out in odd places like a neglected hedge. Then there was the map of route ninety-three and its tributaries that seemed to be etched in red on the whites of his still exploding blue eyes.

"Lay down, you fool," he told the reflection. "Don't you know you died?"

Lenny was just over six feet tall, had the wiry strength of a swimmer, and in his circle of newspaper friends was considered to be a chick magnet. His square chin and easy smile fooled women into thinking that he was just another pretty boy journalist. As he prepared to shave, he wondered where the hell that easy smile was this morning.

While he dried his stubble free face, he made another silent vow. This time forsaking all-night poker marathons . . . at least during the week. Weekends were another matter.

The first cup of java had started the healing process. He returned to the kitchen with a little more life in his step, and slugged down a second cup. The job of the blessed bean juice was nearing completion. He nearly felt human again. But the prospect of another day of excruciating boredom, obfuscating techspeak, and maddening scientific detail still had him considering suicide . . . well, careericide anyway. But there was really no other job he wanted. Just his old one back. And the only way that was going to happen was for him to be a good boy and do what he was supposed to, bear his banishment with humility and grace. The odds of that happening were worse than the inside straight he'd tried to fill last night, but he was trying.

Lenny finished dressing, putting on one navy and one black sock without noticing the difference. His black shoes fought against the brown belt. 'What's clean today' was his fashion style.

He made his way back to the kitchen and started choosing ingredients for his daily breakfast extravaganza. The recipe he ended up with, one-third Rice Krispys, one-third Wheaties, and one-third Cheetohs, topped off with mostly milk (A splash of OJ and the remaining coffee added for effect.) was an especially tasty example of his dietary regimen of, 'what's left in the cupboards today'. Cronin consumed the concoction, complimenting the chef for his culinary creativity. He finished eating, tossed bowl and spoon into the already full sink, and headed out the door.

As Lenny left the small one bedroom apartment, he thought about the phone call he'd received from his girlfriend, Sheila Snow, early the previous evening. She wouldn't tell him what the call was about, but said she wanted to discuss something important with him at lunch the next day. They had agreed to meet at their favorite Mexican place at noon.

Lenny and Sheila had met by pure chance. She had been relaxing over a gin and tonic at a bar near the health club where she obviously exercised regularly. It didn't take an investigative reporter to pick up on the clue that she worked out a lot. Her figure was perfection plus. The historical Irish pub also happened to be near Lenny's newspaper offices. He was sitting at a table enjoying an after work drink with some of his cronies when Sheila first walked in. He had noticed the attractive redhead with the fantastic legs and just-the-right-size breasts (He hated those pumped up plastic bags women were stuffing themselves with these days.) almost immediately, but she seemed to be waiting for someone. He decided against introducing himself, at least until he saw who she was waiting for.

Despite having dated many women, Lenny was not known as a playboy. In fact, he usually dated one person at a time, simply because it was a lot less complicated. But he wasn't partnering with anyone at this junction of his life. He was a gander sans goose, a ram minus ewe, hell he hadn't been laid in three months. And besides, he had an affinity for redheads. So after about a half-hour, when he saw she was still alone, he decided to take a shot.

"Guys, I'll be right back," he said to his pals. "I have a yearning for a certain crimson haired princess."

"Go for it, Len," one of the guys said.

"You going to regale her with stories of you legendary exploits?" another asked. "Or will you stick to the awful truth, Mister Science Reporter."

"Screw you guys," Lenny said as he left the table. Not his best and he knew he'd better sharpen up if he wanted to impress his quarry.

As he got near enough to notice, he saw that the redhead wore a wedding ring. He immediately gave up any hopes of getting to know her. Lenny always tried to live by the golden rule and knew he'd never want anyone fooling around with his wife. But he was too close to her table to turn away without looking awkward (Not to mention the ribbing that awaited him upon returning empty handed.) and she did seem to be waiting for someone who was either very late or wasn't going to show up at all. What the hell, his mother always told him honesty was the best policy.

"Excuse me," Lenny said looking down at her. *Damn she's hot. Hot and married. Bad combination.* "This is a bit awkward. May I join you? "

The flame haired beauty met his blue eyes with her green ones. She seemed surprised to find him next to her.

"Who are you?" she asked in a voice that bypassed his brain and went straight to his solar plexus.

"That's what I'm trying to explain. I was coming over to introduce myself when I noticed your wedding ring and almost changed my mind."

"Almost? So why didn't you?"

Lenny was still standing, and feeling more awkward by the minute. He was wilting under her stare, but was mesmerized by her voice with a throaty timbre so smoky Lenny almost looked for an ashtray.

Lenny wasn't sure how to answer her. Did she want him to turn around and go? Or was she just curious about the fool standing over her, who was beginning to feel like he'd farted in an elevator? Well, tenacity was a good friend of Lenny Cronin's, fart or no he was sticking it out.

"It's just that you seem anxious about something," he answered. "I thought I'd see if I could help in any way?"

Her eyes widened in surprise. "I wasn't aware it was that obvious."

"Every time someone comes through that entrance you look up expectantly, and your disappointed look reminds me of all the extra ties I get each Christmas." He smiled.

She laughed while reaching into her purse and pulling out a cigarette to which he put fire. "You're right, actually. I'm waiting for a friend. We're supposed to go shopping." She lifted a slim wrist and glanced at her watch. "She's nearly an hour late and that's not like her at all. I'm worried something's happened."

Lenny felt like he was walking a mental tightrope; a balancing act was going on. The Clash song, 'Should I Stay or Should I Go?' flashed through his brain. Her Lauren Bacall voice tipped the scales. "Do you mind if I sit down?" he finally asked.

She gestured toward the seat across from her, practically waving the ring in his face. "Sure. But you were right about this too. OK?"

"I kid you not," Lenny said as he took a seat opposite her at the round table. "I don't mess with married women. Single women are complicated enough, thank you."

Lenny lit a cigarette of his own. His senses soaked up her essence. She had on a starched red blouse with her hair bouncing off the shoulders, and a black skirt that showed enough of her racehorse legs to increase his pulse rate. She smelled as fresh as today's edition and projected an aura of sensuality that threatened to suck him in, had the pull of the sun's gravity. *Stop it, you fool. She's married.*

"I wouldn't worry," he said, anxious to get the conversation back on track. "I'm sure your friend will show up. She probably got tied up in a traffic jam or something. Where's she coming from?"

"Medford. I took a cab to work today so we could go together in her car. And now I don't know if I'll be able to get a ride home. Ever try finding a cab driver willing to join the daily mass-migration from the city?"

"I know what you mean," Lenny said with a smile. "I once tried getting a cab to Medford this time of day. The driver looked at me like I was the reincarnation of his mother-in-law."

She laughed a rich deep laugh that nearly hypnotized Lenny. "You have a problem with mothers-in law?"

"Ex mothers-in law," Lenny said. "Let's just say I once knew a woman who could turn wine to vinegar, and not even on purpose. Her evil was just uncontrollable, had a life of its own. Unfortunately, I found out too late that she'd passed down the family talent to her daughter."

They both laughed as Lenny looked at his watch. "Look, my name is Lenny Cronin." He pointed his cigarette-bearing hand toward his friends. "I'll be over at that table for about a half hour longer. If your ride hasn't shown up by the time I'm ready to leave, I'll be more than happy to give you a lift home."

"Oh, you're very kind, Lenny, but I wouldn't want to be a bother," she said.

"I live in Somerville and I can swing through Medford on my way home with no problem at all." Actually, it was quite a bit out of his way, but if she had told him she lived in Seattle, he would have still made the offer.

"Well, thanks a lot for your concern," she said, "but I'm sure my friend will show up."

"I am too. But I'll check with you when I'm leaving just in case." He stood and reluctantly returned to his friends.

A few minutes later Lenny noticed the redhead waving to the bartender for another drink. After the man brought it to her, he saw them look his way and then talk for a few moments. He considered questioning the man about the conversation, but decided that would be too obvious. Besides, he reminded himself yet again, she's married.

Thirty minutes later, as Lenny was preparing to leave, he stopped by her table.

"I see your friend didn't make it. I hope everything's okay. My offer still stands. And by the way, you don't have to worry about me. I really do have a firm rule against getting involved with married women."

"I know," she said with a grin, "I checked you out with the bartender."

Lenny looked like a little boy caught reading dad's dirty magazines. "I hope you weren't too put off by my reputation. I'm really not the world's most notorious playboy. It's not true." He shook his head weakly, looked down with saddened eyes. "In last year's poll I actually dropped to third place, behind Hugh Hefner and that guy who invented birth control pills."

"On the contrary," she said between laughs. "You received a glowing recommendation." Silence reigned over the clinking glasses and mumbling crowd for a few seconds but her smile lingered. "You know, I've laughed more in our two short conversations than I have in weeks. It feels good." Lenny returned her gaze and decided that, married or not, he wouldn't mind drowning in those emerald pools.

Before Lenny had a chance to say something clever enough to make her laugh again, her cell phone rang. While she talked, he looked around the Irish pub's dark paneled walls, covered with photos of the city's greats, near-greats, and wannabes; famous, infamous, and wishtobes. They had all visited the legendary tavern seeking votes, currying favors, or engaging in less benign activities. There were some famous *Chronicle* news articles framed for your perusing pleasure. Many hung adjacent to pictures of the do wells or ne'er do wells they referenced. Two of Lenny's were even up there (Just doing my job, thank you very much.) with his photo sitting between them. How he loved nailing phonies . . . and betting on ponies.

Lenny looked down at her as she returned the phone to her purse and said, "That was my friend. She had to cancel. I guess I'll take you up on your offer."

"Well, in that case shall we go?" he asked.

She stood and he helped her on with her coat. As they were leaving the establishment he said to her in a mock serious tone, "Madame, you have me at a disadvantage."

"How so, sir?" she responded in like manner.

"I'm afraid that while you know my name, I have not the pleasure of yours."

"I'm sorry, monsieur. I was enjoying myself so much I forgot. I'm Sheila Snow," she said proffering her hand.

Since that first occasion, others had arisen when Sheila needed a ride. In a month they were good friends and it became a weekly event for them to ride home together. Within three months Sheila had evicted her philandering husband after one too many episodes of unfaithfulness.

Less than two months later she and Lenny began dating for real, with the "M" word sometimes popping up in their conversations, seemingly of its own accord. Then Lenny made the mistake of writing the story that resulted in his demotion. Now their plans were on hold until the court case was settled.

As Lenny hopped into his car and nosed it into the heavy morning traffic, he wondered again what Sheila wanted to talk to him about at lunch. He also wondered, for the eighteen millionth time, how much longer he'd be suffering the ignominy of reporting geek news.

Later that afternoon, Lenny and Sheila were seated at their favorite table in the attached greenhouse of the Mexican restaurant. They both loved the atmosphere of the hanging plants and a waterfall that misted the air around them as they ate.

As soon as they'd ordered a bowl of guacamole with chips for an appetizer Lenny said, "OK, Red, let's hear it."

"Let's hear what?" She asked, teasing him with her oh-so-innocent smile.

"All right, play it your way, but I know something's up. As a matter of fact if I didn't know better I'd think you were pregnant." He hesitated a moment, studying her smile that projected a certain innocent, yet devilish quality. "You're not are you?"

Sheila laughed. "No, of course not. What makes you think there's anything important at all? Maybe I just wanted a free lunch."

Lenny wasn't sure if he was relieved or not to learn she wasn't pregnant. He wasn't even sure how the idea had entered his mind. "I know you well enough by now. You're holding out on me. So come on. What is it?"

"Tell me something," Sheila said, as the waiter placed their appetizer in front of them. "What would you do if you could get your former job back and maybe even get some well deserved recognition at the same time?"

Lenny cocked his head slightly trying to remain calm, but his palms were already sweating. "You mean after I got up off the floor? Well, let me see. First I'd do an Irish jig, then a back flip or two. And then . . . ," he hesitated as he thought about his reaction to her non-pregnancy, "I'd ask you to marry me."

Sheila's lightly freckled cheeks battled her hair for best shade of red. "Oh, Lenny, I've told you before," in that throaty movie star voice of hers. "It doesn't matter to me what your job is. I love you and I want to be your wife, Pulitzer-Prize-winning writer or ditch digger."

Lenny put his fork down and reached across the table, taking her left hand into both of his. "I know, Red. And I love you too. But we've been through this. I want my old job back first. This science gig has all the excitement of computers playing chess in church. I'm bored out of my personality, I tell ya. I had a hot dog for lunch yesterday? Do you know I actually caught myself gazing at the vendor with envy? His life is more exciting than mine."

Sheila rolled her eyes and laughed. "Green eyed monster scare you, did it? That envy thing sounds Freudian to me."

"It was envy," he said faking perturbed. "At least the hot dog guy's right there in the daily hustle and bustle, getting his fingernails dirty. That reminds me, I need to make an appointment with a doctor. I think I have food poisoning." Sheila laughed and Lenny loved it that she got his joke.

"I'm starting to wonder if I'll ever get my career back on track. Now, are you going to tell me what the hell you're getting at? Or do I have to call in the marines and have them beat it out of you?"

Sheila faked huffy. "The only thing they'll get from me is name, address, and phone number . . . if there are any cute ones," she sighed. "But, to save you all that trouble, I'll tell you what it is."

Sheila began telling Lenny what she had learned at work the previous morning about an expedition to the Middle East. Her boss's foundation would be financing the trip. Two local professors, it seemed, had discovered evidence of the existence of some very old manuscripts near where the Dead Sea Scrolls had been found forty years earlier. As Sheila told him the story of the scrolls and their supposed author, Lenny realized that if true this could be one of the biggest archeological stories of the year. And it might even be one of the biggest news stories as well. But it was still science reporting. He could see no angle that might get him his old job back or even interest him. So far, the best thing about this story was listening to her tell it.

"And the best news," she finished, "is that you get an exclusive."

Lenny played a drum solo on the table with his fingers, and looked at her from beneath scrunched eyebrows. "What's that? What about an exclusive?"

"Your editor will tell you the rest. He wanted to break it all to you, but I begged him to let me tell you this much and he agreed."

"Let me get this straight," Lenny said, the drum solo now a stirring rendition of, 'Wipeout.' "You and my editor have been strategizing behind my back? About my career?" He saw the disappointed look on her face and softened. "All I mean is, don't you think I should have a say in this? I just don't see how this will get my old job back, that's all."

Sheila wiped her mouth with the white linen napkin, pulling her smile into a frown. "Just wait till you talk to your boss. OK? I'd tell you more, but I promised not to. And stop sounding so ungrateful. I thought you'd be happy."

"Okay, you're right. I'm sorry. This is just so surprising and then to find out you're conspiring behind my back . . ." He decided to shut up while he was ahead. They finished their lunch in relative quiet, say a cousin maybe. He thought he should be more talkative, but despite having the most enthrallingly green eyes on the planet staring at him with loving devotion, Mister Laugh-a-minute couldn't really think of anything funny to say. Mirth and words were his currency. The grim silence left him feeling bankrupt.

As the pauperized joke-man saw Sheila off in a cab, he wondered if he should return to the Chronicle Building and confront Perry Hazzard about the big secret. He decided not to as his boss was famous for being closed mouthed and irascible. Lenny knew he'd hear the full story at the right time. His editor was like a clock that way.

He waved a cab over and got in to head for the offices of EuroTech, one of the city's largest hi-tech firms. Yep, off to carry out still another brain frying assignment in the compelling world of science. Jesus, it was time to unsaddle that fleabag and put it out to pasture.

At eleven thirty the next morning Lenny was finally summoned by Perry Hazzard. The editor's office was so cluttered with newspaper memorabilia, unfiled folders, and assorted sports knick-knacks, that Lenny was once challenged by a pal to describe it in two words. He lost ten bucks when his buddy pointed out that retro trash heap was three words, said you couldn't hyphenate retro-trash. He closed the door behind him and was surprised to see Sheila standing there with three others in front of his boss's desk.

Two were obviously a couple, as their body language spoke the vernacular of love. Or was it lust? They were in their early to mid thirties and both were very attractive with black hair and dark eyes. The woman was especially good looking and was also the taller of the two, by at least six inches. They both wore black and white outfits; hers a knee length skirt with a sharply pleated blouse, his a pair of slacks with white shirt and red tie. The colors and height difference reminded Lenny of Mutt and Jeff wedding cake dolls.

The third person, an overweight, gray-bearded man in his early forties, he knew to be Sheila's boss, the Reverend Burl Graves.

"Ok, everybody's here," Perry Hazzard announced while standing behind his desk. "Let me introduce everybody before we get started. Bruce and Roxanne, this is Lenny Cronin. He's the reporter I told you about. Lenny, I'd like you to meet Roxanne Cabrini and Bruce Goldman, both professors at City University."

The three shook hands. Bruce Goldman said, "I think I've heard of you. Aren't you the one who's having trouble with the mayor over that building permit scandal? The false story that almost cost the mayor the primary?"

Lenny shrugged, looked at his editor sheepishly, and then turned back to face the short professor. "I have to admit I jammed the old size elevens right into my yammer on that one."

"Well, it's not my place to judge," Bruce Goldman said. "It's just that Roxanne and I are currently going through a bad experience with the press ourselves. So you'll forgive me if I don't seem thrilled at meeting a reporter right now. In fact, Roxanne and I don't even know why we're here."

"We'll get to that in a moment," Perry Hazzard said. "Lenny, you already know Sheila's boss, Reverend Graves. In addition to his church duties, he also serves on the board of the TUSK Foundation, which is why we're all here."

As they all took seats within the spacious office, Hazzard's secretary entered with a tray of coffee. She poured mugs for everyone, then placed bowls of crackers about.

"OK, Chief," Lenny said. "Let's have it. What's the story?"

Perry Hazzard took a sip from his cup, and began. "Here it is in Reader's Digest format. Bruce and Roxanne have discovered evidence that ancient manuscripts may exist in caves in the area of Jericho in Israel. The TUSK Foundation, of which I too am a board member, has allocated financing for their expedition to find them. I want you to accompany them and report on the search."

Lenny had spent the previous day thinking about hanging around while two scientists dug up old dirt and cleaned off ancient utensils. It sounded less exciting than a worm race, and just as painful to watch.

"Come on, Chief. With all due respect to these people, this doesn't sound like a good idea. I mean, ancient diggings? Why don't you just bury ME out there while you're at it?"

The editor looked at Lenny with focused, penetrating eyes. His buzz cut gray hair and horn-rimmed glasses always reminded Lenny so much of a newspaperman stereotype that he had once asked him if he ever worked at Cliche' Mart. His boss hadn't laughed; no sense of humor, that guy. But Lenny actually liked him.

"Listen to me, Lenny. This is your chance to get back into the fray. You won't be just reporting on what these two are doing. You'll be filing stories on the political unrest in the area as well. I've even got some old contacts lined up for you, from when I was assigned out there."

"What about us?" Bruce Goldman asked. "Don't we have any say in this? Roxanne and I wanted a quiet expedition so we can get in and out without any problems."

Reverend Graves placed his coffee cup on the table and took a cracker from a dish. He looked at Bruce and Roxanne and said, "After that editorial came out calling suspicion on your motives, the TUSK board decided it has to be this way."

"But that was all lies," Roxanne Cabrini sat straight in her chair. "Surely you don't believe that stuff, Reverend? We think my old boyfriend, Young Joe Rizzo, was behind it. He hates Bruce."

"That makes sense," Reverend Graves said. "His father was the board member who tried to get us to rescind our vote. And to answer your question, no I don't believe what that editorial said about you."

"If the story is full of lies," Lenny said spitting out cracker crumbs, "why don't you sue? After all this IS the land of the free and the home of the litigious. Of that I can attest first hand."

Perry Hazzard frowned at Lenny. "Whether they sue or not is up to them. But if they want the TUSK Foundation to finance this venture, they'll have to take you along."

"But, Chief–"

"No buts," Hazzard said. "This is your only chance to get your old job back in the foreseeable future. You taking it or not?"

Lenny considered his options. There was no doubt he wanted to end his expulsion from excitement. His desire to get back in the grease pits with stained overalls was stronger than his aversion to foreign travel and old pottery, or scrolls, or whatever the hell they were looking for out there. He had also heard fragments of information about the recent lull in activity in Israel leading some Palestinians to incite for action. Maybe this was the prescription that would cure his malaise.

"OK, Chief. We have a deal. I go with these two, file a few scientific-like articles plus some political pieces and when I return, I get my old job back."

"And I'm afraid the same goes for you two," Reverend Graves said to Bruce and Roxanne. "This is a take it or leave it proposition."

Bruce looked questioningly at Roxanne, who hesitated, then grudgingly nodded her assent. "OK, Lenny," he said. "I guess you're going on a trip to the Middle East. Luckily, the political situation is fairly quiet right now. We don't anticipate any problems."

THREE

The Avenging Angels

Spring, 1955

In the land of Palestine; where poverty and despair, strife and animosity are as much a part of everyday life as breathing and eating, boredom and oppressive heat, a baby boy was born amidst the squalor of the refugee camp outside Jenin in the northern West Bank region.

One of many throughout the area, both in Palestine and in neighboring Arab countries, the camp had been created as a temporary living compound for the thousands of Palestinians who had chosen to flee their homes in nineteen forty-eight when the Zionists suddenly declared the homeland as the independent state of Israel. Under pressure from their Arab neighbors to refuse life under Zionist control, many of the Palestinians had reluctantly abandoned their homes in favor of the camps. They were assured the move would be temporary and they would soon be returning in triumph. They had only to wait for the glorious and inevitable victory of the Arab armies; war had been declared upon Israel the very day following its declaration of statehood.

Then came the utter defeat of their Arab brothers, and those promises proved as reliable as the visions of a man lost in the desert. By the mid-fifties the camps had begun taking on a sense of permanence. The inhabitants came to hate every day spent in the decrepit confines of these monuments to broken promises and dashed hopes. Every waking moment was a harsh reminder of their loss.

The mother of the baby boy was but fifteen years old and suffered the shame of being unwed. For her sins against Allah she was stoned to death, thereby erasing the shame that stained the family name. The child was sent to live with relatives in the town of Nablus to the south with the cover story that Zionist aggressors had killed his family. He was given the name Achmed.

The fabric of Palestinian society was woven from the cloth of hope and disillusionment. Hope that someday the Zionists would be driven to the sea and forced from the homeland. Disillusionment over the leaders of the neighboring Arab states; they who had encouraged the Palestinians to abandon home and property, to live as refugees rather than under Zionist rule, but then abandoned them to a life of misery.

By the time of Achmed's twelfth birthday in nineteen sixty-seven, the Palestinians were feeling forgotten by the world. The fear of never returning home had inexorably turned optimism to despair as surely as the desert sun bakes a camel's carcass into a heap of bleached bones. Life for many Palestinians had settled down to a state of numbed acceptance. Living under the thumb of the hated Zionists was inevitable. But then, in the summer of nineteen sixty-seven, Israel launched what it called a pre-emptive attack on the Arab brothers in Egypt, Syria and Jordan.

Achmed was a twelve-year-old street urchin at the time, forced to beg and steal for survival. He had been abandoned by his uncle at the age of ten because the man now had sons of his own. Achmed had fallen in with a pack of boys in the same situation. In the ensuing two years, he had risen to the position of Alpha male.

"Achmed, have you heard the news?" a member of his troupe asked one hot day in May. "The Zionists have attacked our brothers. They will rue this day. Surely Allah will bless our glorious armies of brave Arab fighters with a swift and sure victory for such treachery."

Achmed, a tall gangly youth, with eyes like burning coals, looked confidently upon his friend Mazen Mousaka. "The great and blessed armies of our Arab brothers will most certainly send the Zionists marching into the sea as lemmings over a cliff. Our day of reckoning has arrived. Praise Allah."

All around the boys, other groups of Palestinians could be seen in joyous displays of anticipation over the coming victory. Visions of conquest and its attendant return of the homeland danced through their heads. "Praise Allah!" "May the Zionists forever suffer for their dastardly deeds" "Crush the Jews like grapes for the winemaking." "The return of our homeland from the oppressors is nigh." These and other expressions of joy, anticipation and vengeance were heard everywhere in the streets.

Six days later these same people were once again awash in despair and hopelessness. Their dreams of returning home proved no more real than a line drawn in the shifting desert sand. The devastating and humiliating defeat of their heroes by the hated Zionists had revealed the Palestinian's true impotence. In less than a week, those who had enthusiastically endorsed the brinkmanship of Nassar, the Egyptian leader who had instigated the war, saw their world and their last vestiges of hope shattered. And now with the outright seizure of the West Bank, Gaza, the Golan Heights, the Sinai and, most horridly, the holy city of Jerusalem, the twin strictures of occupation and helplessness hovered above the Palestinians like vultures over a dead man.

In the fall of that year, approximately four months after the Six-Day War, a general strike was called. The Palestinians hoped that the Zionists would realize their economy depended on the Palestinian workers. They knew they were being taken for granted.

The strike was a miserable failure. It failed from within, from a lack of unity, as much as from any outside factor.

Nablus, the home of Achmed, was the only city to universally heed the call to strike. For this, the Israelis came down hard. Leaders were deported. A five P.M. to seven A.M. curfew was imposed. Public transportation was shut down. The phone system was turned off. Shops were sealed shut. The town's main outlet to Jordan, the Adam Bridge, was barricaded. Within days of the imposition of these measures, resistance collapsed. All of this became yet more fuel for the fire of hatred that burned in the hearts of Palestinians like the desert sun. They saw these acts as evidence of the Zionist's intent to remain in the occupied territories. Proof of the futility of civil disobedience and the ease with which the Israelis could crush it was all about them. Ominously, many now became convinced that armed struggle was the only hope left for 'The Return' to become reality. Achmed and his band of compatriots were among them.

By the summer of nineteen sixty-nine, two years after the 'Six-Day-War,' Achmed's group of street urchins and beggars had grown into an organized band of resistors. Certain members of the Palestinian Liberation Organization had come to view the group of homeless and hopeless youths as a useful tool in furtherance of the cause. Money began being funneled to Achmed and other similar groups, money gathered from Arab elites in neighboring countries. These wealthy Arabs saw their gifts as a way to appease their own guilt-ridden consciences.

Achmed's group became known as the, "Flaming Arrows of Assad", after their main Syrian benefactor.

In October of sixty-nine, Achmed was called to attend a meeting of resistance fighters. The summons came from Yasser Arafat, the leader of the

Al Fatah faction of the PLO, and the man most Palestinians either feared or revered. The meeting took place in the home of one of Arafat's lieutenants, a small three-room cement block building set in a neighborhood of similar structures. The men crowded into the small living room. Sweet black coffee was served.

The meeting began.

After the general order of business was addressed, Arafat's man called Achmed to stand.

"Achmed," the man began, "your group of strugglers has earned a reputation above all others of your kind. Allah has been kind to you and your fellows. He has heaped upon you many blessings in the way of successes against our oppressors."

The group expressed their agreement with the man's praise by collective head nodding and a general mumbling of assent.

"The time has come for you to expand your activities," Arafat's man continued. "No more will you be satisfied with sabotage. No more will mere destruction of equipment or interference with commerce be worthy of your talents. The time to look at your enemy through the sights of a weapon is at hand. Are you ready for this next step in the struggle? For your entrance into manhood?"

The gangly fourteen-year-old stood rigid before the group. Though his clothing was old and worn, it was clean and well repaired. Pride filled his belly and warmed his insides. He felt like a lion after a fresh kill.

Achmed answered joyfully. "I am ready. Ask of my men and me what you will. The blessing of Allah will most certainly be upon us."

The man running the meeting took Achmed's right hand in his. He looked deep into Achmed's black eyes. His gaze penetrated to the very soul of the young fighter. "The Zionists patrol our neighborhoods like jackals seeking weakened prey. As wild dogs circle their intended victim, do they walk among us with impunity. This must end. They must be taught that Allah's faithful will never submit to their oppression. They must learn that the fires of hell await those who dare offend Allah."

"Death to the Zionists," Achmed said.

The man's lips curled upward as his eyes continued boring into Achmed's inner being. "Yes, death to the enemy who forces us from our homes, who treats us like vermin, who seeks to crush us like the elephant crushes the mouse. They will learn. We are not mice and they are no elephant."

Two nights later, Achmed and his best friend and second in command Mazen Mousaka hid behind a shopkeeper's building in the business section of Nablus. They had determined that an attack on one of the nightly Zionist patrols would send the appropriate message; those who dare walk the streets of Palestine in enemy uniforms risk their lives in doing so.

Achmed peered around the corner of the building. He saw two Israeli soldiers making their nightly rounds. Their backs were to him as they continued down the street lined with small shops. The soldiers turned a corner and began the final leg of their tour, taking them beyond the vision of Achmed and his cohort. The few working lamps and the partially obscured full moon dimly lit the small lane. Achmed signaled his partner and they carefully made their way to the corner around which the soldiers had disappeared. Achmed peered around the corner. He saw the soldiers separate as each took one side of the street to patrol.

When the soldiers were about one hundred feet from Achmed's hiding spot, he waved his hand at Mazen who had made his way to the opposite corner. The hand motion was their pre-arranged signal. Prepare for the moment of truth. Neither fourteen-year-old Achmed, nor sixteen-year-old Mazen Mousaka had ever killed another human being. They had already proven their willingness to do so by hiding a bomb under an Israeli vehicle, but there had been no person-to-person contact on that mission and no deaths had occurred. Both youths anticipated this moment with exuberance and passion.

Achmed and Mazen slithered around their respective corners and drew beads on their quarry. Their weapons were old but reliable and deadly accurate Soviet military surplus. In near synchronization, they pulled their triggers. The two shots rang out with the sound of one overlapping the other. Achmed's target fell to the ground. As the soldier writhed in agony and tried desperately to fire back, Achmed squeezed off two more shots, sending the oppressor to his deserved end. Mazen's target was luckier. He died instantly from a headshot before the reports of the gunfire even reached his ears.

The evening following the shooting, Achmed and Mazen Mousaka were once again at the home of Arafat's lieutenant. The atmosphere was joyful, and the two young killers were congratulated on their success.

"We celebrate our two glorious freedom fighters," the host said, as he clasped his arms around the shoulders of honored guests. "The shining countenance of Allah is upon you. May you both have many sons who will honor you to the end of your days."

"May Allah return our homeland and squash the Zionists like insects," Achmed said. "May our newly elected Chairman, Yasser Arafat, show us the way. May his guiding light be the beacon that brightens our path through these darkened days."

"And now," the host said to Achmed after the celebration had quieted, "I have news that will gladden your heart. Come aside with me."

Arafat's lieutenant led Achmed to a small table with two chairs and bid him be seated. As the man sipped his cup of dark sweetened coffee he said, "Since Yasser Arafat has been chosen as PLO Chairman, he has decided your band of fighters deserves more support. No longer will you dress in rags. No longer shall you carry weapons discarded by others. From this day on your group shall enjoy full status as members of the Palestinian Liberation Organization."

Achmed smiled outwardly, but wondered what this turn of events would mean to him and his group. Would they now be expected to follow orders blindly? Would the PLO presume thoughtless allegiance? Would it mean cutting ties with his Syrian benefactor? Would he lose the independence he held so dearly? "Such an honor comes as a surprise. I fear I must decline."

Arafat's man slammed his cup to the table. Heads turned at the sound of the cup breaking into pieces and scattering on the table and floor. "Curse your arrogance. How dare you refuse such an honor? Chairman Arafat will be mightily displeased. Be warned. Do not cross him. He is a scorpion waiting under a rock. When you least expect it, his sting will come."

"I mean no disrespect to the Chairman," Achmed said. "He is the hero of all true patriots. But I am my own man. My men follow me of their own accord. We do what we desire, when we desire. I am not certain about the benefits of following the orders of others."

The lieutenants' nostrils flared with indignation, like the opening of the dung beetle's home in the sand. "Then why did you take the assignment to attack the Zionist patrol? We were led to believe you would join us if given the chance."

"Forgive me if I misled you or Chairman Arafat," Achmed said. "I took the assignment because it seemed right to do so. The chance to deliver a deadly blow to our enemies comes not every day. But we are not followers of orders." After a moment's hesitation Achmed continued. "I have a counter offer."

Arafat's man stared at Achmed with the look of a man purchasing a camel from an unknown seller. "What kind of offer does a boy make to a man of Chairman Arafat's stature? Your band is but street trash that is occasionally useful, but remains trash nonetheless. You have before you a chance that no collection of vagabonds has had. To become an organized, well trained and effective tool for the liberation of our homeland." His countenance softened and he exhaled a deep breath as he finished. "In the interests of harmony, what is your offer?"

"It is this. My group can indeed become an effective tool. I propose that we do so with your training and support, but as a separate entity. A cell of fighters that remains hidden below the surface. We come into the light only when matters that demand the Chairmen's hands remain clean need doing. Only you and I and the Chairman will know of this relationship. We will be his secret weapon. That way, we remain free to do as we please and the Chairman has a dagger up his sleeve ever ready to deliver a deadly blow in the night."

And so it was that the "Flaming Arrows of Assad" became the secret weapon of PLO Chairman Arafat. Whenever an informant was uncovered, or someone became a threat to Arafat's position from inside or outside the organization, a death would occur that instilled fear in the minds of, and assured submission in the actions of, all who dared oppose the Chairman.

FOUR

A Dawning Light

Spring, 10,000 BC

The ten council leaders approached the meeting hut. Seth, 'Protector of the Scrolls' and hereditary leader of the village, stood outside the entrance to welcome them. They had gathered for the monthly meeting to report progress, or lack thereof, in their efforts to educate and train the most worthy of the outlying tribes in the advanced methods of agriculture, animal husbandry, and manufacture that were the hallmarks of the Edenic League. The eight men and two women returned Seth's greetings as they passed through the arched entryway into the sun-dried-brick building.

The Edenites, as they called themselves, had often been the objects of worship by their aboriginal neighbors. It was easy for the superstitious natives to see them as gods, so much taller were they, so much knowledge did they possess. Their legends, speaking of 'gods walking among men,' had caused a series of problems. The most serious of these was the difficulty some of the fair-haired, light-skinned Edenites had in refusing such head-swelling praise. Oftimes had these propensities led to conflict and turmoil. Five hundred years earlier, the original Edenites had nearly lost all as a result of similar difficulties.

Their settlement was called The Second Garden in honor of the Garden of Eden, the home of their forebears. The village's centerpiece, the golden-domed Temple of the Father, reflected the morning sun onto its neighboring buildings. Rows of small round huts flanked the temple. These were encircled by the agricultural and manufacturing facilities. A high stone wall that had only one gate protected all. Attacks from hostile natives were not frequent, but were violent enough to warrant such precautions.

The physical location of the settlement, just south of where the Tigris and Euphrates rivers meet, had been well chosen. It sat in a lush wedge of paradise that provided everything needed to sustain life; clean water, rich soil, and favorable weather blessed the region.

The meeting hut was constructed of dry laid sun-baked bricks, its straw covered roof protruded by a clay chimney. It matched most of the other community buildings in design and materials. Only the most important buildings, such as the Father's Temple, were constructed from stone with an eye to permanency.

The council leaders entered, gathered around the small fire in the center, and sat on reed chairs in a semicircle facing the flames.

Seth had light brown hair that flowed to his shoulders and hazel eyes as bright as the sun medallion that hung on a gold chain from his neck. He stood upon a small stage between the fire and his audience wearing a multicolored robe that covered him from neck to ankles. The robe, made of finely woven leather and displaying intricate designs, was an indication of this meeting's importance.

"Welcome, brothers and sisters," Seth said. "We begin this meeting with news of great joy. Our population has once again reached a number sufficient to allow the creation of a new Cultural Exchange Commission."

The group applauded. Smiles and congratulatory phrases abounded. Seth smiled down at them as he contemplated their thoughts. He knew each wondered who would receive the honor. Only one council leader would choose fifty associates to follow him or her into the wilderness. Only one would become the bearer of Edenic culture and knowledge to primitive men and women living beyond the current boundaries of the Edenic sphere of influence; the distinction every Edenite coveted.

"How long are you going to keep us in suspense?" asked the tallest man in the party, a bright smile on his face.

Aker's happy expression was immediately duplicated on Seth's face. He said to his best friend, "Have patience, my brother. You shall know soon enough." Seth renewed his attention to the group at large. "Yes the time has come, brothers and sisters. One of you shall choose a new team, organize a fresh commission, and experience the sublime satisfaction of creating yet another stepping stone for the path laid out before us by those on high.

"This joyful news has its sorrowful component as well." Seth stared at Aker with a contemplative frown. "We shall lose some friends and family members for a great period of time, perhaps even unto the time we shall meet on the other side of death's door."

The sun medallion swung against Seth's massive chest as he paced back and forth before the group. Beams of filtered sunlight danced with flickering rays of the campfire upon his colorful robe. Again he gazed upon his lifelong friend Aker. "My brother," he said. "It behooves you to pick a new leader for the Council of Tribal Relations, for you will soon be vacating that position." Seth refocused on the others. "It is my honor and privilege to announce that Aker has been chosen to forge new relations with those beyond our present reach." He gestured for Aker to join him on the small stage.

The broadly grinning Aker stood beside Seth. At nearly eight feet in height, he stood six inches above his friend. Of the Edenites, only the shortest women failed to reach seven feet; many times had they been called giants by the natives, who averaged under five feet. He took Seth's congratulatory handshake and turned to his fellows. "This moment shall live in my mind for all time. I give thanks to the Heavenly Father for His unending love and concern. I give thanks to you, my brothers and sisters, for your unswerving loyalty to God's plan." He placed his arm around Seth's shoulder. "And I give thanks to Seth, our duly elected leader, for his heartfelt friendship and support.

"As we all know," Aker continued, "our task is not an easy one. Danger lies hidden upon the unknown path before us. As grateful as many natives are to receive our assistance, there are even more too ignorant to understand the gifts we bring. Yet others are influenced to the point of belligerence by the nefarious schemes of the Father of Lies. The trail we walk is not without risk. Nonetheless, I accept this great honor with humble joy and gratitude." He turned to Seth. "Where shall this new direction take us?"

Seth placed his hand upon Aker's shoulder. "We have word from our ambassadors to the east that a tribe has settled in a valley by the Sea Without Life. The climate is comfortable and the sea is filled with useful minerals. You shall go there, teach our ways to the locals, mine the sea for exportable products and create another strong ally in our quest to advance this confused world."

The next few moments were taken up with joyful handshakes and backslaps. Aker stepped down and Seth continued.

"I also have news of importance from beyond the garden. Word comes from the west that the Andites and the Nodites are posturing for battle. Their historical animosity for each other is once again threatening to expand from talk to war."

"What cause this time?" asked Aker. He knew his council would bear the primary responsibility for bringing this current episode to an equitable ending. This could be his last chance to bring peace before embarking upon his new responsibilities.

Seth looked at Aker, sadness carved on his finely chiseled face. "The cause of the moment matters not. Since the fall of the First Garden, have these tribes thirsted for the blood of each other. In the five hundred years since that sorrow filled event, their hatred has thrived like a choking vine that if left unchecked destroys the tree which provides it a home."

Aker stood, his golden hair and bright blue eyes sparkled while yet revealing concern. He spoke to his fellow council leaders. "It is a state of affairs that we have toiled long and hard to bring to a just end. It seems each time we gain ground in our battle, the Evil One sows new seeds of doubt and hatred, like a wicked farmer in the night who plants weeds to destroy his neighbor's crop. Often do I despair of ever bringing Andite and Nodite together in brotherhood. This despite the fact that they have sprouted from the same family tree."

Seth nodded his agreement. "Forget not that Lucifer has the natural course of social evolution on his side, but not forever will this be true. The tribal stage of human development is but transitory. The time will come when humanity will remove itself from the darkness of hatred to stand in the light of brotherhood; when all humanity will understand they share the same Heavenly Parent. They must come to know that all religions worship the same Source and Center, no matter how different their traditions may be."

Aker nodded his agreement. "The race is likened unto the man thought blind who had but to open his eyes to see the splendor of the world," he said. "Our task is to help them see the insanity of their hatred."

"The true tragedy," Seth continued, "is that, because of Lucifer's folly, the race may someday achieve technical capabilities its citizens and governments will not be fully prepared to deal with in a wise manner. It has been seen on other rebellion-torn worlds. The ability to destroy grows faster than wisdom. Much suffering results".

"What are we to do in this current matter?" Aker asked. "My network of runners tells me that the Evil One has succeeded in convincing the Andites to embark upon an advance maneuver to thwart a supposed Nodite invasion. We have labored mightily to make the Andites understand that the Nodites plan no such incursion, but to no avail. They are committed to a preemptive strike."

"This we must undertake to prevent at all costs," Seth said. "When our ancestor Adam first arrived on this planet with his loyal and steadfast mate, Eve, their mission was to set the world back on the path that mankind had been diverted from, the way of sure growth through dedicated effort and acquired experience. Adam and Eve's failure to accomplish this weighs heavily upon us now."

"How are we to achieve peace between peoples of such animosity?" Aker asked. "As surely as night follows day will these warring parties cause our destruction if we allow their aggressions to go unchecked. Our history proves this."

Seth knew his friend to be correct in his assessment, understood that flare-ups of aggression were like small fires in a forest. If left on their own, all the trees would burn. "Aker, you and your loyal associates must redouble your efforts to convince the Andites of the folly of listening to the words of the Crafty One. They must come to understand that such a scheme as they are planning can only lead to disaster. I ask that you take on this mission of mercy before embarking upon your new journey."

The remainder of the meeting was taken up with discussions about how to accomplish this seemingly impossible task.

FIVE

The Baker Street Irregulars

Summer, 1985

Two evenings after Bruce Goldman and Roxanne Cabrini learned Lenny Cronin would be accompanying them to the Middle East they were sitting in their living room. The decor of the two-bedroom apartment was a parade that announced its owner's love of, and preoccupation with, ancient history, culture and lore.

The entryway was wallpapered with photos of archeological digs, unearthed artifacts, and framed news articles commemorating their expeditions, experience, and expertise. The show continued on into the living room where artwork from primitive cultures framed windows. South American pottery stood alongside ancient weapons in front of a wall mounted with African war masks. One section of the opposite wall was dedicated to fertility gods, goddesses, and rites. Small models of the gods stood erect on a shelf surrounded by photos of natives engaged in procreative ceremonies.

The TV was on with volume set low, the voices of the talking heads barely audible.

Bruce was sitting on the sofa, bent over the coffee table he was using for a desk. He stood, stretched, and took a deep breath. He wrinkled his nose and looked around for something. "Do you smell anything, Rox?"

She was sitting beside him reading a novel, knees tucked, her feet filling the space between them. She looked up, smiled, and shook her head; her long black hair polished her shoulders. "Not again," she said. "You're always smelling something. What is it now?"

Bruce put his hands on his hips. He sniffed twice, shook his head. "I don't know. It's gone now. I can't describe it. Anyway, what do you think about this guy Lenny Cronin?" He sat down on the black leather sofa and fingered through some his notes arrayed on the steel and glass coffee table.

She moved her bookmark to the current page, placed the hardcover on the table, and sat upright, the soft leather moaning beneath her. She crossed her long legs, nearly banging her knee on the table's sharp edge. "I'm not sure. He seems nice enough. And Sheila speaks highly of him."

Bruce faced Roxanne and rolled his eyes. "Duh? She's in love with him. Hardly objective."

Roxanne laughed. "Still. He seems OK."

"My main concern is his style," Bruce said.

"You don't like the way he dresses?" Roxanne asked, a sly grin plastering her face. "So what if his clothes are from a different era. You like antiques."

It was Bruce's turn to laugh. "You know I didn't mean his clothes style." He thought about how the reporter had been dressed when they had met in Perry Hazard's office. "Although he could use some help in that department. What I meant was he's an investigative reporter. He's only doing science stories as a punishment. This is a delicate situation we're in." He stood and stretched his back again, looked down at Roxanne and said, "We don't want anybody to know what we're looking for. It was bad enough we had to tell the TUSK Foundation. And look what happened there."

Roxanne remained quiet. They both knew there was nothing further to say on that subject.

"Only board members knew we were going to Israel and why," Bruce continued. "Thank God we didn't have to tell them any more. At least nobody knows our exact destination."

Roxanne gazed thoughtfully at Bruce, then smiled, uncrossed her legs and placed the left one between his. She gently rubbed her calf up and down his thigh, her toes inching closer and closer to his zipper. He smiled. She raised her foot to his stomach and pushed him away with a laugh. "You don't have to remind me we want to get in and out of Israel as quietly as possible."

He rebounded from his leaning tower stance and grabbed the exquisitely contoured offending leg. He rubbed her toes. Her eyelids drooped dreamily. "Hell, we don't want anybody. But if we must take a babysitter, I'm still not sure Lenny's the guy we want."

Roxanne pulled her foot back, sat up straight, and went face to face with his crotch. She ran her fingers along his inner thigh, taking up where the foot left off. She adjusted her stare northward, went eye to eye. "What do you mean?" she asked in a double entendre' voice.

Bruce wasn't certain how she meant the question. He decided to take it literally. "It's kind of like a prizefighter entering a cooking contest," Bruce explained. "Yeah, maybe he can cook, but will he take the gloves off?"

Roxanne continued absentmindedly teasing his thigh as she considered his words. They both knew their hopes of keeping the operation from under the microscopes of their competitors were now deader than a mummy. The *City Crier* editorial had assured that. Still, if they could keep the competition from stealing their signals, there was hope yet of completing the task and returning home with the booty before anyone was the wiser, including the Israelis.

"I wish I knew how Old Man Rizzo got that editorial printed in the first place," Bruce said.

"With his money, you need to ask? We know why anyway," Roxanne said. She had already expressed her opinion that the piece, which had painted Bruce and Roxanne with the same brush as famous forgers like Clifford Irving, while carefully refraining from directly calling them frauds, was payback for dumping her old boyfriend, Joe Rizzo, Junior. Roxanne had friends whose former lovers had played Jeckyl and Hyde on them, but despite many ex-boyfriends, and a few acrimonious breakups, this was her first experience with the darker side of relationships.

She had been teaching cultural anthropology at City University for three years when she started dating Joe Rizzo, Junior, namesake and sole offspring of the infamous industrialist. The Italian beauty was twenty-eight at the time and after three months had decided the relationship was a road to nowhere. The incendiary night she told Young Joe it was over made a blazing inferno seem like a campfire.

They had stopped off at a local pub for a few drinks after attending a movie. Roxanne had chosen the film purposely for its subject matter; an easy segue into what she carefully planned for the evening. The bar was crowded. The humming voices, tinkling glasses, and ringing cash registers provided background music for her screenplay. As they began sipping cocktails she said, "That was a pretty good movie, don't you think, Joe? I really thought it was interesting how she figured out a way to move on with her life without leaving any dead ends behind."

Joe Junior, as handsome as he was stupid, looked at her with his trademarked expression of sarcasm; the one he thought sexy but everyone else thought idiotic. He was about as hard to read as a schoolchild's primer. "What was so great about it? He should have tracked her down and dragged her ass home."

"Dragged her ass home?" Roxanne asked, her disbelief showing.

"Damn right. She left him for no good reason."

Roxanne began to realize that she might have made a mistake in trying to delicately ease her way into a breakup conversation with someone possessing the manners and single-mindedness of an elephant in a peanut store. "Well first of all, she didn't leave him for no reason, Joe. He was stifling her. She wasn't cut out to be someone's window dressing. She was a doctor."

"That's the problem with women today," Joe said. "They want it all. Everything has to revolve around them. I'm glad we're not like that."

OK. Here it comes. I'll never get a better chance than this, she thought. "You don't see any similarities between us and the couple in the movie, Joe?"

He took a long slug from his drink, and placed the glass back on the table. He shook his head and tightened his lips. Obviously this thinking thing was tough. "No way. That guy was a wimp. He let her walk out on him like she was the Queen of England and he was a street kid selling apples."

The storm gathering on Roxanne's face nullified her self-promise to remain calm this evening. "You don't see any similarities between them and us? What about the fact that all he wanted her for was to show her off to his friends? What about how he prevented her from taking a better position at the hospital because it would mean more time at work? Or how about whenever they went out it was where he wanted to go?"

"But you like it when I decide where to go. That's a big difference."

Roxanne shook her head in dismay. "I may have liked it the first few times, but in the three months we've been dating, I'll bet tonight's the second or third time it was my choice. And if you'll remember correctly, earlier this evening you complained about going to see this movie."

"No shit." he said. "And now I know why. I see where this is going. You want us to be more like when she found that new guy. Jesus, what a piece of work he was."

Roxanne couldn't believe her ears. Somewhere this dialogue had taken a wrong turn; a fork in the path had appeared when she wasn't looking. But at least the conversation was verifying her decision. "Joe, I'm just going to come out and say it. I'm ending our relationship. If it ever was a relationship. Lately it's seemed more like a dictatorship. I wish you well, but I can't see you anymore."

Joe Junior looked at Roxanne as if she had suddenly appeared out of thin air. As if he couldn't be sure she was real. As if her words had been spoken in a foreign tongue. "What are you saying? That we're through?"

His lack of comprehension jolted her. She began seriously doubting her choice in men. After all, if she could get involved with a lunkhead like this guy, who might be next, Saddam Hussein? "I think I was pretty clear on that," she said through clenched teeth.

"Bullshit. You're not breaking up with me for no good reason. Who is it? Who's the guy?" He slapped his hand on the table causing their drinks to dance. People at nearby tables stared in curiosity.

Roxanne made a gesture of apology to the onlookers, then turned back to face her date from the fiery depths. "Joe, calm down. There's nobody else. These things happen all the time. We just aren't right for each other, that's all." Could she see steam coming from his ears?

"Listen to me, bitch. I know you're seeing somebody else. If you think you can just walk away and I'll play the candy ass nice guy who takes it all in stride, you're farther off base than a peanut vendor in the nigger seats."

"Thanks for the verification, Joe. As if I needed any. I'm not going to sit hear and listen to that kind of talk. I put up with your profanity and crudeness because I thought there was a real person hidden underneath. At times you actually seemed to have a heart beating in that big chest of yours, but now I know it's just a pump. I guess that was my mistake." Roxanne stood and walked toward the exit. "I'm sorry it has to end this way, but I'm even more sorry it ever started."

As Joe watched her leave the table he yelled, "If you think you, or your new boyfriend, have heard the last of me, you're crazy. You'll be back, one way or another." She never looked back.

The next day Roxanne was having lunch in the school cafeteria. Language professor, Phyllis Willette approached her table along with Bruce Goldman, the new head of the archeology department. Roxanne had not yet met him.

"Hi, Roxie, mind if we join you?" Phyllis asked. "This is Bruce Goldman. Bruce, this is Roxanne Cabrini."

Bruce shook hands with Roxanne before taking his seat. "Hi. I hope you don't mind us barging in on you like this, but I insisted Phyllis introduce us."

Roxanne unwrapped her ham sandwich and looked at him closely. He was short and skinny, but attractive in an almost delicate way, with fine bones and features. His piercing black eyes had yet to leave hers. "You insisted huh? Why was that?" she asked.

He continued his deep gravitational stare, she felt its pull, then he released her with a smile that seemed very sincere. "It's because I'm attracted to you.

The first time I saw you, I knew I had to meet you." Only then did he take a bite from his own sandwich.

Roxanne had known teams of men attracted by her good looks. She was used to that. But those shallow encounters never worked out. Last night's fiasco was a classic example. "Look, you seem like a nice enough guy, but I just ended a relationship very badly. I'm not ready to play the Dating Game just yet."

Bruce's quick smile nearly pierced her defenses, caught her unaware. She had just shot the guy down hadn't she?

"You broke up with Joe Rizzo huh? Good for you."

Roxanne leaned back into her seat. She gave him a suspicious look, and tugged at her ear lobe. "How did you know I was dating him? Have you been spying on me?"

"Hang on a minute, Roxie," Phyllis said. "I told Bruce last week when he asked me to introduce you two that you were involved with Joe."

"I know something about him," Bruce said, "and I knew he wasn't right for you."

"Oh really," Roxanne said with a mixture of sarcasm and curiosity. "And just how did you know that?"

"Let's face it," Bruce said. "The guy's father is one of the biggest jerks on the planet. And you know what they say about fruit not falling far from the tree? The way I hear it, Joe Junior's so much like his old man, one time he rented a family and ignored them just to see how it felt from the other side."

Roxanne laughed, almost choked on her food. She swallowed and said, "Rented a family huh? Where'd he go, 'Families R Us'? OK, you called that one right. But I'm still not ready to start dating again."

Bruce gave Roxanne a look she decided lived in the same neighborhood as smug, but was just around the corner from endearing. "I didn't ask you for a date."

Roxanne thought she should have been offended, or at least embarrassed by his statement. Instead, much to her surprise, she felt drawn to this confident little man with the enticing smile. How was it, she wondered, that someone as handsome and financially well-off as Joe Rizzo could be such a world class baby, while someone like Bruce Goldman, who seemingly had far less, could come off as charming, warm, smart, and confident? "OK, you didn't ask me for a date. But you were going to, right?"

"Absolutely. Would you like to go out with me some time?"

Roxanne laughed in spite of herself. Just last night she had sworn off men, at least for a little while. But here she was, less than twenty-four hours later, considering another ride on the relationship roller coaster. "What the hell. Why not?"

Over the next few months Bruce and Roxanne became a couple. One day a friend informed her that Joe Rizzo Junior was telling people that she had dropped him for another man. That was bad enough, according to the friend, but Joe was telling people that she had 'dumped him for a little twerp Jew school teacher' and that was 'too much to take'. Roxanne's was warned to be careful, and she took that seriously. With an enemy like Joe Rizzo, you needed friends.

So what do you think?" Bruce asked Roxanne as he arranged his expedition notes and placed them back on the coffee table. He pulled her hand, still on his thigh, and lovingly sucked on her ring finger. "Should we go along with it? Can we trust Lenny Cronin?"

Roxanne pulled him onto the sofa and rested her head on his shoulder. "We've already said we agreed to this and he's coming over any time now to start the ball rolling. I'm sure everything will be fine."

"I hope you're right," he said, and turned to kiss her.

At that moment, Lenny was standing outside their Baker Street apartment door. He was ready to lay the groundwork for his first article on archeology, whoopee ding. He rang the bell. After a delay of nearly a minute, he rang again. Roxanne finally appeared. Her hair was disheveled, but she smiled and ushered him into the apartment.

He felt sloppy and out of place in the orderly apartment. Even with all the artifacts, everything seemed to mesh, but Lenny thought he smelled something odd. The place had the feel of a museum. He noticed the display of fertility gods, including the graphic photos, and wondered what the hell that was all about. Maybe ancient history wasn't so boring after all.

Lenny had been doing his homework the past few days, boning up on archeology and anthropology. He'd been surprised to learn there were so many inconsistencies in the two sciences. He'd always considered ancient history to be cut and dried; cold, hard facts. When he learned otherwise, he decided he had the basis of an informative and thought provoking article. But it was still science.

Bruce stood when they entered the living room. "Hi, Lenny." As the two shook hands, Bruce crinkled his nose. "There it is again. Do you smell anything, Lenny?"

Lenny sniffed the air like a bloodhound. His eyebrows furrowed. "I think so," he said. "What is it?"

"That's what I'm trying to figure out," Bruce said. "Roxanne can't even smell it."

"It's gone now," Lenny said. "Somehow it smelled OLD. You know what I mean?"

Roxanne snickered. "There are lots of old things in this room. We'll figure it out later. Let's have a drink and get acquainted."

As they sipped their cocktails, Bruce and Roxanne cuddled up on the sofa and explained briefly to Lenny about their work in the Middle East; how they had found a reference in the Dead Sea Scrolls to even older documents. That reference, they said, was what had led them to their current quest. They also told him about an old man they had interviewed, whose family history mentioned some very old manuscripts. They were supposed to be hidden in the caves south of Jericho, near the Dead Sea.

"So that's how you got to this point," Lenny said. "Let me tell you what I've learned about all those mysteries you told me to check up on."

Lenny then shared some things he had discovered during his research. "One of the things I learned is that in Bolivia, near Santa Cruz, concrete roads have been discovered that pre-date the invention of the wheel. Which begs the question; why would people without wheels need concrete roads?"

"I don't know," Roxanne said, "But speaking of Bolivia, did you know there is evidence that the ancient city of Tiahuanaco, near where those ancient roads are, could be over twelve thousand years old? And fair skinned, light haired people, who were much taller than the natives, supposedly built it. There are hundreds of examples like this. We're coming to believe there may have been civilizations on this earth older than anyone has yet been able to prove."

"Those concrete roads are exactly the type of thing we're talking about", Bruce said. "We know much less about ancient peoples than we thought even a few years ago. For instance, there is a map that is hundreds of years old, showing the coastline of the Antarctic land mass, under the ice."

Lenny shrugged. "Yeah, so?"

Bruce was used to explaining, so he didn't hesitate. "That may not sound so impressive at first blush, but modern scientists weren't able to verify the accuracy of this map until nineteen fifty-seven, yet someone from the ancient past knew what Antarctica looked like under the ice."

"But, Antarctica has been under ice for thousands of years," Lenny said. "How could they have such information?"

"We aren't sure," Bruce answered. "But it's a fact. The map exists. It's called the Piri Ries map after the Persian sailor who used it, and who acknowledged that it was a copy of a much older one. There are other maps showing the Antarctic land mass as well, the Mercator Map and Buache Map, to name two. All of them are hundreds of years old at the very least."

Roxanne waited for Lenny to stop scribbling on his notepad before adding, "And how can we explain the sudden emergence of an advanced mathematical system at the very beginning of the first Egyptian dynasty? They used decimals, understood the relationship of pi to the circumference of a circle, and even understood geometry. In fact, nearly every significant aspect of ancient Egyptian civilization, from their worldview to their sciences and arts, was fully formed at the beginning of their history. Not only that, but they never improved after that. How does a primitive culture suddenly transform into a relatively advanced one whose people could smelt gold and copper as pure as we do today? Who gave them this knowledge of metallurgy, astronomy, and mathematics? We don't know, but we are determined to find out."

Lenny had what he came for. "Thanks a lot, you two. My readers will have a lot to think about once this article comes out. I'll see you both in a couple of days." As he stood to leave, he looked around the room one last time to soak up a last impression to include in his article. "By the way, I love your decorating theme. What do you call it, Neo-archaic?" He received a condescending smile for an answer.

After shutting the door behind Lenny, Roxanne turned to Bruce and asked, "That wasn't so bad was it?"

"No, he seems like an okay guy, if you ignore his sophomoric comment about our decorating," Bruce smiled. "Maybe this will work out all right after all."

Roxanne grinned mischievously. "I wonder if he's the adventurous type?"

Bruce smiled in the same manner. "His girlfriend sure is hot," he said as he grabbed her around the waist, anxious to finish what they had started before Lenny's arrival.

Lenny's article created even more controversy and discussion than he'd hoped for. The *Chronicle* story about mysterious ancient civilizations was suddenly a hot topic of conversations around water coolers and over beer and hot wings. Who knew anybody cared about that stuff? The feedback he got revealed that about half the readers thought discovery of new facts could only enhance man's understanding of his place in the universe. One quarter thought it didn't matter one way or the other. There was a highly vocal minority of fewer than ten percent who thought the whole thing was an attempt to undermine the Bible and could only lead to disaster.

Joe Rizzo Senior, reading the article from behind his ornate mahogany desk, didn't care about any of that. The only thing that mattered to him was the ruination of his son's former girlfriend and her Jew boyfriend.

He had grown up blanketed in wealth that had been accumulated by his grandfather during the latter part of the nineteenth century. The majority of that money came from a large textile mill that sat on the banks of the Merrimac River in Lawrence, Massachusetts. The grandfather had stirred up a hornet's nest within his WASP infested social circle when he chose to marry a Jewess, albeit one of extraordinary beauty and personality. The family patriarch's stature had the power to relegate the commentary about his choice of bride to the level of background murmuring. Their son, Joe Senior's father, did not enjoy the same social status and suffered ostracism from the mill-owner's tightly knit society after the potentate's death. This had begotten a hatred in the man for his Jewish heritage.

The next generation, of which Joe Rizzo was the eldest, went beyond hate and erased all evidence of Jewish ancestry from the family archives. By the time the current generation came into being the stain on the family record had been washed clean. This revisionist history was so thoroughly written that Joe Junior had no idea his father's animosity for everything Jewish, a legacy the son willingly carried on, was anything other than logical and based on common sense.

The elder Rizzo dropped the newspaper onto his antique desk and said to his son, "Well it looks like those two are going on that expedition after all. And it's because of the damn Chronicle. After that editorial we planted, I had the board ready to cut off funding. Until that asshole Perry Hazzard convinced that dumb bitch Barbara Peterson to switch her vote, that is."

Joe Junior was sitting in a very opulent, very expensive, and very uncomfortable antique chair in front of his father's desk. "I guess that's it then huh, Dad?"

Rizzo looked at his son with disgust. "Jesus, sometimes I wonder whose kid you are. I don't give up that easily and I better never hear that you do either. There's still plenty we can do. I have contacts in Jerusalem and all over the Middle East."

The son withered under the father's intense glare. He now wondered if it had been smart to get the old man so fired up in the first place. At the time, it had seemed like a good way to win Roxanne back. He'd thought with her new boyfriend's reputation ruined, she'd come running back to him wagging her fine tail like a lost puppy. Now he wasn't sure she was worth the effort. But he knew that once his father's mind was set on something, it became harder than concrete. He decided he'd better go along for the ride. Besides, maybe he'd still get her back. "What do you have in mind, Pop?"

"You leave everything up to me. By the time I'm through with those two, the closest they'll get to ancient artifacts is a museum. Your Jew loving ex-girlfriend will come crawling back begging forgiveness." He leaned forward, fixed his eyes onto his son's, and said, "She better be worth it."

SIX

A Flight for Life

Fall, 1985

The long awaited day of departure had arrived. Lenny met Bruce and Roxanne at the airport terminal and had been annoyed to learn they had changed the flight arrangements to save money. They were twelve hours into the journey to Jerusalem now, and even though they were on the last leg, they still would have to endure the gauntlet of customs and hotel registration. His dream of a non-stop flight, two stiff drinks, and a long nap had turned into a nightmare of rough landings, breath holding take-offs, and an uncomfortable window seat. No wonder he hated traveling. Good thing he was a talented napper.

He woke from his short sleep and looked out through the window to his left. The deep blue Mediterranean Sea was a white-capped carpet. As the plane banked, the shoreline of Israel came into view. He was about to comment on its seeming tranquility when he heard Bruce say something.

"Did you hear me, Lenny?" Bruce said from the aisle seat.

Lenny turned to his right with a surprised look. He looked across Roxanne to face Bruce. "Did I hear what?"

"I just wanted to finalize our deal before we land."

They had decided that each would stay out of the other's way as much as possible. "I'm fine with it, but my boss is still going to expect some articles on you two, so I'll have to come around to your campsite once or twice."

"Fair enough, Lenny," Bruce said. "But you can't let the word out on where we are. Deal?"

Lenny had no problems about keeping their little expedition on the QT. He didn't want to do any more work than possible involving dinosaurs, or whatever they were looking for. He was hunting bigger game. "Deal."

Roxanne tilted to her left and leaned on Lenny's knees as she looked through the window. "It is beautiful isn't it? It's hard to believe the thousands of years of strife that have been going on down there. It looks so tranquil."

As the plane began its descent, Lenny looked to the hills and mountains that separated the sea from the desert. "I was about to say something similar. A lot of history has been written down there. Much as I hate to say it, I think the scribes have a lot more work yet to do."

"You expecting trouble, Lenny?" Bruce asked.

Lenny wasn't expecting trouble. He never did. But, somehow it seemed to know his address wherever he was staying. "I'm not exactly going out on a limb in predicting turmoil," he answered. "Just because it's been relatively quiet for a year or two doesn't mean the party's over."

"That's one of the reasons we want to lay low," Bruce said. "You never know."

"There's so much hatred and mistrust down there, I wonder if they'll ever figure it out," Roxanne mused.

They were silent for the remainder of the landing as each considered the implications of the hatred and mistrust that smoldered below them ever ready to flare up into a firestorm.

After passing through customs, they hopped into a cab. Bruce gave the driver the address of their hotel and the car headed for the edge of the city founded in tribute to God. The cab merged slowly into the clotted traffic, and they were soon engulfed in the noise, clamor, hustle, and bustle that surrounded them.

The buzz of voices speaking in different languages, the church bells ringing loudly in competition with the Muslim calls to prayer barely registered in the minds of the jet lagged archaeologists and their journalist hitchhiker. They were as tired as their clothes were wrinkled and had thoughts only of eating a good meal, followed by a night's rest. They exited the cab in front of the Holiday Inn. As they entered the American style lobby, Lenny thought *Seen one, seen 'em all.* Somehow, though, he was comforted by the familiarity.

Around ten P.M., after dinner at a local restaurant, Bruce, Roxanne, and Lenny returned to the hotel. Jet lag had their bodies feeling like it was early morning and they'd been up all night. Sleep, blessed rest, was their most fervent wish at the moment.

When the trio arrived at the door to the two scientist's room, Bruce opened it and stepped back to allow Roxanne first entry. As she went in, Lenny heard her gasp and say, "Bruce, we've been robbed."

"What?" he said as he followed her into the room with Lenny close behind. Bruce looked around. "Son of a bitch!"

They began to survey the damage. Clothes were strewn everywhere. The bed had been destroyed, with the mattress turned over onto the floor. The desk drawers were upside down and their contents spilled out.

Bruce turned to Roxanne and said, "This is a fine, 'How do you do.'"

Roxanne went to the bathroom. "Oh damn it! They spilled all my cosmetics. Why would anyone do such a stupid thing?"

Before Bruce could comment, Lenny left their room and headed for his own, two doors down. He wasn't sure why, but he just had a feeling he'd better. As he opened the door and looked around, he said, "Shit!" He immediately turned and headed back to the others. "They hit my room too," he said upon entering.

Bruce turned sharply to face Lenny. "You mean you've been robbed too?"

"My room looks like it spawned a tornado." He went to the phone. "I'd better call the front desk. Do you think we're the only ones that have been hit?"

Bruce's face looked like he'd swallowed a sourball. "I sure hope not. I'd hate to think of what it could mean if we were."

Roxanne came out of the bathroom, concern on her face. "You're not talking about Joe Rizzo are you?"

"I'm not talking about Peter Rabbit," Bruce said.

Roxanne started picking up their clothes from the floor. "But, darling, do you really think he'd go through the trouble of having someone half way around the world break into our hotel room just to steal a few things?"

Bruce shook his head slowly. "I don't know, but my grandfather used to say, 'When you step in dog shit, don't get mad at the cat.' Besides, who's to say this person wasn't looking through our papers to find out where our expedition is headed?"

Lenny hung up the phone. "I think Roxanne is right. The manager just told me that some other rooms on this floor were broken into. Looks like we just had some bad luck."

"Let's hope so," Bruce said.

"Your grandfather sounds interesting," Lenny said. "Did he have any other sayings?"

Bruce smiled. "My grandfather had a catchphrase for every occasion. He used to take ordinary phrases like, 'say it with flowers' and turn them around to something like, 'say it with flowery words.' You know, stupid stuff like that."

"That's kind of like me," Lenny said. "I like to take cliches and mix 'em up. Mix-a-phors, I call them."

"Such as?" Bruce asked.

Lenny thought for a moment as he helped straighten the room. He turned a chair back on it legs, then said, "How about this; if Joe Rizzo is behind this, when we get home we'll, 'Send him off with his spiked tail between his cloven hoofed legs.'"

Bruce and Roxanne looked at Lenny like HE had a tail and cloven hooves. Neither said a word.

Lenny stared back at them. Their continued silence was deafening. His fingers filled the void by drumming a tune on the chairback. Finally, he could take it no longer. "Guys, I never claimed they were all winners."

"I'll tell you one thing," Bruce said. "If Joe Rizzo really is behind these break-ins, we better keep our eyes open and our backs covered."

Lenny went back to his own room. He finished cleaning up the mess and decided to give Sheila a call. He mixed himself a cocktail from the mini-bar. *Thank God for American chains that cater to American tourists,* he thought. He'd already had a few after-dinner drinks and was a little buzzed. He picked up the phone and dialed the numbers. "Hi, Red," he said when he heard her voice.

"Hi, there. How was your flight?"

Oh how he loved her voice. Even over the phone it found his heart. "Nothing unusual to report. I'm just relaxing in my room right now." No sense getting her worked up over the break-ins.

"Give me a second to turn the TV down," she said. Lenny heard the noise of the phone being placed on a table and shortly after that, the muffled voices in the background disappeared.

"What were you watching?" he asked when she returned.

"The news. Actually it's a report on where you guys are."

This came as no great surprise to Lenny. The Middle East was in the news almost every night. "Anything new I should know about?"

"A couple of Israeli outposts have been attacked. The report said no one has claimed responsibility yet. The thinking is there may be a new group behind it."

Lenny took a sip from his drink. This wasn't the first time he'd heard speculation about a new faction of Palestinians becoming active in the region. They seemed to pop up like desert flowers after a rainstorm. He said as much to Sheila. "I got some phone numbers from my boss to get me in touch with some of the players out here. Maybe they'll know what's going on."

"Please be careful, Lenny. You could get hurt."

"Don't worry. My editor knows these guys. He says they're word is good. I won't take any chances."

"I hope not. They play by a different set of rules out there, you know."

"I said don't worry. . . . Ma." As soon as he said it, he wished he could take it back. Lenny shook his head disgustedly and took another swallow from his drink.

"Lenny, I'm not trying to be your mother."

Lenny knew this was true, but couldn't help smiling at how much her tone of voice sounded just like his mother's. "I know you're not. Just don't worry, OK? I hate that."

They spoke for a few more minutes but it was obvious to both of them the mood had changed to a darker color so they decided to hang up before it reached black.

As Lenny prepared a nightcap, he chastised himself for getting upset. Why couldn't he just keep his yammer shut? His thoughtless wiseass remarks were always turning sparks into infernos. Where the hell can you buy a fire extinguisher for something like that?

The next morning, while Bruce and Roxanne were purchasing and renting what they would need for their expedition, Lenny went to a pay phone across from the hotel. He dropped some coins in and dialed the number given him by his boss, Perry Hazzard. On the third ring it was picked up and a man said something in Arabic.

"I'm sorry," Lenny said, "but I only speak English. A friend of mine gave me this number. Perry Hazzard? He told me you would be expecting to hear from me."

After a moment of silence, during which Lenny thought the phone was handed to someone else, a heavily accented voice said, "Mister Cronin?"

"Yes."

"Mister Hazzard has told us of you. Do you understand what you are asking? If we take you into our confidence and you betray us, you will die. Do you want to risk this?"

Lenny thought this was a very good question. Taken literally, the answer was a firm and resounding no. Back home, surrounded by tedium and contemplating only theoretical danger, he'd had no problem with that question. Now that he was faced with the reality, he wasn't as certain. His boss had told Lenny these people were serious players. He now knew how serious. This was no Saturday night poker game. But, he was here, and he wanted his old job back more than almost anything.

"As long as we agree beforehand on the ground rules, you won't have to worry about me breaking them."

"Very well, Mister Cronin. Let us discuss what will be required of you. Should you agree to these terms, then we can meet in person."

The next day Bruce found the home of the man he was looking for. His name was Mohammed Abdulah, and he'd been recommended by the car rental agency. After introducing himself and explaining why he was there, Bruce asked him some questions and, satisfied with the answers, offered him the job of camp maintenance. He seemed more than eager for the work.

"Do not worry about a thing, Mister Goldman, sir. I will take care of all your camp needs, and I am very well acquainted with your vehicle. I have worked on these many times," he said while patting the fender of the rented Jeep as if it were a pet.

After agreeing that he would arrive the next morning at eight thirty to pick the man up, Bruce drove off.

After Bruce's vehicle had disappeared from sight, another car approached Mohammed. An Arabic man who'd followed Bruce from the hotel exited the Mercedes and approached Bruce's recent hire. After a few minutes of discussion, the stranger took a large roll of money from his pocket. He peeled some bills from the stack and gave them to Mohammed.

"It will be as you wish," Mohammed said to the man as he started back toward his car.

SEVEN

A Case of Identity

Fall, 1973

In the ensuing years since Achmed had become Arafat's main weapon against dissent, the young man had become indispensable to the chairman. Especially valuable had the band become when the Israelis forced the PLO leadership into exile in Lebanon. Having maintained secrecy, Achmed and his crew were not expelled from the homeland. This meant whenever a threat was posed to the PLO's position, Achmed could be called upon to deal with it. In such a manner did fear become the overriding factor that kept Arafat in power during his forced expatriation.

Throughout the early part of the seventies, the small band of youthful fighters remained a powerful disciplinary tool for the Chairman. In the early fall of nineteen seventy-three, Achmed received word that someone wished to meet with him.

"Who is it that wishes to see me?" he asked the man delivering the message. They were seated in a small cafe.

"His name is Sabri al-Banna," the man said. "His desire is to become more active in the movement."

"I know of him," Achmed said. "He was Chairman Arafat's representative, first in Sudan, and then Iraq. What is it he wishes to see me about? Surely the Chairman is who he should speak with."

The man glanced furtively around the room. There were few customers this early in the morning. At two of the tables old men were playing backgammon, while seated at a back corner table was a single customer reading the morning papers. Apparently satisfied no one was listening, the man leaned forward and placed his elbows upon the table bringing his lips to within inches of Achmed's ears. "It is the chairman he wishes to talk to you about."

Achmed, the beginnings of a scraggly beard betraying his youth, looked at the man with a penetrating glare. "What is it about the chairman he wishes to discuss?"

The man straightened in his chair affecting a pose of caution. "I can say no more. Sabri al-Babba has instructed me to ask only for a meeting."

"Very well," Achmed said. "I will meet with him."

After a time and place were arranged, the man quickly left. Achmed remained at his table. He looked across the room toward the solitary man who was reading the papers. Achmed nodded his head slightly and the man placed the paper on the table, picked up his cup of coffee, and approached Achmed.

"Sit down, Mazen," Achmed said. As the man did so, Achmed explained to him the purpose of the meeting he had just held.

"What do you think this is about?" Mazen asked.

Achmed surveyed the room one more time. Satisfied no spies were listening in, he answered, "I can only speculate. We have heard rumblings recently that Chairman Arafat is not acting forcefully enough. Perhaps Sabri al-Banna thinks I may have some influence."

"I do not think so," Mazen replied.

"And why not?" Achmed demanded. "Do you presume to think I wield no influence with Arafat? Many times has he commended me personally for our efforts on his behalf."

"I meant no insult, brother. But we are just boys in the Chairman's eyes. You are eighteen and I am barely twenty. We are tools for Yasser Arafat and nothing more. He would no more listen to our advice than he would to a woman's."

Achmed's eyes enlarged. His body stiffened. His right hand moved toward his knife. "You dare compare me to a woman? Mind your words well, my friend. An insult of such gravity, coming even from you, will not stand."

Mazen looked calmly at his compatriot. "Sheath your anger, brother. There was no insult in my words. I merely wished to portray how Arafat perceives us."

Achmed's expression softened. His hand returned to the table. "Forgive me. My anger at times knows no control. Like a whirlwind from the desert does it arise within me, seemingly from nowhere and of its own accord."

"This I know well. I have seen men die who have incurred your wrath," Mazen said. "I myself have killed in fits of anger. But there can be no room for animosity between you and me. We are brothers to the end." He raised his cup of coffee and drank.

"Brothers to the end," Achmed repeated, as he too drank the dark sugary brew.

Two days later Achmed was seated at the same table. Across from him sat Sabri al-Banna, Arafat's ambassador to Iraq; al-Banna wore the traditional red and white Palestinian headdress and western style shirts. Achmed's khaki pants and shirt, and black military boots, contrasted with al-Banna's white shirt, black dress slacks and highly polished Italian loafers.

After the usual pleasantries and false compliments had been dispensed with, Sabri al-Banna explained why he had asked for the meeting. "I will be forthright with my words. Times like these and situations like ours demand probity. Can I count on you to do likewise, Achmed?"

Achmed wondered if the diplomat could be taken at face value. It had been his experience that men of words, like al-Banna, often said one thing and meant another. They subverted the beauty of Arabic with their overly colorful phrases and inciting words; eloquence used to manipulate, cajole, incite, and influence. While the fired up mobs responded to the rhetoric, those who uttered it stood on the sidelines. All the while, men of action dealt with the consequences of backstabbing schemes and hidden agendas.

Achmed expressed insult. "My word has never before been questioned."

"I would not think of such a thing," al-Banna replied. "I merely wish to convey that what I am here to discuss with you is very delicate and discretion is paramount. I must ask your promise that what we say here goes not beyond these walls. At least for now."

"Very well," Achmed said. "You have my word. Now what is it you wish to say?"

"I would like to know your opinion of the current state of affairs. How do you feel about the Palestinian Liberation Organization's leadership? Do you think they are doing enough for the cause? Can they get our homeland returned?"

Achmed remained silent for a moment. Was this man expressing dissatisfaction with Chairman Arafat and the other PLO leaders? Or was he testing Achmed for his loyalty at the instigation of those same leaders? "I am sure the Chairman is doing all he can to insure the return."

Al-Banna sipped his coffee. He placed the cup on the table. He remained silent for a moment. Finally he spoke. "I can see you are being cautious. As perhaps you should be. Let me tell you what I, and some others of like mind, think. We believe more must be done. We feel the leadership is growing complacent with the current state of affairs. Arafat walks a fence between those who desire action, and those who betray us with their pleas for negotiations. The leadership is out of touch, exiled, first to Lebanon and now in Tunis. I, and others whom I am today representing, have decided more must be done. Day by day, Arafat replaces action with words. Moment by moment those words become as effective as the bite of a venomless snake."

The young fighter studied the man carefully. The words he'd spoken rang true in Achmed's heart. He too believed that Arafat and his coterie were becoming less and less effective, isolated as they were in Tunis. But he wasn't ready to abandon the PLO. Especially not with money flowing in every month. Achmed knew al-Banna was a man with many connections. He also knew the man was an effective fundraiser. Perhaps a profitable arrangement could be made. "What do you have in mind?"

Al-Banna told of how he had been authorized to finance new activities and groups with the aim of stepping up covert activities against the oppressors. After some intense negotiations, Achmed agreed to throw his support behind the new group. He insisted that his involvement be kept a secret. With this new commitment came more funds for Achmed to use at his discretion. He now had three sources of money; Arafat, his anonymous benefactor from Syria, and this new arrangement. And so it was that the, "Flaming Arrows of Assad," became even more active in the arena, carrying out brazen raids for the cause, and secretly executing Arafat's assassination orders. For ten years, he maintained this delicate state of affairs, ever mindful of the precarious position he was in, but also hungry for the money. In time, his cash account became such that he felt compelled to do more for the cause.

In nineteen eighty-three Achmed decided on a new use for some of the funds. He determined to finance a new direction in the struggle. Modeled on the "Black September" splinter group that had shocked the world during the seventy-two Olympics, Achmed's new efforts would take the struggle outside the confines of Palestine. To the very homes of the Zionist supporting American people would blows for freedom be struck. Achmed and his men would allow no peace, permit no comfort, grant no contentment to those who provided solace, succor, and support to the enemies of Islam. Shortly after this decision was made, Achmed held a meeting with his trusted lieutenant, Mazen Mousaka.

As the two experienced and well trained killers sat at a table in a small cafe, Achmed said to his best friend, "Mazen, it is time for us to part ways."

The surprised and hurt look on Mazen's face touched Achmed's heart. "What have I done to offend you, brother? I would sooner cut off my arm than do wrong in your eyes."

Achmed looked with affection into his compatriot's dark face. He knew that Mazen was being sincere. He knew also that what he was about to say would mean the two, who had shared and risked so much together in the struggle, might never again see each other. He reached across the table and placed his right hand upon his loyal friend's shoulder. "You have done nothing of offense, my brother. Your loyalty has been tested and proven true, even in the pits of despair; your courage forged in the fires of combat; your honor proved beyond question."

Mazen smiled with gratitude and relief. "Then what is the meaning of your words, Achmed? Why must we part? My heart aches to know."

"For over thirty years have our people struggled. Our pain screams to a deaf world day after day. Like a great shadow does it darken our lives. Yet the return of our homeland seems no closer this moment than on the day I was born. The world, and America in particular, must feel our suffering."

"But they do see," Mazen said. "How can they not?"

"They may see, but they do not feel. Like a landowner whose comfort comes on the backs of peasants, the Americans sell arms to our enemies and reap the rewards. Like the caravan owner who ships goods to and fro without dirtying his hands, do they sit on their couches eating pork and drinking wine while others do their dirty work. We must show them their hands are not clean. They must learn that he who sows the firestorm reaps the inferno."

Mazen forcefully nodded his agreement. "Tell me what we must do."

"You must go to America, my friend. Once there you will live the life of an ordinary immigrant. Over the months I will send some of our brothers to join you. Then, when the time is ripe, you will burst from your hiding place like a starved beast. Death and destruction, to the very doorsteps of those who support our enemies, will you deliver. No longer will they feel the pinpricks of faraway strife, for a dagger in their hearts shall you plunge. Eternal joy in the bosom of Allah will be your reward."

And so it was that during the year of nineteen eighty-three, after tearful farewells, Mazen and two others made their way to the outskirts of Boston. Mazen found work as a cab driver. He worked hard, and patiently awaited his date with destiny.

By early nineteen eighty-five, Achmed had become disaffected with Arafat and the PLO leadership. Still exiled in Tunis, the organization was becoming less and less effective, and in the minds of some, Achmed among them, had actually become a hindrance to the cause. The final straw was a rumor that Arafat was considering official recognition of the hated Israel. Achmed decided to disassociate himself from the chairman. Others felt more needed to be done. A meeting was called.

Those in attendance were leery of one another. Many of their fellow outspoken critics of Arafat had mysteriously disappeared or been found dead in the streets bearing signs tied to their bodies warning others of like mind. None knew of Achmed's hand in this. As a hero of the resistance he was above suspicion. His band of warriors had carried out many attacks against the occupiers.

After nearly two decades of turmoil and Israeli occupation following the Six-Day War, there came a period of calm. In fact, it had been so quiet, that many of the local villagers seemed to have complacently accepted the strictures of Israeli rule. This state of affairs was anathema to those in attendance at the meeting. They would not allow their fellow Palestinians, many of whom wanted nothing more than to be left alone, to submit to the Israelis. These radicals were always ready to stir up trouble. They needed no other reason than the complacency of the locals and the ineffectiveness of Arafat to scratch at the thin scab covering Palestinian wounds.

Sheik Ahmed Yasin, a particularly vehement Jew hater, was especially fed up with the lack of action on the part of the Palestinian Liberation Organization and its leader. He had called these men together with the idea of founding a new, more radical group to lead the people in an all out war to end Israeli rule. His aim was the complete annihilation of the Jewish State.

"Let this meeting come to order," the sheik said. "We meet in this holy mosque to praise Allah and beg His help and blessings for our holy endeavor."

"We must act to prevent the Zionist expansion." One man shouted. "While Arafat and his lackeys enjoy the sun of Tunis, the hated ones build settlements on our land. This must be stopped."

"The very reason I called you here this night," sheik Yasin said. "It is time we take matters into our own hands. These Jewish settlements are a threat to our very existence. He who believes the Zionists will live up to their words and relinquish these lands for peace has the brains of an ass. The settlements must be destroyed."

"Arafat and his donkeys sit on their verandas while we suffer," a voice shouted.

"Arafat is a pork eater and wine drinker," sheik Yasin charged. "He offends Allah with every breath he takes. He espouses a separate Palestinian state alongside the motherless Zionists. This will never be. I promise you we will force the Jewish pigs into the sea. Every last one of them."

And so it came to be that a new and more violent group of Palestinians, who took the name Hamas, came to exist. They promised action, and began a more deadly phase of the struggle that seemed without end. Achmed, ever the agile tightrope walker, became one of the new movement's most valued weapons. In order to maintain a level of secrecy, he took a new name, the name of his Syrian benefactor. From this day forward when asked his name he would reply, "You may call me Assad."

Only he and Mazen Mousaka knew of his secret cell in America.

EIGHT

Light in the Darkness

Spring, 10,000 BC

Two days after Aker learned he was to lead a new expedition to unknown lands, following a daylong trek, he and his assistant Lan were entering the hut of Motep, the chief of the local Andite tribe. The chief had agreed to the meeting at the behest of Aker, whom he trusted and honored for his efforts to improve the existence of the Andites. The tribe's abilities to grow food and manufacture implements had greatly expanded with the knowledge imparted by the Edenites and for this the Andites were grateful and had sworn allegiance to the Edenic Code.

Aker and Lan entered the chief's large hut, the construction and design of which were taught them by the Edenites. The inside, however, was pure Andite. Where one would find small individual rooms in an Edenic family structure, those of the natives contained but one large space. Privacy and modesty, while an intricate part of Edenite behavior, were yet ideas beyond Andite understanding. Men, women, and children walked around naked or not, as their spirits led them. Aker could see that sanitation was yet another concept temporarily beyond Andite comprehension as partially eaten food was strewn about with no regard for hygiene.

"Greetings, Aker," Motep said. "And greetings to you, Lan. It is always a wondrous thing for my people to see a female with duties and responsibilities outside the family. Some day we may emulate the Edenites in this manner, but I fear the time for such a radical change is not yet ripe."

"Greetings to you, Motep," Aker said. "We are honored to be welcomed into your home."

"The honor is mine, old friend. Forgive me if I ask that we get to the point of your visit, for many tasks remain to be completed for our planned maneuver."

"That is the very reason we are here, Motep," Aker said as he and Lan sat upon the ground near the central fire. "Word has reached us of your plans and we desire to talk with you about them."

"What is it you wish to say?" the chief asked.

"Let me begin," Aker said, "by recounting how it came to be that the Crafty One and his minions betrayed this saddened world."

Aker began to tell the story of Lucifer, once a high and mighty Son of God, how he first came to this world, and how he had arrived with good intentions. As System Sovereign, with responsibility for one hundred inhabited planets, he and his assistants faired well for thousands of years as they worked tirelessly to prepare the world for the coming of Adam and Eve, who would then take over the reins as the visible representatives of the universe government. Aker explained that, over time, Lucifer had become spiritually insane. He began thinking his own plan to speed up social evolution was superior to the tried and tested ways that had worked out so well on millions of other worlds. Lucifer published his manifesto of unbridled liberty, declaring that all humans were completely free to follow their inclinations. His assistants, Satan and Beelzebub, along with the Prince of Earth, the nefarious one whose name the Edenites refused to utter, bought into the scheme wholeheartedly and sold the planet to the merchant of despair in less time than a lion would take to pounce upon a wounded gazelle.

The tribes, unable to understand the difference between freedom and liberty without boundaries, swiftly turned upon their historical enemies and eventually fell back to the level of existence they suffered before Lucifer and Satan's arrival.

"This I know well," Motep said. "But what has it to do with the coming invasion of the Nodites that we wish to prevent?"

"The Nodites plan no such invasion," Aker said. "Your thoughts have been swayed by Satan. He has convinced you to react to an event that is but a figment of his imagination, that has the reality of a bad dream."

"I have not spoken with Satan," Motep countered. "I have taken well your warnings that he is the Father of Lies and his ways lead only to sad ends."

Aker looked upon the Andite chief with eyes weighted heavy by concern. In a low voice he said, "It is well that you heed my words. Still, you are in danger of falling under the sway of Satan's detestable scheme. Your tribal information system has been corrupted. There are those in your network who unknowingly relay false reports of a Nodite invasion."

"Are you saying, Aker, that some of my messengers are unfaithful and unworthy of trust? Be not concerned. Only my most dependable warriors are assigned to the messenger service. This is a lesson I learned from you."

Aker thought about how he might prevail upon Motep to understand that even those of honest intent can be caught in the snares of Lucifer and Satan's traps. "Let me recall to your mind how my illustrious ancestors, Adam and Eve, two beings of high stature in the universe, were themselves tricked by the Crafty One."

"This too do I well know," Motep said. "My own ancestors, the original Andites, were part of the problem. They saw Lucifer and Satan as like unto Gods and followed them blindly."

"That is true," Aker said. "Lucifer and Satan tricked Eve into executing a scheme she thought would enhance the plan to which she and Adam had sworn allegiance and from which they vowed to never vary. Eve, whom Adam loved and trusted, who had been warned against changing divine plans, who was surrounded daily by evidence of the disaster such foolishness inevitably leads to, still was susceptible to the wily ways of Lucifer. Not until it was too late did she understand that Lucifer had used an innocent earth native of loyal intent to carry out his sinful plan. This man was your ancestor Cano and his liaison with Eve led directly to the birth of Cain, the slaughter of his father's people and the resulting chaos that ended only when the Edenites determined to abandon the first garden to the coming Nodite invaders. Do you see how Lucifer and Satan can use those of good heart? It is their preferred method of execution."

"I take your words as well meant, Aker," Motep said. "You must understand that I cannot take the chance that the Nodites are once again planning an attack upon my village. A first strike is the only way to end this threat to my people. Please excuse me now, as we must prepare."

"But you will be attacking innocent men, women and children," Lan said. She had determined to remain silent for the meeting out of respect to the chief, who never consulted with women over matters of import, but felt the need to interject. "The Nodites are living peacefully in the Land of Nod and have been for nearly two years now."

"You cannot change that which my mind has determined to do," Motep said. "The threat to my village must be dealt with. Once and for all time."

NINE

In Quest of a Solution

Fall, 1985

At eight A.M. the morning after Bruce had hired Mohammed to maintain the camp, and Lenny had made arrangements to meet the secretive Palestinians, they were almost finished loading the Jeep. Roxanne was checking out of the hotel. By eight-fifteen, they were on their way to pick up their campsite assistant who was waiting for them when they arrived. In minutes the four were on their way to the cave strewn cliffs of the Dead Sea.

On the way, Bruce explained to Lenny why the ancient site, ten miles south of Jericho, was going to be the focal point of their explorations. "The old man we met last summer on our first trip here mentioned the mouth of the Jordan River as the area where the descendants of Adam settled. Jericho is also the site of one of the oldest known settlements of solid buildings in the world. As long as ten thousand years ago there was a population of three or four thousand people there. They were called *Anakim* in the Bible, which means, 'Those who from heaven to earth came.' The old man also mentioned caves as the hiding place of the scrolls, and there are plenty of those in the foothills around there."

"Where's the old man now?" Lenny asked.

"He died this spring," Bruce said. "He was the last of his family line. If we hadn't met him, the knowledge of the scrolls would have been lost forever."

"If the site is so old and well known," Lenny asked, "why hasn't anyone found them by now? I mean, hasn't the area been gone over with a comb by now?"

"You would think so," Bruce said. "But remember, it's been less than forty years since the discovery of the Dead Sea Scrolls in nineteen forty-seven. New discoveries are being made all the time at sites previously considered all dug up. Besides, it's the caves we'll be concentrating on, and there are hundreds of them that have never been thoroughly explored."

As they continued eastward from Jerusalem they discussed the desert terrain of the area and its importance to the peoples who had inhabited it since the beginning of known history. So many battles; between Hittites and Semites, Arabs and Christians, Arabs and Jews, had been waged on and over these hills and mountains that Bruce speculated war itself might have originated there. Hatred, jealousy, and bitterness were a pungent presence in the steam bath that blanketed the air-conditioned vehicle.

By mid-afternoon they had arrived at their destination. Bruce and Roxanne decided to establish their operations center at the base of the foothills, far enough from the present location of Jericho to keep their presence low profile. They chose to make camp at a spot just west of the Dead Sea, high enough to provide a view of the surrounding area and anyone who might be approaching. It was time for dinner when they finished setting up camp.

As they sat around the fire finishing their meal, Lenny looked over Bruce's shoulders to the wave of cliffs outlined against the purple sunset and said, "I hate caves."

Mohammed, who was such a chameleon they were forgetting he was around, stirred the coals of the fire. Bruce and Roxanne looked at Lenny questioningly. "What do you mean?" Roxanne asked.

"When I was a kid, I had an experience that I'll never forget." Lenny saw their inquisitive looks and began telling his story.

"Living in the city as a young boy," he began, "I had few chances to experience the great outdoors. Sure, I loved baseball, football and the other sports me and my pals played. But camping or even hiking had never been part of that picture. My parents thought I should have a more well rounded life so they talked me into joining the scouts."

"They had to talk you into it?" Bruce asked. "When I was a kid I loved the scouts."

"Yeah well, I thought the whole thing would never mesh with my personality. For one thing, I've always hated uniforms. I even avoided little league and other organized sports because of this. And another thing, I didn't really think I'd fit in with an organization as tightly structured as scouting. I was never very good at following orders."

"But you joined," Roxanne said. "Then what?"

"Yeah. I joined with my best friend Keith. I was surprised to learn that I really enjoyed the camping trips. Those trips were the main reason I stayed in the troop. Until the spelunking expedition that changed my life, anyway."

"Changed your life?" Bruce asked as he refilled his mug from the coffeepot. "Remember, you're a reporter, no embellishment," he smiled as he took a sip from the steaming cup.

"You'll see. Anyway, whenever pairing up was in the cards, as it often was in scout activities, Keith and I always managed to be a team. We were great friends and had similar personalities." Lenny went to a far off place. Scenes of him and Keith played on his inner movie screen; the two of them playing catch, fishing along polluted riverbanks, sneaking into the movies. Air left his lungs as if forced out by a bellows; his shoulders sagged as if from a great weight.

"What's the matter Lenny?" Roxanne asked.

Looking at the dry dirt beneath his feet, he shook his head slowly. "I miss him. After all these years, I still miss him." He looked up and continued his story.

"We were a pair of outlaws, always getting into trouble for running off on our own. We had learned of a large cave on the side of a hill during an earlier hike. We decided it was our discovery so we would be the ones to explore it." Lenny huffed his shoulders like a peacock in heat. "We were Lewis and Clark, Junior." A small laugh escaped from Lenny's throat.

"It was early spring and the temperatures hadn't yet warmed enough to melt all the snow. It had been a long and colder than normal winter."

"What were you doing out so early in the year?" Roxanne asked.

"The snow was gone where we lived, but this was in the White Mountains of New Hampshire and the trip had been planned for months. It wasn't like we needed snow shoes or anything. It was just a late spring. Anyway, we entered the cave. Keith led the way. Within twenty feet of the entrance the gap between the sides narrowed so much the sharp edged walls nearly touched our shoulders, even as we walked single file.

"Keith suddenly stopped as we rounded a bend in the path. 'Whoa, what's that smell?' he said.

"I took a deep breath and almost gagged. Man, it smelled like something had died in there and forgot to attend its own funeral."

"Was it as bad as Bruce's morning breath?" Roxanne asked with a smile.

"Hey," Bruce said, his face reflecting the mirth in hers, "I can remember a few mornings when clouds of funk came my way. You aren't exactly Miss Minty-Fresh-Breath when you wake up either."

"Could you two hang your dirty laundry another time? I'm telling a story here." Lenny's smile betrayed his serious tone.

"Our apologies, sir," Roxanne said. "Please continue."

"Okay, we smelled something awful. Just then we heard a low-pitched growl. 'What was that?' Keith whispered.

"Another growl, this time an angry, deep throated, rumble bouncing off the walls of the narrow chamber. I swear I almost felt it in my feet. We turned our flashlights toward the noise. The twin beams ricocheted wildly as we each tried to steady our shaking hands. When we finally succeeded in putting light on our target, I found myself looking at the scariest thing I'd ever seen."

"It was a bear, huh?" Bruce said.

Lenny nodded. "Not just a bear, though. A huge black one was looking right at us with fierce yellow eyes. A much smaller bear was cuddled up beside her, beginning to awaken in response to its mother's alarm."

"What did you do?" Roxanne asked, her saucer-sized eyes telegraphing her anticipation. "Did you run? I would have ran so fast the bear would need track shoes to catch me." She looked at Lenny and Bruce and realized she'd interrupted the story just when it was getting exciting. "Sorry, guys," she said contritely. "I guess I got carried away."

"I'll carry you away," Bruce said with a leer. "But we have to wait until everyone's asleep first."

"You wanna hear this story or not?" Lenny wasn't smiling this time. After two quick nods came his way, he continued.

"We were statues at first. We just stood there and stared at the growling mound of fur. 'Oh my God,' Keith said.

"I came out of my stupor just then and threw my flashlight at the bear and ran like hell."

"You threw your flashlight?" Bruce said. "That wasn't the smartest thing to do."

Lenny raised his hand like a school kid. "Uh, excuse me. Professor Obvious?" Lenny smirked. "I was twelve years old. It wasn't like we had bear practice before we took our trip. I wanted to put as much distance as possible between me and that furry Frankenstein. I was scared, man. I didn't even think about it. Just threw the friggin' flashlight and ran. Of course, without it, I soon learned I couldn't see more than a few feet." Lenny grabbed the pot from its seat on a hot rock and poured himself another cup of bean juice.

"I had only run a few feet when I heard Keith scream in pain. 'Lenny! Help me!' I tell ya, to this day that high pitched wail can tear a hole in my heart." Lenny's head sagged as if his neck muscles had lost all strength. When he looked up something wet gleamed from the corner of one eye. "I wanted to go back and help Keith. I really did. But fear kept my legs pumping like pistons. It was like my legs had minds of their own.

"I continued hurtling down the narrow passageway; bumping into the walls, falling down, getting up again. All the time Keith's agonized screams were chasing me." Lenny went silent as he relived Keith's last moments in his mind. He could still hear his best friend's terror-filled cries. He heard them as if Keith was standing behind him this very moment. "Mommmmy! Mommmeee!" were the last words Lenny ever heard from his buddy.

When he returned to the present Lenny realized tears were answering gravity's call. He took a paper towel from a roll and blew his nose. Bruce and Roxanne were caught in rapturous silence.

Lenny continued. "The bear killed Keith. I heard every second of it. That's all I can say about that. In my panic, I made a wrong turn and found myself squeezing through a space so narrow I almost didn't fit. By the time I understood my mistake and knew I'd have to reverse direction, the bear was right behind me with its claws reaching through the narrow opening. I turned to run, determined to put as much distance between me and the maddened bear as possible. I ran right into a dead end and was knocked to the ground in a daze, where I remained in a stupor for what seemed like hours. In actuality, it was probably only seconds, but with the bear's claws only inches from my face, time stood still."

"You were stuck?" Bruce asked. "In a little room?"

Lenny nodded. "I finally managed to crawl to the farthest point from the bear, but that only gave me about three feet of safe space. I huddled up to that wall like it was my mother as the bear furiously tried to reach me. You should have heard it. I tell you it sounded like a herd of bears were after me. The only thing I could see though were its flaming yellow eyes, staring me down with a hatred I could feel in my skeleton.

"After awhile I guess I went into a daze. I have no idea how much time passed before the bear gave up and returned to her cub. The silence, pregnant with dread, made me wonder if it was safe to leave, but there was no way to know for sure, and there was no way I was willing to chance it. Not yet, anyway. For all I knew, that black beast was quietly waiting around the corner, determined to have me for dessert. I just sat there quivering, crying, wanting my friend. I still miss the little guy. Funny, even though he was bigger than me, that's how I remember him."

Roxanne handed Lenny another paper towel.

"Minutes passed, then hours, and the walls started closing in on me. The space I'd felt relatively safe in was now so small it began to feel like a coffin. I was sure that as soon as the bear figured out a way to get to me, I would be dead. I was never very religious, but I prayed. Boy did I pray.

"After who knows how long, I began to hear noises. At first I couldn't identify the sounds. Animal? Human? I strained to listen, then realized I was hearing voices. Then I saw flashes of light and heard our names being called. The voices were faint, but I could make them out. I began to shout. Boy did I shout. I was hoarse for two days after.

"The hardest part," Lenny said as he finished, "was getting over my feelings of guilt. I don't know if I ever have, actually. Despite what everybody from Keith's parents on down told me, I couldn't help but feel I'd abandoned my friend. I vowed never again to back away from a situation where people were endangered."

"And you've never been in a cave since?" Roxanne asked.

Lenny turned from the campfire and looked over Roxanne's shoulder at the cliffside, only a hundred feet away. "This is the closest I've been to one since that day. And I've had bouts of claustrophobia ever since."

After dinner Bruce and Roxanne went for a walk among the hills that were so dotted with caves, Bruce compared them to mottled Swiss cheese.

The vast desert, with its shades of brown, surrounded them; broken only by the deep blue of the Dead Sea to their east. The sun had dropped below the horizon, and black waves of bats began to flow from the mouths of the caves. Little had changed here in the ten thousand years since the first known inhabitants had arrived. They sat on a rock ledge beside a cave opening, holding hands, gazing in quiet awe as the blackness of night pushed away the last pink and purple rays of light.

Roxanne was first to break the silence. "Just think of all the history that's gone on here. Ten thousand years ago people were walking this same path and gazing up at these same stars." They both turned skyward to look in wonder at the uncountable celestial delights blinking newly awakened eyes through the clear desert air. "I've never seen so many before. You know Longfellow called them 'candlelight of the gods'?"

"Let's hope it's a good omen," Bruce said. "Perhaps it means the gods are lighting the way for us." Then in a different tone, "Have you spoken to Lenny yet?"

"Not yet. I thought I'd wait until just the right moment," she said with a mischievous grin. "What about our agreement? Do you think he'll keep our location secret?"

"I have no reason to doubt his word," Bruce said. "I'm beginning to like him a lot. I'm sure everything will be fine."

"I'm starting to wonder if we shouldn't have applied for the proper permits. We could still get into trouble over this."

"We've been through this. Permits take time. We'd have to tell where we were going. Besides, it's too late now."

The next day, after seeing Lenny off in the Jeep, the actual work of mapping out a strategy and exploring the caves and began. Within a few days, they had developed a routine of working, eating, working, eating again, working again and finally sleeping. During these long, difficult and stiflingly humid days, Mohammed would prepare their food, clean clothing and run errands to Jericho, during which he delivered progress reports to the unknown benefactor who paid him well for such information.

Half way around the world Sheila Snow was in the office of her boss, Reverend Graves. She was sitting in a chair in front of his desk and scribbling furiously on a notepad. She finished, and said, "Reverend, can I ask you something?"

The burly man looked up at his assistant and stroked his gray beard in concern. His face showed that he'd recognized the sound of worry in Sheila's tone of voice. "Of course, Sheila. What is it?"

Her shoulders sagged into her chair. "Lenny and I had a fight the night before last."

Reverend Graves leaned forward and placed his elbows onto his desk. He clasped his hands together. "What about?"

"Oh, he called to let me know they'd arrived OK. I was fine at first, but I was just watching a news report from over there and, I don't know, I guess I jumped into my mother hen mode."

"And Lenny didn't like that?"

Sheila shook her head. "It was more than just not liking it. I could tell he was drinking and I think by the time we finished talking he was onto his third at least. He hurt my feelings with his sarcasm too."

Reverend Graves leaned back into his leather-upholstered chair. He tugged at his beard, then said, "This isn't the first time you've had this experience is it? I seem to remember a few times when your, 'mother hen mode,' as you call it, has caused problems. Why do you think you continue to do it, knowing he is turned away by it?"

Sheila shook her head and lowered her eyes. She crossed her legs and dangled a shoe from her left foot, started bouncing it back and forth. "I wish I knew. But is it so bad to be concerned about your loved ones? I do love Lenny. And he is out there in one of the world's hotspots. And he does drink too much sometimes. He's impulsive. That just seems like a dangerous mix to me."

Reverend graves stood and walked around to Sheila. He took one of the office chairs, placed it in front of hers, sat, and took one of her hands into his. "Sheila, you can't waste your energy worrying. It does no good for those whom you worry about and eats away at your own insides. It can be the most wasteful of emotions."

Sheila raised her green eyes to meet Reverend Graves' brown ones. "I know. But it's so much easier to say than to do."

"The story of mankind," he sighed. "Easier said than done. So many times we know what's right, and yet nearly as often it goes undone."

Sheila asked if she could have a cigarette. Reverend Graves reached for an ashtray from his desk and she lit up. "So what do I do?" Sheila pleaded. "Do I go about my daily routine as if nothing is happening? Or do I run around the hen house looking for a fox?"

Reverend Graves remained close to Sheila despite the smoke from her cigarette, which was beginning to make his eyes water. "It doesn't have to be one extreme or the other. Maybe you could do something useful with your spare time. Something that would help you turn your nervous energy into a good force."

"Like what?"

"That's up to you, of course, but what about one of the groups that are helping foster better relations between the Arabs and the Israelis?"

"How would that keep my mind off of Lenny?"

Reverend Graves smiled. "It's just a suggestion. I thought you might get satisfaction from helping make things better. What I'm really getting at is for you to keep busy."

"I'll try something. Thank you, Reverend." She removed her hand from his and stood to leave.

"You're welcome. Feel free anytime you think I can help."

When her hand left his, he felt as if he had dropped a hot coal, such was the heat she impressed upon him. He wondered again how long he could keep his desire for the voluptuous redhead a secret. How long would he be able to control the lust that bubbled like a hot spring just below the surface, threatening to boil over at the touch of even the smallest flame?

TEN

What John Rance Had To Tell

The man who called himself Assad had been gone for the whole day while Lenny was forced to wait in the small farmhouse bedroom. From snippets of conversation he'd heard through his door, he'd gleaned that some of the terrorists had headed for the Sea of Galilee with a plan to waylay some American tourists and take them hostage.

The window had been nailed shut, turning the room into a virtual steam bath. Sweating profusely, and with little else to do, he had spent the day trying to write and dozing off into a miserable, perspiration drenched sleep.

About an hour after dark, he heard the sounds of approaching vehicles. He peered out through the dirty window and thought he could make out Assad and about five men climbing out of two four-door pickup trucks and a car. He could also see the profiles of a man and a woman sitting in the back seat of one of the trucks, leaning forward uncomfortably.

As he watched, they were taken out of the vehicle and led to the barn. He saw their hands were tied behind them. *Poor bastards,* he thought. *They must be scared shitless.*

Moments later, one of the terrorists opened Lenny's door. "You are going to have a busy night, Mister Cronin," the man said. "We have returned with two more guests and you will be able to talk with them and the others. You will also be allowed to ask any questions of us that you wish. As soon as we are done eating, we will begin."

After a bland but filling meal of lamb and rice, Assad and one of his men led Lenny through the darkness to the small barn. They entered the building through a normal sized door that was directly beside the large double doors

Lenny had seen being used for driving vehicles through. The inside of the barn was shadowy and dimly lit by half a dozen oil lamps. There was a typical center aisle, with stalls on both sides. From the bays on the right, where Lenny imagined cows sticking out cud-chewing heads, came instead, dusty bumpers and dirt-gauzed headlights protruding into the aisle. Three small pickups, two sedans, and a military Jeep of undetermined vintage, formed a car lot. Lenny figured the sedans must have belonged to the kidnap victims.

Along the left of the center aisle, eight of the bays had been converted to box stalls. As Lenny and his escorts approached them, he saw that five of the stalls each contained a person handcuffed by one wrist to a chain securely fastened to the outside wall. He could see the shock on their faces, perceive the questions in their eyes, read the fear in their body language.

"As you can see, Mister Cronin, we are taking good care of our guests and they have not been mistreated." Assad said with a smile.

Lenny could not tell if the man was serious or not. He decided not to argue over the semantics of the phrase, 'good care,' or ask Assad what his definition of, 'mistreatment' was. He was overcome by a strong urge to help these people, but knew on a certain level he was just as much a captive as they were. He began talking with the first man he was brought to.

His name was John Rance. He was dressed in a tan golf shirt and gray pants. The wrinkled clothes were damp with sweat, his glistening skin creased with dirt. The man's crusty hair only added more gloom to the picture.

According his story, John and his wife Mary had been taken, along with their daughter Jennifer, three or four days ago. He said he wasn't sure anymore because of the lack of outside light. Lenny noticed that all the windows were blacked out and covered with heavy woolen blankets.

"You mean the only light, day and night, is from these lamps?" Lenny asked.

"That's right," John Rance said. "What's going on? Do you know anything? These assholes won't answer any of our questions."

Lenny wanted to reassure the man that all would be well. He wasn't sure if this was true or not, but thought it best to make an effort to keep morale healthy or, at least from dying. "It looks like they're planning a prisoner exchange for their comrades captured during recent raids in the area. They're returning me tonight with their demands. I guess I'll be coming back in a few days with the answer."

The man looked pleadingly at Lenny. "Do you think they'll let us go?"

"I'm sure they will if their demands are met. And I think our government will be able to exert enough pressure on the Israelis to make them go along with the deal," Lenny said with more conviction than he felt.

Lenny spent the next few hours mining the hostages and kidnappers for nuggets of gold to include in his article. He did this with mixed emotions. He couldn't help feeling that he was exploiting the fear and troubles of these victims, and perhaps even helping the kidnappers by providing publicity for their actions. He'd never felt this way as a reporter before. He was accustomed to exposing corruption and bribery, helping protect the innocent. His only consolation was the fact that he might be helping to affect the release of these people.

"Why do you only kidnap Americans?" Lenny asked Assad when they returned to the house.

"That is very simple. It is because America has the most influence over the Zionists. Without American aid the non—existent state of Israel would not be," Assad said. Lenny's internal editor winced at what Assad obviously thought was perfect logic. Assad looked at his watch. "And now it is getting late. It is time to give you our list of demands and return you to the city."

"OK. I'm ready whenever you are. I hope your demands aren't unreasonable." When Lenny saw Assad's angered reaction to his statement, he quickly added, "What I mean is, I hope the other side doesn't consider them to be unreasonable."

With laser-intense black eyes burning holes through Lenny, the man who reminded him of Fidel Castro said, "We do not care what they think. We demand the return of our brothers."

While preparations for his return trip were being made, Lenny's mind wandered back to the first time his job had gotten him mixed up in a situation where lives were at stake.

Lenny had joined the army shortly after receiving his degree in journalism from Brown University in nineteen seventy-two. He'd joined for two reasons. First because he figured to be drafted anyway, and second because his recruiter had promised him a spot with the army newspaper, Stars and Stripes, if he joined voluntarily. After basic training he'd been issued a camera and notepad instead of a rifle and ammunition, then sent off to Vietnam where he soon distinguished himself as a fearless and honest reporter.

His reputation had caused him to be nominated for a mission that stood outside the parameters of his pay scale. Despite this and the potential danger involved, Lenny volunteered for the mission. His job was to uncover a leak within the press corp. Someone had been passing on information about troop movements that had cost American lives.

Because of the potential for danger, Lenny had been given a crash course in self-defense and covert operations. These lessons stood him well when the object of his investigations came to realize Lenny was a threat. During a situation eerily similar to the current one, Lenny had been forced to kill the man in hand-to-hand combat. Thanks to Lenny, a hostage the man had taken was unharmed. It was his proudest moment and almost made up for the guilt over the death of his best friend Keith that hounded his every step like a shadow. Almost.

Lenny came out of his reverie when one of the terrorists opened his door and informed him that the time to return was at hand.

The next evening, Lenny was in his hotel room, in the same establishment he had stayed in previously, his belongings having been returned to him when he was dropped off. He'd been instructed by the terrorists to stay in the same hotel and to order all his meals through room service. He'd sent off his first article early that morning, but still had to turn in a story on Bruce and Roxanne the next day so began working on that. After a couple of hours he was finished.

He had just completed his dinner when he picked up the phone and asked the operator to put him in touch with Sheila. While the operator was placing the call, he poured himself a scotch and water. He heard the ringing.

"Hello, Red," he said when he heard her melodic voice.

"Oh, Lenny, I've been so anxious to hear from you. Especially since I read your story in the paper today. I hope you're not putting yourself in danger."

"No, there's nothing dangerous about it," he lied. "They just pick me up and take me to their hideout, let me talk to the hostages and bring me back, simple as that."

"The article has everybody talking. You're becoming quite the celebrity."

"I don't know about that. I'm just a reporter who, thanks to his girl, was in the right place at the right time. So I've got you to thank for it. Remember that when all the groupies start hanging around, begging me to sign their breasts and father their babies and stuff."

Sheila laughed. "I'm sorry about the other night. I don't know what gets into me sometimes."

"No need to apologize, Red. I was just as much to blame. You know me after my third drink. The mouth opens up and the stupidity flows like water from a faucet."

They talked for a while longer. Each promised to try harder to make their relationship work. "So tell me what you've been doing with yourself," Lenny said.

"You mean other than worrying about you?" When he answered in the affirmative, she told him.

"Oh yeah, and what movies did you see?" he asked.

"None worth talking about. You know how it is at this time of the year. It's too late for the summer blockbusters and too early for the Christmas releases. I saw two real losers. They were supposed to be funny but I must have left my sense of humor at home. One was a parody of a satire of a farce. It got a thumbs in your mouth from the fat guy and a thumbs stuck in a plumb from the skinny guy," she said, continuing their favorite running gag. "The only reason I went was because I'm so lonely for you and it helps to pass the time. So tell me, are you going to see those terrorists again?"

"They told me I would. I expect to hear from them in a day or so." Lenny hesitated for a moment. "Are you alone, Red?"

In a smug tone, Sheila asked, "Why? Are you getting jealous?"

Lenny smiled as he pictured the teasing look he knew she was giving him. "That's not it and you know it. I just thought I heard something in the background. It sounded like someone dropped something. Was that you?"

"I'm just sitting in my living room chair. All by my little self. Waiting for my long lost boyfriend to find his way back home."

"I guess I'm just hearing things."

A short while later, their conversation ended and they said goodbye to each other. Lenny thought about the noise he'd heard. He knew Sheila hadn't lied. So what was the sound? Was someone listening in on his phone calls?

ELEVEN

The People of the Drama

Spring, 10,000 BC

Two days after returning from their fruitless effort to stop the Andites from making war, Aker and Lan were sitting under a tree on the hillside above the Second Garden. They looked down upon their home. From this vantagepoint they could see the whole settlement, even unto the fields of grazing herds within the stone perimeter wall. It was only from this on-high view that the layout of the compound as three concentric circles could be fully appreciated. The color scheme of bright blues and reds that highlighted the more muted greens and yellows was designed to give the appearance of two rainbows joined together end to end upon the ground, with the golden dome of the sky-blue Father's temple shining brightly at its center. They gazed down upon the temple, a sun in the center of a rainbow, as they etched letters upon leather scrolls with metal tools.

The sounds of playing children reached them. They could also hear adult voices calling the names of the children over the braying of donkeys. Birds sang in the trees and fowl called for their young. Clean, fresh air presented a bouquet of pleasing aromas. The sights, sounds, and smells of peace and happiness touched Aker's soul.

"What are you thinking, Aker?" Lan asked her husband when she determined that his mind was in some far off place.

Aker looked at his wife, one of two females on his council, with a countenance of contemplative sadness. The morning sun reflected from her fair skin and shone through her flowing red hair. The halo of reddish gold around her achingly beautiful face stirred his heart. The natives often marveled at the light colors of the Edenites hair, eyes, and skin. Lan's exceptional fairness had even startled some of them. "I was thinking back to the times of our ancestors and the tragic circumstances of, 'the fall', as we have come to call it."

Lan placed her hand upon Aker's shoulder and gazed deeply into his blue eyes. "You mentioned this at the meeting yesterday," Lan said. "Is it the similarity of our current situation to that far off time that conjures these thoughts of melancholy?"

Aker returned her look with an equally penetrating stare. "You see that which is in my mind as if they were your own reflections. I sometimes feel you understand the inner workings of my thoughts better than I know them myself. How is it you know me so well?"

Lan's complexion took on a hue of red that resembled the apple at harvest time. She took Aker's hand into hers, moved the leather and tools aside, and leaned against his rock hard body with her water soft form. "When a person feels so close to another that she knows not where one ends and the other begins, such things happen of their own accord. Always, do I feel your thoughts as mine, your pain as mine, your joys as mine."

Aker turned Lan's face upward and placed his lips upon hers with the tenderness of a hummingbird seeking nectar from a flower. Lan surrendered herself to the moment and felt her body meld into his. When the kiss ended, he continued to hold her tightly as he said, "It is true we seem to be reliving the history of our ancestors. The Crafty One seeks to destroy that which we have created as surely as a great flood washes away all in its path. His schemes and plots are forever causing us problems. The coming battle between Andite and Nodite surely bodes ill for us."

Lan stroked her husband's arm. "We can do no more to prevent this. We must concentrate on our new assignment. You have chosen from among our brothers and sisters your new team. New copies of the Scrolls of Truth are nearly complete. This one we work on now is the last." She gazed sadly into his eyes. "As difficult as it is to do so, we must look forward and not back."

Aker lay down and stretched to his full length. He drew Lan to him and held her tight as they both gazed skyward. "Your words ring true, my love. It falls upon Seth to carry this burden. We must gather our new team members and their families and guide them on this new leg of our long journey. The scrolls will be ready in two days. Our quest begins then."

The time was at hand. Aker's new team had completed copying the scrolls and final preparations for their expedition were underway. Families were busy gathering possessions. Children were complaining or crying, depending on age and personality. Nuts, grains and other provisions were being packed for travel. Equipment had been repaired and tested. A host of activities and tasks were in the final stages of completion.

Seth arrived at the family compound of Aker. When he entered the living hut, he watched quietly as Aker's wife, Lan, knelt upon the ground to prepare the Scrolls of Truth for travel. She was rolling one of them small enough to fit into the leather pouches that would protect them during the journey. After greeting the woman, Seth said, "There are twenty-four scrolls. Do you have enough pouches?"

"I had to ask my neighbors for some, but we have enough now." She arched her neck, as she looked upward at Seth and asked, "What will become of this village, Seth? I fear the hostilities between Andite and Nodite will cause great distress; may even lead to total destruction, as with the first Garden of Eden."

Seth looked with compassion upon the saddened face of the woman. "It has always been planned that some day we would disperse ourselves around the world, the better to share our knowledge. Should your fears be realized, we shall improvise and implement this plan early. But fear not, as we are told in Adam's own words, in the very scrolls you are carrying with you, 'all things work for the greater good.'"

"Is it wise to send us off like this when such a threat overhangs us?"

Seth had considered this very point during long nights of contemplation. With the threat of expanded hostilities a distinct possibility, first inclinations tilted toward caution. But upon further review he'd deemed it wise to have at least one faraway settlement to carry on the Edenic culture. There were other outlying ambassadorships providing insurance against the complete collapse of the plan, the Sumerians held the most promise at this point. But Seth decided that Aker's new establishment, by the distant shores of the Sea Without Life, would provide the best chances for guaranteeing Edenic culture would live on. He conveyed this to Lan.

"It is the children I worry about," she said. "They are so pure. Why is it that the innocent always seem to get burned by fires started by the guilty? It is a question that vexes."

Seth picked up Lan and Aker's three-year-old son and held him in his massive arms. "What you say is true. You know as well as I that there is no rational answer. It is simply the way things are. When the Heavenly Father created this world and the others like it, He knew that bestowing free will upon evolutionary creatures would provide occasion for such events. We must take our solace in the knowledge that the universe is just and all wrongs will be made right in time."

With a look of weariness, Lan said, "We take solace yes, but it makes our journey no shorter. We look forward to starting a new life with joy. Yet we look back with concern upon the old. In two directions are we drawn."

Seth saw Aker walking towards the hut. He placed the child in his mother's arms, walked outside and greeted his friend. "Aker, a glorious day."

Aker looked at the clear blue sky, arched his eyebrows and said, "A beautiful day yes, but not even the best day can remove the pain that rides upon the joy of this one. I fear I shall never see you again my friend. I will miss you."

Seth took his best friend into his arms and bear-hugged him. "It is true," he said while releasing him, "we may never meet again on this world. We must rely on our memories and our hearts to keep alive that which is between us, until we meet again on the other side of the veil which separates eternal from ephemeral. Nonetheless, it is with true sadness that we separate."

Seth gestured for Aker to follow as he began a stroll down the main path of the settlement. The curved way was one of three that encircled the centrally located Father's Temple, creating the three concentric circles of the village's overall design. "Look around us. Many others are sharing the same feelings and voicing similar words. We Edenites are blessed. We know we shall meet again sometime in the far-flung future. But we also know that many trials and tribulations await us. We must be strengthened by the knowledge that we are carrying out the divine plan as best we can. That our sacrifices will not be in vain."

As Aker gazed upon the activity surrounding them, he said, "Our efforts are indeed not in vain, and such knowledge lightens the burden somewhat. But only somewhat."

Seth knew his friend was right. The weight of the world sat upon the shoulders of the Edenites, and the unforeseen events that had plunged this planet into darkness only made this burden more difficult to bear. Their mission of bringing enlightenment to the citizens of earth was greatly complicated by the efforts of Lucifer and his minions. He who brought the darkness upon this world did all within his power to thwart the Edenites. The primitive and superstitious natives were easy targets for his lies and deceits. The Edenites were tasked with helping advance each tribe, one at a time, from out of the gloom into which their fears had plunged them. The Prince of Darkness and his fellow rebellious ones had the easier task in the short term, but in the end, Seth knew all would someday bathe in the light of truth. This knowledge of certain victory had sustained the noble Edenites through many hardships, and would continue to do so.

"I must tend to the others," Seth said. "We shall say our goodbyes when you are ready to leave." The two men separated as Aker returned to his hut and Seth to his duties.

Bright and early the next morning, Aker and his band of travelers were ready. The Temple of the Father was the site chosen for the last farewells, and everyone came. The adults shook hands, exchanged gifts, and embraced their friends. Many children were in tears, knowing only the sadness of goodbye and nothing of what the future might hold.

Seth spoke passionately of thanksgiving and forgiveness, faith and loyalty, sacrifice and reward, inspiring many to harden their resolve for the trip ahead. Aker and his troupe left through the east gate.

TWELVE

The Episode of the (Gun) Barrel

Fall, 1985

Three mornings after his first meeting with the terrorists and their hostages, Lenny was being escorted into the poorly maintained farmhouse for a second time.

"Hello once again, Mister Cronin. I hope your journey was not unpleasant," Assad said, as Lenny's blindfold was removed.

Lenny squinted in the morning light and stretched his aching back. He looked at the terrorist leader sitting at the kitchen table before him. "You need to rethink your customer service commitment. The peanuts were stale and the pilot never came out back to shake my hand."

Assad and his men looked at Lenny with scorn. "Do you think this is a humorous occasion, Mister Cronin? Because I can assure you, we do not." Assad's tone wilted Lenny's bravado like a blowtorch on a lily.

All his life, Lenny had used humor to relieve tension. He now wondered if his mother's warning that this would get him killed some day might be coming true. Why did his mouth always seem to be faster than his brain? "Sorry. It's how I deal with stress. Sometimes I just come out with stupid things."

"This is not a time for levity. See that you keep it to yourself from now on." Lenny nodded contritely and the terrorist leader continued. "I have read your stories in the newspapers and am pleased. I do think you should be a little harder on the Zionists, however. They stole our homeland and continue to oppress us in every way possible. Try to remember this from now on."

"I'm a reporter, Assad," Lenny said. "I think I gave a balanced presentation of the facts."

Assad pushed his chair back away from the table. The scraping of the wooden legs on the floor gave Lenny goose flesh; at least he thought it was the noise. The black-bearded, khaki-clad, terrorist leader walked toward Lenny and stopped inches in front of him. Of similar height, they looked at each other eye to eye. "Your presentation may have been balanced, as you say. But this fight we are in is not evenly weighted. Try to remember that."

"I call 'em as I see 'em, Assad."

Assad returned to his chair. "This is not one of your baseball games, Mister Cronin. There is more at stake here than who scores the most runs."

Lenny was impressed with the man's knowledge of American trivia. Assad made sure his men spoke English; he was up to speed on Americana, apparently. Maybe he was underestimating this guy. "I understand what you want, but I have to be true to my profession and give a balanced view. If I don't maintain objectivity, then I lose credibility . . . and I'm no use to you."

There was quiet for no more than ten seconds, but it seemed to Lenny as if a day had gone by. He hated the emptiness of silence, so filled it. "By the way, two guys I think were Americans followed me last night. Your men pulled a switch with a decoy like the first time and we lost them, but I just want you to know I had nothing to do with it."

Assad looked up from the table. He studied Lenny in silence. Lenny shifted his feet and waited. "That was expected and is not a concern," he finally said. "We have many ways of confusing those who would try to follow you here."

He stood and indicated for Lenny to follow him to the sitting room. As they entered the room, Lenny noticed a pitcher of water with ice cubes on the table. Assad began pouring two glasses. "As for your articles being unbiased, that is why you are being given such extraordinary access. We have many reporters who would write exactly what we tell them to, but the world would not give their words the credence we desire. Your reputation for fairness is why you are here." He handed Lenny a glass and said, "Still, we hope to convince you of the justice of our cause."

Assad said these last words with a smile that was so chilling Lenny almost asked for a coat, but held the impulse in check. "I can't promise anything." He took a sip from the glass. The coolness felt like honey. Where the hell did they get ice cubes?

Assad continued as if Lenny had said nothing. "We have not yet had a response to our demands and so have been forced to step up our activities. You may have already heard about the French couple we have brought here?"

"I've seen it in the news reports."

"But you couldn't know about our newest arrivals," Assad continued. "After all, we only invited them last night while you were on your way here. In one simple maneuver, we picked up three American students. So you see we now have ten guests." Assad stared at Lenny with pinpoint focus as his voice deepened and took on an even darker tone. "If we do not get a satisfactory response to our demands very soon, we will have to start taking more serious measures."

Lenny frowned. "What do you mean, more serious measures?"

"You are here to verify the safety of our guests and to publicize our demands, but understand that the next time we bring you here, if something hasn't been done to assure us that our comrades are to be released, you will witness an execution."

Lenny's face registered the alarm this statement had set off in his head. "What? You expect me to just watch you kill someone?"

Assad sat and pointed to the empty chair opposite him. Lenny took a seat facing the terrorist leader who leaned onto the card table between them and spoke in a low clear voice. "You are a journalist. You will not be able to resist the fame that such a story would bring you."

Lenny wanted desperately to become a comic book super hero and tear this madman to pieces with his bare hands, but he wore no costume, had no cape flying behind his shoulders. He had no choice but to play along. "I'd like to talk to the hostages as soon as possible."

"They are our guests, Mister Cronin. Hostage is such a harsh word. Don't you think?"

"You say potato," Lenny said.

"What does that mean? Is this another example of your out of place sense of humor?" Assad asked with a scowl.

Lenny repeated his mother's warning to himself like a mantra. *Your wisecracking will get you killed some day. Your wisecracking will get you killed some day.* "It's just an expression we Americans use. It doesn't mean anything. When can I see the GUESTS as you call them?"

"It's been a long night for all of us," Assad answered. "We are hungry and tired. You will see them after we have eaten and rested."

After a breakfast of cheese and bread, they locked Lenny in the same room he'd used on his first visit to the farm. He sat at his "desk" and began composing the opening for the latest chapter of what was rapidly becoming a horror story. He had no intention of witnessing the murder of innocent people. But neither did he have any idea what to do about it.

Later that afternoon he was taken to see the hostages. Most of the barn's stalls were now in use. Seeing the frightened people chained to the walls of the barn, lying in straw, brought the phrase, 'treated like animals' to Lenny's mind, his internal editor changed it to, 'lambs awaiting slaughter'. He was given free rein to talk with any or all of them for as long as he wanted. He went to the couple he'd met on his first visit to assure them and their daughter that everything possible was being done to secure their release. They wondered if their family knew they were safe. Lenny told them he was sure they did because every paper in the country had either printed his story or used it as a basis for their own.

When he went to see the American students, he was surprised by how young they were. He had assumed they would be college age. What he saw were three very frightened high school kids, two girls and a boy. They had been on a day trip while the father of the boy was attending a business meeting. The two girls were his girlfriend and her twin. Lenny did his best to calm them. When he asked them why they had been out at night, they explained they'd had car trouble and were walking back to the city when they were picked up by what they thought were friendly people who took them back to the car and got it started. That was when the guns had been displayed.

Lenny couldn't speak French, but the couple from France spoke enough Arabic to enable communication with them through an interpreter. The man was a petroleum engineer on vacation from his work in the Saudi oil fields. He felt certain that when the Saudis learned of his fate, they would prevail upon their Arab brothers to release him and his wife. He seemed almost sure of himself. He was very important to the Saudis, he said.

Lenny looked at the interpreter, who stood with his AK-47 tucked under his arms, with a questioning glance. The Palestinian said, "Who knows? Perhaps what he says is true. If our Saudi brothers do indeed have a need for this man, then of course, we will be obliged to honor their request. And they would be welcome to him as far as I am concerned. This man has not shut his mouth since we brought him here. He is the most abrasive man I ever met. Much worse than Americans even."

When Lenny finished talking with the hostages, he was led back to the house. Once inside 'his' room, he continued working on his story. This whole saga had been going on less than a week but seemed much longer. He hoped his articles would help end it soon, and without bloodshed.

After a short while, Assad came into the room and started repeating many of the same words and ideas he'd been spouting since Lenny had first met him.

"Assad, don't take this the wrong way, but I need something new to keep interest up, something fresh," Lenny said.

The terrorist leader scowled at Lenny and said, "There is nothing new to say because the Zionists have been taking our land, destroying our homes and crushing our freedom for nearly forty years. The entire world knows this but does nothing, preferring to stand on the sidelines as my people and our homeland fade into history. This will never be allowed. This conflict will never end as long as the Palestinian people are denied their human rights, a term you Americans are so fond of using."

"Do you see any way out of this predicament? Can the Palestinians and the Israelis ever live together in peace?"

"Peace?" Assad spat the word like a sneeze. "How can there be peace when one side seeks only to annihilate the other? How can there be peace when the objective of one is the destruction of the other? How can there be peace when innocent men, women and children are killed day after day?"

Lenny took a risk. "But couldn't you say that about both sides?" He knew he was getting dangerously close to the edge here, but felt compelled to make Assad understand that, as a reporter, he must remain neutral.

"The difference, Mister Cronin, is that we have been forced into our actions by the aggressions of the Zionists." He was suddenly calmer. "They have said they will return the West Bank and Gaza, yet continue to build settlements within those areas. For twenty years now, they have been settling the most belligerent and hardened Zionists on our land. They show the world the face of a people threatened with extinction, while doing everything within their power to bring that very end to the Palestinians. They do not belong here. Why does not the great United States, with its boundless land and immeasurable riches, just take all the Jews in and let them live there? Then we can have peace."

Lenny had heard this solution posed before, and was surprised the first time it had come up. Many Palestinians seemed to think the same way. If only the solution were that simple. Lenny knew it was beyond his abilities to influence the outcome. He also thought he was being served a meal of warmed up leftovers, with some spices added to disguise the flavor, but at least he had the unfolding saga of the hostage situation. He knew he had to try to end this drama without bloodshed.

Assad seemed to tire of the conversation. He told Lenny that he would be returned to Jerusalem that evening, and left, locking the door behind him.

Lenny turned his thoughts to what he might do to diffuse the escalating situation. Should he try to escape with the hostages? He immediately dismissed the idea as unworkable. Even if by some miracle he was able to pull it off, he still had no idea where this farm was located.

That night, as Lenny was being dropped off at the edge of the city, he was told, "Don't forget, Mister Cronin, we will not stop until the Zionist captors free our brothers. The next time we see you we will expect answers, or you will be reporting about executions instead of kidnappings. Goodbye for now, Mister Cronin."

After a night spent tossing and turning, Lenny got up early and ordered breakfast from room service. While waiting for the food to arrive, he took his shower and thought again about his situation.

Like a scientist with an experiment, the role of a reporter was supposed to be as observer only. The journalist was not to affect the story, but merely relay information in a neutral voice, present unbiased facts. He knew and believed this in theory. But like many theories when exposed to the real world, this one held no more water than a sieve. No, Lenny Cronin wasn't going to sit on his ass when something needed doing, journalistic integrity be damned. He made a decision.

As he was drying off, room service knocked and placed the order on the table near the window. He checked under the plate for any messages from the terrorists. He hadn't expected one so soon, but had been told to order every meal this way and to check each time.

After eating and dressing, he decided to act. The time of passively waiting in his hotel room for messages was over. He was not going to be a mere observer of Assad's madness.

As he approached a bank of payphones across the street from his hotel, he noticed a man using one of the phones who seemed startled when he saw Lenny approaching. For a brief moment his suspicions were aroused, remembering the two American looking men who had followed him on his way to being picked up by the terrorists for his second hostage interviews. Even though this guy looked American too, Lenny decided he was just being paranoid. He watched as the man hung up and walked away, then he picked up the phone and dialed a number that one of his editor's contacts had given him. He had been given the number after explaining to the contact that his room had been ransacked, and he was concerned about safety. At the time, that had been his real reason. But now things had changed so he decided to use a pay phone; he had no idea who within the hotel was in contact with the kidnappers, and was afraid they would find out what he was up to. Fifteen minutes after he made the call a cab arrived to pick him up.

"Where to, Sir?" the driver asked as Lenny entered the vehicle.

"Just drive me around for a while. I feel like viewing the city."

"Yes, Sir," the man said as they entered the traffic pattern.

After a few minutes Lenny said to the driver, "I've been told by a mutual friend that you could do a certain favor for me. Is this true?"

"That depends on the favor, Sir. And the mutual friend. Who did you say that was?"

Lenny mentioned the name of the contact and the nature of the favor. When the driver heard what his passenger wanted, he asked to see Lenny's driver's license.

"What do you want that for?"

"So I can tell if you work for my government."

Lenny saw his own surprised look in the driver's rear view mirror. "But how will that tell you? If I was a government agent it certainly wouldn't say so on my license."

The cab driver laughed. "That is true, but it will tell me if you are truly an American. My government cannot afford to hire Americans just to harass poor cab drivers." The man examined Lenny's license and returned it to him. "I can accommodate your request, Mister Cronin"

"I'll want one small enough to hide on my person and yet powerful enough to offer protection. If you can do that, and will take traveler's checks, we have a deal. I'll need bullets too, of course."

"I can supply your needs, Sir. I can get you a Walther PPK .32 caliber, just like James Bond uses. But I won't take your checks. After you accept delivery, I will take you to a bank and you can cash them yourself and pay me then. Is that satisfactory?"

Lenny considered this for a moment, then said, "That sounds fine to me. Except first, you take me someplace private where I can test fire the weapon and reacquaint myself with my aim. Then I'll pay you."

"That is agreeable to me, Sir."

As the cab driver stopped to make a phone call, Lenny wondered if he was doing the right thing. He thought about the childhood incident, when the bear had killed his friend Keith. He had made himself a promise at that time and was determined to keep it. He would never again run from trouble or sit on the sidelines while innocent people got hurt.

THIRTEEN

The Darkest Hour

After ten long days of tiring, backbreaking, heat stressed explorations, all spent in fruitless effort, Bruce and Roxanne finally stood before the mouth of a cave that held promise. They had discovered a secret doorway in this cave late the previous afternoon. Now, before reentering, they turned to enjoy the view from high on the cliff.

With the variant blues of the Dead Sea at its center, the mosaic laid out before them was an impressionist's delight. Frothy whites danced upon the tops of the turquoise waves as if lifelong lovers bonding in ecstasy. Shadow and light played hide and seek on the mottled browns and sparkling salt deposits of the seashore. A warm blanket of texture, color, and light comforted the land. Animal, vegetable and mineral shared the splendor in peaceful co-existence. All seemed right with the world.

"It's hard to believe hatred and animosity can even exist with such beauty surrounding it," Roxanne said.

"It's a shame," Bruce said. "But it has nothing to do with us." He pointed to the cave entrance. "You ready?"

Roxanne turned away from the natural splendor and faced the dark hole in the cliffside before her. Only its small entrance distinguished this particular cave. Bruce surmised the size was one reason it had been chosen by the former inhabitants of the area, as it could be easily defended from inside if the need arose. Perhaps this ordinary-looking cave would be the one that held the ancient manuscripts they were determined to find.

They bent down and entered the womb on the hillside. Their portable lamps illuminated a path in front of them. The beams were concentrated and when focused on the ground did not fully brighten the walls, causing them to feel they were in a smaller and more constricted space than the moderate sized chamber. Shadows formed living companions on the creviced walls as they jumped and frolicked in synch with the light beams.

Two passageways exited this chamber. Bruce and Roxanne had explored both the previous day and found the secret door in the one to the right, which narrowed significantly once they entered. It was so narrow that the walls nearly touched their shoulders. It soon became even tighter and they were forced to inch their way along turned sideways. Finally, they entered a small ten-by-twelve-foot area they'd feared was one more dead end. But then Roxanne had noticed a strange rock that was resting on a small shelf-like indent. She picked it up and saw a lever behind it. She moved the lever and nothing had happened. Just as she was about to call Bruce's attention to it, a section of the wall started pivoting away from her. She had screamed and nearly fainted. Bruce had jumped when the wall began moving. At first, they were afraid to go near it. After a moment of silence, Bruce conjured the courage to peer into the darkness with his lantern. What he saw was another passageway. Since it was late in the day, they had decided to wait before exploring it any farther.

And now here they were once again, staring at the solid stone door that blended into the surrounding wall. All their hopes and expectations could be fulfilled in the coming few minutes. Or they could be taking yet another convoluted route in Mother Nature's granite maze.

"Are you ready, Rox?"

She nodded silently. Bruce moved the lever and the entryway gradually revealed itself as the stone door pivoted inward. Ever so slowly and carefully, they passed through the opening. The narrow hall on the other side turned out to be only about ten feet long before it opened up into another small room about the same size as the area just outside the door. This room had a narrow opening on its right side that went in the opposite direction from which they had just come. Bruce looked through the opening and around the corner.

With his light, he was able to see the mechanism that worked the door, an arrangement of stone weights, counterweights, and levers. He saw how the movement of a very small weight, connected to the outside lever Roxanne had discovered, was used to make the large door move as the heavy counterweights were released.

He showed it to Roxanne and explained it to her. "They were pretty clever weren't they?"

Roxanne's wide eyes conveyed her agreement. "Calling this clever doesn't do it justice. It's like saying the night sky is pretty. You know, I see some similarities to ancient Egyptian handiwork here. Could we be getting close to the mysterious society that helped them?"

"Let's hope so. Bottom line, that's what we're after."

Bruce turned and looked at the exit leading from the area they were in. He saw that the passageway continued through the wall opposite them. He noticed something above the opening. "Look at those markings. Have you ever seen anything like them?"

Roxanne looked where his light was shining. She saw a geometrical symbol cut into the wall consisting of an equilateral triangle with a sun symbol at its center that sat atop a square. "No I haven't. What do you make of it?"

"I don't have any idea," Bruce answered. "I could speculate though. The four sides of a square usually mean the four directions, and is often a symbol of the earth. Living on the earth is something three-dimensional, could be man, whose threefold existence, body, mind and spirit, we've seen signified by the triangle in some societies. And hidden within all this seems to be a center or source. God maybe? I guess it's some kind of religious symbol."

"So God is the center of man as he dwells upon earth?" Roxanne asked.

"Either that or its a slice of pepperoni pizza on a box," he said while smiling.

"I don't think so. A society that old could never have the technology to create pepperoni," Roxanne said dryly.

They carefully made their way through the opening beneath the symbol and onto the pathway behind it. Soon it became as narrow as any they had yet explored, forcing them to inch along sideways.

Roxanne was getting short of breath again. "Bruce, I don't like this. I think we should stop for a minute."

"If we stop now your claustrophobia will get worse. We're moving slowly and carefully. Nothing will go wrong."

They felt themselves going down a slight incline. After about a hundred feet, the path widened and they came to a fork in the way.

"Well, which way do you want to try first?" Bruce asked.

Roxanne chose the left and they continued onward, still going slightly downhill. Soon the path was wide enough for them to walk side by side while they continued to carefully explore all around with the lamps illuminating each step before it was taken.

"No matter how many of these caves we go through, I still get the creeps each time," Roxanne said.

Bruce looked at Roxanne with concern. "As long as we just keep going at the pace we are and check each step before we make it, we'll be OK."

They had gone more than two hundred feet down this passageway when it opened up into an alcove to their right. As they entered this open area, they heard a trickling sound.

"Can you hear that?" Roxanne asked.

"Yeah, it sounds like it's coming from the other side of this room. Nothing to be scared of. I think."

They shined their lights in the direction of the sound and saw a fissure in the ground near the other end of the open area, about twenty feet away. As they approached it, they saw the gash was about five feet across. Their lights revealed a flat area on the other side of the opening, about twenty by twenty feet. As they continued to swing their lanterns from side to side, Roxanne gasped.

There were what appeared to be dozens of human skeletons scattered about the area. The chalky bones reflected the lantern light, making it difficult to tell, but there seemed to be at least forty or fifty of them. Many looked posed, as if they had simply sat or lain down to die.

"What do you think it means?" Roxanne asked.

"Who knows? It could be a lot of things. Maybe we've found the tomb of a great leader and his servants were buried with him. The only way to find out is to go have a look. I'll jump across first and when I say it's all right, you follow."

As Bruce was about to make the leap, he saw the source of the trickling sound. The fissure, about fifteen feet deep, had been carved into the ground by a small underground stream. He made the leap easily and began exploring the area. It seemed safe and he motioned for Roxanne to jump over.

Roxanne stood with one foot in front of the other poised for takeoff. As she pushed off with her foot, she stumbled on a small rock and lost momentum. She landed on the other side of the fissure, but off balance, leaning perilously backward toward the gap she'd just cleared. Bruce grabbed her arm and pulled her toward him.

He hugged her tightly. "Be careful, sweetheart. You scared the hell out of me."

"Yeah, well, I'm okay. Don't let my shaking hands and chattering teeth fool you into thinking I'm scared or anything."

They began to look more closely at the skeletons. Many of them definitely hadn't been moved since their death. Others were stacked haphazardly in a corner.

"It looks as if they were in here hiding from something, or someone," Roxanne said.

"Yeah. I wouldn't be surprised if these were the women and children. Look how small some of these bones are. Those were definitely youngsters. But look at the size of the ones lying stretched out on the ground. They must be seven feet tall." He looked at her. "That can't be right. Can it?"

"They look female by the size of the pelvises. You're right, though. They sure were tall." Roxanne smiled. "This is something new. I just know it."

"It looks like they must have remained hidden in here while the men fought a losing battle outside."

"But after it was over why wouldn't they have gone out again?" Roxanne asked.

"They might have had orders not to come out until the men came for them. Or they might not have known how to operate the door. Or, maybe they did try and saw that the men were wiped out and the victors were still out there. Who knows what kept them in here?"

"They must have starved to death," Roxanne said.

"Probably. You can see by the pile that the first ones to die off were stacked there. Then, as the more hardy ones went, they simply laid down and never moved again."

He saw tears in her eyes. "Sweetheart, it was thousands of years ago."

Roxanne took a tissue from her pocket and blew her nose. "I know. But I can't help thinking of the little ones. They must have suffered so much."

That's just like her, Bruce thought. *Always empathizing with others. Even the dead from thousands of years ago.* "Well this is a dead end," he said. When he realized the terrible pun he'd made, he turned to Roxanne ready to apologize, but she was too distracted to notice. "It is an interesting find though. We'll definitely have to return later. But for now, let's go check out that other passage back at the fork."

Soon they were ready to enter the other path. "I hope this one doesn't lead us to more of the same," Roxanne said.

"So do I. I think it will be different though. I have a feeling that secret door was made to protect something very valuable. Maybe even more valuable than life."

"But what could be more important than that?"

"To quote from our late friend's family tradition that led us here, 'That the truth of the Sons of Light be protected from the lies of the Sons of Darkness.' At least I hope that's why whoever built that door went to so much trouble. There's only one way to find out. Let's go."

Once again, using extreme caution and going very slowly, they continued to explore. This passage too got narrower and narrower until they had to squeeze through sideways. They were not going downhill, however. This time the path remained level. After about fifty feet, the way widened enough for them to walk side by side. After another hundred feet they came upon an open area about twenty feet square. On the wall opposite to where they had entered, there was an exit.

"I'm getting nervous," Roxanne said.

"About what?"

"I'm not sure, but my intuition is vibrating like a guitar string. I just feel a force that I can't identify."

Bruce had a healthy respect for Roxanne's intuition, but he thought that the skeletons they'd found were probably the cause of her concern. "You're not suggesting we stop here are you?"

"Of course not. But let's be very careful that's all."

Bruce looked at her in disbelief. "Are you serious? We can't be any more careful than we have been," he said. "I mean hell, we've been in here almost four hours and haven't traveled more than a couple of thousand feet, if that."

Bruce walked through the opening, and Roxanne followed, lagging about five feet behind. They were both pleased to find this passageway fairly wide. Their joy was short lived, however, as very quickly it too narrowed, causing their shadows to form ghostly companions on the cave walls.

Bruce turned to face Roxanne, and as he did so, he felt his foot kick something solid. His words froze as he saw a look of sheer terror in Roxanne's eyes. She was looking over his shoulder and screamed. He ducked. It saved his life.

Roxanne continued screaming as a beam of wood with sharpened prongs on its end came out of the wall like a giant baseball bat swinging for the fences. It swished over Bruce's head and crashed noisily, but harmlessly, into the wall. Bruce remained on his knees as dust and rock chips showered him.

Roxanne was shaking. "Oh Bruce, I couldn't move," she said in a quivering voice between sobs. "All I could picture was you impaled on that thing."

Bruce stood and embraced her. "It's a good thing I saw the fear in your eyes," he said, still breathless. "Fool that I am, I was going to tease you about your intuition being wrong." He brushed off his pants, and asked, "Do you think there are any more traps?"

"I don't know. Let's just get out of here. Nothing's worth dying for."

Bruce's adrenaline soaked nerves were playing a symphony just below skin level; his arm hairs poised for a standing ovation, but he tried to act calm for Roxanne's sake. "Well, I can't argue with that. But think of what could be so important that someone would go through all this trouble to protect. It has to be what we're looking for." He put his trembling arm around her waist.

"I suppose so. But we have to be more careful. This place is obviously booby trapped."

One look at the spikes lodged in the cavern wall and he knew she was right. "Oh yeah."

Bruce couldn't resist a closer examination of the deadly booby trap. He had to know how it worked. It proved to be another ingenious mechanism of weights and levers, triggered by the lever he had inadvertently kicked. He saw why it had swung so slowly. Apparently a small animal had been digging just above the pivot point and some dirt had fallen into the moving part causing extra friction. "Remind me to make a sacrificial offering to the Mole God," he said. "Would you mind being burned at the altar if it's for a good cause?"

Roxanne was still sobbing slightly. She took a tissue from her pocket and blew her nose. "Don't they always want virgins? I wouldn't do you any good."

He looked at her in mock horror. "You're not a virgin? Oh, how foolish I've been."

"I used to be one, though. Does that help?"

They both laughed, knowing it was forced, but it still helped relieve the tension. When they stopped Bruce tilted his head toward the passageway and said, "You ready?"

Using extreme caution, one lamp held high and one held low, they inched their way past the trap. After about ten minutes, but only about fifty feet, they discovered another small lever protruding into the path. It was just like the one that had nearly cost Bruce his life. Looking all around for what it was attached to, they saw an opening in the ceiling that contained a huge boulder. They couldn't see how it worked, but it was obvious that anyone unfortunate enough to trip the lever would be crushed by the rock.

"Holy shit. Look at that, will ya," Bruce said. "Not only would that rock kill anyone who tripped the lever, but it would also block the path to any others. I can't even tell how the boulder is held in place. It looks suspended, ready to fall. For God's sake, don't sneeze."

"It looks like you were right," Roxanne said. "Whatever they were protecting had to be very important. It must be the scrolls."

"Yeah, I can feel it. We've got to be close now. This trap looks like a last resort, set-up as it is to block the path like that. I don't think we'll find any more. But don't worry," he said when he saw she was about to protest, "I'll still be careful."

"Well, I'm staying here on the safe side of this trap. At least that way if something happens to you, I can go for help."

"Suit yourself, but if that rock falls I don't think help will do any good." He slowly made his way below the boulder protruding from the ceiling and continued on. After only a few seconds, Roxanne said, "Wait! I'm coming with you." She ran to him, and in the process nearly tripped the lever that would have ended their exploits faster than a cobra strike. At the last second she saw what she was about to do and jumped over the protruding trigger mechanism.

Bruce gave her a look that was equal parts fear, anger, and humor. "What are you trying to do, enter us as charter members in the 'Lost Explorers Never Heard from Again Club?'"

This time, she was too scared to laugh. "I'm sorry, darling. I just couldn't stand the thought of being alone back there."

"It's all right," he said as her breathing calmed. "Just stay a few feet behind me."

Once again they continued their way down the passage. In less than another hundred feet, they came to a small room. In it, resting on the cave floor, were about twenty cylindrical vessels.

"Hot damn! We found it. This is it. I know it is. We found it," Bruce said.

As he attempted to approach the clay jars in his excitement, Roxanne grabbed him and wouldn't let go. "Bruce, we've got to be careful. We've come this far and don't want to blow it now. What if they're a trap? Let's just take our time. OK?"

"You're right. It would be kind of foolish to get killed now wouldn't it?"

"Or any time for that matter."

He looked at his watch. "It's late. How about if we look them over very carefully, but we won't touch them? Then we'll head out and see if Lenny has shown up yet. He's due for a visit tonight. Okay?"

Roxanne agreed and they shined their lights over the walls of the ten by ten chamber. The fluid movement of the shadows brought the dark crevices to life, but no traps were seen. They looked at the jars. There were twenty-four of them, each about thirty inches in height, round, with a narrow top about ten inches in diameter. They were wider at the bottom, about fifteen inches. Each jar had a plug in the top that seemed to be made of a waxy substance. They were covered in a fine layer of dust, so it was impossible to see if any inscriptions were on them.

"It's getting late," Roxanne said. "By the time we get back to the camp it'll be after four o'clock. Why don't we head out now?" Bruce agreed and they reluctantly made their way from the small alcove.

As they were leaving the spot where the two paths had forked, one leading to the vases and the other to the collection of skeletons, Bruce thought about the ancient people who had been there thousands of years before them. "Who do you think left those vases, Rox?"

He turned to see Roxanne carefully following his exact footsteps. Bruce smiled as he imagined her wondering what other traps might be lurking about just waiting to drop a boulder on top of them. "Hey, did you hear me?"

Roxanne looked up startled. "I'm sorry. What did you say?"

He took her into his arms and held her close. Her shivering body made his smile change to concern. As much as he loved her, he often wondered how she ever became an anthropologist. On just about every one of their digs they'd come across some underground tunnels or pathways. And every time they explored these hidden passages she'd been a trainload of nerves.

"Sweetheart, we've checked this whole cave out thoroughly. There aren't any more hidden traps."

Roxanne squeezed Bruce tightly. "I know. You'd think I'd be used to this by now. What can I say? I'm just a big baby."

"Anyway, I asked you who you thought might have built those traps and hidden those vases."

They released each other and continued finding their way out of the cave. "That's the question," she said. "Who? It couldn't be the ancient Israelites. At least I don't think so. I've never seen anything like what we found here in any of their sites. And don't forget the height of the skeletons. We haven't seen anything like that before."

"I think you're right," Bruce said. "And don't forget what the old man who got us started on this quest told us last year. He said the scrolls dated from the time of Adam and told his story."

"I'm still having a hard time believing that," Roxanne said. "I'm not sure Adam and Eve were real."

Bruce stopped suddenly and turned. Roxanne nearly bumped into him. "Haven't we been through this already?"

"Bruce, I know you're pretty much convinced that the old man's family traditions reflect true events. And we both know there are plenty of age-old mysteries that can only be resolved by accepting that ancient peoples had advanced knowledge in math, astronomy, metallurgy and other sciences. But Adam and Eve? I mean, what about evolution? Do we just ignore everything science has taught us?"

"I know how far fetched it all sounds," Bruce said as they resumed walking. "But I just have a feeling we've discovered something here that's going to flip the scientific world upside down. Maybe science and religion aren't mutually exclusive concepts after all."

"Well they shouldn't be. In the final analysis, both claim to be after the truth."

When they reached the edge of the cave's mouth and were about to start their descent, Roxanne looked toward their campsite and noticed two vehicles beside the tent. "Oh look," she said, "Lenny must have brought someone with him. Isn't that lucky! Now we'll have some help to carry the vases out. I wonder who it is."

Bruce looked down upon the scene and said, "I don't know, but I don't like it. He wasn't supposed to tell anyone where we are."

"I'm sure he wouldn't have brought anyone who isn't trustworthy, darling. Maybe it's a surprise visit from one of our backers on the TUSK Foundation who wanted to see how we're doing."

"I hope so. Well, the only way to find out is to go see."

As they descended the hillside, they got close enough to see that whoever Lenny had brought with him was a tall Arab. The nearer they approached, the stranger and more sinister the man looked. Also, Lenny wasn't anywhere to be seen. Was he even there?

"I don't like the looks of this," Bruce said. "Don't say anything about what we found today until we see Lenny."

Roxanne agreed and they made their way down the last few feet of the slope. As they approached the camp, Bruce said to the man sitting on the ground poking a stick in the still smoldering campfire, "Hello, can I help you with anything?"

The man looked up at him and smiled. Bruce thought it was the most insincere look he'd ever seen. "Your servant told me that you were Americans before he ran off. I am pleased he did not lie."

Bruce didn't like the tone of the man's voice any more than he liked his looks. "What do you mean before he ran off? Who are you? What's your name?"

The man threw his stick into the fire, stood, and approached Bruce. Two other Arab men came from behind some rocks. Roxanne stayed behind Bruce with her hands on his shoulders; used him as a shield. The tall Arab towered over the much shorter American. He thrust his face to within inches of Bruce's and scowled.

"You may call me Assad."

FOURTEEN

A Break in the Chain

Summer, 10,000 BC

After two long months of difficult travel, Aker and Lan stood upon the edge of a cave filled cliff. Before them stretched the blue Sea Without Life. With a sigh of relief and a heavenward glance of thanksgiving Aker turned to see his troupe struggling uphill to reach him. "We have arrived," he yelled.

His words pulsed energy through the travel weary people. Expressions of relief, joy, and satisfaction appeared on previously downtrodden faces. Sagging shoulders and tired feet suddenly came to life. In short order the fifty commission members and their families stood beside Aker.

"Let us give thanks to the Heavenly Father for guiding us here," he said. "And let us remember our fallen brothers and sisters. The news of the Second Garden's destruction by the invading Nodites came as if a blow from a club. The loss of Seth and the others, the utter destruction of our former home, have left us dispirited. It falls upon us to insure the continued existence of our way of life."

Aker extended his arm over the abyss. As the troupe stared at the sparkling, salt encrusted, rocky shoreline, he said, "A great task awaits us. The primitive people of this area, whose tiny settlement we can see just north of the sea, shall provide fertile ground for Edenic ideals to grow and flourish. They shall be taught of that one God watches over them with love. That God is the Father of all humanity. They shall learn to grow food more efficiently. We shall teach them numbers and letters, the arts of manufacture and trade. Let us pray they accept these gifts in the spirit offered."

After a moment of silent contemplation, Aker turned to his left and started the final leg of their journey. Though optimism was at the fore of his thoughts, he could not help but wonder at the fate that awaited him and his extended family. Would these primitive people open their arms to the Edenites? To those the Sumerian tribes had called the Annanuki, 'Those Who from Heaven Came'? He decided to call the new settlement Jericho, after Jeric, he who had died on the journey.

FIFTEEN

The Great Interpreter

Fall, 1985

Bruce and Roxanne, hands tied behind their backs, were side by side in the cramped jump seat of one of their kidnapper's pickup trucks. The terrorists had taken everything from the campsite, cleaned up the area and left no evidence behind that anyone had been there. Bruce wondered just what the hell was going on. Who were these people? What did they want? What were they planning? What would Lenny think when he arrived at the abandoned campsite and found no evidence they'd even been there? Would he be smart enough to figure it out and warn the authorities? A thousand questions bounced through his mind; zero answers rebounded back.

He turned to his left and looked at Roxanne. He thought her eyes looked as big as the moon that was making its appearance over her left shoulder. Her tight-lipped mouth, flared nostrils and clenched chin, all framed by her black hair, reminded him of a frightened lab monkey he'd once seen at the university. Bruce shook his head and shivered as he forced the image from his mind.

"You okay, babe?" he whispered.

"No talking," the raspy voiced driver ordered.

Bruce turned to face the tall bearded one who called himself Assad, the apparent leader of the group. He was sitting in the front passenger seat. The driver and third terrorist sitting to Bruce's right were both dirty and scruffy looking, exuding enough body odor to gas a small village. Neither of them seemed the least bit interested in personal hygiene. But this Assad guy, he was different. His appearance had more the look of a real soldier. The khaki shirt and pants were well worn, but they were clean and crisp. Despite the oppressive heat, he kept his cap on over closely cropped hair. This guy was serious, no doubt about that.

Assad looked at Bruce and focused his penetrating black eyes on him. "Why do you have no vehicle? How did you get out here with all this equipment?"

Bruce wondered how much he should tell the menacing man. He definitely wasn't going to say anything about the scrolls. But that was all he knew at the moment. "Didn't our camp helper tell you?" He hoped Mohammed had simply run off, as Assad had said, without having revealed anything.

"I will ask the questions. I warn you, do not play games. Should you be so foolish there can be but one winner." Assad held up a Russian AK-47 to emphasize his point. "How did you get here?"

"We rented a vehicle and driver. The driver went back to Jerusalem for a couple of days." Bruce prayed the man would accept this. He wasn't even sure why he hadn't mentioned Lenny, but something told him not to.

The silence that followed had Bruce nearly ready to scream out the truth. He felt like one giant nerve from a day in the caves and a couple of near death experiences. Pile a kidnapping on top of that and yeah, you had a right to be nervous. He turned to Roxanne and saw she was close to the breaking point as well.

Assad's eyes followed Bruce's, then converged on Roxanne.

"Is this true, woman?"

Roxanne nodded weakly. Bruce wondered how much more she could take. Why was this happening? Was it politics? He and Roxanne had always done their best to remain neutral in all political matters. They were after truth and nothing more. What had that to do with politics? Or maybe this wasn't political. Maybe these guys were after money. He decided that given where they were, this probably wasn't the answer.

"What were you doing out here?" Assad asked. "What is way out here that is so interesting to two Americans?"

"The desert, the Dead Sea, the caves. You know, that kind of stuff," Bruce answered.

Assad stared at Bruce with a puzzled expression. Did he know about their search for the scrolls? What exactly had Mohammed told the man before he ran off? "No I do not know. What kind of STUFF?"

"We're university professors in the United States. I'm an archeologist and Roxanne teaches anthropology. We were looking for any evidence of ancient settlements in this area. We have all the required permits and documents." Bruce felt certain the man had no way to verify this last lie.

"And did you find any?"

Once again Bruce had the feeling this guy knew more than he was letting on. But there was no possible way he could know about the scrolls. "Not really."

Assad scowled menacingly over the backrest of the front seat. He stared at Bruce unwaveringly. He asked firmly. "What does that mean, 'not really'? You either did find something, or you did not. Which is it?"

"We didn't find anything substantial. Just some pottery shards from one of the caves."

Assad continued staring at Bruce. After what seemed an hour, but was probably only seconds, he turned to face the front. He looked out into the now darkened sky. "We will be approaching the border soon," he said to the driver.

Bruce looked out into the night. The moon provided enough illumination to highlight the outlines of the hills and cliffs behind them, as well as the stark lowlands where they seemed to be heading. As the cliffs receded from view, he caught sight of the Jordan River. The vehicle slowed, left the road, and began descending toward the river. The driver killed the lights as they approached the riverbank. Bruce looked at the side mirror and saw that the vehicle behind them had done the same. The two late-model, Japanese, four-door, pickup trucks came to a stop beside the swiftly moving river.

Assad took a flashlight from the glove box and got out of the truck. The terrorist beside Bruce followed his leader. Bruce and Roxanne watched as Assad walked to the water's edge and flashed the light three times in the direction of the opposite shore. Three answering flashes were returned.

The driver got out and joined Assad.

"What do you think they're doing?" Roxanne asked.

"I don't know, but that's Jordan across the river. This must be how they cross without being seen."

"Who are these people? What do you think they're going to do with us?"

Bruce looked closely at the love of his life. Her body language; tensed shoulders, right knee bobbing up and down on the ball of her foot, quick abrupt movements of her head as she looked everywhere, all told him how frightened she was. He desperately wanted to comfort her. There was only one problem. He was just as scared as she was. He also knew she wouldn't buy any false assurances. "I wish I knew, Babe. They're obviously Palestinian. From the looks of their weapons I'd guess they might be PLO. Whoever they are, let's just do what they tell us and wait till we find out more."

The door to Bruce's right opened. Assad grabbed him by the arm and pulled him from the truck. He looked to see Roxanne being dragged through the other door. The terrorists manhandled them to the water's edge. In the dim moonlight, Bruce could see the outlines of a watercraft of some sort coming toward them from the middle of the river. As his eyes adjusted and the object got closer, he realized it was a raft. Two men were guiding it with long poles. There was also a rope originating from a strong post in the ground beside him and passing through some type of guide mechanism then disappearing into the water in the direction of the raft.

When the raft was within five feet of the river's edge, Bruce and Roxanne were pulled into the water.

"Sit on the raft," Assad said. He and the driver held the flatboat steady as Bruce and Roxanne followed orders. The two men on the raft pulled them backward until they were seated in the middle, back to back, with a wooden post between them. One of the men wrapped a rope around them, binding them to the post.

"Stay there until told to move, and hold onto the post" Assad said. "It will be a bumpy ride. Do as we say and all will be well."

Bruce and Roxanne instinctively tried to huddle together, but the post only dug deeper into their backs. He did his best to give her some support. He well knew her fear of drowning and wanted in the worst way to assure her that all would be well. He felt her hands clawing, seeking his and moved his own to touch her. He winced as her fingers found his wrist and grabbed like a vise.

"Hang on tight, Rox. This won't take long. It's not that wide a river." He felt her body shivering against his and knew it wasn't from the cold water.

The men started pulling on the rope and they began leaving the shore. For the first few minutes all was fine. The ride was relatively smooth and only small splashes of water came onto the floor of the raft, wetting their legs. As they got further from shore, the current strengthened. So did Roxanne's grip on Bruce's wrist. The ride was getting bumpier as well. As the current grew even more powerful, it fought harder to force them downstream. The resistance it presented to the river's efforts caused a stream of water to wash up onto the raft. Bruce felt the small current trying to force them from their perch and was thankful for the rope holding them to the post.

They were in the middle of the river now and white water was all around them. Bruce wanted to ask these idiots why they were crossing at such a dangerous point. Roxanne's body was shaking violently. Bruce flinched in pain as he felt one of her nails break off in his wrist. "You OK, sweetheart?" he asked.

"No," she said in the most pitiful voice Bruce had ever heard. He looked at the two men pulling on the rope. It was obvious they were struggling against the force of the water. He couldn't tell if it was sweat or water that glistened from their skin in the moonlight and decided it didn't matter. He tried to look to the destination shore to see how close they were. It was too dark to see more than ten or fifteen feet and more whitewater was all this limited visibility allowed.

Bruce needed to distract Roxanne. It was the only thing he could think of to help her. "Hey Rox, remember that time we first found out we were coming here with Lenny?"

"What about it?" she asked in a heartbreaking tone that sounded like a lost child's.

"Remember how I told him we didn't expect any trouble? And how afterwards you said you hoped the nickname I got from all my wrong predictions wouldn't prove true."

Roxanne was silent. "C'mon, you remember. What did you say again?" He heard Roxanne sniff. Was it tears?

"I said, 'Well, Professor One-eighty, let's hope you didn't put your shoes into your mouth this time.'"

"That's right," he laughed. "Professor One-eighty. Every time I make a prediction I'm off that many degrees. It's uncanny, don't you think. I bet we could get rich by betting against everything I say from now on."

Roxanne laughed. It was the sweetest sound he'd ever heard. "Let's try that when we get home. I bet it would work," she said. "You never told me who gave you that name."

"I got it from one of my students. He used to run one of those football pools. I would bet on it a few times. Never won anything, of course, but didn't realize how bad I was doing until he called me in the hallway one day."

"That's what he called you? Professor one-eighty?"

"I didn't answer him, naturally. Didn't even know he was talking to me. He cleared the confusion up when he explained that every team I picked in the pools was a loser. Every single one."

"And what about when we were standing in front of the cave this morning?" Roxanne asked. "When I commented on how the natural beauty was surrounded by all the ugliness. What did you say?"

"I don't remember. What did I say?"

"You said, 'It doesn't have anything to do with us.' Well, PROFFESSOR, the more I think about this the more I realize you really are uncanny."

"It's actually pretty amazing isn't it?"

"Amazing. Yeah, that's you all right." The coolness of her sarcasm warmed his heart.

Bruce's little ploy worked. The raft had stopped thrashing and the current was no longer trying to force them into its embrace. Bruce looked off to his right and could see the outline of two men on the shore coming toward them. He felt Roxanne's back against his and sighed inwardly. Her shaking had calmed noticeably.

The men on shore and the two on the raft maneuvered them to the shoreline. As Bruce and Roxanne were being helped off the raft, two vehicles approached and Assad got out of the first one. He walked up to them and took their elbows, and guided them to the Jeep.

Five minutes later they were on the move again. Bruce had to ask. "Why did we cross the way we did?"

Assad turned to face his two captives. His menacing glare withered Bruce's posture. He should have kept his mouth shut. Surprisingly, the man answered the question. "As you will soon learn, we have other guests. It has become too difficult to cross by the bridge."

About an hour later, the small convoy pulled up to a barn. As the vehicles stopped in front of the large doors, a man from the second truck walked to the structure and opened them wide enough to drive through. Minutes later they were sitting alone in straw, handcuffed to a wall-anchored chain in the semi-darkness.

"Bruce, what's going on?" Roxanne asked in a terrified voice.

"We're being held for ransom," a man's voice said.

Bruce and Roxanne looked at each other in surprise. The voice seemed to have come from the other side of the wall to their left. "Who are you?" Bruce asked.

"My name's John Rance. Who are you?"

Bruce told him their names, then asked, "What kind of ransom? Who are these guys? How many people are here?"

"I know how you feel," John said. "You have lots of questions and you're scared out of your wits. We're all in the same boat, all ten of us, counting you two."

"So what's going on?" Bruce asked.

"They're trying to swap us for some of their friends. I guess the Israelis have them in prison or something."

Roxanne was shivering. "How long have you been here?" she asked.

"My wife and I have been here five days. The others two and three days." John said. He went on to explain all that he knew about the situation. About the reporter who had come to interview them. About the terrorist's promises to let them go once their demands had been met.

"What did you say that reporter's name was?" Bruce asked.

"Lenny Cronin," John Rance answered. "Why?"

Bruce looked at Roxanne in the semi-darkness. She returned his puzzled look in kind. He could tell that she was thinking the same thing he was. Should they reveal their association with Lenny? It seemed like benign information on the surface. But what if one or more of the other hostages were spies for the terrorists? Discretion seemed smarter. He shook his head at Roxanne and placed a finger to his lips.

"Nothing," he answered. "I just thought I might have heard the name before."

"We aren't sure about the guy anyway." John said.

"What do you mean?" Roxanne asked.

"Well, he seems legit. But how did he get the terrorists to bring him here? And why him out of all the reporters in this country. We're just not sure if we can trust him is all."

"Is he coming back?" Bruce asked.

"He's been here twice now. He said he'd probably be returning, but he wasn't sure."

Roxanne turned to face Bruce. "What do you think?" she asked in a low whisper.

"I don't know," Bruce said. "It could be a good thing. But it could also be dangerous for Lenny."

"What do you mean?"

"If the terrorists find out Lenny's with us they might not let him leave. He's obviously gained their trust somehow. But they might think he'd try to help us escape. Let's keep this between us."

Bruce turned the conversation to questions about food, bathroom privileges, and other immediate concerns. He learned that they were fed two small meals a day and allowed to squat over an outside trench once in the morning and once in the early evening. After a couple of hours, the ping pong game of personal questions and answers came to an end.

Weariness came upon Bruce and he felt an overpowering need to sleep. He saw that Roxanne had already drifted off. He lay down beside her and maneuvered as best he could, given their chains, into a spoon coupling. In seconds, he too was fast asleep.

Bruce opened his eyes and saw a man standing over him. The light was too dim to make out facial features, but the man was tall, and as best he could tell, he had never seen him before.

"Who are you?" he asked.

"Names are not important," the man responded kindly. "A name does not reveal who we are. A name is a label of convenience that neither reveals nor obscures that which is within."

"I suppose that's true," Bruce said. "But what is important then?"

"Truth is important."

Bruce looked at the enigmatic figure. "Isn't that obvious? I mean, who doesn't know that?"

"Truth, beauty and goodness are important. Truth, beauty and goodness reveal all that needs knowing."

Bruce shook his head. *What is this platitude machine saying?* Obviously, such a simple condensation of life was no more than words used to cover a lack of understanding. But he felt strangely compelled to continue the line of conversation, to see where it might lead. "How can that be? What about love for example? Where does that fit in?"

"Is not love the greatest expression of truth? Is not selfless love goodness personified? Can there be anything more beautiful than the love of the parent for the child? Truth, goodness, beauty; all that is worthwhile can be distilled to these three."

"That sounds well and good in theory," Bruce said. "But reality all too often kicks lofty concepts right in the ass. How am I supposed to carry this idea into the real world? If I walked around looking for the true, the good and the beautiful all the time, my head would be in the sky while my pocket was being picked by some guy whose noggin was concerned with more concrete details. Like eating breakfast."

"One need not have his head in the clouds to perceive that which is lofty. One need not ignore reality to live a truthful life."

This guy had answers all right. But they sounded like Chinese fortune cookies. "But what about that pick pocket?" Bruce asked. "What's true or good or beautiful about him? How do I deal with someone like that?" Bruce tried to get a closer look at the mysterious person. Why couldn't he see his face? He seemed to be standing in the shadows, yet there were no shadows.

"Life is filled with concerns of this nature," the man said. "Each day presents new barriers to be overcome. Each problem is singular and unique. But the real goal is the same for all of humanity. The trek of every human being is identical, whether they realize it or not. The challenge is to see the good. The quest is to overcome the lie. The goal is to reveal the beauty."

Bruce was getting exasperated. He understood there was wisdom of a sort in the man's words. He even accepted the general idea of what was being said.

If only life were that simple. "You're still talking theory and generalities here. Let's get back to the pickpocket. How do I handle that one?"

"Do you think if the answer is revealed to you, then all understanding will open up before your eyes like a book? That all your concerns and fears will suddenly be as naught?"

"Of course not," Bruce said. "I'm not that stupid. I just want a concrete example of how your theory would play out."

"Do you think this man with his hands in your pocket is completely evil? Do you see him as someone who has no goodness in him?"

"No, no. Nothing like that. The guy's probably just trying to make a living. Maybe he got fired from his job and can't think of a better way to feed his kids. But what can I do about that? Surely you're not saying I have to help the guy out?" Once again Bruce wondered why he couldn't see better. Why couldn't he even see what the man was wearing?

"You do not have to do anything. But know this. Every interaction you have with another human being is an opportunity for inner growth. It is a matter of choice whether or not you take advantage of this gift."

"What kind of opportunity? Suppose I gave the guy a job. What if he stole from the company?"

"What if he didn't? What if the chance you gave him helped him turn his life around?"

"But why should I go out on a limb for a perfect stranger?"

"There are no strangers. Humanity is one big family. If mankind would take those five words and apply them literally, all conflict and animosity would end."

"That'll be the day when that happens," Bruce said.

"A journey to the top of even the highest ladder begins on the first rung."

"Bruce." The familiar, but far off voice said. "Bruce." It was Roxanne. He opened his eyes with a start. He saw her face staring down on him from the dark. "You were mumbling something in your sleep. Are you okay?"

Bruce shook the cobwebs from his mind. "Yeah, I'm fine. I was just dreaming, I guess. It seemed so real though." He thought about the mysterious man. "I think I was talking to Adam."

Roxanne knelt in the straw beside him. The chains rattled with each movement. "Did he say anything interesting?"

In spite of her skeptical tone, he answered her. "It was interesting, but not very helpful I'm afraid. Some stuff about brotherhood and how to deal with the world. Looking for the best in every situation. You know, that kind of drivel."

Roxanne looked around in the small, wooden walled, dusty, dirty box stall. "The best I can see in this is that we're together while the others are alone in their own cages." She looked him in the eyes. "That's not much is it?"

Bruce noticed that Roxanne was no longer shivering and her voice was more normal in tone and tenor. Her fidgety demeanor continued telegraphing her inner fear, however. He smiled inwardly at her attempts, obvious to him, to display a calmness that wasn't there. And why should there be. It was quite evident the terrorists meant business. From what they'd learned, this Assad and his band of thugs were serious players. What would happen to the hostages if the Israelis didn't give in to their demands?

Bruce took her free hand into his own and kissed the back of it. "It's not much," he said in answer to her words. "But I'm grateful to have you next to me."

He thought about the scrolls, wondering if they would ever have a chance to go back for them. The cruelty of coming so close to fulfilling a lifelong dream, only to be snatched from the serenity of scholastic endeavor and dumped into the world of political intrigue and violence was nearly overwhelming. Many times he and Roxanne had talked about their desire to remain outside this arena as dispassionate observers. If they were to succeed in their efforts to unearth ancient sites, they had to remain neutral. To do otherwise was professional suicide. But how could anyone in their situation remain neutral? In addition to the politics, there was the age-old conflict of good versus evil staring them in the face like a prowler peering through a bedroom window. Could that be what had instigated his dream? Was his subconscious telling him that somewhere in this mess there was something good? That good would somehow overcome evil?

It seemed to him right now that evil was kicking the shit out of good. Why did it have to be that way? He felt the Adam manuscripts, if that was what they'd really discovered, had the potential to reveal much in the way of answers to such questions. He had such high hopes for the message they were supposed to carry for mankind, at least as told to him and Roxanne by the old man whose family history led them to the discovery. When they had first encountered the man and heard his tale of ancient documents, written by Adam of all people, they were incredulous. And when the man had told them that the scrolls purported to reveal ancient knowledge of where man came from, why man was created, God's purpose in creating the physical universe, they were equally astonished. So much so they had nearly dismissed the story out of hand. Now it had turned out to all be true. Although he still had no proof of what the manuscripts said, he thought it certain that the old-timer had been revealing accurate information. Again he thought of his dream. Was he somehow receiving messages of what the scrolls said about life and how to approach it? Would he and Roxanne even live long enough to find out?

SIXTEEN

The Valley of Fear

Two evenings after returning from his second visit with the terrorists Lenny left the hotel. It was well past dark and he was again following written directions to walk toward the inner city. As he walked, he thought about what to do once he got to the farm. The Israelis and the Americans had flat-out refused to deal with the terrorists. Where the hell did that leave everybody? According to Assad, this meant they were about to execute innocent people. No way was he going to let that happen. And force him to watch it? Just can't picture it. But all he had was one lousy pistol hidden in an ankle holster. How do you fight a cannon when all you have is a peashooter?

While walking along deep in thought, Lenny accidentally bumped into a man walking in the opposite direction. "Oh excuse me, sir," the man said. "I wasn't watching where I was going."

"That's okay. Neither was I," Lenny said.

A few minutes later, Lenny became aware of two men trailing him on foot. They weren't the SECRETEST of secret agents. It was almost like they wanted him to see them. Lenny wanted to run toward them for help. Was that why they were so obvious? He controlled the impulse, knowing the terrorists were watching from somewhere and any contact would blow things sky high. He continued following directions. Still, he thought this could be a chance to do something. The men on his tail must be American or Israeli agents of some kind. He was considering how he might contact them when, as he rounded a corner, he was jerked into a basement doorway. The door was closed behind him.

Holding Lenny's arm, and smiling like a cat with birdbreath, was the terrorist with the long nose and cracked teeth. This was the guy he'd silently named Wharf Rat. He also noticed they were in a darkened pawnshop. He looked toward the street from behind gauzy curtains, and saw himself, no, his double, walking past. His doppelganger had returned. And, as before, the two men followed the imitation Lenny like greyhounds chasing a mechanical rabbit.

Wharf Rat laughed as he released Lenny's arm. "Ha! Ha! You stupid Americans. How did you ever become a world power with such incompetents on your side?"

The words ate through Lenny like acid. He wanted to put the Wharf Rat down like a rabid dog, but forced himself to shrug meekly and tried hard to quench the fire smoldering below the surface.

Goddamn! What a shithead I am, he thought. He knew he was now a lone sheep in a pack of wolves.

When the cracked tooth terrorist stopped laughing, he said, "Our vehicle will be here in just a few moments, Mister Cronin. Assad is not pleased with the response of the American government or of the Zionists." The man then smiled at Lenny as if he were a long lost buddy, revealing yet more rotted teeth. "That could be good news for you. In the next forty-eight hours, you may have the opportunity to witness executions and you will have the story of the year."

Lenny thought about poker. He had a pair of twos fighting a full house. The first move was to stay in the hand and get to the farmhouse. He had to maintain his poker face to the end. Anything short of that risked the terrorists changing their minds about bringing him back. "I hear you have some more hostages," he said. "I'm anxious to talk to them."

"Yes," the man said. "We have a West German couple and another American couple. We have twelve now. We would have fourteen but we sent the Frenchman and his wife home."

Lenny seesawed about the French couple's release. Good news on one hand, not so good on the other; the gang just went out shopping for more to replace them. "Was it at the insistence of your Saudi brothers?"

"Yes. It was too bad because I had that arrogant son of a pig-eater's whore picked out as the first to get shot. I would have enjoyed it."

From the look of the man's face, Lenny understood he was telling the truth. "Who are the Americans," Lenny asked. "More tourists?"

"We had hoped to hurt the Jews' economy by scaring them all away. These two were camping on the outskirts of Jericho exploring caves. Can you imagine that? What could be more dull? I'll never understand Americans. To look at holes in the ground, they travel thousands of miles"

Jesus, they have Bruce and Roxanne. Lenny's breathing became short and tight. It took every bit of concentration he had to keep his expression from ratting him out. Poker face never meant so much. If he'd had any lingering doubts about attempting a rescue, they were now as dead as he hoped Wharf Rat and his buddies would soon be. He was supposed to have visited Bruce and Roxanne yesterday but had blown them off. Could he have prevented this from happening if he had been there?

The familiar old Mercedes stopped in front of the pawnshop. Lenny was blindfolded, pushed into the back seat, and made to lie down. As always, the driver was cautious and made many maneuvers to assure nobody was following them.

Lenny made a determined effort to figure out the direction they were traveling. After five or six turns he had to give up. For the rest of the trip, the only thing useful he learned was that they had definitely crossed a bridge with fairly rapid water passing under it. This confirmed his earlier suspicions that the Jordan River had been traversed and they were in either Jordan or Syria.

When the car came to a stop at the end of the now familiar gravel driveway, one of the men told Lenny to sit up. "You may remove your blindfold also. You have been here enough times. There is nothing that you have not already seen."

Lenny was surprised that they had arrived so quickly, and realized that much of the first two trips had been camouflage. He was unsure of their reasons for eliminating this ruse, but knowing they weren't as far from safety as he'd first thought made him feel better about the situation. He stole a look at his watch, which they'd neglected to take from him this time, and wondered if the terrorists were beginning to take his cooperation for granted. *I should be so lucky*, he thought. It was three o'clock in the morning. The trip had taken under two hours.

At the speed he estimated they had traveled, they were less than seventy-five miles from Jerusalem, maybe only thirty from the Israeli border. It still meant they were probably in Syria or Jordan, but at least it wasn't an impossible distance.

The three men exited the car and made their way toward the house. As they did so, Lenny noticed the shadows of a forest protruding into the moonlit sky against a backdrop of breezy clouds. It was only a few hundred feet away from the farm property. He suddenly understood where they were. The only large tract of woods in the entire region was in southwest Syria. He knew this from his research. He cursed himself for not having realized this on an earlier visit; the wood stove should have told him. "When will I be able to talk to the hostages?"

"Early in the morning," Wharf Rat answered as they entered the house. "It may well be the last time they will speak to anyone from their own country," the man laughed. Lenny thought he squeaked.

A sandstorm swirled in Lenny's stomach as he realized the little vermin was looking forward to killing innocent people. It further resolved him to his course of action. He didn't yet know how, but he was going to do whatever he could to get the hostages out. *It's a good thing they pay me the big bucks*, he thought, trying to steel himself to the danger, 'cause *I might buy the farm tonight.*

Lenny was led to the small bedroom and locked in. He tried his best to fall asleep, but the man who could nap anywhere anytime tossed and turned like a raft on whitewater.

Lenny was awakened by one of the terrorists. He was surprised that he'd nodded out. "It is time for breakfast, Mister Cronin. Assad would like to talk to you also." It was Raspy Voice. He wondered how many cigarettes the guy smoked in a day, then realized he'd never seen him with one.

Lenny yawned. It felt like he'd only had about an hour of sleep. He looked at his watch. He had. He rolled up onto the edge of the bed and pulled a cigarette from the pack in his shirt pocket. Unsure why, probably just habit, he offered one to Raspy Voice. He declined. Where the hell did that voice come from then? Lenny lit up and inhaled deeply, then exhaled a cloud. This was going to be a long day. He stood and followed his guide.

As they entered the kitchen, Lenny was heartened to see only four others seated around the worn table. He did his best to sound casual as he asked, "Only five of you today? Where's the rest of the crew?"

Assad sneered and for an instant Lenny thought about straws piling up on a camel's back. How many questions could he risk before it broke? But he had to know everything he could if he was going to help anybody this day.

"There are two men out in the barn with the hostages," Assad answered. "The rest are doing errands. They will be back late tonight and tomorrow. And if our demands are not met by then, the executions will begin."

After the men finished eating, Raspy Voice led Lenny to the barn. He had hoped against it, but soon realized the new 'guests' were indeed Bruce and Roxanne. Lenny suddenly realized that back in the kitchen Assad had called them hostages for the first time. Was that another straw for the camel?

He made sure that the two guards were no longer paying attention to him before approaching his friends. At first he was surprised to see them chained together, but then realized there were now more hostages than stalls. They were holding each other and hadn't yet seen him. His heart ached over their desperate expressions. He remembered his dead friend Keith and made a silent vow. *Not again*, he thought. *Not this time.*

"Lenny," Roxanne whispered as he knelt down beside them with his finger to his lips. "It's so good to see you."

"How did you become so close with these animals?" Bruce asked.

"That's a long story. I'll tell it to you later. Right now we have to figure a way out of this mess."

Bruce's eyes opened wide at the mention of a possible escape plan. "What do you have in mind?"

"Nothing yet, but there's only seven of them here until late tonight. And I brought a gun with me."

From the look on Roxanne's face, Lenny knew she wasn't sure if this was good news or bad. She whispered, "But even if there are only seven of them, they each have a machine gun. What could you do?"

"I've been trying to answer that question for days now," Lenny said. "And I don't know yet. Hopefully we'll be able to sneak out of here in the dark. We'll just have to keep our eyes open for any opportunity that comes along. And hope one does."

"Shouldn't we just wait until they exchange us for their friends?" Roxanne asked.

Lenny's first impulse was to tell her what he knew about the terrorist's plans for killing some of them tomorrow morning, but realized no good could come from it. "Who knows when that will be? The Iranian hostages were held for over a year." That seemed to quiet her resistance.

"What can we do to help?" Bruce asked.

"There's not much you can do. If only I could get my hands on the keys to your chains."

"I've noticed they keep them in that small room over there," Bruce said, indicating a door, partially visible through the stall entrance, next to the barn door. "Whenever they unlock us for our walk to the bathroom they always go in there first and then come out with the keys."

"Good," Lenny said. "Maybe I can figure some way to get in there. What time do they usually let you go to the bathroom?"

"About an hour after breakfast and an hour before dark I think." Roxanne said.

"That seems about right," Bruce added.

"Okay," Lenny said. "That's about six thirty tonight. I'll think of some excuse for them to bring me back out here around seven. I'll try to get my hands on the keys then. After that, I'll wait until they're all asleep and then try to sneak back out here."

"Why don't you get the keys when you come back late at night?" Roxanne asked.

Just as he was about to answer, one of the guards came near. Lenny said in a clear voice, "Is there anything else you want me to tell the people of the world?"

Bruce looked up at the terrorist, then said, "I would like you to say this to the Israelis. You are holding freedom fighters, not revolutionaries or terrorists. As such, you should earnestly consider the just demands of the Palestinians. The freedom loving peoples of the world are on the side of the Palestinians. Please release their brothers so that we may return to our loved ones."

A broken toothed smile appeared on the kidnapper's face. "Our leader will be much pleased to read that in the papers of the world. Let us hope for the sake of these people the Zionists listen to reason."

"I'm sure they will," Lenny told the man. "World pressure is building rapidly. Most of the democracies of the world are working on this urgent matter."

"Let us hope so," the guard repeated as he left.

"Laying it on a little thick there, Bruce?" Lenny smirked as soon as the man was out of hearing range. "You may have just given me an idea though." He turned to answer Roxanne's earlier question. "The reason I don't want to get the keys when I come late at night is because I'd rather give them to you earlier so you can free yourselves and be ready for me. Bruce just gave me an idea on how I can get back here later. When they bring me back to the house in a short while, I'll plant an idea in their minds that will hopefully get them to bring me back here after dark. In the meantime, keep your eyes open for anything that might help us."

"Like what?" Bruce asked.

Lenny shrugged and shook his head. "I wish I knew. But we have to be alert to any possibility. Wish me luck and I'll see you later."

"What if they don't let you back out?" Roxanne asked.

"Then I'll sneak back around two in the morning somehow."

"Thanks, Lenny," Bruce said. "I don't know what we can do, but we'll try to think of something."

"Well, if nothing else you can pray."

"You can bet the farm we'll be praying," Roxanne said, as Lenny left to talk to the others.

He spoke with each of the hostages but didn't say anything about his plans for fear they might inadvertently give him away. When he was through, he motioned to the guard and the man escorted him outside.

On the way out, Lenny said, "That last couple that you captured? They are both college professors and speak very well. I asked them to try and think of something to say that might help end this crisis. I told them I would be back this evening to see if they came up with something. Do you think that would be all right?"

The man grunted and said, "That is not for me to decide. It is up to our leader."

"Well, I don't think he'll have any objections. Do you?"

"We shall see."

SEVENTEEN

Danger

Back in the tiny bedroom, Lenny paced back and forth, turning over different plans in his mind for how he might help the hostages. He had mentioned to Assad that he wanted to return to the barn later to talk further with the American professors. The man seemed pleased that he was making an effort to show the good side of the movement. At least he had the murderous bastards thinking he was on their side, his only rationale for optimism so far. He still had no concrete ideas of how he was going to save his friends. He checked the window to his room and confirmed it was nailed securely shut and knew that any quiet effort there would be futile. The camel was breathing heavily; the backbreaking straw seemed closer by the minute. What to do?

Hours later, he wasn't sure how many; Lenny was still walking in small circles inside the room. The weight of the Walther handgun in his ankle holster reminded him with each step how underpowered he was. He had come up with a couple of different plans but had rejected both as too risky. He heard someone approaching his door from the other side. The door opened. It was Assad. As he entered the room, Lenny wondered if he had come to let him talk with Bruce and Roxanne. He looked at his watch and realized with a start that it was nearly seven P.M. He had to get back out there soon or he might not be allowed at all.

"Mister Cronin, I have been thinking about your request," Assad said, as he took a seat on the empty fig crate. "We cannot wait much longer before we start executing hostages or the world will not take our demands seriously. I am a thoughtful man, however, and I have decided to let you talk to the two Americans once more in the hopes that they will have something to say that will help the Zionists see reason."

Lenny hoped his sigh of relief wasn't as obvious as he felt it was. He was anxious not to arouse any suspicions now that the terrorists seemed to trust him.

"But just to make sure that our demands ARE taken seriously," Assad continued, "tomorrow morning at eight o'clock you shall witness the first of the executions, and you shall take that story back with you also. We Palestinians will not give up our cause until our homeland is returned. The world must be made to understand this."

Lenny couldn't hide the inner turmoil. All his poker face work just went bust. He hoped the look of dread on his face wouldn't screw things up. He decided a bit of honesty was needed. "But why do I have to witness their executions? Please realize that, while I understand your position and dedication to your cause, the killing of innocent people is abhorrent to me. I must be honest with you in this. I don't want to witness murder." He hoped he hadn't pushed his luck. After all, if he had anything to say about it, the hostages would be gone before tomorrow anyway.

Assad squinted at Lenny from under a furrowed brow. "Mister Cronin, you are here because we thought you had the stomach for such an assignment. It seems as if we were wrong. If you wish, we can return you to the city right now and you will lose out on the biggest story of your life."

He thinks I'm worried about the story. Probably thinks I'd rather die than lose a shot at it. Lenny decided he'd better play along. "No, you weren't wrong," he said. "I want the story and I'll do whatever you say to get it. I think you knew that."

Assad smiled. "Yes I did. You see I have had experience with reporters before and you are all as alike as jackals. You might talk about your principles as if they were the most important things in the world to you. But I know when it comes to the big story, principles are left behind like a carcass stripped of meat." His laugh sounded so cold, Lenny thought he saw steambreath.

Lenny was relieved. He had nearly blown it with his big mouth. He had to be more careful from now on. Lives were depending on him.

The terrorist leader called to one of his men and said "Abu, take our principled reporter out to the hostages and let him talk to the two American Professors only. Make sure he talks to none of the others. Do you understand?"

The man nodded, and led Lenny out the door.

As they entered the barn, Lenny's escort began conversing in Arabic with the man currently on guard duty. They both looked directly at Lenny and he got the distinct feeling that he was going to be watched very carefully. He went to Bruce and Roxanne.

"How are you two doing?" he asked as he sat down beside them.

"About what you'd expect," Bruce said. "But we found out for sure they keep the keys in that room. The question now is how are you going to get them?"

"I wish I knew," Lenny answered, pretending to take notes.

"There's only one of them now," Bruce said, watching the guards over Lenny's shoulder. "Your escort left. Let's go for it."

Lenny remained silent, thinking. Bruce and Roxanne looked at him expectantly. Then he said, "It's too risky. If he gets a shot off they'll hear it in the house for sure. We'll try to get the drop on him later tonight when he's asleep. But we need those keys now, so you can free yourselves and help me when I sneak back out here."

"I have an idea," Bruce said. "They keep the drinking water in the same room as the keys. As soon as I make my move, Roxanne you say, 'Quick get him some water,' and Lenny you ask, 'Where is it?' and stand up as if to get it."

"What are you going to do, darling?" Roxanne asked.

"You'll see," Bruce said. "Do you both know what I want you to do?" Lenny and Roxanne each nodded. Bruce put the index finger of his right hand into his mouth and swallowed. He immediately began to gag and throw up.

Lenny jumped up and said, "This man is sick."

"Get him some water," Roxanne said on cue.

The guard came over and seeing the vomit made a face of disgust and pointed to the room that held the keys. "The water is in there," he said.

Lenny stood and went into the room. He saw right away where the water was, but couldn't see the keys. He slowly took an empty bucket off the wall, went to the water pump and started using it while his eyes searched everywhere for the keys.

The room itself appeared to be the storeroom for the barn. The walls were covered with garden implements and tools. Lenny made a mental note of which might serve as weapons. A large, metal-lined, wooden box that he assumed once held grain for the farm animals dominated the floor. There were two more buckets on the wall next to where the one in his hands had been. Maybe the keys were in one of them.

As he moved toward the nearest one, he heard the guard yell, "Hurry up in there."

He took a quick look in the bucket. It was empty. Then he saw a cup and poured some water into it. As the guard called once again, he walked out of the room with the cup of water.

"I didn't see this cup until just now and I was pumping a whole bucket full of water," he said for the guard's benefit as he handed it to Bruce. "Drink it and ask for more," he whispered.

Just then, the second terrorist returned and Lenny's stomach suddenly felt like it was about to add its own contents to what Bruce's had spewed moments before. He swallowed the bile in his throat and steeled his nerves; he wasn't about to give up now.

Bruce finished the cup of water greedily. "More please. Just one more cup please," he begged in the most pitiful tone Lenny had ever heard. Bruce looked at the terrorist standing over him. "Just one more?"

Lenny looked at the guard with a questioning expression. He was afraid that Bruce had overdone the acting because the man looked like he was going to refuse the request. But then he said, "Go ahead, but make it fast."

Lenny got up and walked past the two terrorists and once again entered the small room. He quickly poured a cup of water and then began looking for the keys. He checked the last bucket hanging on the wall. There they were. He reached in, quietly took them out and put them in his pocket.

As he spun around, he heard the voice of Wharf Rat. He almost wet his pants.

"So, Mister Cronin. It seems that you want to join your countrymen in chains." Lenny completed his turn to see the man pointing an automatic weapon directly at him.

Lenny tried to bluff. "What do you mean?" he asked.

"What I mean is your little game is over. You have shown us your true colors. Now hand over the keys very carefully, and don't try any other little tricks you might have in mind. I will shoot you dead right here."

"Mohammed," the man yelled to his partner, "You were right. Our reporter friend was ready to betray us. Although what he could have done against you and me I'll never know." He laughed. "Go to the house and fetch Assad. We will show him that his precious reporter is the same as all people from his country."

Lenny couldn't believe his stupidity. Not only had he failed to rescue his friends, but now he was going to join them in chains, if he was lucky. The only ray of hope left was the fact that this guy hadn't thought to search him. He still had his gun in its ankle holster. Assad, though, would not be so careless.

The guard directed his new captive to the stall containing Bruce and Roxanne and ordered him to sit in the hay. Lenny could hear excited voices outside the barn, speaking Arabic.

"I told Assad that you were not to be trusted, but he wouldn't listen to me."

Lenny casually scratched his ankle, the one without a pistol strapped to it.

"What is wrong with you? Can you not take the itch of a little hay?"

"I don't know if it's the hay or not, but my leg is very itchy," Lenny said. The man was facing him and he dared not try anything, but kept scratching the ankle hoping to provide distraction for his real move. But how many more seconds did he have before the others would come through that door?

The terrorist turned to face the source of the outside voices. He began yelling something in Arabic as Lenny deftly pulled his gun from its holster and aimed it at the man's head. He tightened his finger on the trigger. The pressure began building on the mechanism. One more ounce of tension and the man would be dead. Lenny faltered. Shooting someone in the back was harder than he'd thought it would be. The hesitation was enough for the terrorist to turn and see the gun in Lenny's hands. The scowl on the man's face turned to rage as he began raising his weapon. Lenny fired twice. The man fell instantly to the ground like a rag doll as a hole in his forehead trickled blood and the exit wound spurted brain matter onto the wall behind him.

Lenny quickly found the keys in the dead man's pocket and threw them to Roxanne. He picked up Wharf Rat's dropped automatic weapon and gave his pistol to Bruce. "Hurry up and free everybody, Roxie. Bruce, you come with me. We have to guard the doors."

As soon as Roxanne unchained Bruce, he came to Lenny's side. While the other prisoners were being released, Lenny said to Bruce, "There's six of them out there. I'm sure they're gonna come storming in here any second." He pointed to a support column for the structure on the other side of the central aisle. "Hide behind that post and cover the doors. I'll get behind this other one and do the same."

"What else?" Bruce asked.

Lenny shrugged in dismay and said, "I don't know. Maybe we can plow our way out in one of the trucks."

As they were placing themselves in position to provide crossfire cover of the barn doors, They heard a barrage of automatic weapons fire and small explosions coming from outside the barn.

"What's going on out there?" Bruce asked from behind his protective pillar.

Lenny shook his head. "I don't know. That's an awful lot of shooting, though."

"Bruce? Lenny?" Roxanne said from a crouched position within one of the stalls. "Everybody's unchained. What do we do now?"

"Stay where you are," Lenny yelled over the gunfire. Bullets began thumping into the outer wall of the barn. Some flew through the thin walls in a cacophony of buzzing noises, thuds, and metallic ricochets. Wood chips flew through the air. As everybody dropped to their bellies, the shooting level increased, but the number of bullets flying through the barn decreased. Then came a couple of dozen machine gun bursts; none seemed to be aimed at the barn.

"What the hell is going on out there?" Bruce repeated.

"I don't know, but there's a lot more than six of them," Lenny said.

And then all was still.

Lenny, Bruce, Roxanne, and the other hostages looked at each other, grateful for the silence, but afraid to think about what it meant, a stunned audience to a deadly symphony.

The deathly quiet gave Lenny time to ponder what was happening. Were the terrorists trying to trick the hostages? That didn't make sense. They had more firepower and knew it. Lenny realized that those outside the barn couldn't even know their comrade had been killed, although they probably guessed as much.

A loud rapping sound upon the outside of the door suddenly echoed through the barn. "Mister Cronin? Are you all okay in there?" An unmistakable American male voice.

Bruce crawled over to where Lenny was still hidden behind the barn pillar. "Who the hell is that?" he asked.

"I don't have-"

"Mister Cronin. Kidnap victims. This is Captain Ronald Briggs, US Army. We're coming in. Mister Cronin, please drop your weapon to the ground. We don't want any accidents."

"You think it's a trick, Lenny?" Bruce asked.

Lenny returned Bruce's questioning look. He could see behind Bruce. The others were huddled together in one of the stalls. Their expressions were even more bewildered than Bruce's. "I don't know, but I haven't heard anyone around here with an American accent. And what about all that gunfire?"

"Mister Cronin," the American sounding voice interrupted. "Please respond. Time is critical. We must leave now. We're in a foreign country and under orders not to engage the Syrians unless we are forced to."

"He sounds legit to me, Lenny," Roxanne said from across the aisle. Bruce and Lenny looked her way and saw the other hostages nodding agreement with her assessment.

Lenny stood and carefully made his way to the barn door. He stood off to the side in case any bullets might come flying through it. "Slide your ID under the door," he yelled.

Silence followed. In music, Lenny knew, it would be called a break, in a movie, a pause for dramatic effect. In a barn crammed with cowering, frightened people, the stillness was simply nerve shattering quiet. Then it was broken by a scratching noise and a slight movement in the space at the bottom of the door. There it was. Lenny picked it up. The satisfying solidity of the metal dog tags filled him with relief. He read the name imprinted on them. With a resounding, "Yes!" he dropped his weapon and swung the door open.

Lenny instantly realized he'd made a terrible mistake. Half a dozen automatic weapons were trained on him. He slowly moved his eyes upward from the deadly machineguns ready to blast him, to the strange looking faces of those holding them.

EIGHTEEN

The Country of the Saints

Spring, 9,500 BC

In the village called The Home of Jeric, or Jericho, five hundred years after Aker's group had arrived to found the settlement, Aker's descendant, Pap, was officiating at the funeral of his father. The burial was taking place on the outskirts of the village, in the shadow of the cave filled cliffs that had afforded protection for the villagers during many hostile attacks. The presence of these caves was one of the major factors the surviving members of Aker's troupe had taken into consideration when deciding where to settle after the dispersion hundreds of years earlier.

As the mourners gathered around the gravesite, Pap led them in prayer, asking God to watch over his father and all who had gone before him. The purple robe he wore, with the three white concentric circles emblazoned on the front, bespoke his new position as spiritual leader of the village. He was now twenty-seven years of age and had been in training fourteen years, but this was his first official act as Protector of the Scrolls, as spiritual and corporal leader of the settlement.

The suddenness of his father's death had caught the village citizens by surprise, but Pap was well prepared to take over this important position from his late father.

"Brothers and sisters of Jericho," he said. "This day brings both joy and sadness to our settlement. With glad hearts do we wish Godspeed to our father and brother, as he embarks upon the supremely rewarding journey to the center of the universe, to the dwelling place of the Father of Lights. Yet with hearts heavy from sadness and loss, do we contemplate that he is with us in the flesh no longer. We shall miss his wisdom, his encouraging words, his love, warmth, and joy.

"Our ancestor Adam taught us that life is an eternal journey inward, with many stops and multiple pathways, but with one destination. We believe that our departed father and brother even now is choosing the next path on his personal adventure. We have been told the Heavenly Father grants unto all His children the boon of self-determination and free choice. Even as we experience the great adventure of perfection achievement; as we follow the admonishment, 'Be perfect, as I am perfect,' do we exercise these great gifts, by freely choosing the way of service to follow. Therefore join with me now and give thanks to The Maker for His great and unending love. We thank the Eternal Source and Center for this world, darkened though it is by the machinations of the Crafty One. We thank our Heavenly Parent for the very gift of life and the means to achieve eternity and fellowship with the divine."

At the end of the ceremony each member of the village stood by the gravesite to drop a handful of Mother Earth onto the mortal remains of the recently departed as symbolic gesture of the dust from which the body is made and to which it shall return.

That evening, Pap and his advisors held a meeting at the Temple of the Father in the village center. The purpose of the meeting was to discuss relations with the surrounding nomadic tribes who were becoming more and more belligerent of late. After each of the ten council members had taken their seats around the communal fire, Pap said, "Welcome brothers and sisters. It is indeed unfortunate that the death of my father comes at such a time. The raids of the neighboring tribes, which we have endured since the arrival of our ancestors, have been increasing in frequency and intensity.

"Some of these confused people have banded together, giving them increased numbers of warriors with which to defeat us. Our many attempts at negotiating peaceful coexistence have met with rejection, this despite the acceptance of our teachings and knowledge by some of their kinsmen."

"How shall we deal with this threat?" Teth, one of the council leaders, asked.

"That is the purpose of this meeting," Pap said. "We must formulate plans for the protection of the Scrolls of Truth and for the safety of the women and children. The nomads have vowed our extinction for reasons we cannot fathom; others desire our homes for themselves. The new alliance these groups have formed gives them the means to achieve their ends."

"We will fight to the last man if necessary, to protect our families and the scrolls," Teth said as the others expressed their agreement.

"Yes, my brothers and sisters," Pap continued, "we shall indeed fight to the last man if forced to that end. I have a plan that may help us avoid such an event. We will use the caves that have served us so well in the past in a new way. No longer will they serve simply to hide and protect us while invaders plunder and pillage. We will move our village to the caves, where we shall live. The caves will become our homes. Not just our temporary shelter."

"But how shall we feed ourselves?" Sahn asked. He was in charge of agriculture and food production for the community.

"Hear me out," Pap said. "We will live in the caves, but our fields and animals will continue to supply our needs. The houses of manufacture and commerce will remain where they are. The Temple of the Father will stay here at the village center. Each night, or during threats of invasion, will we use the caves. We will utilize the natural contours and passages throughout the cave network for our protection. Secret doorways we shall build. Traps for those who seek our end shall be set. I see this as our only path to safety. The enemy outnumbers us greatly. Our only alternative is to run. But run to where? The world has turned against the way of truth and light. Lucifer and his despised cohorts, Satan and Beelzebub, hold sway for we know not how long. I fear this is our final stand."

"I for one, would rather die fighting than to abandon our home," Sahn said.

When the others expressed their agreement, Pap continued. "We have been taught that someday a Son from Heaven will arrive on this strife torn world to set it back on the path of enlightenment. The Scrolls of Truth tell us this. Also do they explain how the world became darkened by the rebellion of Lucifer, Satan, Beelzebub, and the despised Prince of Earth, whose name we refuse to utter. We know that after the arrival of the Son from Heaven, the world will come to see the light of brotherhood as the beacon of freedom, the lamp of liberty, and the lantern of peace. These truths have all Edenites since Adam pledged to preserve and protect. These truths, which are told to us so vividly in Adam's own words, must be saved from destruction at all costs, that the Son be recognized when he arrives; for we are also told that the foretelling of his coming will enhance his acceptance among his people."

"How are we to protect the scrolls, Pap?" Sahn asked. "How do we assure their survival when our very existence is threatened?"

Pap looked at each of the ten as he said, "We must hide them where our enemies will never find them. They must be preserved and stored where only a few will know how to retrieve them. And those few must be protected to the end."

The plan of creating both living spaces within the cave structures and a safe hiding place for the scrolls was discussed for the duration of the meeting. It was decided that a secure keep for the scrolls would be the first priority. No other work would commence until all efforts had been expended in protecting the Scrolls of Truth from destruction.

Weeks after work had started in the caves, Pap was discussing progress with Sahn. The Protector of the Scrolls said, "Reports come in daily of the hostile attitudes of our neighbors. Attack is imminent. How goes the work in the caves?"

Sahn pointed to the small cave opening that had been chosen as the permanent hiding place for the scrolls. "The men work day and night. Traps have been set. A secret doorway built. Within days, the time for the placing of the scrolls in their new home will be at hand. But nothing has been done for the protection of the women and children. I fear this may cost us most dearly."

Pap nodded. "Your fears may indeed prove well founded. With the forces gathering against us, we may yet see the end of our way of life. For this reason, the protection of the scrolls is even more important. We may die off, but truth must live to see the light of another day."

Sahn shook his head in sadness. "Your words weigh heavily on my soul. How will the scrolls keep truth alive if they are buried and hidden where no man can find them? How will the story of Adam and Eve not die?"

"The tradition of Eden will be kept alive by words and monuments. Forget not that before the destruction of the Second Garden five hundred years ago, ten groups of Edenites were scattered about the earth. Each group has most certainly continued the traditions that we hold so dear. They have built stone monuments. Their storytellers keep tradition alive. We know not where these cousins are, nor how many family branches survive, but assuredly there are other settlements like unto ours."

"Your words ring true in my heart," Sahn said. "I too believe other branches of our family tree are honoring our ancestors and preparing the way for the arrival of the Son from Heaven. From generation to generation will they tell these stories, gaze in awe upon our monuments, and reflect upon deeper meanings."

Three days later, the twenty-four clay jars were ceremoniously sealed with a special wax and placed carefully in their new home. The great hidden door was closed. As Pap left the area, he and his men carefully set the deadly traps that he hoped would never be used.

Five days after, one of the scouts came running into the village. "Prepare! Prepare!" he yelled. "Attackers are coming."

Tension and confusion filled the air as villagers gathered around the messenger. Pap made his way through the crowd to the center of the group. When the messenger saw the Protector of the Scrolls, he said, "The nomads are gathering. Like a thundercloud, they are coming. This day will they arrive, bringing death and destruction. Our end do they seek and are determined to deliver."

Pap started to issue orders. "Women and children to the caves. Teth, see to this and be sure they understand they are not to come out until we send for them."

"What if we should perish?" Teth asked. "What will happen to them?"

Pap placed a tender hand upon the shoulder of Teth. With a stern look he said, "It is better they die from lack of food than at the hands of the barbarians who would enslave and torture them. We face two evils. We choose the lesser."

Teth began gathering the women, the children and the old for the trek up the cliff side. As their mothers comforted the youngest, the frightened troupe began the slow climb. At the mouth of the cave, they looked down upon their settlement and the activities of the men who were forming battle lines. In the distance, to the north of the Sea Without Life, they could see the clouds of dust kicked into the air by the coming invaders. With hearts heavy as stone, they turned from the light and entered the darkness of the cave, never to exit again.

NINETEEN

The Red-Headed League

Fall, 1985

Lenny's shocked eyes moved from the guns, to the faces, and back to the guns. He saw ski masks and bright eyes and small bits of charcoal-smudged skin. The men were clad entirely in black, reminding him of ninjas he'd seen in lousy movies. *Who the hell are these guys,* he wondered, still afraid to speak. Slowly, the guns were lowered to the ground and the blackened lips curled upward. Lenny smiled and took his first deep breath in minutes.

"You gave us quite a scare there, Mister Cronin," the nearest man said as he approached Lenny. "We thought you might get yourself into trouble with that gun you brought."

Lenny figured he must have looked stunned, because the soldiers, if that's what they were, laughed in unison. "You knew I had a gun? Who the hell are you guys? How did you find us?"

As some of the men went into the barn, the man who had first spoken reached toward Lenny and took the dog tags from his trembling fingers. He replaced them around his neck and then reached under Lenny's jacket collar with his left hand. When he pulled his hand away he had a small electronic device between his thumb and first finger. "Big Brother is listening," he said with a smile.

"Where the hell did that come from?" Lenny asked in astonishment.

"Remember that guy you bumped into on the street last night?" the man asked.

Lenny thought about the incident. A light bulb snapped on in his head. "You guys bugged me? You followed me here?" He looked at the man with astonished gratitude and nodded. "AWRIGHT! Way to go."

As the former hostages were being led from the barn, a commando came from the house and spoke quietly to Captain Briggs. "Mister Cronin, would you come into the house with me please?" the captain asked.

Lenny quickly followed his rescuers as they led him into the house. It didn't take long for him to determine that all inside were no longer among the living. But there were only four of them. The one just outside who had apparently been shot first and the one Lenny shot in the barn made a total of six. One was missing. He immediately saw who was not there. "Their leader is missing. He calls himself Assad, the bastard. How the hell did he get away?"

"Over here, Sir," one of the men said.

Lenny and the Captain went to the man who was pointing at a small closet door. "It hides an emergency exit, Sir. We followed it to a tunnel. We're waiting your orders before entering it."

As Captain Briggs thought about what to do, another commando said, "Sir, I don't think we need to worry."

Briggs turned to the man and asked, "What are you talking about?"

"Me and Jonesy found a Jeep hidden in the woods today while we were reconnoitering the area, Sir. We figured it must be an emergency escape vehicle, so we rigged it to-"

A loud explosion came from the woods, interrupting the soldier, who smiled. As Briggs looked through a window in the direction of the blast, the man continued. "That's what I'm talking about, Sir. Whoever escaped from here is no longer a problem."

"Well let's get the hell out of here before that noise brings unwanted visitors," Captain Briggs ordered.

Outside the house, the hostages were clapping each other on the back, shaking hands with rescuers, and generally behaving like people who had been snatched from the jaws of death.

"People!" Captain Briggs shouted. "Listen to me. This operation is far from over." Like a chameleon swaps colors, the hostages exchanged joy for concern. The silent tension became nearly breathable as the captain continued. "We are on foreign soil, almost forty miles from friendly territory. We still have to cross a hostile border." The sound of approaching helicopters broke in above his voice. "The choppers will be here in thirty seconds. Do as we tell you and we should all be safe and sound, happy and healthy within the hour."

As Captain Briggs finished, Lenny looked above the tree line to see four black silhouettes hovering above the barley field in the night sky. As the mechanical birds landed, the commandos started separating the group into four clusters and led each group to one of the aircraft. Lenny stayed with

Bruce and Roxanne. They were helped through the open bay on one of the helicopter's sides by a crewmember. Six commandos followed as Lenny took a seat and strapped himself in. Seconds later, all four choppers, were airborne.

As the CH-47D Chinook helicopter rose above the tree line, Lenny put his reporter's eyes and senses to work. Two of the men, tied to safety harnesses, were sitting by the bay door. Their legs hung over the edge of the craft, swinging in the black emptiness below. Fifty caliber monuments to Freud sat between their legs. Dim reds and greens illuminated the interior of the helicopter. The buffet of gauges and warning lights and the feast of electronics covering the walls of the craft fascinated Lenny. The tips of the treetops, breezy silhouettes against the full moon, reminded him of a wolf pack on the hunt.

Lenny turned to the commando sitting next to him and yelled over the noise of the engines. "Who are you guys exactly?"

The man's grease covered lips turned upward as he removed his shatterproof goggles and ski mask, then donned a red bandanna. Lenny turned to see the others doing likewise. The group of red-banded, black-faced operatives brought images of old vaudeville acts to Lenny's mind. "First Special Forces Operational Detachment Delta, at your service, Sir," the soldier said.

"How'd you guys get here? Where are you stationed?"

"If I told you that, Sir, I'd have to kill you." Lucky for Lenny a big-ass smile came with that threat. "Let's just say, If we go for a long walk we get wet."

"And what's your name, soldier?"

The man shook his head. "Sorry, Sir. I can't reveal that."

Lenny couldn't help himself. He pointed to the man's automatic weapon. "What kind of gun is that?"

The soldier looked at Lenny and laughed. Two of his buddies, sitting across the aisle, joined in. The three men eyed each other. Each man placed his left hand on his genitals and raised his weapon with his right arm. Lenny watched in utter confusion as the three soldiers chanted in unison, "This is my rifle, this is my gun. This is for killing, this is for fun."

While Lenny, Bruce, and Roxanne were still laughing, the helicopter made a sudden violent bank to the left. Captain Briggs grabbed a set of headphones from a rack near his head and began communicating through the mouthpiece. As the captain continued talking, Lenny looked out through the open bay and saw streaks of flashing lights moving upward in the night sky. The helicopter made several more sharp banking turns, then a roller coaster descent and climb. As they leveled out, the two men manning the large machineguns began firing toward the ground.

Briggs turned the mouthpiece away from his lips, but kept the headphones on. "We're coming under fire from the ground." The man's voice was surprisingly clear and Lenny could understand every word over the concert of mechanical sounds. "Nothing serious so far though, just machinegun fire. Those streaks you see are tracer rounds."

Every pair of eyes in the hold of the Chinook turned to watch the light show. Some of the comet-like streaks were coming toward them and others, emanating from the soldier's machine guns, headed groundward. As the helicopter continued its evasive tactics, Lenny could occasionally see one or more members of its flock come into sight. The skyward streaking lights began getting closer to the craft. Suddenly Lenny saw a single large plume of fire moving rapidly upward from the ground. It seemed to travel in a straight line, but within seconds it started veering from its original course and headed directly toward them.

A red light on the pilot's dashboard start flashing brightly and insistently. The helicopter dropped so precipitously that Lenny felt his stomach contents flood his throat. He looked at Bruce and Roxanne and the fearful expression that covered their faces matched what he imagined his own looked like.

As the craft continued making violent changes in direction and altitude, Lenny caught sight of another stripe of light as it passed within feet of one of the other choppers, itself in a rapid descent.

"Are those missiles?" Lenny asked the man beside him.

"SAMs," he replied without elaboration.

And then it happened. The helicopter shook violently. A burst of light, as bright as the sun, lit the insides of the rotary winged craft. A sudden vacuum tried to suck the air from Lenny's lungs. A flash of heat singed his hair. Time stopped. An eternity after the heat, a blast as loud as any he'd ever heard ripped cruelly at his eardrums. Passengers involuntarily tested the strength of their harnesses as G forces tried to tear them free. The Chinook bobbed up and down, tilted left and right, twisted violently as the pilot fought to maintain control.

Smoke began filling the cabin. Captain Briggs spoke calmly into his mouthpiece. When he finished, he turned to the hostages and yelled, "We've been hit," in concise military understatement. "We're leaking oil badly. The pilot says we've got maybe five minutes before we have to ditch."

Lenny watched in fascination as the commandos began what looked like a well-rehearsed dance. In a flurry of activity, men began destroying equipment and removing what looked like emergency packages from metal cabinets, while Captain Briggs set some papers in a metal container and lit them on fire. The pilot continued to fight the forces of nature in a valiant effort to keep the bird aloft.

When Briggs finished burning the papers he battled his way to the cockpit and Lenny saw him in animated conversation with the flight engineer. The two men pointed to a small map laid out on the engineer's lap. After a moment, Briggs returned to the hold.

"We're making an emergency landing," he yelled over the noise. "We're the only craft that's sustained severe damage. We will be okay. But you must move quickly and do as you're told. Can I count on you to follow orders?" Briggs looked at the three former hostages questioningly. He waited until each nodded affirmation before continuing. "We've located an area large enough to accommodate three birds. While the fourth stays aloft and lays down cover fire, we'll be abandoning this craft for the two that will land with us. You three stay together and don't leave the side of this man." He placed his hand upon the left shoulder of the man nearest Lenny. "He'll tell you when to disembark and which bird to jump into. Everybody clear on that?"

While the soldiers continued their emergency dance, Lenny looked at Bruce and Roxanne. "You guys all right?"

Bruce nodded yes, but his frightened expression was anything but positive. To his credit, he had his left arm over Roxanne's shoulder and was trying to comfort her. She was coughing and choking from the smoke that Lenny thought wasn't so bad. The open bay door was continually rushing in fresh air, effectively keeping the atmosphere breathable. "What's wrong with Roxie?" Lenny asked.

"Her asthma is acting up from the smoke," Bruce said. "The stress isn't helping either."

Lenny took a handkerchief from his pocket and turned to the soldier assigned as their guide. "Do you have any water?" The man gave Lenny a canteen and he soaked the cloth, then handed it to Roxanne. "Try this, Rox. It might help."

She took the proffered air filter and put it over her mouth. After a few seconds Lenny saw her visibly relax and take a few deep breaths. Relief filled her eyes.

The machinegun fire had ended and there were no more threatening streaks of light in the starlit sky. They had apparently gotten beyond the range of whoever was on the ground firing at them. Palestinians? Syrians? Does it matter who fires the shot that kills you?

The noise level of the hold had lessened with the end of the staccato gunfire. Then the dying transmission filled the cabin with the sounds of rattling metal and grinding gears that rivaled a student truck driver's first efforts at shifting.

"We're going down," Briggs yelled. "Strap yourselves in tightly."

Lenny tightened the hell out of his lap belt and shoulder harness. As they rapidly lost altitude, an image of Sheila appeared in his mind. He wondered if he'd ever see her again. He realized he'd been foolish to hold off marriage for the sake of his career. What difference did it make what his job title was? Who the hell cared? He loved her and his love was requited in spades. What an ass he'd been. Although not deeply religious, he began praying. But he didn't ask for a safe return home. His concern was not for his own welfare. He prayed that Sheila would be okay, no matter the outcome of this night.

As Lenny finished his first conversation with God in a long time, he looked at his friends. They seemed to be engrossed in the same activity. It dawned on him that not only were no atheists found in foxholes, there apparently were none in crashing helicopters either.

With a mashing of metal followed by a harsh jolt, the helicopter hit the ground. It rolled onto its side and from his strapped in perch, Lenny saw each large rotary blade chop itself to pieces as they contacted the ground and the turf turned them into small projectiles. The dead bird came to a halt on its side with barely enough opening left in the bay to allow the passengers to squeeze out.

Bruce, Roxanne and the others on their side of the craft were on their backs, while Lenny and his traveling companions hovered over them like fellow passengers on a Ferris wheel. The commandos released themselves, then began removing Bruce, Roxanne, and Lenny from their constraints. Once all were free of the crumpled chopper, they took stock of the situation. The pilot had miraculously maintained enough control to prevent serious harm. Bruises and sprains were the only injuries inventoried.

In less than two minutes, the man assigned to them was guiding the three frightened and confused passengers to one of the healthy helicopters. From the corner of his eye, Lenny saw the other soldiers heading for the second chopper. The third bird hovered above the edge of the clearing, its gunners firing into the brush and rock outcroppings, the outlines of which Lenny could see against the starlit sky.

Lenny and the others scrambled on board like snakes were after them. Commandos helped them climb in and as soon as the last man was inside, the overloaded helicopter groaned as its furiously beating rotors sought purchase in the night air. It lumbered off the ground like an albatross with a full belly.

Lenny watched the abandoned chopper go up in a ball of flames as the charges left by the commandos did their work.

The noise inside the Chinook was so loud from the overworked engines it made communication difficult. Lenny thought he heard the buzz of an insect close to his ear. He looked toward the sound and saw a soldier next to him grab his shoulder and roll over with a yelp of pain. Then he saw the left leg of one of the teenaged twins explode in a gush of blood. Only then did he realize they were under heavy ground to air fire. As the helicopter gained altitude and speed, the rate of fire diminished.

Soldiers began dressing the wounds of the girl and the commando. The other passengers slowly regained their composure and watched the sideshow with grim fascination.

Lenny turned to a soldier standing beside him and yelled over the noise, "How close are we to the Israeli border?"

"A bit under ten miles. We just got a report that the Syrians have scrambled extra troops along the stretch they expect us to cross, so we may have to take a longer route though." The man nodded in the direction of his squad leader. Captain Briggs was communicating over his headset and Lenny thought he was as calm as if he were on the phone with his wife. The captain's professional demeanor and the fact that not the slightest hesitation or confusion had occurred, despite the deadly fog of chaos and danger, reminded Lenny how well trained these men were. For sure, he owed them his life.

With no more bullets flying through the cabin and no visible streaks of light coming at them, Lenny decided it was safe enough to try for a look outside. He stood from his jump seat and looked toward the ground. The stars and moon provided enough light for him to see that they were now flying over the rocky, craggy cliffs of the desert. The ground seemed no more than two hundred feet below, at times even less as the hills and cliffs rose upward when they flew over them. He could see one of the other Chinooks up ahead and assumed the third was behind them.

"Listen up everybody!" Captain Briggs shouted. "We're taking a detour. The most direct route is being covered by extra Syrian patrols and it's too dangerous. We should be safe and sound within a half hour." As he was saying this the helicopter banked and headed in a new direction. Lenny, disoriented by the events of the evening, thought they had turned completely around. He knew this couldn't be so and tried to relax a bit.

Lenny asked the soldier sitting next to Bruce and Roxanne if he would swap seats with him. The man obliged and as Lenny sat down next to Bruce he said, "How ya doin', buddy?"

The look on Bruce's face reminded Lenny of a headline he'd once seen on a tabloid that read, 'Man Frightened to Death by Loch Ness Monster'. Despite this, Bruce answered in a steady voice, "Okay. And you?"

"I'm scared shitless."

Bruce nodded as his features softened to something closer to, 'Man Grateful Nessy not Carnivorous.'

Lenny looked past Bruce toward Roxanne. Her face reminded him of a different headline, 'Woman Dazed and Confused by Three-Headed Baby.' He caught her attention and gave her a thumbs up. Roxanne's timid return of the gesture, with her right thumb vibrating like a jackhammer, and tight lipped half smile, told Lenny all he needed to know about her state of mind. He figured they would all benefit from a hot meal and a night in a warm, safe bed.

Fifteen minutes after changing directions, with the desert floor flowing like quick water below them, the helicopters began gaining altitude. Lenny looked questioningly at the soldier across from him.

"We're approaching the Golan Heights," the man yelled. "Safe harbor is near."

Lenny saw Captain Briggs in animated conversation with the pilot. The co-pilot was pointing to a gauge and doing what appeared to be calculations on a hand held device. After a few seconds of this, Captain Briggs spoke into his headset. When he finished he came back into the hold area.

"We have a slight problem," he announced. Like a nest of baby birds begging food, every head turned the Captain's way expectantly. "We're running low on fuel. The extra weight and added distance is costing us. We might even have a small leak because the other choppers are fine."

"What's the bottom line?" Lenny asked.

"We can't make the border. The others can't help us because one's as loaded as we are and the other has sustained damage. They'll be going on ahead while we find a safe place to land."

The three teenagers hugged one another like they were sharing body heat; blood ran down the leg of the wounded twin. Bruce and Roxanne also hugged. The soldiers betrayed no emotions. Lenny sat in silent contemplation, wondering if he should write a goodbye letter to Sheila. He looked out the open bay as the helicopter banked; watched in dismay as the other two birds continued on their way to safety; a place Lenny hoped desperately he and his fellows would also be soon visiting. In less than thirty seconds they were out of sight and the lone copter began descending.

"Stay together as we disembark," Briggs ordered. "We have help coming that should be here within the hour. Follow instructions and everybody will be safe."

As soon as the craft touched ground, four commandos jumped off and began surveying the dark shadowy terrain with their weapons at the ready. When they were satisfied all was quiet, one of the men waved the remaining passengers to follow. As they did this, the soldiers formed a circle with their charges in the center. As one unit, they moved carefully toward a rocky knoll and the relative safety of a natural circle of craggy rocks.

The noise inside the chopper had been loud enough to wake the dead, but this coffin-like silence in the desert night was almost worse. Lenny watched as the soldiers took up defensive positions in the rocky outcroppings. He looked at the huddled rescued as they sat their haunches upon the hard surface and pulled their knees to their chests. He saw it all, feeling strangely detached, like watching a movie, hoping desperately for a happy ending.

"Here's our situation," Captain Briggs said, addressing the rag tag little group. "Two fresh birds are en route here. One will take you folks home while we transfer fuel from the other to our dead one. There are Syrian patrols throughout the area but we've been flying below their radar most of the night so we should be gone before they know we're here."

"What if they find us first?" One of the teenage girls asked in a voice pitched so high it reminded Lenny of a wounded rabbit he'd once heard.

Captain Briggs looked at the frightened girl with compassion. "We don't expect that to happen. If it does, we can deal with it. We own the high ground and can hold off a division from here." He observed the frightened looks these words engendered and added, "Don't worry. We really don't expect anything like that."

"I guess that's good news," Roxanne said. Lenny noticed she seemed calmer since landing.

Thirty-five silence-stuffed, nerve-destroying, minutes later, Lenny heard the approaching sound of helicopters in the night sky. Five minutes after that, two US Army Chinooks were hovering over the area, as the harried former hostages gathered into a small group. As soon as the first chopper touched ground, they scrambled on board. Instantly, the Chinook lifted straight up, then swung west toward safety.

In the woods near the farm, where the explosion had come from, a man began to regain consciousness. He started crawling away from the heat, the smell of burning rubber, and from the acrid smoke that filled the air. Using only elbows and knees, as hands and feet refused to obey his commands, he inched away from the inferno.

He reached the sanctuary of a large tree and struggled to prop himself against its thick trunk. Only then did he take a survey of his body.

His right arm was a bloody mess. His right thigh was attached to the lower part of the leg by little more than flesh and sinew. He took his belt off and used it as a tourniquet on the leg, grimacing in silence from the pain. The bleeding slowed to a manageable drip. He removed the lace from his now useless right boot with his left hand and teeth, and used that to staunch the flow of blood from the right arm. He checked the remainder of his body and was relieved to find only burns, scrapes and bruises. He knew that two of his men, who'd been sent on an errand the previous day, would be arriving back at the farm soon.

"I thank Allah for letting me live to fight another day," the badly wounded Assad prayed.

Three hours after taking off in the reserve helicopter, Lenny was sitting safe and sound at a hotel room desk. Though tired to the bone, he pounded furiously on his word processor. He couldn't seem to get the words from his head fast enough.

TWENTY

The Adventure of the Devil's Foot

The *Chronicle's* International News Editor came charging into Perry Hazzard's office waving a piece of paper he had just torn from the wire service machine in his own office. Hazzard was sitting behind his desk in the process of placing his phone back in its cradle.

"Wait till you hear this, Chief," John Ferrier said. "It just came in. A team of Army Delta anti—terrorist operatives has rescued the hostages in a daring raid. Everyone is safe, but one of the young girls got wounded. Two of our men were hit too, but none were killed."

He paused for a breath, then went on. "But wait till you hear this part. Lenny was there! And wait till you hear this–"

"Goddamnit, John" Hazard said. "If you didn't keep telling me to 'wait till I hear this' and 'wait till I hear that', I'd have heard it by now. Just give it to me straight and cut the drama."

"Okay, okay. Lenny was in on the whole thing. He was actually one of the hostages when the rescue occurred. And wait till, oops sorry, but you're not gonna believe this. He shot one of the terrorists!"

"Holy shit! You mean our man Cronin actually shot a terrorist during a rescue mission? I never would have thought he had the balls." Hazzard tilted his chair-back so far he nearly tipped over backwards. He thought about the implications for a moment. "It's still early enough to get this in today's edition. Get your ass in gear." Hazzard became a drill sergeant, snatching up the phone and issuing orders. A blizzard of visions filled his head, each snowflake a Pulitzer Prize. For his whole professional career the spectre of the illusive award had prowled his psyche, lurking in hidden corners, surfacing at the most surprising moments. Could this be his moment in the sun, the *Chronicle's* chance to shine?

Reverend Graves was sitting at his desk preparing a sermon when Sheila Snow came through the door to his inner office. He thought she was as agitated as a loaded washing machine set on high.

"Look at this," she gasped, dropping a copy of the *Chronicle* on his desk. "Bruce and Roxanne were kidnapped, and then rescued, and Lenny was there, and he shot someone, and they're all safe now, and it all happened in only three days, and we didn't even know about it and–"

"Hold on, Sheila. Calm down and let me read this," the Reverend said, as he picked up the paper.

Sheila's hands were shaking so much they looked ready to jump right off her wrists. She took a cigarette from her pack and fired up. As Reverend Graves read, she paced back and forth in front of his desk; a smoke breathing mother hen. She'd been right all along; there was a fox out there. "I KNEW Lenny was taking chances that he shouldn't have. What would I have done if he had gone and gotten himself hurt? Or Worse? I swear, I love him so much, I could just kill him for nearly getting himself killed." She stopped pacing and smiled at her own ridiculous statement.

Reverend Graves looked up from the paper, "I'm sorry. Did you say something?" Sheila stopped wearing a path in his carpet and sat down in the chair in front of his desk. She crossed her legs, and started chewing her fingernails while he returned to his reading.

When the Reverend finished the story he said, "That was quite an adventure wasn't it? There's no mention of any manuscripts though. I wonder if they had any luck."

Sheila jumped up and placed her hands on her hips, every bit the angry mother about to scold her child. "Shame on you, Reverend. I'm surprised that's all you can think of at a time like this. Don't you know they could have been killed?"

The anger in her deep sexy voice was a slap in the face. His head snapped back into the chair's backrest with a thud. After a moment, he stood and lumbered around to the front of his desk, took her hand into his.

"You've never spoken to me like that before, Sheila. I'm sorry. I didn't mean it quite as callously as it sounded. All I meant was that it would be a shame if they went through all this without getting what they went after."

Sheila's anger cooled. She took another drag on her cigarette, blew the smoke away from his face and cast her eyes downward. "I'm sorry, Reverend." She freed her hand and held out her left arm. "Look how nervous I am. I'm shaking like I mainlined pure caffeine."

He took her quivering hand into his own again and stroked the soft palm. Were his hands shaking as well? Or were they resonating to hers? "Why don't you take the rest of the day off and try to relax? I can handle things here."

"Are you sure?"

After receiving his assurance, Sheila left his office to go home for the day. Reverend Graves sat at his desk and remembered when he first met Bruce and Roxanne. It was when they made their presentation before the TUSK Foundation for the funding of their expedition. Like the other board members, his first inclination was to reject the possibility of such a find as impossible. Their insistence that the author of the scrolls might be Adam seemed so far from the realm of possibility that he'd thought they must have been kidding. But their sincerity, impeccable research and well thought out presentation had won him over.

He dried his sweaty palms on his pants. He thought it strange that this only happened when he touched Sheila. He pictured her trim figure. *Not so strange, really,* he thought.

Reverend Graves looked out the window. The afternoon light warmed his black clothing. He gazed skyward and silently thanked the Heavenly Father for the safety of Bruce, Roxanne, Lenny, the other hostages and the soldiers, and finally prayed for strength for the families of the dead terrorists. That these were men of the sword, and had died by the sword, meant nothing to him. Their families still loved them and undoubtedly missed them.

In a small house, on a farm a few miles from where the rescue had taken place, a tall man convulsed on a short cot. His bloodied and torn clothes lay like a sleeping animal on the floor; his untrimmed beard, matted with sweat, spittle, and blood, a barber's nightmare. A battle waged under the bloodstained and vomit-caked sheet covering the thrashing body. His head rolled left and right as lightning jolts of pain ripped through him. A bloody, bandaged stump replaced his right arm. The right leg ended just below the kneecap, its bandages yellowed and darkened with puss-blackened blood. One man stood over him.

"Tell me what to do, Assad, to avenge this monstrous deed."

Assad looked up at the man, fire burned in his bloodshot eyes. "They will die for this. Find them before they leave Palestine. Kill them slowly."

"But how? Our brothers are dead or rot in Zionist prison. Some have shamefully abandoned us. You and I are the last of the 'Flaming Arrows' to breathe the air of our homeland with honor."

"I have heard from Mazen in America. The story the infidels told the press was a lie. They are not tourists, but are on an expedition. Why would they keep it secret where they were picked up by us?"

"I know not why, Assad."

"Because they found something there of importance. That is why. They will return there. You know where the campsite was. You have but to wait for them to return. Then the death of your cousin and of our brothers will be avenged." He held up his stump and grimaced as the phantom hand taunted him with a pain all too real. "Make them pay in blood, my brother."

The evening after being saved, the rescued hostages and their rescuers, as well as most of the important dignitaries in the city, were present for a lavish banquet at the American embassy in Tel Aviv. Bruce, Roxanne and Lenny were seated together at the table reserved for them. Between debriefings and press conferences, they hadn't had much chance to talk to each other privately. During after dinner cocktails in the ballroom, they finally had time for some conversation.

"So tell me," Lenny said, looking around to make sure they weren't being over heard. "What are you two going to do now? I'd guess your hunting trip is over."

"Lenny, we found the scrolls," Roxanne said.

"Easy now, sweetheart. We're not positive," Bruce said. He looked at Lenny and said with a sly grin, "We're pretty sure though." He then went on to describe their harrowing experience in the cave.

"Sounds like your trip to Adventure Land, by way of Zealot's Island, might be worth the price of admission," Lenny said.

Bruce smiled. "We've got our fingers crossed."

Lenny looked around the room. He noticed someone watching them. "See that guy?" he said. When they both nodded affirmation, he continued. "His name is Jim Gallant. He's a freelance reporter. Watch out for him. He's as tenacious as a bulldog and almost as smart."

Roxanne thought she noticed a hint of familiarity in Lenny's tone and inflection. She smiled. "An old friend of yours?"

"Let's just say I thought I had a friend who could find dirt under a freshly scrubbed surgeon's fingernails. When he believed he'd found dirt under mine, things changed. He'll go to any lengths to dig something up. Especially since I'm involved."

After the dinner party was over, the three friends went to the lounge in their hotel for a few drinks and to discuss plans for the upcoming days.

Bruce and Roxanne were anxious to return to the foothills along the Dead Sea shore before anyone should discover that they had been there when they were kidnapped, instead of Qum Ran, which was what they had told everyone.

"It looks like you two found something that will turn the world on its ear," Lenny said. "How do you plan on keeping anyone from finding out about it until you get to the states?"

"We're not sure," Bruce said. "While we were captives, we weren't even sure we'd get home at all. And since the rescue, we haven't had a chance to formulate any plans yet. We're hoping you might have some ideas."

"Well, for the first couple of days I wouldn't do anything," Lenny said.

"Nothing at all?" Bruce asked.

"No matter where you go, you'll have the press up your ass. Why not simply return to Jerusalem and relax for a few days. Then when the heat is off, we can sneak back to the site."

"But what if someone finds the cave in the mean time?" Roxanne asked.

"I wouldn't worry about that too much," Lenny reassured her. "You said the terrorists made off with all your camping gear and your jeep, so there's no evidence of your having been there. And after all, those scrolls have been safe for thousands of years haven't they?"

"I guess you're right, Lenny," Roxanne said. "But what about our servant Mohammed? He knows we were there. I can't help but be nervous about the whole thing. What do you think, Bruce?"

Bruce scratched his chin. He took a sip from his drink. "I think we should take Lenny's advice. After all, he knows what the press is like. As for Mohammed, he ran off like a scared rabbit. Plus, he has no idea that we found anything. I don't think he'll be back there any time soon."

"After a few days," Lenny said, "or when a new crisis arrives, the reporters will move on. Believe me, they'll dump you faster than a new politician dumps his morals. Then you'll be able to head back to the cave without anyone being the wiser."

"I guess we'll be playing tourists for a few days," Bruce said.

"That will give me a chance to put a little something I'm planning into action," Lenny said.

"What's that," Bruce asked.

"Let me make a call to my boss first. If he agrees, then I'll tell you about it."

A half-hour later, while Bruce ordered their third round, Lenny returned from phoning his office. When he approached the table he was smiling. He took a sip from the drink Bruce had placed in front of his seat, sat down and said, "Boy, getting that old sourpuss to spend money is harder than getting a politician to retire."

"Who are you talking about?" Bruce asked. "Your boss?"

"Yeah," Lenny said. "It was like a tug o' war against a football team, but I finally convinced him it was in the paper's best interest to do it my way. So, by this time tomorrow night, there'll be a private jet at our command."

Bruce looked at Lenny with amazement. "You got us a jet to fly home in? Way to go, Len. How did you do that?"

"I just dangled a picture of him holding the Pulitzer Prize before his imagination. He's so hung up on winning that thing he'd swim us across the Atlantic on his back if he thought it would get one for the Chronicle."

"Let's drink to that," Bruce said as he lifted his glass.

After a couple more drinks, the conversation turned maudlin. "I'm starting to wonder if all the danger and risk is worth what we're after," Roxanne said. "I mean, what we're seeking could be very important, but we WERE nearly killed after all." Her voice was beginning to slur and take on a distinct whine.

Lenny placed his glass on the table. He leaned toward Roxanne and said, "Just because something is distasteful at first, you can't give up. Eventually, you'll break through the unpleasantness of the task, reap the rewards of your efforts, and see it was worth the risk."

Roxanne looked at him with deep respect. She turned to Bruce and saw he too was impressed. She turned back to Lenny and said, "That's very profound, Lenny. Is that how you became such a good reporter?"

Lenny held up his nearly empty glass of single malt and smiled. "Actually, it's how I learned to drink scotch in college, but the principle's the same."

After a few more drinks they returned to their rooms on legs less than steady.

As Bruce was opening the door to their room Roxanne asked, "Want to join us for one more, Len?"

The red-eyed reporter responded, "Does the Pope shit in the woods?"

Roxanne and Bruce stared at Lenny. Their slack-jawed silence told him they were trying to figure out what the hell he'd just said.

"Sorry," Lenny said, "When I have a few drinks in me my mixaphors tend to have lives of their own."

Bruce remained silent for a few seconds. "Well, you didn't exactly kick a home run with that one," he said with a smile.

"Maybe you should have asked if a bear is Catholic," Roxanne tried.

They entered the room and Bruce went to the courtesy bar to see what was available. As he began mixing three gin and tonics, Roxanne called out from the bathroom, "Do you two mind if I slip into something comfortable?"

Bruce looked at Lenny and smiled like the Cheshire Cat. His eyes never wavered as he said, "Get as comfortable as you want, sweetheart. Lenny doesn't mind."

Lenny staggered to a chair near the curtained window. He grumphed into the seat and placed one elbow on the round table between himself and the other chair.

Bruce finished mixing the drinks and placed them on the table. Lenny chose one. Just as he was taking his first sip, he saw Roxanne coming from the bathroom and nearly choked on the liquid as it caught in his throat. "Geez, Louise," was all he could get out between choking gasps.

"Sweetheart, you look hotter than the desert sun," Bruce said as he sat in the chair opposite Lenny.

Roxanne was wearing very little, but what she had on was something Lenny thought was called a Teddy. The black silky gossamer fabric barely reached her upper thighs; her long shapely legs alabaster pillars fashioned by the world's best sculptor. Full, round breasts strained against the thin fabric, the bullet-point nipples a testament to the air-conditioner's effectiveness. Or were they sending a different signal? Lenny's eyes were magnetically drawn to the dark triangle that defined alabaster-pillar junction. He couldn't tell if she was wearing a slingshot or nothing at all down there.

The phrase 'Heavenly Creature' entered his mind. His internal editor changed it to, 'Devil's Playground'. Look at *those balloons,* he thought.

Lenny's imagination was flaring like a blowtorch. His little soldier was snapping to attention. *What the hell is she trying to do,* he thought, crossing his legs and trying to will himself to stand down.

"Lenny, I asked you a question," Bruce said.

Lenny turned to face him. "Huh?" He tried desperately to clear his head, to understand, but his intellect had apparently hung up a 'Gone Fishing' sign. *Poker,* he thought, *think of poker.*

"I said, isn't she something?" Bruce repeated.

Roxanne handed a drink to Bruce, making sure she bent over to reveal yet more cleavage; the damn things were defying gravity now. Then she spread her legs and straddled Bruce's lap, while giving Lenny a look that made, 'come hither' about as accurate a description as, 'wet' would be of the ocean. She reached for Lenny's soldier area with her foot (or was it the devil's?) and began a teasingly slow rub.

Lenny's soldier mutinied against the stand down order.

Lenny's fire blazed to inferno status.

Lenny's will power fought the battle single-handed, a candle in a hurricane.

Roxanne slowly stood and swung her leg away from Bruce. Lenny's eye caught sight of the slingshot as she did so. At least she wasn't totally naked down there. He caught himself wishing she were. He shook his head, but desire refused his eviction attempt.

When Lenny regained focus, Roxanne was standing in front of his face. She smiled down on him like a goddess from above. She bent and reached out one hand toward Lenny, Cleavage City mapped out before him. *How the hell are those two things staying in there?* She placed both hands on his shoulders and mounted.

Lenny was still trying to think of a poker game, but his internal editor kept changing it to a Poke-Her game.

He tried to picture his resolve as a solid piece of ice, but the blowtorch of desire had it pouring water in no time.

When she began grinding her slingshot area into his little soldier and riding him like a hobbyhorse, his menagerie of tricks surrendered en masse. She apparently saw this as she took his hand and led him into the bedroom. Lenny barely noticed Bruce following behind like a kid on his way to the candy store.

Lenny watched as she slowly and tantalizingly removed the lingerie. The excitement of the previous week, which had been simmering beneath the surface, began stirring an almost primitive passion in him. He wanted to grab her and take her right then, right there. He looked into her eyes and knew she was having similar thoughts. He quickly stripped and pushed her onto the bed. They joined bodies violently in a naked embrace that fueled the blast furnace that was their lust. Hungrily and wantonly he began to kiss and caress her, to roughly run his hands over her writhing body. As he bent to kiss the nape of her neck, he inhaled her body's natural scent and wondered at the intoxicating effect it had on him. The volcanic pressure that had been trapped within longed for release.

Then they were joined, and in what could have been seconds, hours, or eternity, they were at the height of ecstasy, climaxing together. It was the most explosive orgasm Lenny had ever experienced.

After catching her breath Roxanne said, "Boy, we're going to have to get ourselves kidnapped more often."

Lenny was confused. As his breath came in more normal cadence, he looked over his shoulder to see Bruce sitting in a chair with his Cheshire Cat face still smiling away like there's no tomorrow. *Oh God,* he thought.

"I just remembered something," he said as he grabbed his clothes and bolted out the bedroom door.

TWENTY-ONE

The Adventures of the Mazarin Stone

Two days after the party, and after the other former hostages had left the country; Lenny, Bruce, and Roxanne were able to slip away from the few remaining reporters.

The three intrepid wanderers were once again on the road from Jerusalem to Jericho in a rented Jeep. Bruce was driving, and Roxanne was in the front passenger seat. From the back seat Lenny had extracted a promise from them to not mention the other night. He'd decided that the excitement of what they'd been through, coupled with having a few too many drinks, had been the stimulus driving everyone's behavior. But he still couldn't get the picture of Roxanne's writhing naked body out of his head. It would take a long night with Sheila to do that.

For the hundredth time he thought of Sheila. He'd spent to two intervening days alternately beating himself up and attempting to justify his actions. Try as he might, he knew no jury would return a verdict of justifiable homicide in this case. And homicide was just how he felt the situation should be described, for he felt certain he'd killed any chance he had of making a life with Sheila.

She'll never understand it, he thought. *Why was I such a wimp? Why didn't I just get up and walk away?* He asked himself for the millionth time. *I swear; I love her so much, I'll never forgive myself if I lose her.*

He promised to quit drinking, knowing full well that alcohol wasn't an excuse for his actions, but it had certainly added fuel to his fire. *Please, God. Just don't let her find out. I'll never touch another drop.*

It was late afternoon when the trio arrived at the former campsite. After a little more than an hour their tent was up and a fire warmed the dusk. Soon they were enjoying what Lenny described as a delicious meal of beans and hot dogs with a bottle of vintage mineral water.

"A gourmet delight," Bruce said, wiping his mouth with the back of his hand.

"I'm glad you appreciate it," Roxanne said. "It wasn't easy picking out the proper mineral water to go with beans and hot dogs."

Lenny groaned. "You guys need to work on your pointless banter," he said with a smile.

"Sorry, but we aren't professionals like you," Roxanne smiled back. "Maybe someday, after years of hard work and dedicated effort, our inane conversations will be a match for your well thought out, precisely articulated banalities."

"See, you're getting better already," Lenny laughed. He looked up at the cave-strewn cliffs that rose behind Roxanne, and marveled at how the red sunset painted them in pinks, mauves and rusts. "Which cave are the scrolls in anyway?"

Roxanne turned around and pointed. "See those two openings very near each other up to the left? And then, just above them, the small one? Well, it's the small one."

About a quarter mile away, hidden behind a rock at the crest of one of the hills, a pair of binoculars was trained on the campers. The watcher even saw Roxanne pointing toward the cliffs, but he couldn't tell which cave she was pointing at.

A few hours later, he saw that the campers had turned in for the night. After waiting another hour to make sure all was quiet, Assad's man began to walk stealthily toward the campsite. His plan was to hide out in one of the caves until daylight, and then watch to see which cave the three went into. He wasn't sure what exactly he was going to do after that, but knew his gun would play a role. For inspiration, he carried a picture of his cousin's death and beloved leader's maimed body in his heart.

He began ascending the cliff quietly and carefully by the light of the half moon, using climbing skills he had honed since a boy.

An hour later he was safely hidden in one of the caves. He'd been able to tell the general area the woman had pointed to earlier, and made certain that he stayed away from there. He didn't want to be surprised by the three people stumbling in on him.

The sun rose with a harsh brilliance seen only in the world's desert regions. The three campers awoke and began daily preparations while movies ran through their heads. The films were independent productions, but they echoed similar themes; recognition, redemption, and reward. Over a breakfast of coffee and sugary rolls, they discussed plans for the day.

"It's going to take four trips up and down for the twenty four vases, assuming we can each take two at a time," Bruce said. "At that rate it will take all day to get them down here. It might even be dark by the time we get the last ones out. But no matter how late it is, I don't think we should spend another night here. Even if we have to sleep on the plane, I say let's head right for the airport as soon as everything's loaded."

Roxanne and Lenny agreed. As soon as they finished eating they assembled their gear and began the ascent to the cave that held so much hope for them. After about thirty minutes of careful climbing, they were in front of the cave entrance. As far as Bruce and Roxanne could tell, there was no evidence of anyone having been there during their forced absence.

"Everything looks the same as when we left here," Bruce said.

"How can you be so sure?" Lenny asked.

"I can't really," he said with a shrug. "I'm just trying to keep my confidence up. But I don't see anything out of the ordinary anyway."

Bruce dropped his load on the ground in front of the cave opening. "We won't need the blankets and rope until we bring the vases out." Lenny and Roxanne mimicked him and they headed into the cave.

Lenny felt a constriction in his chest as he entered a cave for the first time since his friend Keith's death. The walls seemed to be closing in on him. "Let's go nice and slow, okay, guys?" he said.

Roxanne saw Lenny's nervousness and thought he was thinking of the traps that they had told him about. "Don't worry, Lenny. We've checked out this part of the cave thoroughly and there's nothing to be afraid of."

Lenny decided to let her think that was what was bothering him. He hoped she didn't notice the army of sweat-beads he felt popping out of his forehead.

As Bruce and Roxanne headed deeper into the cave, he followed them like a cat burglar. No matter how hard he tried, Lenny felt his thoughts race back to his boyhood loss and the horror of his young friend's death. His breath shortened and his throat constricted as he fought to control the panic.

Assad's man was now outside the cave entrance. He listened carefully while standing off to the side so as not to be seen. He could hear only the mumble of their conversation but could tell they were out of sight of the opening. Slowly he made his way into the cave using the sound of the voices as his guide.

As they neared the secret doorway, Bruce and Roxanne stopped, stared, and said nothing. The doorway that hid the passage to all their hopes, the doorway behind which awaited the fulfillment of lifelong aspirations, the doorway that they had left open, was now closed. Roxanne's chin began to quiver.

Seeing the look of total dejection on their faces increased Lenny's nervousness. His fearmometer was nearly redlined. "What's the problem, guys?" he asked in a vibrating voice.

"The problem," said Bruce with a disheartened tone, "is that someone has been here since we were kidnapped."

Bruce decided to try the lever to see what would happen. As he lifted it, the heavy stone door slowly began to open. Lenny jumped backward. "I'm almost afraid to go in there," Bruce said, cautiously peering into the opening. "But from here everything looks all right. Lenny, let's you and I go check it out."

Lenny's eyes exploded with anxiety. "What about Roxanne?"

"Yeah," Roxanne's falsetto voice squeaked. "What about me?"

"You can wait outside the door, Babe. Just in case."

Lenny hadn't been concerned about Roxanne when he'd blurted out the question. He was actually offering her up as a viable substitute. He calmed enough to feel ashamed and followed Bruce, leaving the doe-eyed Roxanne standing beside the door looking like she was caught in headlights.

Slowly and carefully, Bruce made his way through the opening. Slower and more carefully, Lenny followed. Bruce went to the area behind the door where the mechanism could be viewed. He noticed something he hadn't seen the first time he and Roxanne had been there. Poised above the counterweight that moved the door sat an hourglass shaped device that was, even now, slowly sifting sand from the counterweight. Bruce realized that once the sand had shifted itself onto the smaller weight, it would reverse the process that opened the door. It was an ingenious timing device that made sure the door was never left open for too long.

"Hey you two, come look at this," Bruce called.

"Are you sure it's all right?" Roxanne asked from outside the doorway.

"Don't worry. Just come look at this."

Roxanne joined Lenny and together they stealthily approached the small entrance to the room Bruce was in. As they crowded up to Bruce, he showed them the mechanism.

"It looks like we have underestimated our ancient friends once again," he said, as he explained how it worked.

"Does that mean nobody's been here?" Lenny asked.

"I'd say so. At least we know we can open the door from the inside if we have to," Bruce said.

"How much time do you think it takes to close the door, sweetheart?"

"That's hard to say," Bruce said. "But from the size of that pile of sand, and the rate at which it's flowing, I'd say at least several hours."

"That means we must have barely gotten out of here in time the first time doesn't it?"

"Well yeah, but it's nothing to be worried about. Just look at it. We could simply reverse the tilt of the platform the hourglass is on, and the door would open again. So let's go."

Lenny saw the look of relief on Roxanne's face and smiled at the thought of her standing alone at the entryway, jumping at every little sound. "What's the matter? You weren't afraid or anything were you?" he joked, trying mightily to camouflage his own fears.

"And what if I was? Would you have cared?"

"Not at all," he said with a smirk.

She hit him on the shoulder and laughed. The tension relieved, they continued inward. When they came to the two entryways, Lenny asked about some symbols carved into the wall above the entry. He was proud of himself, being able to forget his fear long enough to observe his surroundings.

"We're not sure, but we think it's a warning of some kind," Bruce answered.

"You'll see why in a few minutes," Roxanne added.

"What's down that other path?" Lenny asked.

Roxanne's eyes fell and her shoulders sagged. "That's where we found the mound of bones we told you about."

"Oh yeah," Lenny said. "The women and children, you said. What do you think happened?"

"We have no idea," Bruce said. "Our best guess is a battle took place outside while those who couldn't fight waited inside."

"That must have been pretty bad for them." Lenny said as they entered the passage that led to the vases.

A short while later, just as Roxanne had promised, Lenny saw why they thought the symbols were a warning. They were standing in front of the spiked booby trap that had nearly killed Bruce. Lenny whistled.

"These people meant business didn't they?"

"We've got to be very careful from here on in," Bruce said. "There's another trap up ahead, and if we set that one off, we won't be leaving here."

A few moments later, Bruce was shining his flashlight on the small lever protruding into the path; the lever that would release the large rock onto their heads if moved. "This little baby could trap us here for a long time. I can't find out how to neutralize it either, so we just have to be very careful."

"Maybe Roxanne should stay here just in case. That way she can go for help if it should come to that," Lenny suggested. Bruce nodded in agreement.

Roxanne frowned however, and said, "We decided not to do that last time. Why now?"

"Because," Bruce said, "this time I won't be alone inside. And besides, with everything that's gone wrong so far, maybe a little extra caution is in order."

Roxanne seemed as happy with that decision as a prisoner just learning she was about to spend some time in front of a firing squad, but reluctantly agreed it was a good idea. Bruce and Lenny made their way farther into the cave.

Following behind them carefully, Assad's man listened to the conversation of the Americans. He realized that whatever had been discovered was valuable and would also take four round trips to remove from the cave. He decided to wait until they were on the last leg before making his move. That way, he wouldn't have to do any of the work.

* * *

Bruce was showing the vases to Lenny. "There they are, our pride and joy. If those vases contain what we hope they do, people will be talking about this for a long, long time. This is what every archeologist dreams about, a discovery that will tell us more about our ancestors and their way of life," he said proudly.

"How should we get them out of here?" Lenny asked.

"Let's start by seeing how much they weigh. We should be able to carry two at a time, but I want to make sure." He bent and gently lifted one of the cylindrical jars. "Yeah, we can carry two at a time easily. They're even light enough to carry three, but that would be too clumsy."

"Want me to call Roxanne?" Lenny asked.

"No. I want her to stay on the other side of that booby trap. We can carry three each to her and then we'll each carry two outside. How's that sound?"

Lenny agreed and they each carried three vases to where Roxanne stood. Lenny smiled at the look of relief in her eyes when she saw them with the jars. Bruce and Lenny each gave Roxanne one and the three continued on until they were outside of the cave.

"One down, three more to go." Lenny said.

"That wasn't bad at all," Roxanne added.

"At this rate we'll have them all outside by noon." Bruce said. "We're a little ahead of schedule. Ready for round two?" Roxanne and Lenny nodded and turned back into the darkness.

Two hours later, they were standing outside the cave entrance after having placed eighteen clay jars on the ground.

"Whatta ya say we break for lunch before making the last trip?" Lenny asked.

"Sounds like a plan," Bruce said.

While Bruce and Roxanne unwrapped sandwiches and opened water bottles, Lenny looked at the eighteen vases lined up in front of them. "So what do you think you really have here, guys? Are you expecting to see Adam's handwriting, or what?"

Roxanne handed Lenny a sandwich and some water. The three sat down near the edge of the cliff and looked out over the foamy Dead Sea as they ate.

"In all honesty, Lenny," Roxanne said between bites, "we don't really know what's in those vases. The old man we interviewed last summer told us what his ancestors had passed down through the generations. Of the many stories handed down, the one that fascinated us the most, and the one that led us here, was the tale of the 'Anakim', the 'Heaven Sent' and how they arrived here long ago."

"You're talking about Adam and his descendents supposedly. Right?" Lenny asked. When they both nodded Lenny continued. "You've already told me that story. What I want to know is what you think these scrolls actually say."

"That's the sixty-four thousand, make that million, dollar question, of course," Bruce said. "Let me answer you with a quote from the old man. He told us this was supposed to be one of the traditions preserved in the scrolls. 'On this world man has been deprived of superhuman leaders and rulers as a result of the Lucifer Rebellion, and therefore will humanity constantly seek to make good this loss by enshrouding his human leaders with legends pertaining to supernatural origins and miraculous careers.'"

"What the hell does that mean?" Lenny asked.

"We think it was meant as a warning against mythologizing our rulers," Roxanne said. "You know, like how the Egyptian Pharaohs were supposedly descended from God? That practice started about forty-five hundred years ago. If these things," she nodded toward the vases, "are as old as we think they are, that's quite a prediction."

Lenny looked skyward and marveled at the hundreds of birds heading south. "Look at that," he pointed. "They look like eagles."

Bruce and Roxanne looked at where Lenny was pointing. Roxanne said, "They're lesser spotted eagles, a cousin of our golden eagle. They fly over Israel by the thousands every year on their way to Africa."

"Thousands of years ago their ancestors flew over this same location," Bruce said. "It's kind of a link to the past don't you think? They could have witnessed famous battles. Perhaps seen the Exodus from Egypt. Maybe even flew over the head of Jesus as he gave the sermon on the mount."

"They might have even taken a dump on Herod's statue," Lenny laughed.

Inside the cave structure, Assad's man was carefully exploring the area he'd seen the three American's traverse. He realized that his quarry was taking more time than usual for this last trip and was worried that he might have miscalculated. He'd decided to make his way in the opposite direction from which they had returned with their armloads of objects to make sure they hadn't left with everything yet. Suddenly he bumped his head on something.

He pointed the narrow beam of his small flashlight and its weak rays illuminated something that startled him. At first he could not tell what it was. Then he understood. He was looking at a spiked beam that had been somehow embedded in the cave wall. It excited him. What a marvelous device! He silently commended those who had created it, thinking they were his own ancestors. Believing the Americans had neutralized any other traps that might be ahead, he continued rapidly onward. As he lurched forward along the path, he began to hear voices coming from behind. He increased his pace and soon found himself in the small alcove in which the remaining six vases sat. He snapped off his flashlight and carefully hid himself against the wall to wait for his prey.

Lenny, Bruce and Roxanne were standing in front of the lever that would drop the huge boulder onto the path if it were tripped. "I'll be glad when we don't have to worry about that thing anymore," Roxanne said.

Bruce was no longer concerned about the trap. They'd traveled past this point enough times now to see it as more of an inconvenience than a danger. Something else was on his mind. "I want you to come all the way this time, Babe," he said. "I almost dropped one of the vases last time. Carrying three is too clumsy."

"Are you sure?" she asked with a slight quiver.

"Don't worry about it. Just be careful."

They each cautiously stepped over the small lever. Roxanne asked, "Why do you think the thing is so small? It doesn't protrude all the way into the path. Someone could walk right past it without knowing it was even there."

"I wondered that myself earlier," Bruce said. "I think it's because they weren't worried about one person sneaking in here. They were concerned with a fighting force. One of them would definitely set it off."

At last they entered the small alcove for the final time. They stood with the entrance to their backs and looked at the vases. "This collection is priceless," Bruce said.

"Do not worry. I will find someone willing to put a price on it."

Roxanne, Bruce, and Lenny wheeled around as one at the sound of the oddly familiar voice, and saw a man aiming a handgun at them from the shadows. Roxanne screamed.

Bruce took Roxanne in his arms and hugged her tightly. She was shaking and crying in his shoulder. He turned toward the man and demanded, "Who are you and what do you want?"

"Who I am is none of your concern. And as for what I want, I think that is obvious. I will do the questioning from now on. Just what is this priceless discovery of yours?"

When he received no reply, he pointed his gun at Roxanne's head. "In my homeland when you are asked a question, it is polite to answer."

"We're not sure," Bruce said. "But we think they're ancient manuscripts from the first people to inhabit this valley. But they would be of no value to you. If someone were to merely show up with them, without the proper credentials, they would be branded fraudulent."

"I shall determine if that is a problem," the man said.

"I represent one of the largest newspapers in the United States," Lenny said. "My publisher will pay anything you want for the exclusive rights to this story."

"Yes, I know who you are, Mister Cronin," the man said. He stepped forward out of the shadows and smiled. It was 'Wharf Rat.' "And I have a special interest in you. I am not so stupid as to fall for your obvious scheme. I have not decided whether to kill you yet. I can always say that I discovered this cave before you and caught you trying to steal the contents. So don't do anything foolish and you may live."

Bruce knew the man would probably kill them as soon as all the vases were out of the cave. But he didn't know what to do about it. He needed a plan.

The man waved the gun at the trio of captives and said, "Take two of those items each and stay in front of me."

Bruce was desperately trying to come up with a plan. He decided that the safest route was to be patient and wait until they were outside. Then they could look for an opportunity to push the guy off the cliff or something. But then again, what if there were more of them out there waiting? His mind continued working on the problem as he picked up two vases and watched Roxanne and Lenny do the same.

"Don't get too far in front of me," the man said. "I won't hesitate to shoot if I am forced to. But no one will get hurt if you do as I say."

While the man was giving the orders, the three captives formed a line. Lenny hesitated so Bruce took the lead, with Roxanne in the middle. Bruce half wondered if there wasn't some ancient curse on the damn scrolls. Like the one that was supposed to protect King Tut's tomb. It sure seemed like it. Nothing but trouble since the day he'd first heard about them. As they left the little alcove and entered the small passageway, they maintained their positions in front of the terrorist.

The going was slow, the passageway narrow, and the vases bulky. Soon they were approaching the lever for the trap.

"Be careful," Lenny warned Bruce and Roxanne.

Bruce was allowing himself to get into a funk, and he didn't even bother turning around while responding to Lenny. "Don't worry about me. Worry about yourself." Then his flashlight beam illuminated the lever and he realized what Lenny was talking about. He turned to face Roxanne. "Be very careful not to TRIP, darling. You could hurt yourself."

"Be quiet and keep moving," the gunman said.

Ever so cautiously, and as unobtrusively as possible, Bruce and Roxanne stepped over the protruding lever. As Lenny came upon it, he stumbled and kicked it.

"Whoops! I almost fell," he said, as he stopped and turned toward the man. The terrorist stopped just behind Lenny.

Wharf Rat looked up at the sound of rumbling. The look of horror on his face showed he was fully aware of what was about to happen to him. He made a move to get out of the way of the falling boulder, but it was too late.

The echo of the crashing boulder rolled through the cave complex like thunder on a summer night. Bruce and Lenny stared at each other, clutching the vases, and looking at the only thing remaining of Wharf Rat. One leg, already turning black, stuck out from underneath their side of the boulder.

Bruce began to come out of his trance. He placed his load carefully on the ground. He took Roxanne's vases from her and put them beside his, then hugged her tightly.

Lenny was the first to speak. "Damn, this is getting to be habit forming. I thought being a science reporter would be as dull as a year old razor, but now I just want to get home in one piece."

Roxanne turned toward Lenny while maintaining her tight hold on Bruce. Between sobs she said, "It's turned out to be more than we bargained for too. What should we do now? Do you think there are others outside?"

Bruce was almost as nerve-wracked as Roxanne. This was just too much to bear. He wanted nothing more than for it to end, and forced himself to ponder Roxanne's question. "I doubt it. If he had help, he probably wouldn't have come in here alone. And we probably would have seen someone during lunch."

"I just want to get out of here. I'm not used to any of this," Roxanne said.

"What do you think he meant when he said he had a special interest in me?" Lenny asked.

"He must have wanted to avenge Assad or something like that," Bruce speculated.

"You think Assad's still alive?" Roxanne asked.

"No," Lenny said. "He must have returned to the farmhouse and found them all dead and sworn revenge when he read in the paper about how I was involved. I agree with you, Bruce. I don't think there are any more of them out there either, but let's be careful."

They cautiously made their way to the cliffside with the remaining scrolls.

"I don't see anything," Lenny said, slowly surveying the area from the mouth of the cave. "Let's get these things down to the damn car and head for the airport."

Moving as quickly as they dared with their precious cargo, they were loaded up and on their way back to the city within an hour.

The next day, as the sleek private jet taxied to its assigned gate at Boston's Logan Airport, Bruce, Roxanne and Lenny were surprised at the number of reporters awaiting their arrival. They were further shocked to learn that everyone knew about the vases, and that there were pictures of them loading the objects onto the jet in that day's edition of the *Chronicle's* cross town rival, *The City Crier.* After passing through customs, they were deluged by the press. From the nature of the questions thrown at them from every angle, they soon determined that speculation was running as wild as the bulls at Pamplona.

After running the gauntlet of flashbulbs and pushy reporters, they entered the car hired to ferry them home.

"How the hell did word leak out?" Bruce asked. "And where did those pictures come from?"

Lenny looked at the newspaper photos and said, "Judging by the angle these were taken from, it looks like someone followed us to the airport and hid behind a maintenance building. The byline for the story is Jim Gallant's. He's the guy I warned you about at the embassy party. I can see how he earned his bull dog reputation. I gotta tell you guys. This is the second time I've been on the flip side of a press feeding frenzy and I don't like it."

"You thinking about changing professions?" Bruce asked.

Lenny shook his head. "Not that. Exposing crooks that betray public trust is too important. But I'm definitely thinking about how I go about it. I have a new perspective on the trouble I caused for the mayor. I'll have to send him something when the lawsuit is settled to show him I'm sorry."

"The mayor isn't exactly a babe in arms, Lenny," Bruce said. "He's like a damn puppeteer. He controls so many things from behind closed curtains he reminds me of the Wizard of Oz."

"I know," Lenny smiled, "but he was innocent of what I accused him of. I owe him for that."

* * *

The Joe Rizzos, Senior and Junior, were in the older mans' richly adorned office. Young Joe was sitting in a chair facing his father's imposing mahogany desk. He fidgeted while his father read the morning paper.

"Well, it looks like the guy I hired to harass your two friends didn't do very well. If he thinks I'll be sending him any money for his failure he's dumber than you are."

Young Joe winced inwardly at the insult. He'd learned long ago to hide his feelings when his father was throwing barbs his way. The more he reacted, the more it fired up the old man. "What do you think those funny shaped things they're carrying are?"

The old man placed the paper on his desk and crumpled out his cigar in the ashtray. "Who knows? I'm going to find out though. If it's those ancient manuscripts they went out there looking for I've got an idea."

"Maybe we should just drop the whole thing, Pop. I mean yeah, Roxanne's a hot piece of ass." He shook his head slightly as he remembered some of their wild nights. "I'm talking real hot. But I'm starting to think she isn't worth all this trouble."

Old Man Rizzo grabbed the recently stubbed out cigar butt and fished for his lighter. "You little snot. You ready to give up so easily? Your mother was soft like that too. And what did it get her but an early heart attack?"

Young Joe had heard this crap about his mother's fate before. Too many times, actually. As far as he was concerned, his mother had died from a BROKEN heart not a soft one. She had never badmouthed his father in front of him, but he'd been able to pick up enough innuendo to realize she had become very sorry that she'd married such a hardheaded, vindictive, blowhard.

The old man ruled his little fiefdom with an ironclad fist, always forcing young Joe to acquiesce to his father's wishes, but now he had his own plans. As soon as the old man was dead, (hopefully from a painful, debilitating, disease), he would be living such a high life on the old man's riches that the dead fuck would be spinning down there in his new home before they could throw the dirt on his still warm corpse. But until that day, he knew he'd have to shut up and play along.

Young Joe had actually calmed down from his initial outburst of anger and desire for revenge over Roxanne having dumped him. It still bothered him that she'd hooked up with a Jew like that, but fuck it, it was her funeral. His father, though, had taken up the cause like a damned holy warrior. What the hell, he figured, whatever the old man had in mind might be fun. And it might even get Roxanne back. He felt an erection coming on as he thought about her. Oh yeah, what a piece of ass she was.

"What do you have in mind, Pop?"

"Just leave it up to me. I'll take care of those two."

On the other side of the planet, the man who called himself Assad was reading the news reports about the three Americans returning to their homeland. The story, written by another American reporter, somebody named Jim Gallant, mentioned strangely shaped objects being loaded onto their private plane. He threw the paper on the floor. The anger welled up inside him began mixing with the phantom pains from his missing limbs to create a potent revenge cocktail. He swore to himself that he wasn't through with them yet.

TWENTY-TWO

The Problem

In the cab line at Boston's Logan Airport sat a yellow taxi, undistinguished amongst the hundreds of others just like it throughout the city. Its driver, a man of indeterminate Middle Eastern origins, blended easily with the dozens of others who operated similar vehicles. The driver's looks, demeanor, and activities had never once in the two years he'd been in the United States elicited the slightest bit of notice. Not from government officials, not from fellow immigrants, and certainly not from his passengers.

As travelers poured from the terminal and entered the cabs ahead of his, the nondescript driver slowly made his way to the front of the queue. When his turn came, a man waved at him and he pulled up beside the potential fare. The man entered through the rear passenger side door.

"Where to, sir?" the driver asked.

"Downtown," the well-dressed man said. "The Copely Plaza Hotel."

"Yes sir," the cabbie said, as he pulled out into the moving traffic. Moments later the vehicle was entering the tunnel that connected the suburb of Revere to Boston's famed North End. As they were passing under the city, the driver asked his passenger, "Are you here for business or pleasure, sir?"

"Both, I hope," the man responded with a smile. "I'm here for a sales meeting that will provide a big commission if it goes well. If it does you can bet I'll be celebrating. You know any places in town where I can have a good time?"

The driver smiled as he pictured the many strip clubs he'd visited since his arrival. Yes, many times had he enjoyed the sensuous pleasures of the flesh that the harlots of this country provided for mere money. As a Muslim, he knew this behavior was not permitted. He knew many of those who frequented the mosque would be scandalized at his propensity for earthly pleasures. But they did not understand. They did not know. He was on a mission. All his sins would be forgiven and he would be welcomed into the arms of Allah for all eternity. The sacrifice he was planning would gain him admission into the inner sanctum of heaven where virgins awaited him. Where a house of gold awaited him. Where his every wish would be granted, every desire fulfilled.

All he awaited was a phone call. One call and he would be given the chance to leave the sinful denizens of this godless country for eternal bliss. One phone call and the temptations of the flesh, the drug addicts, the liars, the thieves, the boy lovers, the child abusers, and all the other sins and effronteries to Allah would be washed from his memory like flotsam carried away on the ocean tide. One phone call. He dropped his fare off and headed home for the day.

As the cab driver entered the small apartment he shared with one of his compatriots, he removed his shirt and placed it on one of the kitchen chairs. He could hear the television playing in the living room.

"Is that you, Mazen?" a voice asked from the room.

"Yes, it is me. Who do you think it is?"

The man came in from the living room and sat down at the kitchen table. "I was not sure. Mahmud is coming by. We have plans to work on." He looked at Mazen and bowed his head. "We have received a phone call. Soon you will be glorified."

Sheila walked into Reverend Graves' inner office. It was the end of the day and she knew he was probably finishing up the last of his day's work.

"Have a seat, Sheila, I'll be finished in just a moment", he said, never too busy or too tired for her.

Sheila made herself comfortable in the red-leather upholstered chair that matched the one Reverend Graves occupied. She had been debating with herself all day about whether or not to bring her problem to the Reverend. The two of them had a friendly relationship and had discussed many things over the years, but she had never come to him with her personal problems out of concern for their professional relationship. She had finally decided to talk to him because every person involved in her current predicament was known to him, and he could hopefully give her some sound advice. The problem had her stymied and she had to turn to someone.

Sheila squirmed from side to side in the chair. She tilted forward then pushed her back into the seat. She crossed and uncrossed her legs. Reverend Graves glanced up from his paperwork. His gray-framed, grinning response to her fidgeting only made her more nervous. She was beginning to have second thoughts. Maybe she should just forget the whole thing.

Finally he put his paperwork aside, removed his wire rimmed glasses, stroked his beard, gave her a Papa Bear smile, and said, "OK, Sheila. What can I do for you?"

She continued trying to find a comfortable position in the very comfortable chair. Her lightly freckled face took on a reddish tinge. "It's uh. It's uh. Uh."

Reverend Graves snickered and asked, "Who are you today? The Wizard of Uhs?"

Sheila laughed and felt better. A laugh was just what was needed right now. "I got a visit last night that really disturbed me."

"Who from?"

"Bruce and Roxanne."

"How are they? I haven't spoken to them since their return."

"I'm not sure how they are. That's what I wanted to talk to you about."

"OK. It looks like whatever it is has you pretty worked up. What happened?"

Sheila straightened her back. She placed her hands on her lap. She cleared her throat. "They tried to seduce me last night."

Reverend Graves sat ramrod straight in his chair. His expression changed from anticipation, to surprise, to thoughtful contemplation, to bewilderment. He scratched the back of his neck with his right hand. "Well. I have to admit that if I'd been forced to guess what you were so nervous about, that would not have even made the list. I'm not sure what you mean by 'they'."

"I know." Sheila said with vigorous head nodding. "It blew me away too. And the most shocking part of it was the 'they' part."

"Are you sure you didn't misunderstand?"

"How do you misinterpret something like that, Reverend? No. There wasn't any confusion. They're swingers. They told me so in no uncertain terms."

"All right then. Am I right in assuming you turned them down?"

Sheila was in the act of lighting a cigarette. She coughed out a cloud of smoke. Her naturally pink cheeks turned as red as a sailor's delight sunset. "Reverend, how can you even ask such a thing? I would never do anything like that."

Graves held up both his hands defensively. "Whoa, hang on a second. I didn't mean it like that."

"What did you mean then?"

He lowered his arms onto the desk, and leaned over them as far as his belly would allow. "I just meant that you're so fidgety and embarrassed over this I thought it possible, just possible, Sheila, that you might have given in during a moment of weakness. I should have phrased it differently." He looked at her contritely. "Sorry."

Sheila took a deep drag, and let it out slowly. "I'm sorry too. You can see how upset this has me."

"Why don't you start at the beginning, Sheila."

She stood to take the ashtray he offered her and then started walking circles around the chair, smoking, flicking ashes, smoking, flicking ashes. Finally, she crushed out the butt and sat back down in the chair. "They came by my place about seven, after having called first saying they wanted to see me about something. It all sounded mysterious, so I said okay. When they arrived, I could tell they'd been drinking. Not too much. They weren't staggering or anything, but it was obvious they had a slight buzz going, so I didn't offer them any of my own liquor. They flat out asked for a drink though, so I mixed us some weak cocktails.

"We just talked for a while. They told me about the scrolls they found and how they had learned what language they'd been written in."

Reverend Graves perked up a bit at the news. "Really. What did they say?"

"I forget actually. Some language I never heard of. Poko-European or something."

"Proto-Indo-European? Could that be it?"

"That was it. You've heard of it?"

"Yes," Reverend Graves replied. "It's the mother language from which dozens of European languages have evolved. If those scrolls are in that language, it's pretty significant."

Sheila nodded. "That's what they said too. So anyway. We talked about that and their trip for a while. All during this time they kept telling me how fit I was, how good I looked. I just thought they were being nice."

"Maybe they were. You are a beautiful woman after all." His eyes seemed to Sheila to be taking on a dreamy quality. "And I've noticed over the years that you have a difficult time accepting compliments."

Sheila's complexion had nearly normalized, but now it started turning pink again. "I know," she said demurely. "But this was more than just being nice. You'll see."

Reverend Graves folded his hands into a tent over his lap as he leaned back and rested his elbows on the chair's armrests. "Go on."

"Well, we talked some more. We drank some more. Bruce mixed the next two batches." She shook her hand back and forth. "Those weren't weak, let me tell you. After about an hour the compliments for my body and looks started coming faster, and more direct."

"What do you mean more direct?"

Sheila looked at her feet. "Oh, Reverend. This is one of the reasons I was so hesitant to come to you." She remained silent for a few seconds. Her eyes moved to her fidgeting hands. "Roxanne complimented my breasts. Then she started talking about her own. Do I have to go into all this?"

"Of course not, Sheila. Just what you're comfortable with."

"Humph," Sheila laughed. "I'm not comfortable with any of it. Let's just say they told me they were both attracted to me and wanted to know how I felt about them."

"I think I have enough now." He smiled when he saw how relieved Sheila was to hear those words. "You said you weren't interested and then what?"

"They seemed disappointed, but didn't get mad or anything. We talked some more, I think they were smart enough to see how uncomfortable I was though, because they left shortly after."

"It sounds like there are no hard feelings. Why are you so upset?"

Sheila's eyes expanded. Her eyebrows arched in surprise. "I'm shocked over the whole thing. I never in a million years would have guessed they were like that. And I really liked them too. It makes me wonder if I'm a complete idiot when it comes to judging people. I mean, the only way I met Lenny was because my irresponsible and self centered best friend didn't show up for our shopping date."

"And now you don't like them or trust them any more?"

Sheila remained silent for a minute. "I'm not sure. I think I still like them. I just don't know right now. I guess I'm annoyed, too, that they think I'm that type of person."

"You're a very beautiful woman, Sheila. And I'm sure you're a fine judge of character. Similar things must have happened to you in the past. Haven't they?"

Is that curiosity I hear in his voice, Sheila wondered? *Is this conversation getting him worked up*? She immediately dismissed her speculations as a silly reaction to her own discomfort.

"Well sure, I mean, guys are hitting on me all the time. You've witnessed that yourself on more than one occasion. And in college I was tempted to try a threesome onetime with my roommate and her boyfriend when I was drunk. But I never actually went through with it." She remembered that time back in school. Now that she thought about it, the circumstances weren't all that different from last night. Sheila started wondering if there might be something about herself that brought this out in people. Was she sending out some kind of weird vibe she wasn't aware of?

Reverend Graves unfolded the hand tent and clasped them together behind his head. His weight made the position look awkward to Sheila, but he maintained the position for a full minute without saying anything. Sheila sat silently, wondering what he was thinking about.

"Bruce and Roxanne are respectable college professors," he finally said. "I had them checked out before we granted them the funds for their expedition. Nothing like this came up, so apparently they are discrete about it. I think you just need some time to get over the shock. They're still a very nice couple, after all. You can certainly drop them as friends if they continue to make you uncomfortable."

"Are you condoning their life style?"

He shrugged. "I'm not saying I approve, no. But what I am saying is that it's not the worst thing in the world. What they do privately is their own concern, as long as they don't harm anyone. Live and let live, that's all. Would you say they harmed you?"

Sheila shook her head a few times. "No, no. They were very polite about the whole thing. And actually they were their usual funny selves. That's one of the things Lenny and I have come to like about them very much. They can be quite a hoot when they want to be."

"Speaking of Lenny, have you told him?"

"No. I don't think I will either."

"So why don't you give this a few days and you'll probably see it for what it was. Two people very attracted to you tried to take that attraction to the next level. You weren't interested and they were fine about that. I think you can all still remain friends. After all, if we dropped our friends every time they did something we didn't agree with, nobody would have anyone to hang around with."

Sheila stood. She still wasn't sure she agreed with the Reverend's advice, but thanked him for his time anyway.

After Sheila left his office Reverend Graves continued the dialogue internally. He wondered what the gorgeous redhead would do if she knew of his own secret attraction to her? He certainly couldn't blame Bruce and Roxanne for making a play. Many were the times when he wished he'd had the nerve to do the same thing, but his conscience always prevented it. He'd been fighting this battle with his better self for a solid two years now.

Reverend Graves had never cheated on his wife, whom he loved deeply, and was determined not to give in to this temptation. But it was getting harder and harder by the day. And speaking of harder, the very thought of the two luscious women getting it on had him as hard as he'd been able to muster in a long time. Good thing his desk had been between himself and Sheila, he thought.

It wasn't easy being a spirit in a physical mechanism. The human body was a machine designed for sensuous existence, but forced to live within strict moral confines. He well understood what his Catholic brothers must go through. At least he had his wife to occasionally vent steam with. Yes, 'the spirit is willing, but the flesh is weak.' How true, he thought.

TWENTY-THREE

The Science of Deduction

Sheila had decided that she would take Reverend Grave's advice and not let her and Lenny's friendship with Bruce and Roxanne be undermined by what had happened. As long as they didn't try something like that again she would continue to enjoy their company. They WERE a lot of fun, after all. When they invited her and Lenny for a Saturday night dinner at their place, she gladly accepted. She'd almost said something about them not trying anything funny, but decided to give them the benefit of the doubt.

On the following Saturday night, three weeks after returning home with the twenty-four scrolls, Lenny and Sheila arrived at Bruce and Roxanne's apartment.

After enjoying great conversation and a delicious meal of boiled lobster and steamed corn, they carried a bottle of white wine out to the patio.

"Thanks for the great meal, Roxie." Lenny said, as he leaned comfortably back into his wicker chair and patted his full stomach. "Ya gotta love the lobster. That ugly little crustacean, with its spiny shell, dangerous claws and creepy face, tastes a lot better than it looks. Just proves one of my favorite mixaphors, 'You can't judge how it will cook by its cover.'"

"Wouldn't that be more of an adage, or maybe a proverb?" Roxanne asked as she filled glasses.

Lenny shrugged. "Probably, but who ever heard of a mixadage, or a mixaprov? Actually, that last one isn't too bad. Honey," he turned to Sheila, "what sounds better, mixaphor, or mixaprov?"

Sheila looked at him with an exaggerated grimace. "I have a better question," she said, rolling her eyes. "Who do you think could help you more, a psychiatrist, or a psychologist?"

While the other three enjoyed a good-natured laugh at Lenny's expense, he turned back to his hosts. "Something tells me our legendary wit is only a part of why you invited us here tonight. Do you have some good news about the scrolls?"

Bruce and Roxanne looked at each other and smiled. "That's very astute of you Lenny," Bruce said. "But of course you've got the best nose for news I knows of." He smiled, but all it got him was a collective groan. "C'mon you guys," he pleaded. "It's at least as good as Lenny's was."

"Lenny's schnozzle is the best," Sheila added as she gave the reporter's famous proboscis a loving kiss and smiled. "I love his nose for news."

"I have to agree," Roxanne said. "As a matter of fact, I propose a toast to Lenny's famous snout, without which we wouldn't be here tonight. And furthermore, without which we wouldn't have tonight's news either."

Roxanne raised her glass and toasted, "To Lenny's wondrous olfactory organ. Never has so small done so much for so few."

"Now wait a minute," Lenny complained with a smile. "My smeller may be small but it's not that small. Is it, honey?" he asked Sheila.

Sheila made a great show of donning her glasses and putting her eyes right up to his face. She studied him for a moment and said, "Oh, there it is. I think it's perfect."

They were all still laughing when Lenny said, "Enough of the nose jokes already. What's the good news you have for us?"

Roxanne turned to Bruce and said, "You tell them, sweetheart."

"Okay," Bruce said, and he began telling them about the translation work that had been done so far.

As Bruce finished, Lenny whistled and asked, "But are you sure that it's the real Adam we're talking about here?"

"That's the best news," Roxanne said. "Just yesterday, Phyllis, from our languages department, gave us some more of the translation. It definitely confirms that it was 'THE Adam' who wrote the manuscripts."

"At least the author CLAIMS to be Adam," Bruce said. "There's still the possibility that whoever wrote the scrolls could be someone else."

Roxanne got up from her chair and went inside to the roll top desk in the corner of the living room. She pulled open one of the drawers and took out a piece of paper, returned to the patio, and handed it to Lenny.

"Here's a copy, read it for yourself."

"Speaking of copies," Lenny said, "Are you working from the original scrolls? Or from copies?"

"We made photographic images to work with," Bruce said. "The original leather scrolls are locked in a climate controlled container in my classroom."

"Are they safe there?" Lenny asked.

"As safe as anywhere. We've hired a night watchman just for them. Now there are two men in the science building all night," Bruce answered.

Lenny took the paper Roxanne had handed him and started reading. As he did so, his eyes began to look as if he were in a far off place and time.

"What does it say, Lenny?" Sheila asked. He didn't respond immediately and she had to repeat her question.

"Huh?" he said. "Oh yeah, I'll read it out load. 'Know you all who read this, my name is Adam. My mate Eve and I are nearing the end of our days on this planet. It has been over five hundred years since we came unto this world. Our bodies are tired. The ravages of time take hold.

"'The Sons of Darkness are strong, but they shall not prevail, for truth is eternal and the lie ephemeral. To keep truth alive, to help the Sons of Light in their never-ending quest to preserve knowledge of The Heavenly Father and His plans, are the reasons for these writings. Our story must be kept alive through the coming times of darkness.' That's as far as it goes for now," Lenny said. "I guess that's all they've translated so far. I wonder who those Sons of Darkness were."

"Apparently the 'Edenites', as they called themselves, had some enemies," Roxanne said. "But that's all we know right now."

"What do you think, Lenny?" Bruce asked.

Lenny stood and headed for the kitchen phone. "I think I should call my paper right now. It isn't too late to get this in tomorrow's edition."

Bruce held his hand up like a traffic cop. "I'm afraid not, pal. We've decided to wait until more of the story is known in order to forestall as many adverse reactions as possible. As it is, we expect talking heads to pop up like jack-in-the-boxes over this."

Lenny came back to the table, the reporter in him disappointed that this story had to be kept under wraps. But the man in him knew that loyalty to friends was more important than his work. It was a difficult situation, not uncommon to reporters. Lenny realized that not too long ago he might have gone for the story, but not anymore, not after the life threatening experiences he'd shared with Bruce and Roxanne. "Well, as much as I hate to admit it, I think you're right."

"What do you think Adam meant," Sheila asked as she took the notes from Lenny, "when he said," she read from the paper, "' five hundred years since we came unto this world'? Is he saying he's five hundred years old? And 'came unto this world'? What does that mean?"

Roxanne took the sheet of paper from Sheila's hands. As she re-read the words, she said, "There are theories that Adam and Eve came from another world. Have you heard that?" When Sheila and Lenny nodded, she continued. "And of course, the Bible claims Adam and Eve lived for hundreds of years. This could add veracity to both schools of thought."

Lenny wondered how much of this Bruce and Roxanne were buying as fact, and how much was wishful thinking. Sure, he'd heard those theories before, but nobody in their right mind actually believed them. Did they?

"Don't take this the wrong way, guys. But have you thought about the implications of all this? I mean, the academic community will fry your asses. Won't they? Ancient astronauts? Five hundred year old people?"

Bruce and Roxanne nodded slightly. "We'll have to be certain before we let any of this out. That's why we can't have you doing any stories just yet. But so far it's all falling into place. The scrolls and vases have been carbon dated. They're written in Proto-Indo-European. We think this is the real deal."

"You said they've been carbon dated," Lenny continued. "How old are they?"

Bruce looked to Roxanne who said, "Twelve thousand years old."

Lenny whistled.

"That's pretty old," Sheila said.

"My grandfather's pretty old. We're talking Neolithic here, or monolithic, some kind of lithic," Lenny joked. He turned to his hosts. "That's the age of the scrolls themselves?" When Bruce and Roxanne nodded, he did some mental math and said, "So what's that mean? That Adam and Eve supposedly came here in ten thousand five hundred BC?"

"That's right. And wait till you here what I've found out," Bruce said. "Three of the most impressive and mysterious ancient mystical sites on the planet have ties to that date."

The others looked at Bruce like puppies awaiting a bone. "When did you learn this?" Roxanne asked.

"The day before yesterday. When I first heard the date from the lab last week, it rang a bell in my mind, but I couldn't place it. I've done some research since then and found out I was right."

"So out with it, man," Lenny said.

Bruce led them into the museum-like living room and poured some more wine for each of them. He sat down on the couch beside Roxanne, placed a hand on her thigh, and began.

"Let's start with the pyramids at Giza," Bruce said. "It's been known for quite some time that the three great pyramids are laid out as an earthbound representation of Orion's Belt, the three central stars in the constellation of the Great Hunter. Their physical relationship to each other, in both size and orientation, is an exact duplicate of what we see in the sky above. You guys with me so far?" After they each affirmed they were, he continued. "Now, if you draw a line through the pyramids it describes an angle of twenty-seven degrees from north. Everybody still with me?"

"So," Sheila asked. "If you look along the line drawn from pyramid to pyramid, it points northeast?"

"Almost," Bruce answered. "True northeast is forty-five degrees. This is more north than that, but you have the right idea. So anyway, you all know the stars move in the sky right?" Again they all nodded confirmation. "Well, it just so happens that the last time Orion's belt was positioned twenty-seven degrees from north was ten thousand, five hundred BC, when it was at its exact lowest point in the sky. In other words, the layout of the pyramids is an earthbound representation of Orion's belt as it looked at that time."

"You're saying that Orion's belt matched the pyramid layout in ten thousand five hundred BC?" Lenny clarified.

"Exactly," Bruce said.

"But, Bruce darling," Roxanne said, "surely that's a coincidence."

"You could be right. In fact, if that were it, I'd say it probably was. But there's more, lots more. Have any of you ever heard of Angkor Wat in Cambodia? Other than Roxie, of course."

Sheila and Lenny both shook their heads. Bruce continued, "Well, Angkor Wat is the second most impressive architectural wonder of the ancient world according to the opinion of many. Most scientists date it around the twelfth century, but some people think it was built around twenty-five hundred BC, about the same time as the pyramids are supposed to have been built."

"Didn't you just say the pyramids were built in ten thousand five hundred BC?" Sheila asked.

"That's not what I said. I said it was oriented to represent what the sky looked like at that time. To the best of our knowledge, the pyramids were built forty-five hundred years ago, although there is scant evidence to back that up. Some people think Angkor Wat was built much later than the pyramids, but when they were built doesn't matter. What they represent does. Anyway, Angkor Wat has seven structures that are a mirror image of the constellation Draco, which is in the exact opposite position from Orion in the sky. Now here comes the good part. The orientation of Angkor Wat exactly matches what Draco looked like in ten thousand, five hundred BC."

"So both may have been built around the same time," Lenny said. "And both call attention to the same date, ten thousand, five hundred BC. That's a coincidence and a half."

"There's more," Bruce said. "Now we come to the sphinx, the most mysterious and enigmatic of the ancient monuments. Most Egyptologists place its construction at about the same time as the pyramids, even though there is no, and I repeat, no evidence to back this up. There are absolutely no written records regarding its construction, despite the fact that the ancient Egyptians are justifiably famous for their record keeping."

"Are you going to tie the sphinx into the same date?" Sheila asked.

"You tell me," Bruce said. "Let's start with this fact. The sphinx shows unmistakable evidence of water erosion from precipitation. Most reputable geologists who have studied it agree on this. I can see this surprises Roxanne. Does anybody know why?"

Sheila and Lenny both shook their heads.

"Why don't you tell them, Roxie?"

"Well, to begin with," she said, "Egypt is arid, and it has been for thousands of years. How could the torrents of water required for causing erosion have happened?"

"Here's how," Bruce said. "Thousands of years before the sphinx was SUPPOSED to have been built, Egypt was not arid at all. In fact it was semi-tropical and had plenty of rain."

"So the sphinx may be, and I say may be, thousands of years older than suspected," Lenny said. "But does that mean ten thousand, five hundred BC."

"Not yet," Bruce answered, "but here it comes. The sphinx is facing directly east so that on the morning of the spring equinox, the sun rises directly over its head. In twenty-five hundred BC, when it was supposedly built, the constellation Taurus arose just ahead of the sun where the sphinx is looking. Everybody knows how well the Egyptian astronomers followed the stars. If it was built in the age of Taurus why isn't the body of the sphinx a bull instead of a lion?"

When Bruce saw they had no response to this, he continued. "I don't know either, but which constellation do you think the sphinx would be looking directly at on the spring equinox in ten thousand, five hundred BC?"

A smile of satisfaction came over each of their faces. Roxanne's hand shot up like a schoolgirl's. "Leo?" she asked.

Bruce smiled, leaned toward her and planted a big kiss on her forehead. "Leo the lion, give the girl a gold star. One final note. The sphinx is famous for having the head of a man on a lion's body, but evidence suggests that the face was re-carved at some point. Maybe it was originally the head of a lion as well. That's speculation on my part. But we have absolute proof that for whatever reason, the ancients wanted to recognize or honor the year ten thousand, five hundred BC, the exact date that Adam arrived, according to our scrolls."

Lenny asked if he could light up a cigarette. After Roxanne said he could, he took two from his pack, lit both and gave one to Sheila. "Interesting stuff. And when you tie it to what I've learned about other ancient mysteries, it presents a hypothesis for ancient civilizations that's pretty amazing."

Sheila blew smoke toward the ceiling. "Have you learned anything new in that area since you've been home, honey?"

"I've found out there's a small model of a counter dihedral winged aircraft in the Cairo Museum that's thousands of years old."

"A what?" Sheila said.

"It's kind of like a delta winged aircraft." He took his small notebook from his back pants pocket and leafed through it. "It's in room twenty-two, exhibit number six-three-four-seven. Discovered in eighteen ninety-five and is over two thousand years old."

"Are you saying the ancients had airplanes, Lenny?" Sheila asked in astonishment.

Lenny laughed. "No, of course not. You have to admit it's pretty interesting though."

"This is fun," Sheila said. "Got any more, Mister Ancient Detective?"

Lenny turned to a different page in his notebook. "Here's a good one. In the Berkshire Museum in Pittsfield, Massachusetts there's a working model of a twenty-two hundred year old battery."

"A working model?" Roxanne asked. "What happened to the original?"

"The original was discovered in the ruins of an ancient Parthian village in present day Iraq and is still on display in the Museum of Baghdad. This working model, when filled with fruit juice, produced one and a half volts for eighteen days, and they actually strung some together and used them to silver plate some objects as a test."

Sheila stubbed her cigarette butt out in the ashtray, and stood to stretch. It was a very sexy move, and it didn't go unnoticed by Roxanne and Bruce.

"Are you saying they had electricity? Aren't we going overboard here?"

"I know about this one," Roxanne said, never taking her eyes off Sheila. "And it actually helps clear up another old mystery."

"What's that?" Sheila asked

"No evidence of soot from candles or torches from the era of the pyramids has ever been found inside the pyramids themselves," Roxanne said. "I've often wondered how the builders were able to see what they were doing inside them during construction and their ceremonies."

"Couldn't they have just used torches and then cleaned the walls?" Sheila asked.

"They could have," Roxanne said. "But some of the ceilings are very high. And it would have taken a super-cleaning job to get rid of all the soot that hundreds of lamps and torches would have thrown off. Basically, what we've got are two big questions. What did the ancients know? Answer, a lot more than we thought. And how did they come to know it? Answer, we may have just found out."

That same Saturday night, while Bruce, Roxanne, Lenny and Sheila were enjoying an evening of discovery and conversation, a man dressed completely in black, and with a grease and soot smeared face, waited on the roof of the science building that housed Bruce's classroom. The man, hired by Joe Rizzo Senior for this mission, had climbed the side of the building and hidden his scaling equipment from view. As he carefully surveyed the surrounding area, he took a small transceiver from his pocket. "I'm all set," he spoke quietly into the mouthpiece. "Phase two now."

Rick Smith, the new night watchman for the science building, was making his rounds. He'd been on the job for less than two months and was already bored stiff. After all, what is there to do except to get a little reading in, or maybe catch a West Coast ball game while fighting off sleep by sucking down gallons of coffee.

His usual procedure was to walk the halls and randomly check doors to make sure they were locked. Since last week there had at least been another person to talk to at the end of his rounds. Ever since the two professors came back from Israel, there had been a man hired to watch over the archeology department all night.

Since the new man's post was on the fourth floor, it was convenient for Rick to kill a little time playing chess with him. His name was Tony and he seemed like a stand up guy. He played a pretty fair game of chess too.

They played their games by taking two moves each at the end of Rick's round. This way, he wouldn't be away from his post at the entrance to the building for too long. Then, after he had returned to his desk, he would set up his own board in the present position of the game and mull over his next move. Tony would keep the active board and consider his own options upstairs. They would then continue the game over the phone. They were usually able to get in at least two games each night, occasionally more.

Sometimes they would leave their shifts in the middle of a game and finish it the next evening.

"Hi, Tony," Rick greeted him as he entered Bruce's classroom. "How's it going?"

"Pretty good, man. How about yourself?"

"Same old, same old. You ready to continue our game?" Rick asked as he took a seat next to Bruce's desk. As he was about to make his move, a loud screeching of tires, followed by crunching metal and breaking glass interrupted the silence of the night.

"What the hell was that?" Rick asked.

"Sounded like an accident."

They got up and went to the side window nearest to where they had been playing. Through the trees on the campus road, they could see two cars against each other, nose to nose.

"Whatta ya think?" Tony asked.

"I don't know. It's too hard to see anything from here. I see some people moving around though."

"That's a lot of smoke. Think there's a fire?"

"I don't think so," Rick said. "That looks like radiator steam. I'd better get back downstairs to my post in case someone needs help. If they don't have cell phones, my phone is the nearest one."

"You gonna call the police?" Tony asked him as he was leaving.

"No, not yet, they might only want a tow truck or to call some friends. It doesn't look all that serious."

"Okay. If you need me for anything give me a call," Tony said.

"Sure. In the meantime, look over that board. I've got a surprise waiting for you."

"Yeah, well I'm sure you do. I may not be a magician, but I've got a trick or two up my sleeve."

Rick laughed. "That's what makes it such an interesting game," he said as he took one more look out the window. He was surprised to see someone walking toward the building from the scene of the accident. "I better get going."

Rick got to his desk just as the man he had seen from the fourth floor was knocking on the front door.

"Mister," The man yelled through the glass, "there's been an accident. My wife's stuck in our car. We need help."

"Should I call an ambulance first?" Rick asked as he opened the door.

"That's already been taken care of. The other car has a cell phone and we called the fire department and the police. But we need help right now," the man said, while breathing heavily.

Rick noticed the blood on the man's clothes and hands and felt weak. The sight of blood always caused his stomach to threaten eruption and his head to feel light.

"Is there somebody else who can help us?" the man asked.

"There's someone on the fourth floor. I'll call him. Wait right here."

Rick ran to his desk and dialed the number for Bruce's classroom. When Tony answered, Rick spoke rapidly. "They need our help. Get down here right away."

"I'm on my way."

Rick ran back to the man at the front door. "He's coming. It'll take a couple of minutes."

The man began running back toward the scene of the accident. "Let's go now," he said. "He can catch up to us when he gets here."

Rizzo's hired burglar looked at his watch as he listened to the message coming in over the radio informing him phase three was a go. They were within thirty seconds of his schedule.

He made his way to the spot over the fourth floor bathroom window. He removed a small rope, with a metal hook on the end, from his tool bag. After setting the metal grappler securely into the lip of the roof, Rizzo's man swung over the side and lowered himself to the window. He tore strips of duct tape from his chest and covered the glass in a silver web. With one quick blow, he shattered the pane as quietly as possible.

He reached through the broken section, unsnapped the swing lock, and opened the window. After gaining entry, he dropped a stone on the floor. Anyone investigating would think a thrown rock had broken the window. In moments, following a carefully sketched floor plan, he was inside Bruce's lab. Rizzo had told him that he was to steal some ancient documents hidden in a locked and sealed chamber and to leave the place as if nobody had been there. He was the best money could buy for this type of operation.

Outside the building, the man with the bloody clothes was running toward the crash scene, with Rick and Tony trying hard to catch up to him.

"Hurry," he turned and yelled to them.

"Hurry," he said again, this time weakly. He began to stumble. Suddenly he collapsed. By the time Rick and Tony caught up to him, he was motionless.

"Damn," Tony said as Rick bent over the man, "he must have been hurt more seriously that he thought."

"No shit, Dick Tracy. Help me roll him over onto his back. But be careful, he might have internal injuries."

The man seemed to be all right; breathing normal, skin color OK, no drool or spittle, so Rick decided to see what was up with the cars.

When he got there he saw an unconscious woman behind the wheel. She wasn't pinned in any way though. What had the guy meant when he'd said she was? He opened the car door and pulled her out onto the ground. He decided to wait for the ambulance the man had said he'd called.

After ten minutes with no signs of the police or an ambulance, Rick was beginning to get suspicious. The woman hadn't moved, the guy was still on the ground beside Tony. Something just didn't fit. The fact that there was a lot of blood, but no apparent injuries also weighed into his thoughts. When two tow trucks pulled up and began hooking up the cars, he made a decision. He called Tony over.

"Man, I don't feel right about this," Rick said.

"What do you mean?"

"I'm not sure, just a gut feeling. You stay hear, I need to check something out." Rick turned and headed back to the science building.

The first place he went to was Bruce's classroom, having decided that if anything was up, it probably had something to do with the scrolls. He held his breath as he entered. He looked around the interior of the room, checked the lock to the small enclosure that contained the scrolls. As far as he could tell, all was fine.

Shortly after Rick got back to his desk, Tony returned and reported that everybody had been driven off in the tow trucks. "Remind me to never get in an accident around here. I can't believe I just saw three accident victims drive off in tow trucks."

"What about the police?"

"They never showed up," Tony answered.

"Well it's the strangest accident I ever saw," Rick said.

Tony laughed. "Why, how many have you seen?"

Rick laughed too. "Actually that was the first one. Except for driving past one on the highway now and then. Maybe that's why it all seemed so strange. Well whatta ya say we finish our chess game?"

* * *

The following Monday morning, in the city of Malden, Massachusetts, Mazen Mousaka, the ostensible cab driver, and two members of his cell were sketching out the operation for which they'd been activated.

"We have the information we require on the three infidels," Mousaka said. "We must now formulate a plan that will send them to hell and will also free our brothers."

One of the others smiled. He held up a copy of the *Chronicle.* "Praise Allah. The reporter's own newspaper has shown us the way. The University at which the two professors work is advertising for janitors. With your green card, you can get a job their, Mazen."

Mousaka grabbed the paper and read the want ad that had been circled. He smiled. "Who can doubt that Allah is on our side?"

That afternoon Mazen Mousaka was sitting in front of the Human Resources manager at City University. The man finished studying the application he held in his hands. He placed the papers on his desk and faced the man he'd just interviewed. "I see you have excellent references."

"Yes, Sir. I would still be at my last position if my wife had not lost her job. Now that we have only one car, I must work closer to home."

"Well, we need someone who can start as soon as possible, we're three men short right now. We have openings in the gymnasium, the administration building and the science building. Do you have any preferences, Mister Mousaka?"

"I have always had an interest in science, sir. If you don't mind I would like to work there," Mazen Mousaka said.

"Not at all. Can you start tomorrow?"

"I will be here first thing in the morning."

TWENTY-FOUR

The Crooked Man

A week after Mazen started work at the university, ten days after the scrolls had been secretly stolen, Bruce, Roxanne, and Phyllis the linguistics professor, were sitting in the school cafeteria sipping coffee and discussing their next move.

"We've just about got the translation work done now," Phyllis said. "It's quite a story. Some of the things contained in those scrolls have already helped me in my personal life."

Roxanne looked at Phyllis as if her friend had just said she'd found salvation in a crossword puzzle. "What do you mean?"

"I've often had doubts about God," Phyllis said. "I mean, I would sometimes wonder if He created evil? If so, why? If not, who did? And of course being a scientist, I often had trouble comparing the facts of evolution with the story of Genesis. You know, things like that."

Bruce thought about this. He knew Phyllis's head to be as level as a master carpenter's baseline. And from what she'd told him previously about the scrolls, there were indeed important messages of brotherhood and tolerance in them. But as for helping in her personal life, well he wasn't too sure about that scenario. He'd often thought that people tended to find answers to their deepest questions wherever it seemed easiest and to see signs where none existed. If one was pondering the death of a family member, for instance, and a bluebird landed on the porch during such a moment, it was easy for some people to see such an event as spiritual symbolism rather than temporal realism. To certain people there was no such thing as a coincidence, while to others, there were nothing but. "Could you be reading more into them than is really there?"

"Definitely not." Phyllis responded. "The answers to these questions are in the scrolls. They have actually helped rekindle my faith in God and humanity."

"So," Roxanne asked, "Did God create evil?"

"According to the scrolls," Phyllis said, "there is a difference between sin and evil. Evil is the misadaptation of divine plans to local circumstances, the inadvertent introduction of error. Sin, on the other hand, is deliberate and conscious. God gave humanity free will knowing full well that we would make mistakes. We created sin and evil on this world. God allows it because this universe is designed to teach lessons through experience. Adam and Eve's mistake was the commingling of good and evil. They-"

"Hold on a minute there, pard'," Bruce said. "What was that about mixing good and evil?"

"Adam and Eve made a big mistake. They tried to carry out their own plans in conjunction with those they were given to execute. They mixed good with evil and ended up having to leave the Garden of Eden as a result."

"It almost sounds like the eating of the apple story," Roxanne said.

"That's pretty heavy stuff," Bruce said.

Roxanne looked at him with a smile and said in a slow cadence, "Bruce, what did we say about the seventies? Didn't we agree they're over?"

Bruce laughed and said, "Sorry, gorgeous. At least I'm not wearing my bell bottoms to work anymore." He returned to his conversation with Phyllis. "What more can you tell us about this?"

"Adam was dying when he wrote his story. He knew that the truth of his and Eve's mission would very likely be distorted over the ages. That's why he wrote it in the first place. Very few people at the time were literate and he had the wisdom to realize that oral history gets changed from generation to generation. He understood this. He accepted it. But he wouldn't allow the truth to die."

"And twelve thousand years later we find it," Roxanne mused. "It's quite a story. And with all the intrigue and action that's been going on, it would make a great movie."

"The only trouble is, no one would believe it. It's too fantastic. Too far fetched," Phyllis said.

Roxanne smiled and nodded in agreement, then turned to Bruce. "You know, Bruce, we've said this before but now it's even more true; a lot of people aren't going to accept this. They'll see it as an attempt to change the Bible and undermine their faith. As Lenny said the other night, 'They're going to argue over this like politicians fighting lawyers over money.'"

"If you two don't mind me sticking my nose in," Phyllis said, "I think you should consult a reputable clergyman before going public. Not someone who has a reputation as a liberal, but you don't want someone who'll label you the spawn of the devil either."

"I think that's a good idea," Roxanne said. "And we know just the person don't we, Bruce?"

"Reverend Graves, of course," he said. "That's excellent. When do you think you'll have the translations ready, Phyllis?"

"We're almost done now. A couple more days and they're all yours."

"That's great!" Bruce said. "Thanks for everything Phyl, you've been a great help. Things are looking up," he said as he clasped his hands together.

The following morning, Wednesday, Sheila Snow answered her office phone. "Reverend Graves' office. Can I help you?"

"Hi, Sheila, it's Roxie. How are you?"

"Oh hi, Roxie. I'm doing fine thanks. How about yourself?"

"Just hunky-dory," Roxanne said as she explained the purpose of her call. "So you see, Sheila, we thought if Reverend Graves could come by our classrooms for a meeting, he could read the scrolls and we might be able to come up with a plan for taking this public."

Sheila consulted the office schedule. "I think Reverend Graves would love to be involved in this. He's never been one to interpret scripture literally, without errors. He's often told me that anything touched by human hands has fingerprints; you know, has been changed in some way. Anyway, he's not in right now. Why don't I set up an appointment for him to meet you guys at the university Friday morning? That's the day after tomorrow."

"I know when Friday is," Roxanne laughed. "We covered the days of the week in graduate school."

"Very funny, wise guy. I just didn't want you to think I meant next week or anything. How about ten in the morning? You can have a couple of hours if you want."

"That would be great. It's school vacation week so we won't have to worry about interruptions. Thanks, Sheila."

The next afternoon, a bright and sunny Thursday, Phyllis came into Bruce's classroom and said, "Did Roxanne arrive yet? I called her and she said she'd meet us here."

Bruce was seated at his desk. He finished putting the papers he had been working on into the drawers. "She just called me, she'll be right up". Noticing that Phyllis was carrying a stack of computer printouts, he asked, "Is that what I hope it is?"

"It sure is."

As he walked over to take the documents from Phyllis, Roxanne entered the room. "Look what we've got, Babe. We've waited a long time for this haven't we?"

"I know you'll enjoy reading it," Phyllis said. "Picture 'War and Peace' written by Moses, inspirational and thought provoking, yet tragically historical."

"I can't wait," Roxanne said. "It seems as if our whole life has been tied up in this. Has it really only been six months or so?"

"I know what you mean. It seems like forever," Bruce said.

"I don't know how we'll ever be able to repay you for all your help, Phyllis," Roxanne said.

Phyllis smiled, thought for a moment, and said, "Just give me a credit when you write the book, and make sure Jane Fonda plays me in the movie."

"You got it. Even though I was kind of hoping for Jane Fonda to play me," Roxanne said as they both laughed.

"Seriously though," Phyllis said, "it's still too early to go handing out accolades. You two still have a lot of work to do before you'll convince the world these scrolls are telling a true story, and it won't be easy. Here's a quote from Adam that might help you while you think about all the trouble you're having with this thing. He says, 'All things work toward the light in the long run, no matter how dark it may seem in the present.' He also said something to the effect that if he and Eve had kept that thought in mind, they wouldn't have failed in their mission."

Bruce and Roxanne both looked at her in surprise. "Are you talking about that mixing good and evil stuff again?" Roxanne asked.

"Don't worry, you'll find out soon enough. I'll tell you this much for now, though. The part about Eve being tempted by the serpent in the garden has more truth to it that you might think."

"I always considered the whole Garden of Eden thing an allegory," Bruce said. "To learn those two actually existed, is a revelation to me. And now you're saying the temptation and the fall and all that stuff really happened?"

"That's right, although it wasn't a snake of course, there was no fall of man, and it wasn't about eating an apple either, but I've said too much already. I don't want to spoil it for you. I have to get back to work now. Have fun, and good luck."

"Thanks again, Phyllis," Roxanne said. "We'll see you tomorrow morning." After Phyllis left the room, she turned to Bruce and said, "Boy, she's got me more curious than a litter of kittens."

Bruce smiled. "I know what you mean. I'm fired up. I feel like dropping everything and jumping right into them. But I think we should wait until tonight, when we can devote our full concentration to it. What about you?"

The look of disappointment on her face said she was not in total agreement with this. "Yeah, I guess so."

Slowly, and with obvious hesitation, Bruce placed the papers in his desk. "I have a lot of work to do."

"I have to get back too," she sighed. "How is it that we have more work during vacation weeks than during school weeks?"

She walked up to him and kissed him lovingly on the mouth. "See ya later, alligator."

"Roxanne," he said slowly and condescendingly, "what did we say about the nineteen twenties? Didn't we agree they were over?"

She laughed. "You got me there. At least I'm not wearing my flapper skirt to work anymore."

As Roxanne walked away, he said, "Hey." She turned to face him.

"In a while crocodile," he said with a big smile plastered on his face.

Joe Rizzo Senior sat at his desk. He had just taken delivery of the leather scrolls his rent-a-crook had stolen for him. As he sat there he thought about what he would do with them. Were they worth much in terms of money? Even if they were, could he market them without getting caught? It would be nice if he could do that, no sense wasting the ten grand he'd spent getting them if he didn't have to. That wasn't the important thing, though.

What mattered to Joe Rizzo Senior was teaching lessons. He knew many people considered him to be a ruthless son-of-a-bitch, and worse. That didn't bother him one bit. Truth be known, he was ruthless. He was a son-of-a-bitch. So what? That was how you got ahead in this world wasn't it? What did bother him was the fear that his son would become weak like the boy's mother had been. He was determined to show his namesake that the only way you got respect was to instill it in your adversaries. It didn't matter whether you were competing for money, power, or love. If he lost his sexy girlfriend Roxanne to a simp like Bruce Goldman, there was no telling how far down the slippery slope of wimpdom the boy would go. A lesson must be taught. The strong and the committed won every time, while the weak and wishy-washy sat on their asses and complained. That was a lesson well worth ten lousy grand if it found its way into his son's dense skull.

He stood and took the scrolls, which were now in a single leather case, and carried them to the large built in bookcase behind his desk. He moved a leather first edition book and the bookcase pivoted, revealing a narrow alcove fitted with a massive combination locked stainless steel door. Rizzo entered the combination, walked into the safe, and placed the leather carrying case with the scrolls inside a drawer.

After returning the bookcase to its original position, he thought about how satisfying it was that no one knew what he had done; and no one, not even his son, knew the safe even existed. He imagined with glee, the scene where the two college professors learned their precious cargo had gone missing.

TWENTY-FIVE

His Last Bow

During the pre-dawn hours of Friday, Mazen Mousaka was in the kitchen of his small apartment. He was preparing for his last day on earth. For more than two years he had been anticipating this moment of glory. The day on which he would surrender earthly existence in the name of the Prophet, and in the service of Allah. Only those with the will and strength to sacrifice all, would reap the rewards of martyrdom.

He took the tan colored canvas vest, with its many tubular pockets, from one of his associates.

"Allah wills the death of infidels everywhere," said his team member, Ali, in Arabic with deep-voiced poetic cadence, as he helped Mazen strap on the vest. "Those who hate heaven must be sent to hell."

Mahmud, the other team member present this day said in a hypnotic voice, also in poetic Arabic, "Allah wills the destruction of all who support the Zionists, and those who seek our end." Ali and Mahmud started filling each pocket with three sticks of dynamite. In movements evocative of a religious ceremony, they inserted a detonator, with its attached wire emerging, into one stick from each pocket. As they quoted suras from the Koran in Arabic, their beautiful and musical mother tongue, the expressive language of Allah, they wired the detonators to a battery and then to a red button.

Mazen paid little heed to their actions. It was the words that penetrated his soul; the almost musical rhythms that resonated to the very core of his being. The lyrics of Allah, in the language of Allah, produced the song of Allah. A powerful rendition of hope played upon the instrument that was his heart. Revenge was its drumbeat.

The voice of his people echoed deep within him. A song for salvation, for the return of the homeland, for relief from despair vibrated within him. Retribution was its chorus.

He pictured his homeland as honey filled meadows, saw olive groves far into the distance. He envisioned children playing in the streets, old men sipping coffee, all in harmony with Allah. The heartfelt scene of imagined days-gone-by became engulfed in flames of Zionist origin. Reprisal emerged from the blaze like a newborn Phoenix. It arose and flew off into the night sky to deliver its message of doom. Its name was Mazen Mousaka, holy warrior. He was ready.

Ali held the small, red, thumb actuated switch in front of Mazen's eyes. "You are now a force capable of complete destruction. A weapon of God. A deliverer of holy vengeance. Allah will be pleased. The Prophet will smile down on you. Islam will praise your sacrifice. You will be blessed with eternal happiness and fulfillment in the bosom of Allah, as will each of your family members."

Ali placed a small electronic device in his pocket. "I will be vigilant and ready with our insurance policy to guarantee success."

Mahmud said, "You will seek the release of our comrades in arms before carrying out your mission of revenge. Remember that you are to give the Zionists forty-eight hours to release our brothers and no longer. Take these pills. They will keep you awake and alert for two days. After that time, no matter what stalling tactics the infidels use, even should you gain our brother's freedom, you are to carry out the final step of your journey to heaven, the complete and utter destruction of the blasphemers who maimed our beloved Assad."

Without another word, Mazen put on his overcoat and walked out the door, heading to his appointment with mortal eminence and heavenly bliss.

Later that same Friday morning, Bruce and Roxanne entered Bruce's classroom about five minutes before their meeting was scheduled to begin. Lenny, already seated at Bruce's desk, looked up as they entered.

"Hi, you two," he greeted them. "I hope it's all right that I told Sheila she could join us."

"Of course it is," Roxanne said.

"By the way, have you seen today's paper?" Lenny asked. He held up the morning edition of the *Chronicle* with its usual complement of dire headlines.

Bruce read the lead story concerning Israelis fighting in Lebanon and Jordan. Syria was heavily involved also. "I wonder if we'll ever get an opportunity to return there."

"I know," Lenny said. "This thing looks like it could go on forever. Both sides are convinced they're right and both sides think God is on their side."

"How can anybody in their right mind think God is on the side of violence?" Reverend Graves said as he entered the room in the middle of the conversation.

Bruce shook his head and shrugged. "Well anyway, we're glad to see everybody here. Today we all finally get to see what the scrolls say. Where's Sheila?"

"She's taking care of business," Lenny said, meaning the ladies room.

As if on cue, Sheila entered the classroom. "Good morning, everybody," she said. "Are we all here? Boy I'm really looking forward to reading those scrolls."

Bruce said, "We're just waiting for Phyllis, our language expert. She's making copies for each of us."

"How long do you think it will take to read them?" Lenny asked.

"Phyllis said it took her about an hour and a half," Roxanne said.

"So she's already read them then." Reverend Graves said. "Did she give you any hints about what they say?"

Bruce and Roxanne looked at each other and smiled. "She sure did," Roxanne said, "but only hints. She said, for instance, that some of the contributions Adam and Eve made to world culture are still significant to this day. Bruce and I were going to read them last night, but decided it would be more fun to share the experience with you guys." She looked at Bruce and gave him a lascivious smile.

Lenny thought that whatever they DID end up doing last night must have been a LOT of fun. Certainly more fun than reading old documents. He thought about the night after their rescue when Roxanne had, what? Raped him? That was a bit much. Acted like a slut? Well, maybe, but Lenny hadn't exactly been Mister Faithful. Taken advantage of the moment? That was better. He wondered if he would ever mention it to Sheila. *Don't think so*, he decided.

Reverend Graves missed the significance of Roxanne's smile completely. "That must have taken quite a bit of willpower," he said.

"We left our copy here so we wouldn't be tempted," Roxanne said.

Reverend Graves crossed his arms and gazed at the ceiling with a faraway look. "I wonder what significant cultural contributions Phyllis was referring to." He lowered his eyes to ask Bruce, "What do you think that could be all about?"

Before Bruce could answer Phyllis entered with an armful of papers. "Hey everybody. Sorry I'm late but these just got finished." She started handing out a copy to each person. "I have the advantage of familiarity with these so I'd like to fill you in a little if I may."

"If you can do it without giving anything away it's okay with me," Bruce said.

"I can do that," Phyllis said as she continued dispersing the copies. "First of all, what you're about to read is not like anything you've ever come across before. I know there are plenty of theories out there regarding Adam and Eve, but I've never heard of one that comes close to this. But who they were and where they came from pale in comparison to what they accomplished."

"I thought you said they failed at whatever it was they were trying to do?" Roxanne said.

"In a way they did," Phyllis said. "Their goals were so lofty that I saw their inability to meet them as a failure of their mission, as they did themselves. But they introduced humanity to so much during their lives, that the world would be a very different place today if they hadn't come here."

"From what you're saying, Phyllis," Reverend Graves said, "I think Bruce and Roxanne are wise to take the cautious route about publicizing all this. To simply come out with it and say 'Here it is, take it or leave it', could easily offend a lot of people. They'll think you're treading on their turf, questioning scripture. Some will go so far as to call this the work of the devil. You'll need to walk softly if you want support from certain quarters."

"We're hoping you can come up with an idea to help us do just that," Bruce said. "We almost lost the game before the first pitch. We don't want to take any unnecessary chances now."

"I have a question for Phyllis," Lenny said. "What kinds of things did Adam and Eve introduce to this world and how did they know this stuff?"

"Why don't we just read this ourselves right now," Bruce said. "After all, that's what we're here for."

Phyllis finished handing out the copies. "I've decided to stick around for this, if it's all right."

Bruce nodded and Phyllis took a seat. Everyone began reading their copies, and for over an hour the only noise in the room was the turning of pages and the clearing of throats. No one even noticed a man enter the classroom.

Bruce looked up when he heard the click of the door being locked. He recognized the new janitor and figured he was just mistaken about what his duties were. "Hey, what are you doing there, Mazen?" he said. "We don't need to be locked in while you're working." Bruce saw him putting a key back into a pocket in his heavy overcoat, but he didn't answer. Bruce was about to repeat his words, when the man pulled a pistol from his pocket and aimed it at the group.

"Nobody is to move," the wide-eyed Palestinian yelled, waiving the gun at the group. "I have a bomb and you will all die if you do not do what I say." He opened his overcoat to reveal the dynamite laden vest.

Roxanne looked up and screamed. Lenny's first instinct was to attack. After all, they had the guy outnumbered. Then he saw the small brown plastic cylinder with the red button in the man's hand and decided to stay put. The women instinctively looked to Reverend Graves.

Bruce asked, "What's this all about, Mazen?"

"Silence," he said. "I will do the talking. If any of you try to escape or in any way try to prevent my mission, I will push this switch," he held up his right hand with the thumb resting on top of the red button. "I mean every word I say. Now, all of you gather together behind that large desk in the front of the room."

The six hostages did as instructed and stood in the small space between Bruce's desk and the blackboard covered wall four feet behind it.

The terrorist then took a roll of silver duct tape from his overcoat and threw it at Lenny. "You," he said, "tape the wrists of the others. And do a good job. I will be watching closely."

Lenny began to follow his orders, starting with Reverend Graves who had proffered his hands first. "Let's just stay calm and do what he says," the Reverend said. "Then maybe we can find out what he wants so we can end this without violence."

"That is good advice," Mazen said. "If your government and the Zionists meet our demands then you may indeed live to see another day. But make no mistake, I will not hesitate to detonate this device, and destroy this building along with all of you."

"What about your family?" Reverend Graves asked. "Surely you want to spare your loved ones the sadness your death would bring." He reacted to Mazen's look of contempt like it was a slap in the face.

"Quiet, you silly man. Do you really think you can play your idiotic mind games with me? You know nothing. My family will be proud of my having gone to Allah as a martyr. You foolish Americans think you understand my people and our faith. What will it take to make you realize that the world does not work the way you think? That it does not revolve around the minds of westerners?"

Lenny finished taping Reverend Graves' wrists together. Mazen Mousaka aimed his pistol at the man of God. "As each of you has your wrists taped, come around to this side and sit at one of the student desks near the front."

Reverend Graves, wrists taped together in front of him, slowly walked around the teacher's desk toward one of the smaller ones as instructed. The words, 'condemned prisoner' entered Lenny's mind. His internal editor searched valiantly for more optimistic phrasing, but failed. He shuddered as he forced the image from his mind's eye.

"Stay right there," the man said, causing the Reverend to stop just as he was about to take a seat at the front center desk. "The rest of you stop while I check this man's wrists." He walked to Reverend Graves while keeping a wary eye on the others. When he was close enough to reach the reverend's bound hands, he stopped and said. "Hold out your arms so I can test the tape." The wild-eyed terrorist held his right hand up high where all could see, thumb positioned on the red button. He placed the pistol in his waistband, grabbed Reverend Graves' wrists and shook them vigorously with his left hand. When he finished he said, "Very well. Sit down and do not move. You," he said to Lenny. "Do the others just as well. I will be testing each one, you can be assured."

Lenny resumed wrapping his fellow hostage's wrists with the strong tape.

"When you are all tied and seated the reporter will make some telephone calls."

"Who will he be calling?" Bruce asked.

The bomb-garbed man removed the gun from his waist and waved it in Lenny's general direction. "The reporter will start with a call to his newspaper offices. Our demands must be made public for all the world to see. Then he will speak to the Zionist ambassador who will contact his government with our demands."

"You keep referring to your group," Lenny said, "who are you and who do you represent?"

"I represent the Palestinian people and all Muslims everywhere who are oppressed by infidels, false leaders and thieving governments." He looked directly into Lenny's eyes as he continued. "You are already familiar with our leader, since you are the reason he now has but one arm and one leg."

Lenny looked surprised for a moment. Then his expression changed to shock. "You mean Assad isn't dead?"

"Did you really think Allah would call him home before his time? Let me tell you something all Westerners must realize. Our struggle will not end until all peoples accept Allah as the One God and Mohammed as His Prophet. Allah wills this and it shall be so. You cannot stop this from happening. You can only delay it."

Lenny finished his assignment. All the other hostages were now sitting at student desks with hands and wrists tightly bound together. Mazen carefully inspected each while still holding his thumb over the button that could convert their bodies to hamburger in an instant. He walked toward the teacher's desk, keeping it between himself and Lenny, and said, "Come around to this side slowly with your hands held together in front of you." Lenny followed his orders as Mazen took the tape from the desktop and said, "Wrap this around one of your wrists at least five times then put your free hand next to the taped one." Lenny did as instructed and Mazen finished the job. Within seconds, Lenny was as tightly bound as his fellow POW's were. "Now take that telephone and call your office. Tell your boss what is happening and make him understand that if he does not do everything I tell him to, you shall all burn in hell this day."

"What about the police?" Lenny asked.

"They will be called as well. The whole world will be watching us in a short while. Now make the call."

Lenny picked up the phone with both hands, put it on the desk and started dialing. In a moment Perry Hazard was on the line. Lenny filled him in on what was happening.

"Great Gobs of Horse Shit!" Hazzard said. "Is everybody okay? How the hell did he get in there? Who else knows about this? Wha–"

"Hold on, Chief," Lenny cut him off. "This guy wants to speak with you."

Mazen Mousaka took the phone from Lenny and told him to sit with the others. "You will do everything I say. Is that understood?" he said into the phone. Lenny assumed his boss had replied in the affirmative as the man said, "If all goes well and our demands are met, you will see your friends again. If not, then you will next see them in the Devil's living room. We demand the release of the Palestinian freedom fighters unjustly held hostage by the Zionist government. You will call your White House and the Zionist ambassador and tell them this. Only upon their release will your friends be allowed to live. Do you understand?"

A moment of silence ensued as the terrorist listened to Hazzard's response. "You may contact the local authorities and evacuate this building. But no one must enter. If I see even one person coming into this building I will destroy it and every one left inside. Do not think you can do such a stupid thing without my knowledge. I have friends watching all sides of this building. Call back here when you have done what I've told you."

He hung up and said, "Now we wait, but not too long or I will end it."

"May I ask you something?" Reverend Graves said.

The terrorist stared at him with hollow black eyes, seemed about to say something, then shook his head and said, "What do you ask?"

"I would like to talk about Allah."

Before the Reverend could say another word, the terrorist quickly covered the ground between the two of them, brandished his handgun and pointed it directly at the reverend's forehead saying, "Do not blaspheme the name of The Maker. You shall meet Him here and now if you should be so foolish."

Reverend Graves remained calm in the face of death, but Lenny saw the beads of perspiration forming in the folds of his neck. "I would never blaspheme or take the name of God in vain," he said. "I've dedicated my life to serving Him and to serving mankind in His name. I only wish to understand. Any questions I ask, I assure you, are in no way meant as aspersions on Allah."

The terrorist kept the gun aimed at Reverend Graves. "What is it you wish to ask?"

"Do you really think Allah desires His children to kill and hate one another like this?"

Mazen pulled the gun from his captive's head and walked to the front of the room. "That is a stupid question. Of course He does not. But for those who refuse to recognize Him as the One True God there are no other options. The choice is simple. The way of Allah, or the path of annihilation."

"What about those who worship God in their own way? Does not Allah hear their prayers?" Reverend Graves asked.

"Infidels! They are all infidels and will burn in the eternal fires of damnation."

Lenny could see Reverend Graves wanted to say more, but was being cautious. He hoped his friend wouldn't go saying anything foolish like, 'No book is perfect,' or 'Don't follows the words in a book, follow the poetry in your heart,' both of which Lenny had heard from the Reverend. This wasn't the time to convert anyone.

Before Reverend Graves could continue, and to Lenny's immense relief, the telephone rang. Mazen waved for Lenny to answer. "Yeah, Chief," he said, standing at the side of the big desk. "We're all okay so far. What's going on?"

As his editor spoke, Lenny heard the scream of sirens approaching. The next thing they heard was the sound of car doors slamming, then the voice of a police officer speaking into a bullhorn.

"Attention! Attention! All students and others in the science building. Evacuate immediately. Calmly and quietly leave the building now. This is not a drill. I repeat, this is not a drill."

Within a couple of minutes, a trickle of people began to leave the building. Soon, the number was in the dozens. As this was happening more vehicles were arriving with sirens screaming like banshees. Less than five minutes after the announcement, there were four fire trucks, two fire department cars, and six police cars scattered about the front of the building. Lenny assumed, hoped actually, that there were others around back.

"Don't worry about what's going on outside, Mister Cronin. Ask of him what information he has?" Mazen demanded.

"The guy wants to know if you have followed instructions, Chief. Also, do the police understand that no one is to enter this building?" Lenny asked. He listened intently, then told Mazen, "He says he followed your instructions. The police have orders only to evacuate the building and not to enter under any circumstances. He also says, however that if anyone is hurt, all bets are off."

Mazen Mousaka's neck muscles tightened into knots. He covered the ground to Lenny in an instant and grabbed the phone from Lenny's hands. "I will make the threats, Mister Hazzard," he yelled into the phone. "What about your government and the Zionists?"

Lenny cautiously edged his way over to the window as the terrorist spewed his venom at *The Chronicle's* editor. He saw the crowds beginning to gather under the trees and along the demarcation line the police had created with yellow crime scene tape. He saw a black panel truck with no police markings. Men carrying automatic weapons and who were obviously wearing body armor began swarming from the truck. A SWAT team. *Great,* Lenny thought. He took a deep breath. *What a month this has been.*

The walking bomb took a piece of paper from his overcoat and handed it and the phone to Lenny. "Get away from that window, and read this list of names to him."

Lenny, with wrists still taped, clumsily took the phone and paper. He started reading the names to his boss. The terrorist went to the edge of the window, peaked out, and quickly snapped his head back as if shot.

He turned to Lenny and said loudly, "Tell your editor to call the police and order them to remove the SWAT team. There will be no snipers and there will be no sneak attacks or all will die."

Lenny looked at the man as he said into the phone, "Did you hear that, Chief?"

* * *

Outside the building, newly appointed Chief of Police, Kim Donavan, was busy commanding his men and the firemen. His first responsibility was to cordon off the immediate area to assure nobody entered the building. He also had to keep curious bystanders at a safe distance.

"Jerry," he called to the SWAT commander, "we just got a call that you guys have to go, but just make it look as if you're leaving. How about packing up and driving off behind the administration building. You should be able to stage your team from there while staying out of sight. Where will you be putting your sharpshooters?"

The SWAT commander placed a small map on the hood of the nearest police car and while pointing out various buildings said, "We can cover all four sides of the science building with eight shooters. Two will be in the fourth floor windows of the administration building. They can stay hidden there while maintaining visual contact with the room the hostages are in. These other buildings on the opposite sides will provide the same coverage. Our assault and rescue team might have a hard time approaching the building unseen, though. It's pretty open ground all around it."

"What about the back side?" Kim asked. "That guy can't watch both sides of the building from where he is."

"That's what we're planning right now. The only problem is, he may not be alone. He claims to have accomplices."

"We have to consider that, of course." Kim said. "For now, get your men out of sight so this guy will think we're complying with his demands, then get your sharpshooters in position. It's too early to talk about an assault just yet anyway. There's a hostage negotiator on the way. We have to give him a chance to end this peacefully."

The head of the SWAT team ordered his men into their vehicle and they headed beyond the sight of anyone inside the science building or its immediate vicinity.

Inside the classroom, the six captives and their captor were discussing ground rules. Lenny had assumed the position of lead hostage more by circumstance than conscious decision. "What about bathroom privileges?" he asked. "We're certain to need access before this is over."

"Where is the nearest facility?" the terrorist asked.

"Just down the hall," Bruce said. "It's the third door on the left."

"That will not do," Mazen said. "No one is to leave this room. Come up with something else."

Bruce pointed at a door on the side of the classroom with his bound hands. "That's a janitor's closet with a sink in it. Maybe we could use that."

The terrorist went to the door and opened it. From his seat, Lenny could see that it was as Bruce had described it, with cleaning supplies, mops, buckets and the sink. "This will do. You may urinate in the sink. If you have to do anything else use the mop bucket."

With that matter settled, Lenny turned to his captor and asked, "Can we talk to each other?"

"Talk all you wish, but they will be your last words if I suspect you are planning anything. And no whispering, all talk must be loud enough for me to hear."

Reverend Graves asked, "How do you plan on getting out of here if your friends are released?"

Mazen approached Reverend Graves and bent down nose to nose with his captive. "You need not worry about me, false man of God," he said in a low, hateful voice. "What I do is no concern of yours. All shall be carried out according to Allah's will. Ask no more foolish questions of this sort."

He looked at Lenny and said, "You, go to those windows and close the blinds." As Lenny did so the man continued, "Your stupid police most certainly wish to try a shot at me. Rest assured that should something so foolish be attempted, you will all be dead before the echo of the shot ends. Your lives will be spared only if the Zionist government accedes to our demands and releases my brothers."

Sheila raised her hands and said, "I have to use the janitor's closet. May I?"

Mazen looked at her with disgust and tilted his head toward the closet door. "Go."

As Lenny watched his girlfriend make her way to the makeshift bathroom, he asked, "What about food? We'll get pretty hungry before long. Have you thought of that?"

"All is planned for. As you Americans like to say, we shall cross that bridge when it comes to us."

Lenny almost laughed out loud at the foreigner's misquote, but caught himself in time. He looked at the others and saw they were too frightened to see anything humorous. He realized he'd seen the same look, on some of the same faces, only a month ago in the barn in Syria. As dire as their straits had been on that occasion, looking back on it now made it seem like a day in church. At least he'd had a gun then...and there hadn't been any hot-tempered bombs walking around.

Lenny's stomach started tightening into a knot. He clenched his fists. This was the third damn time his life was in jeopardy over those scrolls. What the hell was going on? Were they jinxed by some ancient curse? He knew that was ridiculous, but still you had to wonder. Or could it be something even more insidious? From what he'd just read, Lucifer was a real spiritual being. That had been a shock. Real, but not the devil, that was even more surprising. It turned out that Lucifer, Satan and Beelzebub were actually different entities. And according to the scrolls, they were still roaming the earth encouraging wrongdoing, or at least had been when Adam wrote his words. Could they be behind this? Was this an actual battle between good and evil? Was he really asking himself these questions?

He thought about everything he'd just read; about Adam and Eve on a mission from the universe government to advance the planet, assigned to take the reins from the defaulting ruler, Lucifer and his crew. Earth darkened by isolation from planetary spiritual communication circuits because of Lucifer's default. Holy shit! Phyllis had sure been right when she said this was all new stuff. It seemed so far fetched at first blush. But so many of the ancient mysteries he'd been studying about had been explained by the scrolls that he had to seriously consider everything they said.

Lenny refocused his thoughts on the moment at hand. He wasn't about to give up after what he'd already been through, but he needed a plan, or a weapon. One way or another, he was determined to get everybody out of this pickle.

He had no illusions about this guy giving himself up, even if his friends were to be released, which they probably wouldn't be. Lenny knew the man was a fanatic. He saw it in his eyes. He'd seen that same look in the eyes of Assad's men back at the farm in Syria. This guy would kill at the drop of a hat and what's more, Lenny was sure he was looking forward to blowing himself up for the glory of Allah. What a crock that was. But what to do?

The first thing was to convince the others that this guy was hard-core and had no plans to release anybody. As he looked at each of his fellow captives, he realized that Bruce and Roxanne would probably understand. But what about Sheila and the Reverend? And what about the other teacher, Phyllis? They all probably think this can be talked out and everybody will be home on time for dinner.

Back in his army days, he had been taught that in such a situation you had to enlist support, to develop a strategy based on your strengths and the enemy's weakness. And execute your plan to perfection. The phrase, 'easier said than done', crossed his mind. His internal editor changed it to, 'mission impossible.'

Outside the building, Captain Donavan was receiving reports from his men. They had evacuated not only the science building, but all surrounding buildings as well and had cordoned off the immediate area. The small crowd that Lenny had seen beginning to form behind the yellow ribbon fence, was now in the hundreds. The hostage negotiator had arrived and was in the process of setting up a dedicated phone line to the classroom.

His name was Joe West, and while the technicians were setting up the phone line, he said to the man in charge, "Kim, have you spoken directly to the bomber yet? I need to know everything that's been said so far."

"The only one who's spoken with him is Perry Hazzard, the editor of the Chronicle. He's expected here in a few minutes and can get you up to speed."

Joe West picked up the handset to his portable phone and dialed the number for the classroom. "Who's this?" he asked when it was answered.

"This is Lenny Cronin. Who's this?"

"Mister Cronin, my name is Joe West of the state police. My job is to establish and maintain communications with your hostage taker. Could you please ask him to come to the phone?"

He could hear mumbled voices then a male with a Middle Eastern accent spoke. "Who is this? Why does not your government call here directly instead of sending an errand boy?"

The negotiator was too experienced to let a little name-calling rattle him. "Sir, my name is Joe West and my job is to make sure you get what you want so nobody gets hurt. My government is even now speaking with the Israeli government and conveying your demands and the list of names. I'd like you to permit something that will help expedite this matter."

"What is that?"

"I'd like to send up a second phone that will allow us to remain in contact while keeping the one we're now using open for other calls."

"What other calls are you talking about? I see no need for a second telephone."

"What if someone from my government needs to contact you or me while we are talking? Or what if you wish to make a call to verify something we tell you? Or what if something goes wrong with this phone? There are good reasons for having a backup line. I can tie the second phone to a rope and throw it up to someone in the window. No one has to enter the building for this."

"Very well. I will send the reporter to the window. But no tricks."

Joe West hung up and turned to Chief Donavan. "Okay. He's letting us put the second phone in. Is the bug in place?"

"My man is just finishing up now," Kim said. "We'll be able to hear everything that goes on in there."

Lenny walked to the window and raised one of the blinds. He watched as a man came towards the building with the cellular phone and a thin rope. He caught the rope and lifted the phone into the room and untied it.

The phone rang immediately, and Lenny answered it. He handed it to Mazen and said, "It's for you."

"I just wanted to make sure it's working," Joe West said. "What can I do to make this go as smoothly as possible for you?"

"You can contact your President and tell him he will lose some citizens if he does not do as I say."

"Yes, Sir. We're already working on that, as I said. I meant, what could I do to help you personally? What is your name, by the way? I like to know what to call people I speak with."

"Try none of your mental games on me. You are not dealing with some olive-growing peasant who knows nothing about psychology."

"I'm not playing games, I assure you. But I've told you my name and I just wanted to know yours. It's strictly for conversation."

"My name is Mazen, but do not ask for my family name. You will not get it."

"That's fine, Mazen. Like I said, it's only for conversation. Now, what about food and water? Can I get you anything like that?"

While Mazen was occupied on the phone, the SWAT team used the opportunity to set up in the administration building, preparing to execute their plan for covering the science building.

"Let's start making our way to the back of the building, said the squad leader. "Remember we don't know if there are any accomplices, so we have to assume there are. We can't let anyone see what we're doing. That includes the press. For that reason, we must wait for dark before we can try mounting an attack. That's still over six hours away, but we can get ourselves in place in the meantime. Any questions?" He looked at his men, determined there were none and said, "Let's get to it."

The eight men left the room one at a time and emerged from the building from different exits and at different times. They slowly and methodically began making their way to pre-assigned positions to wait for nightfall. It took nearly an hour for this to happen but when it did, they were sure that no unauthorized person was aware of their presence. Assault Team B was in place. Some were dressed in camouflage and had hidden themselves along the ground at strategic locations in trees or shrubs. Others remained in street clothes and blended in with the uniformed police manning the demarcation lines. All were ready to go on the offensive the moment orders came.

In the crowd of onlookers, maintaining a view of the front of the science building, stood Ali, Mazen Mousaka's roommate and co-conspirator. He had delayed his arrival until after a crowd had developed in order not to draw any unwanted eyes his way. He realized, as he strained to see past those in front of him, that this was a mistake. He and Mahmud, the other member of the small cell, were supposed to keep an eye on the police, especially the SWAT team. He had seen the members of the elite unit pulling out of the area just as he arrived. That was according to plan. But he could not tell if they had completely left the area or were just pretending to do so. He hoped Mahmud was having better luck from his location.

Mahmud had also arrived after people had gathered. He was hidden within a crowd to the right of the building. He had also seen the Swat team leaving the scene. He watched as the panel truck parked beside one of the other school buildings and the heavily armed men disembarked and entered the building. He did not see them exit the building. But he did see something that aroused his suspicions. Something about the almost forced casualness of some of the men leaving the building singly and in pairs a short while later struck him as false. He watched as these men, each one tall and athletic looking, certainly not school professors or students, cautiously made their way to different places around the science building. He felt certain that something was in the works. He took out his cell phone and called the number of Bruce's classroom, which he had committed to memory.

TWENTY-SIX

The Solution

Lenny had been thinking about what he and the other hostages could do to save themselves. It was now almost three o'clock, over six hours into the crisis, and no new information had been forthcoming. He imagined the governments of the world discussing the situation and looking for ways to stall the terrorist and maybe talk him out of his plan. He knew damn well where that line of reasoning would lead everybody. Right to the morgue, that's where. He knew no government was about to release a bunch of Palestinian terrorists.

A plan was beginning to form in his mind. He'd used the janitor's closet to relieve himself and had seen something in there that might give him the leverage he needed. Now if he could just convince his fellow captives.

The other hostages started asking about food. "Very well," Mazen Mousaka said. He looked at Lenny. "Use that phone to order something to eat. Tell them that anything I eat will be tested by one of you first, so no games. And no pork."

Lenny made the call and ordered the food. He hung up the phone and took a seat next to Bruce. "You must have to go to the bathroom by now don't you Bruce?"

"No, not really," he said. "I didn't have my coffee this morning."

Lenny gave him a stern look. "Are you sure?"

Bruce was unsure of what Lenny was getting at, but turned to the terrorist and asked permission anyway. Upon receiving a nod, he went to the closet, opened the door and entered.

What he saw was no more or less than he'd seen dozens of times over the years. There was the stainless steel sink for filling and emptying the bucket that was used when mopping floors. The wheeled yellow bucket with a mop in it sat on the floor, with a spare mop in the wall mounted holder. The shelves contained the usual assortment of cleaning agents such as bleach, floor detergents, drain cleaners, and the like, along with assorted paper goods such as toilet tissue, tampons for the dispenser in the lady's room, and paper towels. He shrugged, grunted and, realizing he did need to pee, relieved his bladder into the sink. What could Lenny be getting at? What did he have up his sleeve? It better not be anything dangerous. As grateful as he was for Lenny's help in their first two encounters with Assad's group, this one was sure to work out. After all, they were in the United States now. Our government would take care of everything. Or would they? He started thinking about the age-old battle of good versus evil yet again.

It seemed that evil always won out over good. Why did it have to be that way? The Adam manuscripts revealed much in the way of answers to such questions. He had such high hopes for the message they carried for mankind. If they were destroyed in a blast, that message would be lost forever.

Of course, they still had the translations on computer files. And it is, after all, the message that's most important. So many times throughout history, the personalities of great men, or the circumstances surrounding their lives, had become more important than their words, he thought. Reverence for Moses had become more important to many Old Testament Jews than his revelation of the One God above all others. The extraordinary circumstances surrounding the life of Jesus had become more important to those who professed to be his followers than the beauty and simplicity of his utterances. Even Mohammed had become revered as almost superhuman over the ages, to the near obfuscation of his sublime message.

Perhaps he could learn something from these and other similar episodes of history. The message of the Adam scrolls is what's important, more important than the scrolls themselves, their author, or the events surrounding their discovery. But the story they told was so different from the prevailing theories about Adam and Eve that Bruce felt certain nobody would believe them without hard evidence. Without the actual scrolls for people to see, he was sure the message they had carried for thousands of years would be lost.

Upon returning to his seat, Bruce looked at Lenny with a puzzled expression. Lenny returned the look by remaining silent and arching his eyebrows in the direction of the terrorist who was close enough to hear anything they might say.

* * *

The outside scene was now a full-blown national news event with satellite dishes and reporters scattered about the area. Microphones were in the faces of police officers, firemen and just about any other official looking person. News helicopters were flitting about the sky like seagulls over a dumpsite. Some were shooting aerial footage; others landed to disgorge more news teams. The crowd now numbered over two thousand and was still growing.

Perry Hazzard arrived at the police barrier outside the building. He approached Chief Donavan, who had just finished giving orders to some new arrivals, introduced himself and asked, "Anything new, Chief?"

The police officer took out a cigarette, offered one to Hazzard, who accepted and said, "Call me Kim, it looks like we're in for a long one and we might as well be on a first name basis. The hostage negotiator just got off the phone with the guy and he's rounding up some food for them. We've got our sharpshooters in place should an opportunity present itself, but that's between you and me. We can't let that get out. I don't think we'll be able to use those guys anyway." He lit his cigarette and held the lighter in his cupped hands for Hazzard.

Perry took a drag from the butt and asked, "Why not?"

"The guy's got a thumb actuated switch wired to the bomb. He explained it to our negotiator. Luckily it's not one of those that work by releasing thumb pressure. We'd have to worry about an accidental explosion if it was. But still, it only takes an instant to push that button and send the whole building up."

Hazzard wrote some notes on a pad and asked, "What about the sharpshooters? Can't they get a spinal cord shot? That would stop him from detonating the bomb."

Kim chewed on the filter of his cigarette. "A perfectly placed shot would do that."

"Right," Perry Hazzard said. "Sever his spinal cord and he wouldn't be able to press the button."

"But that's extremely risky. We haven't ruled it out, and we have our best men placed around the building, but it's our last option. For now, we're hoping the governments can get this settled peacefully. That's where you come in I guess. What's the latest on that?"

Hazzard leaned against the hood of a police car, took another drag and said while exhaling smoke, "It doesn't look very good. I just spoke with someone from the Secretary of State's office who told me the Israelis are adamantly opposed to releasing any terrorists."

"You can't blame them. It would just encourage others to try the same thing," Kim said.

Perry nodded his agreement. "You're right. And besides, our government has been saying the same thing for years."

"Part of me agrees with that position," Kim said. "More of me wants to see those people walk out of there in one piece, though."

"So where does that leave us now?" Perry asked. "It's three thirty in the afternoon and we seem no closer to a solution."

"We're leaving it in the hands of the hostage negotiator for the near term. That's him there, let me get him over here." The Captain waved for the negotiator to approach. "Perry Hazzard, this is Joe West. Joe, Mister Hazzard is the editor of the Chronicle. He has some questions for you."

Joe West looked at Hazzard, who wore a light blue shirt and a red tie, with navy blue jacket and pants. West, five foot six and dressed in jeans and a green flannel shirt, had to look up while shaking hands with the six-foot tall editor. "What can I do for you, Mister Hazzard?"

"For one thing, as Kim here said, we might as well be on a first name basis so I'm Perry and you're Joe. How are the hostages doing? One of my reporters is in there, as well as some friends of mine."

"They seem to be holding up well, Mist..., I mean, Perry. They assure me nobody's been harmed and they're allowed to use the bathroom when necessary. I just ordered some food and I'll try to convince him to let me bring it up to them."

"Why would you want to do that? What if he doesn't let you come back out?"

Joe West looked Perry Hazzard in the eyes and shrugged. "That's part of the job. If I can get in there, maybe I'll be able to see a weakness, or an opportunity for neutralizing the situation. It's also better to have hostage takers know what the person they're negotiating with looks like."

Perry remained silent for a moment. "I can see where that might help in some situations, like if you're dealing with a foiled bank robbery or something where the perpetrator is hoping to get out alive. But do you really think this guy cares about anything like that?"

West folded his arms across his chest and shrugged. "You're probably right, but it can't hurt for me to get in there. Anyway, when the food arrives I'll give it a shot."

Perry took a last drag on his cigarette and stomped it out. "What else are you doing? Will you be telling him about the Israeli's refusal to deal?"

Joe West shook his head. “No point telling him anything other than good news at this point. I did tell him this could take days. After all, we’re dealing with two governments. He didn’t want to hear that.”

“Do they ever?” Perry asked.

“Not really. But it planted the idea in his head that we might need an extension of his deadline.”

“How do you think he’ll react to that?” Hazzard asked.

“You’re asking questions I can’t answer, Perry. Let’s just see how it goes.”

Lenny answered the phone. Joe West told him the food had arrived. “He wants to talk to you,” he told the terrorist, holding the phone out toward him. While Mazen talked to the negotiator, Lenny decided to take the opportunity to speak with Bruce. “Bruce,” he quietly said, “did you see the stuff in the janitor’s closet?”

Bruce looked at Lenny with eyes askance and in a cautious tone asked. “What about it?”

Lenny checked to make sure Mazen was still engrossed in his phone conversation. “We can use some of those things to make something useful.”

“Useful in what way. You aren’t planning anything dangerous are you?”

Lenny decided to ignore the second question. “There’s bleach and drain cleaner in there. That’s a volatile mix. If we could somehow get them into a couple of glass containers, like jars or something, they’d make a pretty good chemical grenade we might use.”

“What about the dynamite on his body? Wouldn’t that go off too?”

Lenny shook his head slightly. “What I’m talking about wouldn’t explode. But it would create an acid that we could use to blind and confuse him for a while. Maybe long enough for us to overpower him.”

“Are you sure?”

“I took some chemistry courses in college. It’ll work. What do you think?”

Bruce, while carefully assuring himself the terrorist was still on the phone, said, “I don’t like it. It’s too risky. We need to trust the government to get us out of this.”

“What if the Israelis don’t release their prisoners?” Lenny asked. “We’ll be up Shit Creek then.”

“We’re all ready in Shit Creek now. What you’re talking about could get us killed. What if we get the jump on this guy and he sets the bomb off?” Bruce asked.

Lenny wanted to kick Bruce in the ass. He'd been through this kind of thing twice now. He should know the only chance the hostages have is to take matters into their own hands. He thought of a compromise. "Why don't we start making our chemical grenade? That way we'll have it if we need it."

Lenny saw that the others were listening in as well and said to them, "Reverend, you, Sheila, Phyllis and Roxanne need to keep your eyes facing front so that guy doesn't get any ideas about us planning anything."

Reverend Graves passed this on to Sheila and Roxanne, who were on his other side, while Lenny and Bruce continued talking quietly.

"What are you talking about?" Mazen said in a loud voice.

Like a six-headed, twelve-eyed, fear-ridden creature, the row of hostages looked in the direction of the terrorist. Lenny was relieved to see that the man was still talking into the phone. Apparently something the negotiator said had angered him.

As Lenny was about to resume their planning, he heard Mazen say, "Very well, but I will be watching your every move and you are to wear shorts and shoes only, nothing else. Is that understood?" The terrorist hung up the phone. He turned to his captives and said, "One man will be bringing the food. He will leave it outside the room and exit from the building before we open the door." He worked his way to the side of one of the windows and peeked through the curtains. Lenny looked at Bruce questioningly. Bruce discretely nodded his assent to the first step of the plan.

On the ground, Joe West was removing his jacket, pants and shirt while explaining the situation to Chief Donavan. "He won't let me into the room. I was hoping I might get a face to face with him."

West had just left for the school building with the food when Special Agent Dan Murphy, of the Boston FBI office, approached Kim Donavan and said, "Chief, can I speak to you for a moment in private?"

"Why don't we sit in your car," Donavan said.

Agent Murphy slammed the car door, then said, "I just got off the phone with Washington. The news isn't good. The Israelis have refused to even discuss releasing any terrorist prisoners."

"That's pretty much what we expected wasn't it?" Kim asked.

"Yes it is. The question now is what do we do about it. I've been ordered to take command of the situation as of five o'clock." He looked at his watch. "That's a little over twenty minutes from now."

"What are you talking about?" Kim asked.

Special Agent Murphy turned sideways to face the cop. "This comes from the White House. They want to make sure nothing goes wrong."

"What the hell does that mean? My men are all professionals who know their jobs. This isn't some backwater county with a part time rag tag sheriff running things. We're a major city police force, some of my men have even trained at Quantico," Kim said.

Murphy sighed. "Look, we don't want any conflict here. We both have our jobs to do. Your men will be responsible for maintaining the perimeter. Your SWAT team can stay in place along with your sharpshooters, but they'll be acting under my orders. Is that clear? Civilian lives are at stake and we can't afford to let personal disagreements interfere."

Captain Donavan remained silent. Finally he said, "I could fight you on this. But you're right about the safety of the hostages. I'll inform my men that you're in charge. Just remember, if anything goes wrong it's gonna be your ass, not mine." He left the vehicle, slamming the door a little harder than necessary, and informed his men of the change in command.

The classroom smelled like a fast food joint, and the hostages hungrily attacked the pizza and burgers laid out on Bruce's big desk. They had been allowed to get food one at a time. The terrorist was not allowing more than one person out of his or her seat at any time for any reason.

Sheila looked at Reverend Graves. She frowned. "Are you okay, Reverend?"

The Reverend looked at her with hound dog eyes. "I'm confused and saddened," he said. "I just don't see how somebody can use God as an excuse for violence. It's opposed to everything I believe."

"What do you believe, Reverend?" Lenny asked.

"It's a little complicated, Lenny," he answered. "I was raised in a strict fundamentalist family. Faith, morality, and just about everything else were colored black or white in my home. My parents brooked no behavior that even hinted we might be questioning the word of God. As a youngster I accepted this philosophy without question and tried my best to live up to my parent's expectations." His head sagged, shoulders slumped. "Until my brother got sick, that is."

"You never told me the story of how he died, Reverend," Sheila said. "What happened?"

"Timmy was two years younger than me and could do no wrong in my eyes." A smile appeared on his round, gray-beard-framed face. "He was quite the kid. We never engaged in the petty squabbling that our friends with brothers seemed to constantly enjoy. We were so much alike. The number of times we were compared to peas in a pod earned us the nicknames, 'Pea' and 'Pea-Wee'" He nodded with pride. "We wore those names like badges of honor."

"I'm guessing you weren't Pea-Wee," Lenny said as he grinned.

Sheila shot him a grimace in return.

"Sorry. Just trying to lighten the mood."

"That's all right, Lenny. I'm not offended. My weight is a burden in more than just a literal sense, but I've come to terms with it. Anyway, when Timmy came down with a bad cold, nobody thought much of it. As the symptoms grew worse and he lost strength and weight, some of our neighbors said that he should visit a doctor. My parents refused to even consider it. I asked them why.

"'God will cure him,'" they said. "'Prayer and faith are all that's needed.'"

"They really believed that?" Lenny asked.

Reverend Graves nodded. "So did I at the time. I took their words as literal truth and prayed my heart out."

He faced each captive before continuing. Lenny could see the others were as touched as he was.

"I pleaded with God, as Timmy got worse. I begged God, as Timmy got weaker." His voice lowered in volume and strength. His lungs deflated as if from an outside force.

"I volunteered my own life in exchange as Timmy's ebbed away." He looked at the ceiling, remained silent, and finally said, "I turned on God in wrath as Timmy died."

Sheila awkwardly took his taped hands into hers. "You had a right to be angry, Reverend," she comforted.

Lenny was touched by the look of appreciation?, acknowledgement?, adoration?, the Reverend gave Sheila. There was obviously a deep-felt response to Roxanne's kindness.

"I had a right to be angry, yes," he said. "But not at God. Nonetheless, it was God who in my ignorance was the focus of my wrath. My parents said that lack of faith and straying from the path of righteousness had caused God to take away that which I loved most. I knew better than that." His look hardened. "I had never lost faith. I never strayed, or if I had, the infractions were so minor that the punishment was all out of proportion to the crime. No, my parents had it all wrong, I thought. Only two options presented themselves to my young mind. Either there was no God. Or He was an asshole."

Sheila removed her hands from the Reverend's and covered her gasping mouth. "Reverend, how could you say such a thing?"

With a contrite expression he explained. "I was twelve years old, Sheila. My little brother had just died."

Sheila's look softened. "I'm sorry. I didn't mean it like that. I was just a little shocked to hear those words from you. Go on."

"As I grew older, the memories of my beloved brother sometimes dimmed, but like a perpetual candle, they never extinguished. I came to understand my childish reaction to Timmy's death. But I continued denying God's existence. The daily business of bad things happening to good people provided all the evidence I needed to verify this decision.

"I turned a small corner in high school science when we studied atoms and molecules."

"How the hell did that help you?" Lenny blurted.

Reverend Graves gave Lenny a benevolent smile. "I learned that the infinitesimal, lifeless things that make up our bodies never touch each other, yet work as an organized entity. This caused me to consider what life was. Where did it come from? How could a bunch of dead particles become animate and sentient?"

"I never thought about it like that," Lenny said. "How DOES that work?"

"That's one of the great mysteries, Lenny. We know these particles never touch each other. We know they're dead. How do they become living, breathing organisms?"

"Are you going to tell us?" Lenny asked.

"I would if I could."

"Isn't it your job to answer questions like that?" Lenny asked. "I mean, isn't this where God enters the equation?"

"I was still in high school, Len. I have theories now, but not then. Anyway, when I got to college as a liberal arts major, I met a girl." His eyes took on a faraway look. "Diane was a brown-eyed beauty with an outlook on life that said anything was possible."

"Mrs. Graves," Sheila said to Bruce and Roxanne.

The Reverend smiled. "I fell for her hard. This caused me to consider what love was. Where did IT come from? How could a bunch of dead particles, spinning around each other like tiny solar systems, never coming any closer to each other proportionally than the sun to the earth, produce the experience of caring for another so deeply that you'd sacrifice your own life to protect her? I couldn't fathom such emotion coming from itsy bitsy little dead rocks. There had to be more.

"These questions began eating away at my determination that God was a figment of man's imagination. There had to be something more than what met the eye. But if God did indeed exist, was He an asshole, as my youthful temper had imagined?" He looked around the room, gazed into the eyes of each hostage.

"There certainly was enough evidence around me in the guise of suffering innocents, high living gluttons, and war mongering despots to support such a thesis. But what about love? Compassion? Happiness? Joy? These too must be taken into consideration. I decided to seek answers."

"How do you research something like that?" Roxanne asked. "I mean, they're age old questions even the most revered philosopher's have wrestled with."

"Indeed," he said. "It wasn't easy. I started by exploring the world's religions. It wasn't long before I was struck by the many similarities they shared. Each attempted to guide its adherents to a better life. Most of them professed a belief in one God above all others; one who loved His children. Even many of their allegories and parables sought to teach similar lessons and followed related themes. Why was it their adherents couldn't get along with one another?" He looked at Mazen Mousaka with a gaze heavy with compassion.

"It is because the world sees not Allah as the One True God. When all call His name in brotherhood we will get along."

"But that's just it, Mazen," the Reverend said. "God cares not what you call Him. He cares only that you call."

"Foolishness," Mazen said.

Seeing no indication that he had to stop, Reverend Graves continued. "On the surface the answer to my question seemed simple enough. It was the sacred texts, ancient documents that purported to be the word of God to the exclusion of all others. At least that's what I thought at first. But upon further reflection I came to understand that it was those in positions of authority; they who claimed to understand what these texts said who were the root of the problem."

"What do you mean, Reverend?" Sheila asked.

"People who place themselves over others, Sheila. Like small time kings and potentates, they secure their personal fiefdoms from threats by dividing the world into we and they, us and them, insiders and outsiders. Do you see how, as long as there is a THEM to blame the trouble of the moment on, then WE have something to band against, to distract us, and a reason to relinquish control of our lives to the religious dictators?"

"Isn't that a little simplistic?" Lenny asked. "I think the world's problems are a bit more complicated than that."

Reverend Graves nodded. "Sure. I knew this was an oversimplification. But nonetheless, it boils the problem down to a manageable essence. Certainly race, class, geography, and many other elements are also contributing factors to the, 'us' vs. 'them', controversy. But think about it. Religion is the tool most readily used to propagate this mindset. It hovers over mankind like a mushroom cloud. Power hungry autocrats shamelessly manipulate the natural human quest to find, 'something more,' to feel a part of the whole. The religious impulse and its hope of life eternal is continually being subjugated to the fears of the small-minded."

"So how did that bring you to your faith?" Lenny asked.

"After years of thoughtful research and contemplative study, I came up with what I still consider an elegant solution. Everybody is we. Nobody is they. I found ample confirmation for this theme in many scriptures; the Koran, for one, says, 'All people are a single nation.'" He looked at Mazen with careful eyes.

"All people must form a single nation under Allah. That is the answer to your blasphemous questions," he said. "Go on. I am interested in your ramblings."

Reverend Graves looked as if he was going to say something to the terrorist. He must have thought better of it, Lenny conjectured, because he just frowned and continued his story.

"Since most of the world believed in one God, it seemed to me that it must be the same God. Whether She or He was called Allah, Jehovah, Earth Mother, Jesus, or any other name mattered not a wit to me, nor, I decided, to God. I came to understand that all religions had truth; some more than others, some with kernels of wisdom buried deep in the earth of strange tales, but truth was there to be discovered in all of them. To my way of thinking, it followed that all religions had error."

"But how do you separate truth from error, Reverend?" Roxanne asked. "That seems like the hard part to me."

Reverend Graves smiled at Roxanne. "You'd think so, wouldn't you. It was simple, really. It was just a matter of eliminating references to THEM wherever I found it and in whatever guise it wore. It doesn't matter one bit to me, nor to God I'm certain, what men eat, what women wear, or how people worship. What mattered were results. As Jesus put it so succinctly, 'By their fruits will you know them.'"

"But he was warning his followers about false prophets," Sheila said.

"True, Sheila. But those words are as concise a rendering of moral filtering as I've ever heard."

He sat straight and tried to arch his back, but Lenny could see his size and bound hands prevented relief. "I've taken part in many debates over this theory, and people say over and over that I can't pick and choose from the Bible, the Koran, the Torah, the Vedas, the Book of Mormon and other scriptures, what I want to believe and then discard the rest."

"Can you?" Lenny asked.

"Why not?" He said. "No one ever gave me a satisfactory answer to that question. Besides I wasn't picking what I WANTED TO BELIEVE. I was picking what I THOUGHT RIGHT AND GOOD. There's a world of difference."

"You have not the nerve to follow even your Christian religion," Mazen Mousaka said. "You choose what to believe like you choose food from a grocery store shelf. You are pitiful."

"It isn't like that, Mazen. It's more like entering a vegetable garden. You certainly wouldn't expect me to pick and eat everything growing from the ground. There are weeds and stems and hidden insects lurking about. One must be careful what one picks to nurture the body. You have to be more careful what you choose to feed your soul."

"Even so, Reverend," Roxanne said. "It can't be easy to pick the right from the wrong."

Reverend Graves finished his sandwich and clumsily gathered the wrappings into a ball. He smiled at Roxanne and continued. "Actually, my criteria is simple. Whatever tends to separate God's children from one another is wrong, or has been misinterpreted, or is being misapplied. Whatever tends to bring us together into the family of humanity is right. Exclusionary words and rhetoric are out. Inclusionary teachings are in. And from what I've just read in these extraordinary documents you have discovered, I'm right."

"I have to admit everything you've said fits in with what we've just learned," Bruce said. He flipped through his copy of the scrolls with his greasy hands. "Listen to what it says here, 'Mankind has but one Heavenly Parent. The One Source and Center desires that all humanity live as a family.'" He looked at the Reverend. "So how did you end up where you did?"

"I married Diane right out of college. Together we discovered a church that fit in with my ideas. We became active members of the congregation. In fact, we became so involved that when the church pastor retired, the job and title, Reverend, were offered to me. I was overjoyed."

He grinned such a huge smile that Lenny was reminded of Santa Clause. All he had to do was dye his beard white.

"I joyfully accepted, of course and have been at the Church of the Shepherd ever since."

"And you went on to author several well-accepted books expounding on your theory of choosing what to believe based on your conscience, moral compass and good sense," Lenny finished.

"That's it," the Reverend said. "My story in a nutshell. He turned to the terrorist. "Mazen, may I ask you something?"

The man looked at his captive and sneered. "What is it?"

Reverend Graves said, "As you've just heard, I've made it a point in my life to study the religions of the world and I would like to learn more about Islam if I could."

"It is wise to seek knowledge of Allah and the Prophet, peace be upon him. You may be meeting them very soon. Perhaps the Maker will show you mercy for this."

"I've heard you use that name twice now. Is that one of the ninety-nine most beautiful names of Allah?" the Reverend asked.

"It is indeed," Mazen said between bites of his sandwich. "It is my favorite. Allah made everything. The Maker is an appropriate name."

"I've heard the most common of the ninety-nine names is Allah the Compassionate and Merciful. As a man of the cloth, I know in my heart that God is all-merciful. Do you think He would condone what you are doing here? Do you think you are acting in compassion and showing mercy?"

"Do not presume to know the mind of Allah. Have I not allowed you food and drink? Do I not allow the use of the bathroom? Is that not compassion? Would you prefer that I end these privileges?"

Reverend Graves looked at his fellow captives and observed their different expressions, ranging from concern to out right hostility. "No, no, that isn't what I meant. Certainly we are grateful for your kindness. What I meant to ask is, shouldn't all Muslims, and indeed all who profess to do God's will, attempt to show mercy and compassion in their daily lives?"

Mazen put his sandwich in its wrapper on the desk and began walking in small circles at the front of the room with his hands clasped behind him, thumb ever present on the fatal red button. "I could as easily ask you where is mercy and compassion when the Zionists kill innocent women and children in my homeland. Where is mercy and compassion when a whole people are living in occupied lands, forced to exist in squalor and on handouts? Where is mercy and compassion when the Muslims of Afghanistan are invaded by the Soviet Empire, whose soldiers also kill and rape women and children? Must I go on?"

Reverend Graves nodded in sadness; the wrinkles under his large chin folding like an accordion as he did so. "We all understand that injustices abound in the world. But does that excuse the killing of more innocents? Do two wrongs make a right?"

The terrorist was now pacing back and forth. As his steps quickened so too did his words. "The governments of the infidels understand only one language, that of force. They talk of peace. They talk of cooperation. They talk of economic assistance. But their actions make lies of their words. Ask your native citizens, the American Indians. Do they not have a saying that the white man speaks with a forked tongue?"

"But that was during the early days of our country," Reverend Graves countered. "We have learned from our past. Things are different now."

"Are they so different? Throughout history westerners have sought to control and exploit others for their own purposes. It is time for this to end. Allah wills it and it shall be so."

Roxanne interjected. "You speak of westerners as if we are not children of Adam. Have you ever heard this quote from Mohammed? 'The Arab has no superiority over the non-Arab and the non-Arab has no superiority over the Arab. They are all children of Adam.' That's a direct quote I came across one time that has always stuck with me."

The terrorist stopped his pacing, stretched to his full height and looked directly at Roxanne with his black, penetrating eyes. "This is not a matter of superiority, woman. We are talking about respect and humane treatment of women and children. My people want and deserve to be treated with respect in our own homeland. The occupying Zionists humiliate us and denigrate us every day. They force us to beg for what is rightfully ours. They took our country from us and we will not rest until the day we have it back."

Reverend Graves said, "The Koran also says, 'Allah does not change a people's state until they change what is within themselves.'"

From the front of the classroom, Mazen Mousaka pointed his right index finger at the Reverend like a schoolteacher pointing at a miscreant student. His nostrils flared and his jaw clenched as he said, "Are you trying to say that my people brought this state of affairs upon themselves? Be mindful of your words. My patience is not without limits."

"Forgive me. My words are clumsy. What I was trying to say," the Reverend said, "is that a peaceful solution can be found if the people involved desire it. And I mean both sides, not just one or the other."

"There can be no peaceful solution. The Jews must be expelled from the Palestinian homeland. They have no right to be there and must be forced into the sea."

"But surely," Reverend Graves persisted, "Allah wants His children to live in peace and harmony. The true purpose of religion is to bring people together, after all, not set them in conflict with each other."

Mazen was pacing back and forth in ever quickening steps. His arms were flailing about as he accented his words with finger pointing and fist clenching. "False religions separate men. Islam seeks to protect all under the umbrella of Allah. It is only the stubbornness of the blind that keeps them from seeing this. When all accept Allah and the Prophet, peace be upon him, then you shall have peace."

Reverend Graves said, "My parents used to voice similar arguments, but while espousing a different God. Don't you see that there is only one Creator and what He's called is unimportant? You call Him Allah. I call Him God. The Jews call Him Yahweh. We're all praying to the same being."

"I warned you to be mindful of your words," Mazen said. "Allah is the one true God and I will hear of nothing else. Do you understand?"

Reverend Graham nodded his understanding as his shoulders drooped. He thought he should know how to handle this disagreement. After all, it was his life's work to help people to understand God's love, to understand that all of humanity shared the same parent. "We both agree that Allah created everything and everyone. It follows then that even the Jews are His children and therefore your brothers."

With cat like quickness and athletic grace the terrorist took his pistol from his overcoat, pounced to the front of Reverend Graves' seat in three steps, cocked the hammer and placed the muzzle to his forehead. "I warned you about blaspheming. This talk is ended."

He pulled the trigger and the room echoed with the sound of the discharge and the screaming of the women as it filled with the smell of burned gunpowder. The body of Reverend Burl Graves slid out of its seat and dropped to the floor like the piece of meat it now was.

"Oh my God," Sheila screamed as she rushed to the body and tried to comfort her dead boss and friend. She knelt down and cradled the blood soaked head in her lap as best she could with her taped hands. She looked at the hole just above the left eyebrow from which a trickle of blood was dripping, even as a river of blood flowed from the exit wound and soaked her dress, then she looked at the killer. With tears streaming down her face, she screamed, "You bastard! He never harmed anyone in his life. He was a man of God who always tried to do the right thing. You killed him because you think you know God and he didn't? How dare you!"

The murderer stood over the two bodies, one dead, the other quivering with too much rage to know fear. He calmly aimed the gun at Sheila's head. "You may join him if you wish. It matters not to me."

Roxanne and Phyllis clamored for Sheila to get back in her seat, while Lenny was being physically constrained by Bruce from making matters worse. "Mazen," Bruce said while holding Lenny with his back. "Please let her get back to her seat. She's upset. Please forgive her."

He looked at Bruce and said, "First, she and you will dump the body out the window. I do-"

"Noooooo," Sheila screamed before the man could finish.

Bruce turned to look at Lenny who seemed to be in control of himself at the moment, then made his way toward Sheila and the body of Reverend Graves, carefully eyeing the terrorist as he did so. He knelt beside her and said, "Sheila, he's dead. His body doesn't matter any more."

Sheila looked at Bruce with fierce determination and gasped through her tears, "How can you say that? He was your friend too."

He tried to hold her, to comfort her, but his taped hands would not allow it. "It's because he was my friend that I know he wouldn't want any of us to get hurt over this. We have to do what this man says."

She took Bruce's hands into her own and they hugged each other as best they could. For the next minute her sobs were all that could be heard in the room.

TWENTY-SEVEN

The Resident Patient

Nestled within a neighborhood of nondescript concrete block two-level homes on the back streets of Nablus, in the West Bank region of Palestine, the house presents no external clues to its true purpose. Its drab color scheme and uninspiring design lack character and distinction; just another mongrel among littermates. Only those allowed within its confines know for certain what goes on inside. The neighbors conjecture. They gossip. But they can only guess.

When the tall bearded man was carried in on a stretcher in the middle of the night, few noticed. When more people than usual began trekking into and out of the home shortly thereafter, none cared. When well-known faces began to come and go, the local doctor, the Imam from the nearby mosque among them, some speculated.

When one man came to the house, the neighbors knew for certain that an important personage was recuperating inside. That man was Sheik Ahmed Yassin, the founder of HAMAS and the second most influential Palestinian after Chairman Arafat. Sheik Yassin did not waste his valuable time on unimportant people, they knew. Whoever the mysterious patient was, he had to be a man of value to the cause.

Inside the small house, the recently arrived man lay upon the narrow bed in the back bedroom. He moved in fitful sleep, mumbling incoherently about infidels, death, and revenge. His wounds were covered with bloody bandages. The look on his face, as he jerked his head left and right, was of desperation and loss. Filthy, sweat soaked military fatigues covered the fever ravaged, one-legged, one-armed body of the suffering man. He awoke with a start and sat upright against the headboard, using his good arm for support. "Sami!" he yelled. "Sami, come in here."

A young boy of about thirteen came running into the room. "How can I be of assistance?" he asked with downcast eyes.

"It is time for my medicine. Why did you not wake me for this? You know if I am to recover, I must fight off this infection that is ravaging my body."

"Forgive me," the boy said. "You were sleeping and I feared disturbing you. You called upon Allah in your dreams and I prayed He was with you in your time of need."

Assad's expression softened. "Come to me," he said in a warm voice, beckoning with his stump. When Sami approached the bed, Assad placed his hand upon the boy's head and tousled his hair. "You are a good boy. I only wish your thoughts of my dreams were true. But, such is not the case." He removed his hand from the boy's hair and looked out of the small window to his right with a far off gaze. "I was out there. With my men. We were exacting our revenge. All was going according to Allah's will. Then suddenly, without warning, we were outnumbered. Chaos ensued, and once again I lost my arm and leg." He returned his eyes to the boy. His lips tightened and his jaw clenched as yet another jolt of pain circuited through his body. "How many times must I relive those moments? When will Allah grant me peace? How much longer will He punish me for failing Him?"

The boy Sami shook his head vigorously. "You have not failed Allah, Assad. You are mujahedin, a warrior of God, a son of our homeland. Palestine is blessed to have you fighting on the righteous side of our Holy War."

"Blessed? Better you should say cursed. Bring to me today's newspaper with my medicine."

Sami left the room and returned moments later with a battered metal tray, upon which sat a glass of water, three pill bottles and a newspaper. He left the tray on the small table beside the bed and exited the room. Assad opened the bottles using his teeth and his good hand, took out varying numbers of pills from each and swallowed the mouthful with a large gulp of water. He picked up the paper, clumsily opened it onto his lap, and began reading.

There was the usual coverage of local and international events of importance to Palestinians. On most days, Assad would immediately devour the stories of attacks and excursions against the Israeli oppressors. Despite the fact that more of his brothers died in these operations than Jews, he considered each Zionist death a small triumph, the laying of another paving stone on the beaten path to victory. But today he was looking for another story. Today was the day that Mazen would exact his revenge upon the hated American reporter who had twice escaped Assad's clutches.

He rapidly turned the pages in search of what he was looking for. On page five he found it. Mazen had done it. He had the reporter Lenny Cronin in his grasp. He also had the two American professors, a bonus. Allah be praised.

He thought about his lifelong friend. He remembered when they were street urchins and had first competed for leadership of their small band. Over and over again, Assad had beaten the smaller Mazen into the ground. Each time he seemed on the verge of defeat, the determined Mazen Mousaka would somehow wrangle out of Assad's grip and continue fighting. Even when it was obvious that he had no chance of winning, and when three boys held him down so that he couldn't continue with a losing battle, he had managed to free himself to renew the fight. Yes, Mazen was a very determined soldier of Allah. If anyone could be relied upon to carry out this mission, it was he, whom Assad considered his one true brother.

How he missed his compatriot. Ever since Assad had sent Mazen on the secret mission to the United States, he'd felt the loss of his closest confidante. Assad was a hard man. Death and danger were travelling companions every step of his journey. He had allowed himself no wife, no personal involvements of any kind, knowing full well that the Israelis retaliate against family and loved ones. But Mazen was different. He too was an orphan. He too was without family. They had only each other. That was enough.

When Assad had sent the order for the phone call to be placed, he had wanted to speak with Mazen directly. He resisted the desire for fear he'd be overcome at the sound of his brother's voice. Somehow Assad's missing arm and leg had come to symbolize the missing fraternity of the two freedom fighters. A part of him felt that if Mazen were to return, the void created by the absent limbs would be less empty, less cavernous, less devastating. He feared that his will would falter if he spoke directly with Mazen. As badly as he wanted to see his brother in the flesh, he wanted revenge even more. And Mazen was the last weapon in his arsenal. He was also the most reliable.

Assad reflected on the visitor who had come to him four nights ago. Sheik Yassin was paying his respects to Assad when he had casually mentioned Mazen and asked what he'd been up to the last two years.

"He is in America," Assad said.

"That is a surprise indeed, my friend," Sheik Yassin said. "Why have you not told me of this before? What is he doing there? Training partisans for the cause, I hope."

"He has been living the quiet life, keeping his presence unknown. Certainly, he has been recruiting at some of the mosques. But his main task is to lie in wait, to disappear into the underbrush of American society, only to emerge as a Lion of God delivering death to those who wantonly seek our destruction."

"And he has accomplished this, your Lion of God? He has been able to keep his presence and plans a secret? And if so, what can we learn from this?"

Assad nodded slowly. For the first time in days his lips curled upward. "None are aware of this except you and I. We can duplicate this maneuver. We can have small groups of assassins in waiting throughout America and Europe ready to wreak havoc at our command. We shall exploit the weakness of their so-called open societies. It will lead to their downfall. Mark my words."

Sheik Yassin nodded thoughtfully. For a full moment only the sounds of the street could be heard from outside the bedroom window. Assad listened to the voices of the children playing with sticks in the dirt. He wondered how much more time would pass before his people would be allowed to live life as it was meant to be, as Allah meant it to be.

"We need to test your theory," the Sheik said. "After all, Mazen has been living among the ungodly for two years. His resolve may have weakened in that time. Before I commit to this plan, I want to see action. If Mazen proves worthy and carries out his orders, we shall finance more of these cells."

"He only awaits the day of my call," Assad said. "And I know just what task to request of him. Mazen will achieve martyrdom, Allah will be pleased, and I," he held up his right stump of an arm, "will have my revenge."

The phone call had been placed. The orders delivered. And now here it was in the world's newspapers. Mazen had proven his faithfulness just as Assad knew he would. His heart swelled with pride at the great gift Mazen Mousaka was about to present to Allah.

As Assad continued reading the news reports, he wondered if the Israelis would release his fellows. The effectiveness of hostage taking had yet to be proven, he knew. Some of his brother fighters from Hezbollah had hijacked a jet plane with its passengers while enroute to Athens from Rome during the previous summer. Seeking the release of their Shiite brothers, they had not accomplished what they set out to. And just last week, sixty people had died in a hail of commando bullets when Abu Nidal had hijacked an Egyptian airliner to Malta. Assad thought the suicide bomber was the missing ingredient. Pack enough explosives onto the body of a holy warrior to do some serious damage and the governments would listen. If they knew they would be seeing God that day, by way of dynamite, commandos would think twice before storming the scene. The suicide bomber was the weapon of choice, the ultimate weapon against which no strategy could be effective. Then governments of the west would be forced to address his people's concerns. They would have no choice but to reconsider their moral and material support for the hated Zionists that infested his homeland.

Half way across the world, Joe Rizzo Senior was driving home from his Boston office. As he sped north on Route ninety-three toward New Hampshire, he was listening to the news reports about the hostage crisis. What a turn of events that was. He thought about the ancient scrolls hidden in his secret wall safe and wondered if anyone had yet discovered they were missing. Probably not, he decided. The reason he'd had them stolen in the first place was because he'd learned that copies were being used for the translation work and the originals were just sitting in a drawer. Hell, if the place blew up with everybody in it, no one would ever know they'd been stolen. Wouldn't that be something? When the station he was listening to changed to another topic, he began searching for more news on the crisis.

"Hey, fuck you, asshole!" he yelled, as a car passed him on the left with horn blaring. When he returned his eyes to the road he realized he'd wandered into the other car's lane while fiddling with the radio. He swerved back into his own lane and continued searching for news on the hostages.

Another car passed him with its horn screaming. He looked up. Once again his car was wandering from its lane. Jesus, he hated his daily commute. There were plenty of times he'd considered moving his business to the suburbs, but had decided against it. Too many meetings in the city to bother doing business elsewhere.

Joe Rizzo found a station covering the hostage situation. He picked up his cell phone from its cradle and began calling his office.

"Rizzo Companies," his secretary answered.

"Shirley, is my dumb-ass son there yet?"

"No, Mister Rizzo. I haven't heard from him today. It's almost five-thirty and I'll be going home soon. Do you want me to page him?"

"Never mind. I'll page him myself. The dumb shit was supposed to be back with the Jensen contract signed, sealed and delivered by now. If he screwed up again I swear I'll boot his ass out of the house and disown him." He hung up without saying another word.

Rizzo took his right hand off the steering wheel and reached over to the passenger seat of the Mercedes to open his brief case. It was uncomfortable trying to look for his address book due to the constraints of his seat belt. He unhooked the safety harness and leaned toward the passenger seat while rummaging through the valise. As he tilted more to the right, he unknowingly turned the steering wheel in the same direction.

Suddenly he felt a force from the right front of the car pushing it to the left. As the black Mercedes bounced off the car in the right lane, he felt it veer more sharply to the left. His natural response of pulling the car away from the impact, combined with the momentum of the rebound, caused an over-reaction and he found the car forcefully entering the left lane where it caromed off a large delivery truck.

The force of the impact with the truck turned Rizzo's vehicle sideways. The car behind him slammed into the passenger side of the Mercedes, which was now totally out of Rizzo's control and under the influence of the laws of action and reaction. In a matter of seconds, car after car joined the tire-screeching, glass-shattering, metal-crunching melee like football players piling onto a fumbled ball.

All became quiet, except for the sound of the cars passing in the opposite lanes. The pileup of vehicles sat with steaming radiators, flattened tires, and hanging metal parts. Slowly, people began climbing from cars and trucks as traffic in the rear ground to a halt.

Good Samaritans began helping the injured and the trapped.

Joe Rizzo's unconscious body was sprawled face down on the hood of his big black Mercedes. His life's blood flowed down the car's bonnet and dripped onto the ground, where it mixed with the green radiator coolant to form a macabre cocktail.

TWENTY-EIGHT

The Final Problem

At the police barrier, the sound of the gunshot that had killed Reverend Graves instigated a flurry of activity. Men were talking on their radios or cell phones, others were huddled in small groups to discuss possible responses; still others became more determined than ever to get a clean shot at the terrorist.

FBI Special Agent Murphy, State Police hostage negotiator Joe West, and local Police Captain Kim Donavan were discussing the implications of the pistol report when their attention was drawn to a window of the classroom that was the center of the mounting crisis. "Holy Shit," Murphy said, as they watched a corpulent male body being dumped to the ground. "Who is that?"

Perry Hazard approached the group. "Damn. That looks like Reverend Graves." He lowered his gaze to the ground. His shoulders lost all pretenses to good posture. He expelled a deep breath. "Why would that maniac kill him? He was a good man."

"This changes everything," agent Murphy said as he headed for his car. "West, get on the horn with that guy to find out what happened. I'm going to contact Washington. Don't do anything 'til I get back."

Joe West didn't need some know-it-all Fed telling him how to do his job. He was already on the phone dialing the number. The answering voice was that of the terrorist.

"Your call was expected," Mazen said without preamble. "You now know we mean business. What news have you for me? I warn you, my patience is wearing thin."

"Why did you kill that man?"

"Better you should ask, why haven't I killed others," the terrorist responded in a voice coated with false charm. It chilled the experienced negotiator to the bone.

"Don't you understand this has undermined any leverage I had in getting your demands carried out?"

"Do you not understand that the death of the false man of God is but the first of many if my demands are not carried out?"

Joe West knew that under normal circumstances he needed to stall for as much time as possible. The longer these situations took to play out, the better the odds of a satisfactory outcome. But the game had entered a new phase now, and normalcy had been thrown out the window with Reverend Graves' body. Investigation had revealed the name of the janitor and a report had just come in about the killer from Israeli sources. Mazen Mousaka was no psycho on an imaginary mission from God, as Joe had hoped. This guy was a stone cold killer whom the Israeli's suspected of being involved in many brutal murders.

Joe West had already decided it would be too risky to let the terrorist know about the outright refusal of the Israelis to release any prisoners. At the same time, he had to be careful not to get caught in any lies. That might lead to more deaths. But lies were needed right now. Lies that would hopefully give the authorities time to formulate an effective rescue plan.

"The Israelis have decided to co-operate and will be releasing your comrades as soon as they can co-ordinate the logistics of the process. It's going to take time though."

"You know exactly how much time you have. It was forty-eight hours from this morning. It is now down to approximately thirty-nine. My demands have not changed."

Joe West looked at the window of the university building. The bastard was brazenly peering out from behind the closed curtains. Joe wondered if this might present an opportunity for the SWAT team. He spoke into the phone. "We're doing all we can to expedite the release of the prisoners, but it's a larger task than you might think."

"This is a simple matter. The Jews open their doors and my brothers walk out."

"Don't forget your friends are scattered throughout the country. The word I have is they haven't even confirmed the whereabouts of some of the names you've given us. Are you sure you spelled all of them correctly?"

"The list of names is accurate. The Zionists are playing games. I warn you I will not be toyed with. Take heed of my words or more will die. The next time I talk to you, I want to hear that the freedom fighters have been released."

Joe kept the conversation going for a few minutes with more questions about Reverend Graves and why he had been killed. He was trying to continue stalling when the line went dead. He called Agent Murphy over to relay the gist of the conversation.

"What do you think the bottom line is?" Murphy asked.

"We can't stall much longer. He gave us permission to remove the body so let's get that out of the way."

Murphy relayed instructions for this over his command radio, then asked, "Do you think this guy will kill anyone else before the deadline? There's no way I'm going to just sit here and let that happen."

Joe looked at Agent Murphy shook his head and said, "Your guess is as good as mine. I told him I couldn't promise anything if any more killings happen. I also told him his comrades would definitely not be released if anyone else gets hurt. I came up with an idea while we were talking."

"What kind of idea?"

"His attention when speaking on the phone is divided between talking and watching the hostages. I think that might allow us to make a move or two."

"What do you mean?" Murphy asked.

"If we can keep him on the phone long enough, we might be able to get the SWAT team into the building without his knowledge."

"That would be nice," Agent Murphy said. "But he never stays on for more than a minute or two. That might not be enough time."

"If we could get someone he knows, or knows of and respects, to talk to him we could get more time."

"Who would that be?" Murphy asked.

"There's a local Muslim cleric on the way here. The guy's a moderate, but still commands the respect of the radicals. When he gets here, we'll ask him to call the guy and keep him on the phone for us."

"If he can do that, the shooters can be in place within minutes. I'll relay the orders to get this going," Murphy said. "You let me know the minute that cleric gets here."

Lenny needed to convey his plan for creating a chemical grenade to the others. He also had to do this covertly. How the hell was he going to get them to understand what he wanted without slipping up? Bruce already knew, of course. But how could they have an innocent sounding conversation without clueing in the killer? Then he thought of something. "Hey Bruce. Did you watch TV last night?"

A surprised Bruce looked at Lenny and said, "A little bit. Why?"

"Did you see that movie, 'The Breakfast Club'?" Lenny studied Bruce's face and knew he wasn't getting it. He seemed to know Lenny was trying to say something, but had no idea what. "You know. The one about all the kids in Saturday detention. It was on last night."

"What are you talking about?" Mazen demanded.

Lenny looked in the direction of the dark-eyed man, but saw only the pistol muzzle aimed at him. He then looked at the puddle of coagulating blood only inches from his feet. His stomach suddenly seemed as empty as a fresh dug grave. His initial impulse was to sink quietly into his seat and shut the hell up. Why should he always be the one to put his life on the line? Let the pros do the rescue work. He saw Mazen waiting for an answer. Screw it, the pros were going to need inside help and he was drafted to fill the position. "I'm just trying to pass some time. I saw a good movie on TV last night, that's all."

He turned to Bruce after the terrorist, seemingly satisfied with the answer, had turned toward the window. "Did you see it?"

Still sending Lenny a confused look, Bruce answered. "No. But I've seen it before. It is pretty good." He turned to Roxanne. "We've watched it together a couple of times, right, Babe?"

Lenny looked at Roxanne expectantly. He could see it was now her turn to play–What the hell you talkin' 'bout? "Yes . . . What about it?" she answered.

"Remember how they handled their boredom?" Lenny asked. "They secretly fashioned a pipe so they could get high in the closet?" Roxanne seemed about to protest so Lenny started nodding vigorously. The last thing he wanted was a disagreement over what the movie was about. Of course there had been no such scene. Lenny's stupidly clownish expression, on a head bobbing up and down like a recently sprung jack in the box, had the desired effect and Roxanne said nothing.

Lenny turned to Bruce, who seemed on the verge of saying something, and signaled to let him carry the ball for now. "You remember, Rox." Lenny turned toward the terrorist who was looking outside through the window and was apparently still satisfied at the inanity of the conversation. "They took turns making the pipe out of things they had hanging around in the coat closet." He looked at the terrorist again to make sure that last word hadn't set off any alarms. So far, so good.

Roxanne's puzzled expression shifted gears to neutral. Lenny could almost hear the squirrel running on its little wheel as options ran through her mind. Then her lips started curling upward slightly. "I think I remember," Roxanne said very slowly. "Was that when they were so bored they felt they had to do something or they'd just die?"

Lenny laughed. "Yeah that's it. They just had to do something. That was pretty funny." He faced Sheila and Phyllis. "Did you two see it?"

Roxanne turned toward them as well. "You remember. They were all just hanging around in detention. Bored silly. They made a pipe out of tin foil, using pencils and whatever else they could find to make something that would save them from the boredom."

Roxanne had the right idea. Bruce had picked up on it too. Lenny decided not to push the conversation too far. He feared Mazen might also lock onto the gist of it. It was time to do something. He asked permission to use the janitor's closet. Mazen nodded absentmindedly, and Lenny made his way to the small room. Once inside, he quickly began assembling a crude device from the articles stored on the shelves.

He took two latex gloves from a box and laid them over the lip of the stainless steel sink. He opened the bottle of bleach and poured as much of it into one glove as possible while leaving room to tie the top tightly. He pulled the strings from some tampons, and used one of those to seal the glove. He then filled the other glove with drain cleaner and tied it off tightly.

His next task had not yet been thought out. He only knew he must somehow tie the two gloves together in such a way as to insure they remained a single device while not hampering the mixture of the two chemicals when the gloves burst. He couldn't tape them together, as the tape would strengthen the glove's surface and prevent it from rupturing. Tying the two gloves together with string would create too many small pockets within the gloves, hindering the release of the chemicals. He thought of a way, but it required starting from scratch and he feared being in the closet too long would arouse suspicion. He decided he must try.

Lenny took two more empty gloves, and carefully tied the thumb and pinky finger of each to its twin. He tested the knots and was satisfied that he now effectively had one device with two separate compartments. He was about to fill each cavity with chemicals when he heard Mazen's voice.

"What are you doing in there? Come out now." The murderer said.

Lenny quickly placed everything behind the toilet paper box and turned on the sink's water faucet. "I'm just finishing up now," he said through the closed door.

Lenny opened the door and found himself looking down the barrel of the terrorist's pistol yet again. Muzzle-staring was beginning to feel like some macabre ritual.

"Get out here." Mazen ordered, while standing aside for his captive to pass. As Lenny walked to his seat, Mazen looked into the closet and carefully surveyed its interior. The hostages eyed each other nervously as their captor slowly looked at everything he could see without leaving the confines of the classroom. He slammed the closet door and made his way to the front of the room.

"From now on, there will be a time limit when using that room," he said. "Two minutes only will be allowed."

"What about the women?" Lenny asked. "They need more time than that." Lenny knew that Arab men were notoriously shy regarding anything to do with a woman's private parts. He guessed that this man was no different and would be uncomfortable even discussing such a horrible thing.

Mazen looked disgusted as he said, "Very well, three minutes for the women and two minutes for the men. That is the end of this matter. I will talk about it no more."

Bruce asked, "What about sleep? Can we get some blankets and pillows sent up for the night?" He looked at the clock on the wall. "It's almost seven o'clock and it will be dark soon."

The others expressed agreement, both verbally and with vigorous body language. "I'm already getting tired from sitting in this chair all day," Roxanne said.

Mazen looked from hostage to hostage as they continued clamoring for the blankets. "Enough. You are worse than children." He faced Lenny. "You, get on the phone and tell the man who brought the food what you want."

Lenny made his way to the phone and dialed. He spoke to Joe West for a minute then handed the handset to the terrorist who took it and began issuing orders for the way he wanted the pillows and blankets delivered.

Lenny returned to his seat and quietly informed the others how he had tied the two gloves together but they still needed filling with the chemicals.

"I'm still not on board with this plan," Bruce said. "Something could go wrong."

Lenny kept his eyes on the terrorist as he said to Bruce, "Go wrong? Look around you Bruce. We're all gonna die if we don't do something. Besides, it's just for insurance. Maybe we won't need it. But if we do, we'll have it."

Bruce remained quiet for a half minute. It seemed like an hour to Lenny. "Okay," he finally said. "But only for insurance."

They decided to wait until the arrival of the blankets before anyone would ask permission to use the closet, in the hopes that the terrorist would be too distracted to pay attention to the clock.

"How much of the translations did you read?" Roxanne asked Bruce.

"I read the whole thing," he answered. "Why?"

"What do you think of the description of the first Garden of Eden? And the location?"

Bruce shrugged. "Interesting, I guess. A little too early to tell if it's meaningful though. Don't you think?"

"Did you pick up on the resemblance to Plato's description of Atlantis? I found quite a few similarities. And the scrolls claim the original garden sank into the Sea in the Middle of the Land, which was formed by the Great Ocean rushing in. Sounds like the Mediterranean to me."

"What are you saying, Rox? That Atlantis was real? That the Garden of Eden was Atlantis?"

Lenny listened as Roxanne listed a litany of cross-references between Plato's depiction of Atlantis and the Garden of Eden as described in the scrolls. He was impressed by her catalogue-like memory. Between particulars of temples, locations of geographic reference points, and the names of inhabitants, she ticked off more than a dozen similarities. Could she be right? Shit, this science stuff was getting more interesting by the minute. But would they live long enough to verify any of this?

"I'm telling you, Bruce," Roxanne finished, "We went looking for Eden and found Atlantis too. They are one and the same."

About an hour later, while the blankets, pillows and some more food were arriving, Sheila received permission to use the janitor's closet. A few minutes after that she emerged and, while seating herself, discreetly nodded to the others, indicating she had completed the task of creating their home made chemical grenade. Lenny still had no idea how they would utilize the device to free them from this nightmare turned real, but at least it was ready.

Joe West was talking to the Muslim cleric who had just arrived at the police barrier. The well-respected man was fingering his long, gray, beard as he listened to the hostage negotiator's request for help. "So you see, sir, if you can convince this man to give himself up, I guarantee he will be treated humanely and in full accordance with our laws."

"I understand what you ask, Mister West. Islam abhors the killing of innocents. I pray for God's mercy on the Reverend Graves, whom I knew as a good man. I will do what I can to help end this with no more deaths."

Joe West handed the phone to the Imam and winked toward Agent Murphy, who began speaking into his command radio.

Five minutes later, Murphy received confirmation from the SWAT team leader that his men were at the back of the building ready to enter. The spectators weren't allowed on this side, as the shore of a small lake came within two hundred feet of the back. "Is there anything, and I mean anything, to indicate you were seen?"

After a delay of a few seconds, the reply came. "No, Sir. Everything looks calm and quiet back here."

"All right then, make your way into the building and then up to the third floor. Don't go any further until ordered to. Understand?"

When he was assured that the man understood his orders, Murphy put the radio down and said to Chief Parolisi, "The SWAT team will be in place soon. We still don't have any idea if we can use them, but if needed they'll be ready."

"What time do you figure they'll be in position?" the Chief asked.

Murphy looked at his watch and said, "They'll be on the third floor in a few minutes. From that point on I'll issue orders to go very slowly and carefully until they can cover the classroom from all angles. They should be in position before that priest gets off the phone."

"He's not a priest, Murphy," Kim said. "They call them Imams."

Murphy smirked and said, "Okay, so they should be in position before the IMAM gets off the phone. Does that satisfy your little PC mind?"

Joe West had just approached the two men and hadn't heard what was said. When he saw Parolisi lunge at the FBI agent, he grabbed the captain and held him before any damage could be done. "C'mon Kim. I don't know what this asshole said, but he isn't worth it. Let's concentrate on the situation and forget personalities for now. How about it?"

"You're right," Kim said. "We need to think about the hostages. He just told me the SWAT team is almost in position."

"So then we'll have to make a decision pretty soon," Joe said, as he released Kim from his grasp. "The guy's getting antsy. While the blankets and pillows were being brought up he told me they might not be needed."

"You think he might not give us the amount of time he promised?" Murphy asked.

Joe West threw up his hands and said, "Who knows for sure. I'm just passing on what the guy said. One thing's certain though, without a change in position by the Israelis, we'll be either blasting our way in there in a rescue action, or the hostages will be blasting out of there in pieces. Either way, innocent people are going to die."

Mahmud was still standing in the crowd to the side of the building. He'd called Mazen and warned him that he thought the SWAT team was still somewhere in the area. He had also seen some movements that caused him concern. The men he'd earlier observed trying to blend in with the crowd had disappeared. He looked everywhere but could not find one of them. Something was definitely afoot. He hit redial on his cell phone.

During the activity of bringing in the blankets, pillows, and food, the phone rang. It wasn't the cell phone the hostage negotiator had brought, though. Mazen was currently using that one. The ringing was coming from Bruce's classroom phone. When Lenny went to pick it up, the terrorist gave him a withering look and gestured that he'd take this himself. Mazen spoke on the campus phone while holding the cell phone in his hand. Lenny used the opportunity to continue the earlier discussion. He hoped that keeping the level of their voices low enough to sound like mumbling, while above the level of a whisper, would allow them to converse without arousing the terrorist's suspicions.

"We're going to have to take this into our own hands," Lenny said. "There's no way the Israelis will release their prisoners."

"You don't know that," Bruce said.

"They had two weeks when we were in Israel, and they didn't even consider letting any go. And there were more hostages then."

Lenny could see that Bruce was giving this serious thought. Then his expression softened, his shoulders sagged visibly. Lenny realized Bruce had just understood they might not get out of this alive. When his features hardened and a look of determination came over him, Lenny knew Bruce was on his side. "Okay, we're a team." Bruce said. "What do we do next?"

Keeping their voices low, they began formulating an action plan. They decided that during the night their captor would need rest, or at the least, he would be less alert due to lack of sleep. This would be the best time to attempt something. They decided that they would have to keep themselves awake and aware at all times, for any opportunity that might present itself, as there was no way of foreseeing such a thing.

The group began moving all the student desks, save the five they were using, to the back of the room according to instructions given before the terrorist had answered the phone. They spread out the blankets and pillows in the vacated area, being careful not to get Reverend Graves' congealed blood on anything. The five remaining desks were arranged in a line directly in front of the teacher's desk.

When everything was in its place and the hostages were in their seats, the terrorist hung up the second phone and made his way to the window from an oblique angle. With his head against the wall and to the side of the window, he moved the blind just enough to see outside. He resumed speaking into the cell phone. He hung up after speaking for only a few seconds.

Lenny was suddenly struck with an idea. Now, if he could just convey his plan to the others.

"What's it look like out there?" Lenny asked.

"No different than the last time," Mazen answered. "They are all just standing around like a pack of jackals waiting for the kill. They will get just that if they try anything foolish." He held his left hand up for all in the room to see and said, "My thumb is ever present on this switch. They think they fool me with their pretenses. I know that men are even now waiting in the halls outside this room, anticipating the opportunity to kill me. They too shall perish when the moment is ripe."

"Do you really think they'd be so stupid as to risk that? After all, if Israel releases your comrades this will all end peacefully, won't it?" Lenny said.

The terrorist approached the reporter with a menacing glare and said, "Do not insult me with your obvious attempts. We both know there are men out there who will not let me live through this. No matter the outcome, they will kill me if given the chance." Once again he held his hand up to display the button. "Only this is preventing them from carrying out their desires."

"I really didn't mean to be insulting," Lenny said. "We're all on your side when it comes to ending this peacefully."

"The peace of Allah is all I desire."

Lenny looked at his fellow captives as the terrorist made his way to the front of the room. Did they understand what the man had just said? Was this guy planning to send himself to heaven even if his friends were released? From the looks on their faces, it seemed that each had indeed read enough between the lines to understand that, if they wanted to live through this, they'd have to save themselves, and they had better act quickly.

"I have to go to the bathroom," Lenny said.

"You just went an hour ago. What is wrong with you?"

"I don't know. Nervous I guess. But I have to pee real bad."

"Very well, but remember the time limit. Two minutes and no more."

As soon as he was inside the closet, Lenny removed the twin-gloved device that Sheila had finished filling with chemicals. It needed something, but he wasn't sure what. Then he realized that latex had a certain amount of give to it. For his plan to work, the makeshift grenade would have to burst when thrown against something. This thing looked like it would just bounce like a beach ball. He found a razor and very carefully cut thin score lines along the sides of the latex. All he could do now was hope it would work.

He had barely finished when he heard Mazen saying from just outside the door, "Your time is up. Come out here now."

Lenny quickly hid the homemade chemical grenade inside his pants front. He left his shirt hanging out to cover the small bulge that this created and hoped for the best while holding his stomach muscles in. He'd just gotten the grenade hidden when the door flew open and Mazen stood there glaring. His dark eyes slowly surveyed the interior of the janitor's closet.

Lenny pretended to be in the process of tucking in his shirt and said, "Sorry I took so long. But it's not easy when your wrists are taped together like this. I just barely got my pants back up when you opened the door."

The terrorist remained quiet as he continued looking inside the closet. His eyes darted from the sink to the walls to the shelves. He seemed to sense that something wasn't right. The questioning look in the man's eyes gave Lenny his only hope that he did not know what was going on. He pointed to Lenny's chair and said, "Go sit down. Bathroom privileges are no more. I don't care if you wet yourself."

Lenny took his seat, being very careful not to dislodge or damage the package hidden in his pants. He noted Bruce's questioning look and covertly nodded. He saw Bruce's relief as the archeologist turned to convey this good news to the others. The plan now was to keep constantly on the alert for an opportunity. Lenny knew Bruce and the others would jump into action as soon as he made the first move. The deadly contest entered a new phase. Unbeknownst to the hunter, he had now become the hunted.

TWENTY-NINE

Three Broken Threads

It had been over an hour since Lenny had emerged from the closet with the chemical grenade hidden in his pants. No opportunity had yet presented itself to execute their risky plan and he was beginning to think this wasn't such a hot idea. What if the fucking thing burst in his pants? He thought about his two previous escapes and began to realize how much luck had played a part in the fact that he was still breathing. As a gambler, he knew that all winning streaks must end sometime. Had his stream of good fortune run its course?

Bruce was also a bundle of worms. Lenny watched as his friend continuously squirmed in his seat. Then Bruce apparently thought of something. His expression took on a more optimistic tone and he said, "Mazen, do you know what the scrolls say that we found in the caves outside Jericho?" He held up his copy of the translations to emphasize his point.

"I know they are filled with Jewish lies. Why should I be concerned with fabrications the Zionists have been telling forever?"

"It's true that the scrolls were discovered at the site of a Jewish settlement. But the story they tell is about Adam and Eve. Did you know that?"

"Destroying these lies will be an added pleasure for me. When this building is ruined your precious manuscripts will also be destroyed. The falsehoods of the Zionists and those under their control, like your government, must be revealed for what they are, carefully constructed fairy stories designed to further their agenda. The day will come when these dark tales are exposed to the light of truth."

"But the scrolls tell a different tale of Adam and Eve." Lenny hoped Bruce knew he had to be careful if he didn't want to end up like Reverend Graves. "They tell of God's goodness and of His plan for the brotherhood of man. They inform us of the truth, beauty and goodness hidden behind the veil of lies."

Mazen looked at Bruce with scorn and said, "What truth, beauty and goodness do my people share in? Is it beautiful when a mother must watch her child grow up in squalor? Is it good to see a whole nation humiliated every day by the occupying Zionists? And truth? What is truth? Is it truth when Jewish controlled media throughout the world collaborate in the crushing of a people? Is it truth when politicians march in a parade of lies? A procession their citizens blindly watch from the streets while waving false flags of patriotism?" The man made his way to the side of the window while he continued. "Is it truth when our own leaders pretend to follow in the path of the Prophet, peace be upon him, while living in sin and debauchery?" He stopped beside the window and sneaked a look outside.

Lenny saw this as his chance. He carefully pulled his shirt out of his pants and took the small chemical grenade into his taped hands. As he was thinking about leaving his seat to get close enough to throw the device, the killer pulled back from the window.

"You speak of truth, goodness and beauty as if they are real things," Mazen continued. "In actuality, they are but words without meaning. In my world, in my homeland, in my life, I have seen only lies, bad intentions and horror. What will it take to end it?" He looked at each of his captives individually. "I ask you, what will it take?"

Lenny knew he had no answers to such a complicated question. He only knew he needed to keep the man talking and, hopefully, distracted. "It will take people of good faith, on both sides, to sit down and talk rationally."

"Talk!" the terrorist bellowed. "You think this situation can be wished away with magic words? It has already been talked to death. And where has it gotten my people?"

"But the killing must end," Bruce said.

Mazen walked to the front of the classroom. He took a piece of chalk and began drawing figures on the blackboard. "This is a map of Palestine," he said. "And this is the surrounding area of Zion. Look how they have divided my people. We cannot even go from Gaza to the West Bank without having to subject ourselves to the humiliation of military checkpoints. We cannot visit our beloved capital of Jerusalem unless the Zionists grant us passage. Can any of you understand what it is like for my people? Do any of you even care? Does anyone in the West care?"

The hostages looked at one another with downcast expressions. "Many people care, Mazen," Roxanne said gently. "But most of us can't even understand this whole thing. The Western world, and the United States particularly, thinks of this almost like a conflict between cousins." Upon seeing Mazen react to this with a hard look she hastily added, "Well, after all Abraham is the father of both Jew and Arab."

"Forget not that Sarah forced our father Abraham to expel Ibrahim and his mother from the family tent, thereby starting this eternal conflict. That was the beginning of it all. The Jews are to blame and must die."

"All I know is, more violence won't settle any of this," Roxanne said.

"And all I know," Mazen said, "is that force is the only language they understand. Enough of this silly talk."

Fifteen minutes later Lenny was still holding the small package of chemicals in his hand. Twice he'd thought he had an opportunity to use it, and twice he'd been wrong.

Suddenly the phone rang. "Should I get that?" Bruce asked, knowing what Lenny was holding. When Mazen nodded, Bruce picked up the phone. "This is Bruce Goldman."

Bruce listened and then handed the phone to Mazen and said, "There's someone out there who wants to talk to you. It's the Imam you spoke with earlier. He said he has some answers for you."

Mazen approached Bruce and took the phone. He watched to make sure Bruce returned to his seat, then spoke into the handset.

Lenny watched carefully as the terrorist began pacing in small circles. The man started talking in his native tongue. Lenny wondered who the cleric was. Whoever he was, he obviously had the respect of the terrorist; whose demeanor quickly went from a near boil to a serenity that amazed Lenny. Mazen went to the window and looked outside as he continued talking in his calmest voice of the day. This was Lenny's chance.

Very carefully he left his seat while Mazen continued peering outside through the small opening between window and blind. He saw the looks of fear and concern on his friend's faces as he crept up behind the living bomb at the window. Suddenly Mazen stopped talking. Lenny feared the conversation was ended and he was not yet close enough to throw the grenade accurately with his taped hands. He stood motionless for a full ten seconds in the silent room. He thought about quickly returning to his seat. He turned to look at his fellows.

Roxanne's visage was a sculptor's study in fear. Sheila and Phyllis were both as frozen as statues too, with eyes squinting to the point of near closure. Bruce was subtly trying to encourage Lenny to proceed. Lenny turned around to face the killer's back. The man was still silent and Lenny decided to return to his seat. Just as he was about to do so, he heard Mazen say something in his native language. The telephone conversation continued and Lenny breathed a sigh of relief as he stealthily resumed his trek to the window. When he got within three feet of the back of the man he raised his taped hands above his head. The killer continued looking out the window; he continued speaking into the phone.

A full minute later, nothing had changed. Lenny's shoulder muscles were burning with the strain of keeping his arms raised. *Come on. Come on you bastard.* He could feel the strength beginning to leave his arms. *Fucking cigarettes.*

Just as Lenny was thinking of giving up, Mazen pulled his eyes from the window and Lenny threw the device with all his strength. It splashed against the wall in front of the terrorist's face.

Mazen screamed in agony as both hands instinctively reached for his eyes and tried to remove the burning liquid. He dropped the button in the process. He stumbled against the wall while furiously rubbing his eyes. Lenny thrust his shoulders into the terrorist's body and forced him against the wall.

"Get his arms," Lenny said, as he tackled Mazen by lowering his body to the level of the screaming man's knees and tackled him to the floor. "Don't let him get his hands on anything."

Bruce threw his body on top of the falling men and grabbed the terrorist's left arm with all his might. His hands were taped together and Mazen was trying to kick him, but Lenny was holding the legs firmly with his body weight and the kicks were ineffective. Sheila and Phyllis put all their effort into immobilizing his right arm and shoulder while Roxanne grabbed his right wrist and held on tightly. In a matter of seconds the man was under their complete control.

Lenny worked his way up from the knees to the waist, completely restricting any lower body movement on their captive's part.

"Sheila, go get help," he said. "We've got him under control."

Mazen had stopped struggling and was reduced to whimpering in pain. "My eyes! My eyes!" he said while shaking his head with lids tightly closed.

"Shouldn't we wash his eyes out?" Sheila asked as she rose and made her way to the door.

"Screw him." Roxanne said. "Let them burn."

Sheila hesitated at the door. "We can't do that. Lenny get some water for him."

"I suppose you're right," Lenny said. He made sure Mazen was still under control while he stood and went to the janitor's closet.

Sheila opened the classroom door and was immediately overrun by the SWAT team as they rushed into the room. One of the men took her away from the scene by grabbing her arm and dragging her down the hall and out of the building.

Outside the building, Joe West was listening to the Muslim cleric speaking over the phone while he watched the window through which the terrorist was peering. He saw Mazen's face disappear immediately after a look of shock had come over it. At the same time, he saw the Imam remove the phone from his ears. He had a puzzled expression. West took the phone from the confused man and listened. What he heard made no sense to him at first. Then he understood.

"Kim," he called to the Chief of Police. "I think they've overpowered the guy." As Kim approached, Joe West listened further. "Yup. They've got him under control. I can hear our guys rushing into the room. It sounds like everything's okay. Hey every-"

Before Joe West could finish his intended announcement of a satisfactory and happy ending to the crisis, his words were cut off.

Before his mind could process what was happening, his face contorted in horror.

Before he could react to what his eyes had seen, he was thrown to the ground.

Before he could get up, he was covered in dust and debris.

A powerful blast had blown out the front of the classroom and sent building parts, classroom parts, and body parts flying through the air like pieces of wood spewing from a large chipper.

The crowd was struck silent and still. All eyes were drawn to the gaping maw from which smoke, ash, and small particles floated skyward, a malevolent plume. None moved except one man.

Ali turned away from the smoking pit. He placed the small radio transmitter back into his jacket pocket and calmly fought the tide as the crowd came out of its trance and rushed in a screaming frenzy through the police barriers toward the building.

* * *

Six months after the funerals for Reverend Graves, Bruce, Roxanne, Phyllis, and the six policemen who had been killed in the explosion, Lenny and Sheila were having dinner at Sheila's apartment, which they had been sharing for three months.

Lenny's wounds were healing nicely; only a few small scars would remain. He wondered for the thousandth time why he had been the one who had gone for the water to wash out the terrorist's eyes. Being in the closet had saved his life. He was grateful of course, but survivor's guilt sometimes reared its ugly head. He was very thankful that Sheila has been pulled away by one of the SWAT team members. She had gotten away without a scratch.

Lenny was playing with his mashed potatoes, forming small hills with caves in them. He placed pieces of carrots onto the edible hillside and called them Bruce and Roxanne. "I miss those two," he said.

Sheila put her fork down and clasped her hands together in prayer-like fashion with her chin resting on her knuckles. Her lips tightened, turned downward. She sighed. "Me too. They were a lot of fun. How are your notes coming along?"

"Not very well. I can't seem to remember anything about what those scrolls said, other than general thoughts. You know, brotherhood, tolerance, stuff like that."

"Me too," Sheila said. "It's such a shame everything was destroyed. What a waste."

"I read something interesting today about Young Joe Rizzo," Lenny said.

"Oh yeah?" Sheila said as she cut her steak. "What's that idiot been up to since his old man died?"

"He's been living high on the hog, for one thing. He put the mansion up for sale too. Says he wants to erase every memory of his father that he can."

"How are things going with your story on election fraud? Have you found anyone yet who'll help you on that one? By the way," Sheila continued as she ate a bite of mashed potatoes, "have I told you how proud I am that you're getting promoted?"

Lenny swallowed a mouthful of food and said, "Thanks. I can't believe Perry Hazzard chose me to be his Assistant Editor. I'll still be able to do my investigative reporting too, that's the best part."

"Perry told me that your decision to stop drinking had a lot to do with his choice."

Lenny remained silent as he remembered his promise of abstinence after the night with Roxanne. He wondered if he would ever tell Sheila. He certainly wanted to, but decided only anger and hurt feelings lie on that path.

"Have you thought about our wedding plans?" she asked. "Do you know who you want for your best man?"

A forlorn look came over Lenny. "I sometimes wish it could be Bruce."

The man who calls himself Assad was reading a six-month-old copy of the *Chronicle*. He lay in the bed he'd been confined to since the hostage rescue; the mucus stained sheets under his back absorbed the seepage from his bedsores. He read the articles about the explosion for perhaps the hundredth time since the day it had happened. There had been speculation over how the bomb had gone off when all had seemed under control. The radio-controlled detonator had never been discovered amongst the ruins.

His misery over losing his arm and leg was festering as badly as the infection in his stump. He carefully folded the newspaper with his remaining hand and placed it on the bedside nightstand.

"As long as the American reporter still lives," he said to the empty room. "I swear to Allah I will have my vengeance upon him."

Epilogue

They sit in a cool, dark, steel and concrete encased tomb within a man made structure that provides a perfect environment for their preservation.

The twenty-four scrolls lie quietly inside the modern cave designed by engineers to withstand nearly any disaster. The leather from which they were fashioned thousands of years ago has regained some suppleness. The lettering remains faded but legible. More have died in the effort to uncover their secrets. None left alive on earth know of their existence.

Their temporary emergence from darkness was premature. The time for their message not yet ripe. Humanity's appetite for destruction and chaos not yet satiated by the truth of fraternity. They wait, isolated from the light, until the inevitable coming of their day.